A Duke Is Always Dangerous

REBECCA LEIGH

A Duke Is Always Dangerous

©2023 Rebecca Wood

print ISBN: 979-8-35091-046-9

ebook ISBN: 979-8-35091-047-6

Chapter One

1816, The Rose and Thistle Inn, Scotland

The wind had picked up and whistled through the branches of the trees that lined the roadway. And the drizzle of rain that had been bothersome for the past hour had now turned to sharp prickles of ice as the temperature began to fall. The village and inn were just ahead and Camden Davenport, Duke of Stafford would be glad to get out of the inclement weather. This was the last stop on the journey back to McDonough Castle. The trip from Edinburgh to the Highlands had been long and tiresome with the ever-changing weather of Scotland, at times he had wished that they had traveled by carriage rather than on horseback. Traveling by horseback was faster and preferred by his friend and traveling companion, John Cavendish, and he did have to admit that being cooped up inside a conveyance for days was never something he enjoyed, besides the fact that he was anxious to reach their destination.

Cavendish disliked being in a carriage even less than he did himself. He and Cavendish had been through much together over the past eight years. During the war with France, when Napoleon tried to conquer Britain, Cam served as a spy and an assassin. For many years he had lived in the shadows, walking a fine line between being a hero to his country or becoming a monster. He had killed many men, all in service to the crown, and had even become known to the French as *Ange de la Mort*, the Angel of Death. Through everything, John Cavendish had been his right-hand man, from smuggling goods, as well as information, through the French lines to nursing him back to health after being shot after a mission didn't go as planned. Now that the war between France and England was over and Napoleon was exiled, John was still by his side and would serve him as his estate steward.

It was estate business that had brought them to Edinburgh and now that it was concluded, Cam thought it would be an excellent time to return to the home of his good friend Ian McDonough, Duke of Sunbridge. Ian had recently married and was in residence at his estate, McDonough Castle in the Scottish Highlands. Cam wanted to spend at least a month there hoping to find some time to relax and perhaps enjoy some fishing before it was time to return to his estate in Sussex and then on to London for the season.

Another cold gust of wind seemed to go through him as they neared the village. He could see smoke billowing from the chimney of the small two-story white stone building with a thatched roof where Cavendish had already secured them a room for the night. As they rode up to the *Rose and Thistle*, Davenport could hear voices coming from inside the inn the moment his horse stopped out front. The sun was just beginning to set leaving the sky bathed in a deep purple hue, and the wind was getting colder by the minute. He was glad to have finally reached the inn and was looking forward to a hot meal, some hearty ale, and hopefully some peace and quiet. Judging by the sounds coming from inside the establishment, he doubted the latter would be possible. Suddenly he saw a bag being tossed out the door and a flurry of brown muslin retrieve it before marching back inside the establishment. He dismounted and looked over at his companion.

"I'll go speak to the innkeeper." He handed the reins of his horse to Cavendish. "See to the horses and take a look around. I'll meet you inside."

As he walked closer to the entrance, he heard the voices again, only this time he could make out the soft almost pleading voice of a lady. He stepped closer to the door and peered inside curious as to what all the commotion was about. Standing in front of the large unfriendly looking innkeeper was a petite lady wearing a plain drab brown traveling dress with an equally dowdy little bonnet to match. Her hands were clasped tightly in front of her and there was a sense of desperation in her voice. He moved further into the inn to better hear their conversation.

"Please, sir, there has to be a room somewhere I can stay," Abigail Bailey pleaded with the innkeeper who stood before her as an unmovable mountain.

The man was wiping his hands rather aggressively on the worn-out rag he was holding. "I dun told ye, lass. There be no rooms left for the night. You can either sleep on the floor by the hearth or go out to the stables."

Abigail felt the blood leave her face. How could he even suggest such a thing? "Is there another lady that is traveling alone? Perhaps she might be willing to share a room with me. I simply can't accept what you are telling me."

The man pushed back his long unkempt red hair from his face and shook his head. "There be no ladies traveling alone. Now be off with ye, I have work to do. Don't make me throw ye out along with yer bag."

Camden watched as the lady's shoulders slumped in defeat and knew it was time for him to step forward and take charge of the situation. "The lady can take my room."

Abigail spun around quickly at the sound of the man's voice behind her. She stared at him for a few minutes as her memory began to register that she had seen him before. She kept silent as he stalked forward removing his riding gloves as he did so to confront the innkeeper.

"What kind of a man would even suggest a lady sleep in the stables and to suggest bodily throwing her from your establishment is not tolerable." The innkeeper narrowed his eyes and he continued. "I have a room reserved for the evening, and if the lady has no objections, she may have it. I will sleep elsewhere."

The innkeeper threw his dirty rag down on a nearby table and crossed his arms over his chest letting them rest above his bulging belly. "And who might ye be?"

Abigail raised her head to study her rescuer's reaction and saw his lips quirk up on one side as he leveled the man a fierce stare. "I am the Duke of Stafford."

Abigail's head swiveled back to the innkeeper in time to see his face pale and felt a little bit of satisfaction at the fear clearly registered in his eyes.

The inn keeper immediately bowed deeply. "I'm right sorry, I am, your grace. I will certainly see that the lass has one of the best rooms in the inn, and I will have a private dining room prepared right away for the two of you."

Camden nodded his approval and watched as the man rushed off to prepare the rooms. He then turned to look at the lady standing by his side still clutching her hands tightly before her. Her pink lips parted in surprise. "I hope that we now have this matter settled to your satisfaction…Miss Bailey. Am I wrong to assume you are on your way to McDonough Castle?"

Abigail's eyes widened before she hastily remembered to drop into a curtsey. "You remember me, your grace?"

Her smile spread wide across her face, and he couldn't help but think that if she were dressed in something other than the dreary drab ugly traveling dress, she was wearing, she would be quite pretty.

"Now how could you think I would ever be able to forget a lady so lovely, Miss Bailey?" It had been the unique violet color of her eyes that first drew his attention when he initially met her several months ago when he and Ian had travelled to her cottage in Somerset in search of Emma, Ian's runaway betrothed. Emma and Miss Bailey were close friends and Ian had hoped that after discovering the fact that Emma had written to Miss Bailey often while in London, the young lady would perhaps have an idea as to where Emma might have disappeared.

Abigail blushed at his compliment and turned her gaze away. "I hate to take your room, your grace, but I am most thankful for your assistance."

"What kind of gentleman would I be if I permitted any lady to sleep in the stables with horses while I had the luxury of a private bedchamber?" He took her arm and led her off to the side of the room as another gentleman passed by them. "However, you must appease my curiosity, Miss Bailey. How is it that you come to be traveling alone? As you must know, it isn't exactly safe."

Abigail shrugged her shoulders. "Well, as it were, there was a young lady from the village traveling with me, your grace. I had employed her to be my companion and lady's maid for the trip. Unfortunately, I discovered that she had bouts with her nerves and became homesick after the first day. She did not even make it four hours down the road. I could not bear it, so I sent her back to Somerset. She was young, and it was her first time to leave home. I felt I would rather take my chances on my own, even if I had to fight off a group of highwaymen myself rather than listen to her cry and snivel about missing her family the entire trip. Traveling by public coach isn't exactly a pleasant experience, I didn't need her shrieking and sobbing on my shoulder the whole way to make it worse. As it was, I had already been sandwiched between two very unpleasant smelling traveling companions, one of which constantly belched and the other snored quite loudly. Thankfully, they did not journey the whole way to Scotland."

Camden arched his eyebrows. "You paint a vivid picture of the trials of traveling on a public coach, Miss Bailey. So, you have traveled the entire way from Somerset alone?"

She nodded. "Yes, and I am grateful that the journey is almost over. My fellow passengers have not been the best company."

"I'm sure it has been an ordeal." He watched as other passengers came through the door, and his senses instantly heightened. After working for eight years as a British spy and assassin, being suspicious and wary was second nature. He surveyed the room and decided he would prefer to continue their conversation somewhere less crowded and more private.

"My steward is traveling with me. Give me a few minutes to tell him of my plans and then I will see if the innkeeper has the private dining room ready. I'm sure you would enjoy some refreshment after being confined inside the traveling coach."

Abigail smiled sweetly. "Thank you again, your grace. Perhaps you can tell me news of Emma. Is she as happy as her letters to me indicate?"

Camden chuckled softly as he took her hand and placed it on his arm to lead her toward the dining rooms. "She is most definitely, and I'm sure she will be ecstatic to see you. Wait here and I will return shortly."

He led her away from the others and then went to find Cavendish who was still outside the inn getting their bags. The rain was now mixed with snow flurries, and he did not relish the idea of telling his friend that they would need to find other less appealing accommodations for the night.

"There has been a change in plans, my friend."

Cavendish narrowed his eyes hoping he was not about to hear that the inn was full or the arrangements he had made ahead of time were not acceptable. "It's colder than a witch's tit tonight, I hope those plans don't include sleeping out in this shite."

Cam grinned knowing his friend would not be pleased. "There is a young lady traveling alone that does not have a room. She was begging the innkeeper for a place to stay and since the inn is full, I gave her our room."

Cavendish frowned as he scratched the scruff of his beard. "A young lady you say."

Cam nodded. "We will need to acquire lodging elsewhere for the night. Perhaps the stables will be acceptable. It will not be the first time we have bedded down with horses." He heard his friend grumble his displeasure under his breath. "I did acquire a private dining room if you would like to join us for dinner."

"Does this young lady happen to be attractive?"

Cam shrugged his shoulders. "I did not take notice of her looks. I was simply helping a damsel in distress."

"Hmm, a damsel in distress you say. If I am going to be freezing my arse off, I would at least like to know that the girl is bonny."

Cam grinned. "Join us for dinner and you can see for yourself."

"Nah, no need in getting all warmed up just to freeze again. I'll eat in the public room and then bed down for the night." He took a few steps back toward the stables before turning back around. "Please give the lovely lady my regards, your grace, and bring a bottle of ale or whiskey out to the stable when you come. We will need it to ward off the chill."

Davenport nodded in agreement and walked back toward the inn to find the innkeeper, whose attitude had changed dramatically since Cam revealed his identity. It still surprised him how people reacted to finding out he was a duke. Even though his father had always acknowledged him as his son, he was still illegitimate. Being a bastard son, he had never aspired to the title, but after the death of his father and seeing there were no other heirs apparent, he was fortunate enough to have gained the Prince Regent's favor and friendship. In recognition of the work he had done in the protection of the crown during the war with Napoleon, Prinny granted him the dukedom, and now he had risen from the depths of obscurity to being a very influential and powerful man, not only in London but throughout the country.

He had to admit that it would have been much more difficult assuming his new role, had it not been for the friends he had recently made in London. One of those friends was Ian McDonough, Duke of Sunbridge and Chieftain of Clan McDonough. Ian was now married to the lovely Emma Presley and was at present happily living at McDonough Castle in the Highlands. It was Emma that Miss Bailey was traveling so very far to visit.

After helping Ian find his runaway betrothed some months ago, Cam had traveled north with the happy couple. He had even stayed a few weeks at McDonough Castle before returning to London. While in Scotland, he had decided to invest in a few new ventures with Ian and had finished up some business with his solicitors in Edinburgh. Now that business was concluded he planned on returning to McDonough Castle to spend a few quiet weeks in the beautiful Scottish Highlands before returning to resume his duties to the dukedom.

When he entered the inn again, he found Miss Bailey right where he had left her, standing outside the private dining rooms, wringing her hands nervously, as if she were afraid he would change his mind and not return.

"Miss Bailey, if you will follow me, the innkeeper has everything prepared for us."

Abigail walked with the duke into the private dining room, hesitating at the entrance as if she was debating on the wisdom of being alone with a man she had only met briefly. Then she heard the raucous laughter coming from the taproom and thought it would be much wiser to be alone with the duke, than in a room full of travelers and strangers that might not have her best interests at heart.

"Will your steward be joining us?"

Davenport shook his head slightly. "No, he prefers to eat in the public rooms and then bed down early."

"Do you also live in Scotland, your grace?" She moved over to the table and removed her bonnet before taking a seat.

Camden watched her as she walked across the room to stand before the fire. Now that she had removed the ridiculously ugly, and at least twenty years out of style bonnet, he could see that her hair was fair, so blonde that it was almost white. "No, my estate is in Sussex, like you, I am traveling to McDonough Castle."

Abigail looked over at him, noting the way his clothes fit him perfectly, the way his eyes crinkled at the corners when he grinned, and how his arm had felt so warm beneath her touch. He was much taller than her and appeared so much more sophisticated. She shook her head and quickly looked away embarrassed when he caught her staring. Thankfully the innkeeper entered with their dinner before he could remark on her lack of manners. The duke took the seat across from her and poured her a cup of cider.

Abigail gazed at the feast before them. There was roast chicken, potatoes, and fresh bread and butter. It was the most appetizing meal she had eaten since leaving Somerset. "My goodness, is all of this just for the two of us?" She raised her eyes from the meal set before them and looked across the table at him surprised at the amount of food that had been brought to them.

"I hope you are hungry." He leaned back in the chair but didn't reach for any of the food.

Abigail felt a little uneasy being the only one to eat, and while her stomach rumbled as the smell of the roasted chicken drifted up to her nose, she simply reached for a slice of the bread and spread some butter on it.

Camden held out the plate of chicken to her. "Don't be shy, Miss Bailey. You must be hungry."

Abigail resisted the urge to lick her lips and took a small piece of chicken. "I would feel better if you would partake with me."

"As you wish." He took a plate with some chicken and bread but only took a small bite to encourage her to eat.

He watched as her tongue flicked out to lick some butter from the corner of her lip. "How long do you plan on staying at McDonough Castle?"

Abigail took a sip of her cider before answering. "I am not certain. Emma asked me to come to stay with her after the death of my father. He passed away a few months ago."

"Emma mentioned that your father had died, my condolences."

Abigail lifted the cup to her lips again. "Yes, he had been sick for a very long time."

Camden noticed the frown form on her lips and the light in her eyes dimmed slightly so he thought it would be a good idea to change the subject. "What do you think of Scotland so far?"

"I'm not sure I can make a decision yet. I have seen very little of it from the coach windows. Since I was the smallest person on the coach, I had to take the middle seat every time." She squinched up her nose. "It doesn't allow you to enjoy the scenery, but I do know it is rather cold, and it has rained almost every day since I crossed the border."

He saw her shiver just a bit and noticed that her cloak was thin and threadbare and could not possibly be warm. At least not warm enough for an early Scottish spring.

"You said that you were also traveling to McDonough Castle, your grace. Do you plan on staying there for a time or is it to be a quick visit?"

Camden watched as she continued to eat tiny bites of food. It was no wonder she was so small. "I had planned on staying a few weeks before returning to London, but that could change."

She took another sip of her cider, then pushed her plate away. At that moment, the wind picked up outside and the windows of the inn creaked. She glanced toward the windows and then back to him. "Where will you stay tonight, your grace?"

He shrugged his shoulders. "I will stay here by the fire for a while until I decide to make my way to the stables."

Abigail frowned drawing her brows together. "I can't let you do that. The weather sounds like it will be most foul tonight, and I simply can't ask you to give up your room for me. It would be terribly selfish. I'm sure I can stay here by the fire. Sleeping in a chair here can't be any worse than trying to sleep on the coach." She gave him a slight grin. "At least the smells would be better."

He grinned slightly. She was worried about him. It had been a long time since someone was concerned with his welfare, but he could see that her eyes were growing heavy. The food in her belly and the warmth of the fire were taking their toll on Miss Bailey. She was getting sleepy.

"I am afraid this is an argument you will never win, my dear. Allow me to escort you upstairs. I already had the innkeeper take up your trunk. I also ordered a hot bath; they should be seeing to it now."

Abigail's eyes widened. "I never expected that, your grace. The room was enough."

He raised an eyebrow. "Shall I cancel the tub? I thought you would enjoy that small luxury after traveling so far."

Abigail couldn't help herself. "I know I shouldn't accept, but it does sound delightful. Are you certain you don't mind? I am rather tired."

Camden stood from his seat and offered her his hand. When she placed her small hand in his, he couldn't suppress the shiver that moved through him.

"Are you cold, your grace?"

He looked down into her eyes and then quickly looked away. "No, certainly not. If you need anything, Miss Bailey, and I am not here in the dining room, you will find me in the stables. Hopefully, you will get to enjoy a peaceful night's sleep, and I will see you in the morning before your coach departs."

Abigail allowed him to lead her down the darkened hallway and up the stairs to the room he had reserved. As she reached for the door a young girl came out carrying an empty bucket.

"Water is ready and hot, mi lady." She looked over at the duke. "Tub isn't big enough for the both of ye and it'll be a tight squeeze for ye."

Camden chuckled at the girl's comment and saw that Abigail's cheeks blushed brightly. "It's alright. Thank you. We will not be needing anything else for the night."

The woman didn't bother to curtsey, just barged between them and back down the hallway. Cam opened the door and allowed Abigail to walk inside. He thought it best not to follow. It had been a long time since he had been in a bedroom with a woman and Miss Bailey was proving to definitely be a temptation.

Abigail looked around the room. The small wooden tub was sitting in the middle of the floor, there was a fire burning in the hearth, and a bed closer to the window. "Thank you again, your grace."

Cam bowed to her. "It is my pleasure, Miss Bailey. Be sure to lock the door behind me and do not open it for anyone."

He closed the door, and Abigail walked over to do as he suggested. She saw her bag sitting by the bed and went over to retrieve a nightgown. The buttons of her traveling dress were a struggle, but she finally managed to get them unfastened. She shimmed out of her chemise and walked over to the tub. The water was still very hot, but she didn't want to waste a minute of it, so she gingerly stepped into the tub and slowly sank down letting the water envelop her. The maid had not been jesting about the size of the tub. There was no room for Abigail to stretch out her legs, in fact, her knees almost touched her chest, but the water felt amazing, and she knew that she would sleep better after a long soak.

Cam didn't go out to the stables right away. If he was truthful, he was not looking forward to bedding down outside in this cold. Even though it was the beginning of spring, it seemed as if winter was not quite ready to give up its hold on the Scottish Highlands. This wouldn't be the first time he had slept in a stable or with horses for that matter, but it had been a few years. He went back to the private room that had been provided for him and sat beside the fire while he finished off the ale that had been brought to him. It was barely tolerable, and he was thankful for the flask of brandy he had tucked away on the inside of his coat. He propped his feet up into the chair opposite him and stared into the flames. The laughter and raucous voices coming from the public dining room were beginning to encroach on his privacy. Since he knew it would still be a few hours before the noises from the inn began to fade as people either retired to their rooms or drank themselves into unconsciousness, he decided it was time for him to seek rest somewhere quieter. He took a swig from his brandy and grabbed a bottle of ale to take out to the stables to Cavendish. As he buttoned up his coat and braced himself for the biting cold, it occurred to him how fortunate it was that he had been there at the right time to help Miss Bailey and frowned as he thought about the dangers she could have faced traveling alone. Tomorrow he would make certain she arrived at McDonough House safely, after that she would be under Ian and Emma's care.

Upstairs alone in the room the duke had relinquished to her, Abigail brushed out her hair and slipped into her nightgown before climbing into the bed. It was small and the mattress was lumpy, but after being crammed inside a traveling coach, it felt like heaven. As she lay back against the pillows and closed her eyes, she reminded herself of how fortunate it was that the duke happened to be at the inn at the same time that she needed his help. It did prick her conscience that she was the reason he was probably sleeping out in the cold, but her guilt did not outweigh her exhaustion, and she soon found herself drifting off to sleep.

Chapter Two

Abigail's eyes flew open as the sound of angry voices roused her from her sleep. The voices seemed to be right outside her door. She blinked her eyes a few times and pulled the covers closer around her. The room was plunged into darkness. She had blown out the single candle that had been burning on her bedside table before she went to bed. Now the only light illuminating the room was from the full moon shining through the window. She heard the voices again and rolled to her side hoping to block out the noise so she could get back to sleep. The fire had burned down, and the room was much colder than it had been when she had first climbed into the bed. She fluffed her pillow and pulled the blanket up over her shoulders, but despite her efforts to ignore the conversation, she still found herself listening. She heard the sound of what she thought was someone picking the lock of her door. She remained absolutely still, terrified of what the men would do if they knew she was awake. The door opened and then closed again quickly. She could still hear their whispered voices on the other side of the door. When one of the men mentioned the name Davenport, she realized they had not come for her. Keeping the blanket wrapped tightly around her, she listened.

"I thought you said he would be here tonight." The man's voice was gravelly and harsh.

"That's what I was told, and he is here…somewhere. The innkeeper said this was the room he was given, but upon arriving he gave up the room to a lady who needed lodging for the night," another man replied nervously and in a much softer voice.

"Hold your voices down, all we need is for the chit to wake up and start screaming her bloody head off. He isn't here," the other man whispered.

The conversation continued in the hallway outside the door. They were whispering and it was hard for her to make out what was being said. She very quietly swung her legs to the floor, and as soundlessly as she could, tiptoed closer to the door so she could hear better. She placed her ear against the wood panel and listened.

"If he gave up the room he isn't here, idiot. I swore to that French frog that we would take care of this Davenport for him. He is paying us well." The first man's voice sounded more aggressive.

Abigail thought she heard a scuffle between the two. She chewed her bottom lip and pressed her ear harder against the door.

"He is still here, boss, just not in this room. I'll find him."

Abigail heard flesh hitting flesh and thought the other man must have struck the one giving the excuses.

"We can't barge into every room, you fool."

"No, but we can wait till morning. The innkeeper said that Davenport had dined with the lady this evening. Perhaps he will join her for breakfast."

"Hmm, is the lady anything to him?"

"The innkeeper said that she came in on the stage begging for a room. The duke gave up his room to her, but that doesn't prove she means anything to him."

"We can't be certain of that. If they dined together, and he was willing to give up his room to her, it could mean they are familiar. Could be that he plans on visiting her room later tonight. Stay here outside her room, and if she leaves, I want to know. Don't let her out of your sight. As soon as Davenport shows his face, we kill him. We can't take any chances."

Abigail covered her mouth with her hand. The two men she heard were there to kill the duke. It was imperative that he be warned. She waited till she heard footsteps receding down the hall as one of the men walked away. While she only heard two voices, there could be more men involved, and she knew at least one of them had been instructed to wait outside her door. So, she would have to find another way out of the room. She tiptoed back across the floor, trying not to make a sound hoping the man outside would not discover that she was awake. She moved to the window and looked down at the ground below. It would be quite a jump, but she felt she could make it without injury. She quietly moved back over to the chair where she had draped her traveling dress. Going out in her nightgown would be the height of stupidity, even if she was trying to hurry to warn the duke that his life was in danger. She would have to change quickly and silently. Thankfully, the rain had stopped but judging how cold the room was, she knew it must be freezing outside. She used a ribbon to tie back her hair before slipping on her dress and shoes as noiselessly as possible before making her way back to the window.

At first, when she tried to open it, it didn't budge. She pushed against it once more with as much force as she could muster and cringed at the squeaking sound it made. She closed her eyes and silently prayed the man outside her door didn't hear the noise. When the window was open just enough for her to squeeze through, she stuck her head out and looked around. The darkness loomed before her and there was no one about, but the moon offered enough light to allow her to see the stable off to the right of the inn. There was no guarantee that she would find the duke there, but she was certain that if he had been downstairs in the inn, the men would have discovered his whereabouts by now.

She lifted her skirts and put one leg over the side of the window, then climbed through the rest of the way. She clung to the window's edge with her fingers as she dangled above the ground. With a deep breath, she prepared herself for the fall but before she could drop to the ground, she noticed the hem of her skirt was hooked on something. If she let go now, it would either rip her skirt or she would hang upside down until the fabric gave way.

"Oh for the love of heaven," she mumbled as she pulled at the material trying to get it to give way when she heard the sound of voices headed in her direction. Providentially, the fabric released just as she let go of the windowsill and dropped to the ground. Thankfully, she landed softly on her feet but then dropped to her knees keeping very still as two men walked by the inn. From the way they were slurring their words and their staggering gate, she knew they were foxed. So, she remained silent until they were out of sight. When she felt it was safe, she made her way toward the stables, keeping in the shadows and out of sight as much as possible. The way was dark, and she was terrified that she would be discovered before she could warn the duke, but she managed to make it to the front entrance.

When she first opened the creaking door of the stable, she thought no one was there. It was dark and quiet. Even the horses were still as she crept slowly inside, careful not to make too much noise. She looked in each stall and had almost given up hope thinking he must have gone somewhere else for the night. Then she saw a lump covered with a blanket lying in the corner. She moved over to it and reached out her hand. Everything else happened in a blur. Her feet were knocked out from under her, and she was tumbled over onto her back knocking the breath from her lungs. The heavy weight of a body held her down as a hand covered her mouth while she struggled to catch her breath. Something cold and hard was pressed into her throat. There was no need to muzzle her, the shock had robbed her of any sound she might have made. Then just as quickly as she was attacked, she was released.

"Christ!"

She recognized the voice but remained still.

"Bloody hell, woman! Has anyone never told you that sneaking around in the middle of the night could get you killed?"

Davenport raked a hand through his hair and breathed out a frustrated sigh before reaching down and lifting her back to her feet. "What the hell are you doing out here?" He held up a hand as Cavendish came rushing forward a pistol drawn.

She put a hand over her chest, looking from one man to the other surprised that they could not see the way her heart was thumping, but still could not find the words.

Cam prowled away, then back to her again. "Do you have a reason to be stalking about at night?" When she didn't answer, he reached down to grip her arm. "Come on, I will walk you back inside."

She pulled back from him. "No! You can't go inside. I can't go back inside," she said frantically as she finally found her voice.

He dropped his hands glancing quickly over to Cavendish before looking back at her wondering if she was just a bit touched in the head. It was dark in the stables, and while he couldn't see her face very well, her voice implied that she was in a state of panic. He supposed she was still in shock, but hell, who wouldn't be? He had knocked her to the ground rather violently and put a knife to her throat for Christ's sake. The moment he heard the stable door open his training had taken over, and when he felt the presence of someone approaching him unexpectedly, he did what came naturally, and now he felt like a beast for frightening an innocent young woman.

"Miss Bailey, I am sorry, I didn't know…"

She frantically grabbed his arm. "There are men inside the inn looking for you and from the things I heard them say, they are not your friends."

She couldn't see his face, but she could tell that from the casual way he was standing that he wasn't convinced. "I was in bed, and they opened the door to see if you were inside. I pretended to sleep, but I listened to their conversation."

"I told you to lock the door, Miss Bailey."

"The door was locked! They must have picked the lock to get inside, but seriously the door is not the issue here." She was beginning to get irritated with him. Here she was trying to save his life and he was speaking to her as if she were a simpleton. "When they realized you were not in the room, they left but continued their conversation in the hallway outside my door, please do try to pay attention."

He heard Cavendish chuckle at her remark, and Cam found that he couldn't help but smirk at her cheeky behavior, although in the dark, he knew she didn't see it. "By all means. please continue, Miss Bailey." He motioned for Cavendish to move forward so that he could better hear her story, as it was sure to be entertaining.

Abigail frowned as she looked at the two men who she was certain didn't believe a word she was saying. "The men I heard were upset that you were not in the room. The innkeeper told them that you had given the room to me. Two different people were speaking." She waved her hand around. "Well, there were two distinct voices I heard, I suppose there could be more. One of the men was very angry, and I think they may have scuffled. It sounded like he may have struck one of them. He told the other man to watch my door, and they would be ready for you in the morning. They are planning to kill you." She took a deep breath after such a lengthy and somewhat rambling explanation and waited for their reaction.

At this, Camden instantly became more alert as did Mr. Cavendish. This was not the first time he had found his life in danger, but it was the first time a lady had become tangled up in the plot. There was one thing that puzzled him. "If they were watching your room, how did you get here?"

"I was very quiet. I jumped from the window." She watched as his head dropped and he covered his eyes with one of his hands. "I had to find you first before they discovered that you were in the stables, and I couldn't leave the room via the door as they were watching."

"What is it with ladies from Somerset, do you all have a penchant for climbing out of windows?" Camden asked her before turning back to look at Cavendish.

Miss Bailey crossed her arms over her chest. "What else was I supposed to do? Open the door and say, *Excuse me, sir, do mind if I step out for a few minutes to find the duke so I can warn him of your plot to murder him?* I'm certain he would have been most obliging."

Cavendish chuckled again, but then quickly covered it with an awkward cough. This woman took cheekiness to a whole new level. Any other time, Camden would ready himself for a fight and dispatch the men without haste, but Miss Bailey had risked her life to save him, and he could not risk something happening to him, and her being left on her own unprotected.

Cavendish came toward him and leaned over to speak softly hoping not to alarm Miss Bailey. "Do you believe her?"

Cam took his arm and led him away so they could talk privately. "I'm not certain, but I can't take the chance that she is wrong."

"What are you going to do with the girl?" Cavendish asked as he glanced over to where Miss Bailey stood.

"I can't leave her here. They know about her, and you know what men are capable of when they are trying to extract information from someone. I'll take her with me. You stay here and see what you can discover and then meet me at McDonough Castle. If you are not there by tomorrow night, I will return to find you."

Cavendish tucked his pistol back under his coat. "There won't be a need for that. I know what to do. You get the lady to the castle, and I'll investigate to see if what she says is the truth. Ladies do have a tendency to exaggerate at times."

Cam nodded and went back to where he had left Miss Bailey. It was cold and he could see her breath coming out as vapor in the air. "We leave now." He walked over, grabbed the saddle, and moved toward his horse.

Abigail moved behind him. "Please do be careful. I will worry about you, but if you leave now, I'm sure you can escape before anyone notices."

He stopped what he was doing and looked at her. "You misunderstand, Miss Bailey, you are coming with me."

She heard the words but thought he could not be serious. "I can't go with you."

"You can and you will."

"But..."

He didn't have time for her arguments. He walked over and put his hands on her shoulders. "If I leave you behind, what makes you think they will not hurt you to find out information about me? It is much too dangerous for you to stay here. Cavendish will stay and discover who these men are and what they are after. I'm taking you to safety. You are leaving with me, and I don't have time to listen to your refusals."

Abigail had not thought of it that way. "What of my trunk? It has everything I own in the world inside it. Can I at least go grab my bag?"

He rolled his eyes and sighed at the absurdity of her question. "And how will you do that? Climb up the wall and back through the window, then back down again? No, we will leave your bag and trunk behind. Cavendish will bring what he can to the castle when he comes and make arrangements for the rest."

He continued saddling the horse then grabbed the blanket he had been sleeping beneath and moved towards her. He wrapped his hands around her waist and easily lifted her into the saddle before lithely jumping up to mount behind her. He pulled her closer to him and wrapped the blanket around her. In her haste to find him, she had left her cloak behind, and the night air was cold. It would not do for her to fall ill before they reached the castle.

Cavendish moved to his side and shook his hand. "Now don't you worry miss, his grace will take care of you."

Abigail pulled the blanket tighter around her shoulders but was in too much shock to respond.

Cam looked around before urging his horse further. He kept the animal at a walk until they were out of hearing then nudged him into a canter.

Miss Bailey was sitting before him, her bottom pressing delight-fully into his crotch, if it had not been for the fact that someone might be trying to kill him, he would have taken the time to appreciate that feeling just a bit more. Her body was rigid, but she had not protested further once he explained the direness of the situation. This was an unexpected change in his plans. He had not had word from any of his contacts that his life might be in danger. Could it be that Miss Bailey had misheard the conversation taking place in the hallway outside her room? Maybe she had dreamed something so fanciful. Regardless, he couldn't take any chances with her safety. Cavendish would find out what he could, and then they would make their decisions about how to handle the situation. Once Miss Bailey was safely out of the way, things would be much easier.

They had been gone from the village for over an hour now, and even though they were trying to avoid dangerous men determined to kill the duke, Abigail found her eyelids growing heavy as they rode on through the night. The small blanket the duke had wrapped around her gave little protection from the crisp cold winds. In order to get warmer, she found herself leaning back against his hard body relishing in the warmth it provided and after a time she did close her eyes as the rhythm of the horse's movements and the warmth from the duke's arms as they held her against him, lulled her to sleep.

Cam decided to keep off the main roads as much as possible. He wrapped his arms tighter around Miss Bailey as shivers continued to rack her body while she slept in his arms. The blanket was not nearly enough to keep her warm. She had slept most of the way since they left the inn only waking long enough to reposition herself, instinctively pressing her body tighter against him in her sleep searching for warmth.

The sun was beginning to rise casting the sky in a pink and purple hue and with it came warmth. Hopefully, the rain would hold off until they reached McDonough Castle. The quiet of the early morning gave him some time to think about the incident at the inn. For the past eight years, he had served his country as a spy and an assassin. He had killed men and fought the devil, so it was entirely possible that his past had come to seek revenge.

Miss Bailey stirred against him pressing her hand against his chest. Her fair hair fell along her face. He frowned when the sun allowed enough light for him to notice that her lips were slightly blue, and he could hear her teeth chattering. It angered him that she was in this situation. At least once he had her at McDonough Castle, she could bask in the luxury of Ian and Emma's estate and would no longer be his problem.

Abigail couldn't remember a time when she had been so cold. It seemed to seep through her bones. She blinked her eyes remembering where she was and what had happened at the inn. The blanket the duke had wrapped around her before they rode out of the stables was not much, but she was grateful for what protection it had offered.

"Are we getting close?" She could hear the shiver in her voice.

Cam shifted and pulled her tighter. "We have a few more hours. The temperature will rise once the sun is fully in the sky.

Abigail sat up feeling the loss of his warmth. She put her hands to her lips and blew her warm breath against them. "Will your friend Mr. Cavendish be alright?"

Cam nodded. "He is experienced. I expect to see him again very soon."

Abigail looked back to study the duke's face. He was not what she imagined a peer of the realm to be. His features were hard and severe. His jaw was firmly set, and his eyes were intense as he faced forward not glancing at her. He looked like he would be more comfortable on a battlefield than he would be sitting in the House of Lords.

"Can I ask you a question, your grace?"

She noticed one corner of his lips turn up slightly.

"I'm not certain I could stop you even if I wanted, but you may ask."

"Why would anyone wish to kill you?"

Cam kept his eyes focused ahead. "You don't beat around the bush do you, Miss Bailey?"

She waited for an answer, but he remained stoic as they continued to ride.

"Are you going to answer me?"

He let his dark amber colored eyes look down into hers. "I said you could ask, I never said I would answer."

Abigail huffed out a breath in agitation. "It just seems that if someone were trying to kill me, I would at least have an idea of who it could be and the reason behind it." She craned her neck around to see him better. When he still did not bother to answer she said, "Could it be that you have an overabundance of people who wish to do you harm?"

He couldn't help but grin at her estimation of his character. "I imagine I have more than most."

Her forehead crinkled slightly as her brows drew together. "I was only jesting."

He glanced down then and raised an eyebrow before replying, "I wasn't." He grinned at the worried look on her face. "Would it ease your mind if I told you that the list of suspects is much shorter than you think?"

"Hmm, not particularly. I do hope you are taking the threat seriously."

"I take everything seriously, Miss Bailey including my obligation to see you safely to McDonough Castle."

Abigail turned back around deciding that this conversation was not making her feel any better. She raised her face to the rays of sunshine peeking through the trees as they continued to ride. Despite the cold of last night, everything was so green and lush. The trees were full, and the meadows were covered in the first buds of spring flowers. It was a beautiful country despite the miserable rain and cold winds they had yesterday.

They rode on in silence until they came to a large loch and the duke pulled his horse to a stop. "This will be a good place to take a break, get a drink, and stretch your legs before we continue."

He dismounted then and reached up to lift her to the ground. Abigail found herself clinging to his arms to hold herself upright as her legs began to tingle from being in the same position for so long. Once she felt confident that her knees would not buckle underneath her, she made her way to the edge of the water where she bent down and cupped her hands, bringing them to her face. The water was cold. She splashed a small amount on her cheeks, then looked up quickly when a pewter cup was held out in front of her face.

She took it from his hands. "Thank you."

He nodded and went over to where the horse was drinking. Abigail took the small cup and took a drink of the cold clear water. "Where are we?"

"We are getting closer to being on McDonough's lands."

She refilled the cup and walked over to him offering him a drink. He took the cup from her, his fingers grazing hers as he did so, then lifted the cup to his lips. She watched his throat as he swallowed the water, then he took the cup and tucked it back in the small bag attached to his saddle.

"I suggest you walk around a bit Miss Bailey; we will not be stopping again until we reach the castle." Cam watched as she walked away stretching her arms over her head and turning her face to the sun. She was quite lovely, and he thought once again that he would like to see her wearing some of the more fashionable gowns worn by the ladies in London. He would bet money that if she was dressed in something more fashionable and not outdated, she would be even more beautiful than he suspected and would cause quite the sensation among the ton. He watched as she ran her fingers through her long flaxen tresses, then turned his back to her. He didn't have time to think of this, of her. He needed to get her to the castle and then concentrate on the threat at hand, if indeed there even was one. He was not yet convinced that Miss Bailey was not exaggerating what she heard. Once Cavendish finished snooping around the inn and asking questions, he would know how to handle it.

"We should start moving again."

Abigail turned and walked back over to him noting that his eyes seemed to follow her movements. When she reached his side, he put his hands around her waist and lifted her onto the horse as if she weighed nothing at all. He then mounted behind her. His right arm held the reins while the left wrapped around her holding her closer. She still had the blanket around her shoulders but with the duke's body so close to hers, she wasn't sure she would need it.

"How much longer before we reach McDonough Castle?"

Cam nudged his horse forward. "We should arrive just before dark. Are you growing tired of my companionship so soon?"

She laughed softly, not trying to hide the sarcasm in her voice. "That's not the reason, your grace. What girl doesn't dream of fleeing from would be assassins in the middle of the night with a handsome duke?"

His arm tightened around her as he leaned down to say softly by her ear. "So, you think I'm handsome then do you, Miss Bailey?"

Abigail felt the warmth of his breath against her neck and shivered slightly. "I think you are dangerous, your grace."

"Of that, there is no doubt, my dear." His lips hovered above her ear and the temptation to press them against the pulse he could see throbbing in her neck was almost more than he could resist.

Abigail closed her eyes trying to still her rapidly beating heart. His lips were close enough to her skin that she could almost feel them.

She needed this journey to end soon so she could put some distance between her and the duke. The man was dangerous, in more ways than one. She couldn't afford to lose her heart or her virtue to a man who had people trying to kill him, no matter how handsome he was.

Her friend Emma, the Duchess of Sunbridge would think this whole ordeal quite amusing. When Emma had left Somerset for London, Abigail had warned her of the dangers and trouble she could get into if she were not careful, and now here she was being held entirely too close in the arms of a man she scarcely knew, a duke nonetheless, as they tried to make it to McDonough Castle before the men that wanted to kill him discovered their whereabouts. Yes, Emma would declare this a glorious adventure and tease her for being the one to find trouble as soon as she left Somerset.

She settled back against him noting that he seemed a bit distracted, as she guessed anyone would be that had someone trying to kill them. For the remainder of the ride, she remained silent until they topped a hill and she saw the most magnificent castle in the glen below. She sucked in her breath and put a hand to her lips.

Cam chuckled at her reaction. "Welcome to McDonough Castle, Miss Bailey."

"Oh my, Emma lives there?"

"She does indeed, or at least she was the last time I saw her. Of course, there is the distinct possibility that she has grown tired of McDonough and his incredibly possessive personality and decided to leave."

Her head snapped around, and he couldn't help but smile at her stunned expression.

"Your ability to jest when we are in such a precarious position, surprises me, your grace."

He chuckled again as he urged the horse forward. "Trust me, Miss Bailey, I am full of surprises."

As they got closer, Abigail marveled at how beautiful everything was. Pink and purple heather covered the glen surrounding the castle. There was a large ancient crumbling turret off to the right covered in vines. While the turret looked to be several centuries old and quite dilapidated, the rest of the castle was much different. The gray stone buildings were darkening with time, there were dozens of windows which amazed her. She supposed she had imagined a medieval castle with few windows and slots where archers could defend the occupants from invaders, maybe even a murder hole inside to stop attacking forces. But no, that was not the castle that stood before her. McDonough Castle was very different from her imagination. There was a large stone entrance that led to a beautiful courtyard. The front of the castle had massive granite steps that led to two huge front doors made from heavy oak. There were turrets on either side but certainly not dilapidated. She guessed every castle must have a turret.

"It looks like something from a storybook," she said as a cool breeze blew her hair back from her face.

"You seem shocked, Miss Bailey. Were you expecting something different?"

Abigail shrugged her shoulders. "Well, yes, I pictured Emma living in a dark, crumbling, tower in a castle surrounded by a moat. This is more of a palace."

He chuckled again the sound reverberating through her own body. "There was an ancient castle on this sight years ago, but Ian's great-grandfather had it torn down and rebuilt a more modern version. It is just as lovely inside as it is on the outside. You will be very comfortable here."

Abigail put a hand over her heart. "I will be so out of place."

Cam frowned at her remark. "I am inclined to believe the opposite. You may stand out from the others, but only because you are so beautiful."

Abigail was stunned by his words. No one had ever said she was beautiful before, but before she had time to think about what to say in response, the front doors were thrown open and Emma bounded down the stairs toward them.

"Abby!"

The duke dismounted and lifted her to the ground just before Emma rushed headlong into her, wrapping her arms around her and squeezing her tightly.

"I had no idea you would arrive today!" Her friend looked to Davenport and then back to her. "And I certainly didn't expect you to arrive with Cam."

Abigail smiled at her friend thankful to have finally arrived. "It's a long story, but it is safe to say that I am thrilled to be here, Emma." Her gaze drifted to the top of the steps where a large mountain of a man stood waiting for them.

Emma must have noticed that she was staring and took her hand to lead her up the steps. Abigail took a second to look behind her to see if the duke would follow and much to her relief he did.

"Abigail, I know the two of you have met briefly before, but this is my husband, Ian."

Abigail dipped into a curtsey. "There is no need for that, lass. My Emma thinks of you as family and there is no need for formality where family is concerned." He reached for her hand and placed a light kiss on her wrist before releasing her.

"Thank you for letting me stay here with Emma. I have missed her a great deal since she left for London." She saw a smile spread across his face, and it made him even more handsome. He was a very large man with sandy brown hair and when his eyes looked at Emma it was obvious that he loved her. He wrapped an arm around her friend's waist possessively pulling her to his side.

"Emma has talked so much of you, and she is excited to have you here and even more excited to take you to London for the season, and whatever Emma wants, Emma gets." He leaned forward and placed a kiss on his wife's forehead.

Abigail blushed and lowered her head; she then felt a hand at the small of her back. "We have had a rather long tiresome journey, and I am certain that Miss Bailey would like to wash up and rest."

Both Ian and Emma gave him an odd look.

"Certainly, Emma why don't you show Miss Bailey to her rooms and introduce her to Persephone and Catherine. Davenport and I will join Hawk and Leicester in my study."

Emma took Abigail's hand. "Are you hungry, Abby?"

Abigail put a hand to her stomach and just realized that she had not eaten anything since the dinner she had shared with the duke last night before everything went so terribly wrong. "I am famished." She looked back to Davenport. "I'm sure the duke is as well."

Emma nodded. "Ian will take care of Cam, and I will take care of you. Let's get you cleaned up, and I will have some food brought up to your rooms."

Abigail was grateful. She turned around one more time to thank the duke. "Thank you, your grace."

Davenport bowed to her. "It is I that is grateful to you, Miss Bailey."

Abigail gave him a timid smile before Emma could drag her away.

Once the ladies were out of sight, Ian turned to him with a frown. "Now do you want to tell me what the hell is going on here?"

Cam narrowed his eyes and his frown became more pronounced. "Yes, but I do not wish to discuss it here. Let's move somewhere more private. Your study will do nicely. I could use a drink as well.

Ian held out his hand. "You know the way, and I hope there is a good explanation."

Davenport growled at his friend. "There is, but you aren't going to like it."

"I was afraid of that," Ian said as he followed behind him into the castle.

Chapter Three

Cam entered Ian's study not surprised to see the Duke of Hawksford and the Duke of Leicester lounging about drinking Ian's best liquor. Ian moved to the decanter of brandy that was sitting on the table between them and poured his own drink.

"Davenport, I wasn't expecting to see you here today," Hawk said as he stood and offered his hand to him.

Cam shook it and inclined his head slightly. "As I thought you would be in London."

Hawk's mouth turned up in a lopsided grin. "Persephone has been wanting to visit McDonough Castle ever since she found out Ian was her cousin. I put her off for as long as I could."

Cam nodded knowing exactly how persuasive the Duchess of Hawksford could be, then looked to Leicester who dipped his chin in greeting but remained quiet. The duke had never really forgiven him for stealing his duchess away after they had been married to accompany him on a mission that resulted in a night of unexpected adventure that put Catherine's life in jeopardy. Davenport had been shot but managed to kill the man before he could hurt Catherine.

Ian moved further into the room after firmly closing the door behind them. "Start talking Cam, why did you arrive here with Miss Bailey astride your saddle?"

Cam took a seat and stared into his glass. "I met her at the inn last night, the *Rose and Thistle*. She was traveling by coach here. The inn was full, and she was having difficulty convincing the innkeeper that a lady should not sleep in the stables. I offered her my room."

"Good God! Please tell me you slept elsewhere," Ian replied pinching the bridge of his nose between his two fingers.

Cam frowned at his friend. "Believe it or not, I'm not nearly as lecherous as the three of you. I slept in the stables along with Mr. Cavendish. He was traveling with me." He took another drink of the brandy.

"I saw that she had a meal, and then escorted her to her room where I reminded her to lock herself in. Later that night Miss Bailey claimed that she heard voices outside her door."

"Bloody hell, women should know better than to travel alone," Hawk said clearly irritated.

Cam sighed heavily knowing his friend spoke the truth, but right now that point was irrelevant. "The men she heard claimed they were there to kill me. She then preceded to climb out her window and come to the stables to warn me."

"She did what?!" Ian said almost choking on the brandy he had just sipped.

Cam swirled the amber colored liquor in the glass he was holding and grinned at his friend's shocked expression. "Yes, apparently it is common for ladies from Somerset to climb out of windows." Reminding Ian of the time Emma had climbed out of her uncle's window to sneak away to see the Prince Regent's firework celebration. Luckily, they had seen her make her escape and decided it would be prudent to follow her in case she ran into trouble, which she did, and they were able to intervene before she was hurt.

Cam smiled at the memory before continuing with his explanation. "After discussing the situation with Cavendish, I decided that I couldn't leave her there. The men knew I had given her the room and might have assumed we knew each other. I couldn't take the chance of her getting involved. Cavendish stayed behind to gather information. He should arrive later tonight. My main concern was getting Miss Bailey here to safety."

"Bloody hell! Are you certain she heard what she thought she did?" Ian asked as he tried to make sense of the situation.

Cam shrugged his shoulders. "I am not certain, of course. That's why I left Cavendish behind, to see if he could discover the truth of it."

Ian began pacing the room. "Damn, Emma isn't going to like this at all."

Cam raised an eyebrow at the remark. "I wasn't exactly pleased with the circumstances myself."

"Just how many people want to kill you, Davenport, or should I say Stafford now? I would be interested to know the number." Michael Shelbourne, Duke of Leicester finally asked as he watched him over the rim of his glass with narrowed eyes.

Cam was not intimidated in the least. "I would say more than most. Am I to assume you are still among their number?"

Michael took another small sip of his drink. "No, you are safe from me. My wife would be most distraught. She still thinks of you as some bloody knight in shining armor. I prefer not to play the part of the villain where she is concerned." His lips curled up in a smirky grin. "Of course, you know my mind would be swayed if you were to disappear again with my wife."

Cam grinned slightly. He couldn't blame Leicester for his malice. There was a time when he had thought of claiming Catherine as his own, but it was obvious that her heart belonged to her husband and Leicester wouldn't have hesitated in killing him if he had tried.

Hawk stood from his seat. "I believe it is time for you to forget the past, Michael. Besides we aren't discussing Catherine, we were discussing the dilemma with Miss Bailey."

"There is no dilemma. Her reputation is safe, no one knows that she was with me alone overnight except for the people in this room. I delivered her safely into Ian's hands, and there should be no further need for concern." He saw the others relax a bit, but in the back of his mind, he had a feeling it would not be that simple.

Abigail hungrily eyed the plate of sandwiches and cheese that Emma's lady's maid had brought up to her room. She put her hand over her stomach once again as it growled louder this time. Her hand itched to reach for a sandwich, but every time she moved to do so, Emma or one of her friends would ask another question that required her to answer.

"So, you really did climb from the window at the inn to warn Davenport?"

Abigail glanced toward the lady who asked the question. If she remembered correctly, it was Catherine, Duchess of Leicester. "Yes, there was no other way to leave the room without being seen." She quickly grabbed a sandwich from the platter and took a bite before another question could be asked. It was a matter of self-preservation at this point. If she waited till all their questions were answered, she would starve to death.

Persephone, Duchess of Hawksford moved to sit beside her. "And after you found Davenport and warned him, he swept you up on his horse and rode away with you in order to keep you safe, bringing you here to McDonough Castle?"

Abigail took another bite of her sandwich and nodded, covering her mouth with her hand as she answered. "Yes."

Catherine began to pace the floor in front of her. "My goodness, what an exciting adventure! I must admit I am a trifle bit jealous."

Emma sat beside Abigail and took her hand. "I'm sure it was more terrifying than it was exciting. Were you terribly afraid, my dear?"

Emma reached for the glass of water the maid had brought with the food and took a long sip. "Not very. It all happened so fast and when we were traveling here, I was more cold than afraid. His grace seemed most capable of getting us here safely."

Catherine looked at Persephone grinning mischievously. "Oh, he is capable all right. So, tell us, what happened next?"

Abigail took another bite of her sandwich. "Well after riding through the night, only stopping once to rest, we arrived here."

Emma sighed before clasping her hands together. "Oh, Abigail that is so…exciting! You have had your first adventure before you even arrived."

Abigail couldn't help but roll her eyes knowing Emma would find all this fascinating. "I knew you would feel that way, but honestly Emma, I could do without the threat of murder in my adventures."

"Hmm, I wonder who could be trying to kill him?" Emma asked, ignoring Abigail's comment as she looked at her friends.

Catherine stopped before them her hands going to her hips. "He is a very dangerous man with a very dangerous past, I'm certain he made more than a few enemies in his line of work."

Abigail coughed as she choked on her sandwich. She grabbed the glass of water taking a sip. "What exactly do you mean? What has he done in the past?"

Persephone looked at her sister-in-law and shook her head slightly. "I don't think it's our place to say, but everything he did was justified and in service to his country."

Emma stood. "I'm sure you are exhausted from the journey not to mention all our questions. I had the maids prepare you a bath, and I'm certain you would like to rest before we have dinner. We will go through my dresses and find you something suitable to wear. I know you had to leave all your things behind, but if I am correct most of your dresses are outdated and worn thin. We will see you dressed properly now that you are here." She wrinkled her nose as she looked at the drab brown dress Abigail was wearing. "Besides, I have always wanted to see you in colors other than brown and gray."

Abigail's cheeks colored slightly at her friend's perusal. Persephone came forward and took both her hands. The duchess had such a sweet genuine smile, it could put anyone at ease.

"My sister-in-law and I are so happy to meet you, Abigail, and I know that we may seem a bit much at times, but we only mean well."

Abigail returned the duchess' smile feeling oddly comfortable with her. The Duchess of Hawksford was a high-ranking member of the ton, and as such held much power, but her kind nature belied her commanding presence.

Both Persephone and Catherine turned to leave the room. Emma stayed behind. Her friend gave her a long hug.

"I am so glad you are here, Abigail. And I am sorry about your father's passing. By the time I got your letter, the funeral had already occurred."

Abigail gave her a sad smile. "He had suffered for so long, it was time."

"I am glad that he insisted that you not mourn his loss."

"He told me that I had mourned him for the past three years, and I was too young and full of life to waste another minute mourning someone that had been dying for so long."

Emma gave her another tight hug. "I will go through my dresses and see what will look best on you and when we get to London, I will have my Madame Lacroix design some gowns just for you."

Abigail opened her mouth to protest, but Emma held up her hand. "I know what you are thinking, you are concerned about your finances, but we will not talk about that now. Come, let me show you the dressing room, you can bathe and then come back to rest before dinner. I'm anxious for everyone to see my beautiful friend looking her best."

Abigail smiled and allowed Emma to lead her to the room next door. There were so many things going through her mind right now. She couldn't help but wonder about Davenport and if she would ever find out what Mr. Cavendish discovered about the plot to kill him. All those thoughts flew from her mind, however, when she saw the giant copper tub filled with steamy water and an array of scented soaps and oils. She sighed heavily and the sound caused her friend to chuckle softly.

"Take your time, my dear. Dinner isn't for a few hours yet. There is plenty of time to indulge." She gave her a wink and left closing the door behind her.

Abigail moved over to the tub letting her fingers skim the warm water. It had been a long journey trapped in a public coach for most of it and then fraught with danger after running into Camden Davenport, a mysterious man with a dangerous past, or so she had been told. But all of that was behind her now, and a long hot soak sounded heavenly.

Abigail followed the sound of laughter and voices as she made her way down the stairs to the great hall below. After her bath, Emma had returned with a few dresses she had selected for her to wear and had instructed her lady's maid to curl and style her hair. She had decided upon a lovely pink gown of soft muslin. It had a modest neckline but was cut in the popular new style of dresses with an empire waist that didn't require a corset. There was delicate lace around the edge of the bodice and the tiny puff sleeves. Abigail hardly recognized herself as she stared into the mirror and thought how easy it would be to become accustomed to such things. She had to remind herself that this was not her life, and when she returned to her own, she would not have the same luxuries that currently surrounded her. Now as she stood only a few steps away from the drawing room where her friend Emma and her high-ranking important friends from London had gathered, she froze. When she had arrived, she had been much too tired to think about the differences between herself and the ladies that were Emma's new friends. She was the daughter of a vicar. Her father was considered a gentleman, but the thought of conversing and mingling with dukes and duchesses had always seemed beyond her reach.

Her breathing increased as she took one more step forward and stopped again. Perhaps she should return to her room and request to have her dinner brought to her there. No one would question her if she claimed to be too tired from her journey to socialize with anyone tonight. The idea was becoming more appealing by the minute when she felt a hand at the small of her back propelling her forward.

"Where is your courage, Miss Bailey? It's too late to back out now," a voice whispered in her ear.

She glanced around quickly to see Camden Davenport standing beside her. His dark eyes peered directly into hers. He took her hand and placed it on her arm. "You look lovely by the way."

Abigail felt her cheeks blush, but before she had time to respond to the compliment, he had ushered them forward into the drawing room. Upon seeing her, Emma rushed to her side, and he relinquished her hand to her friend. Abigail smiled as Emma gushed about how wonderful she looked in her dress, but she couldn't keep her eyes from following Davenport as he moved to stand on the opposite side of the room beside Ian McDonough. He had changed as well and was dressed as elegantly as the other gentlemen. Of course, he was a duke after all, what did she expect?

"Abigail? Are you feeling alright?"

She forced her gaze away from the duke and back to her friend who was watching her with concern evident in her expression. "I'm sorry, I was distracted."

"Yes, I can see that." She frowned as she looked over to where Davenport was talking with her husband. "I know this has been an ordeal for you and if there is something you would like to talk about…"

Abigail gave her a small smile. "There is nothing more to say, Emma."

Her friend didn't appear convinced, but luckily the Duchess of Leicester came to her rescue. "Miss Bailey, that color suits you well. You look lovely."

Abigail returned the duchess's smile. "Thank you, your grace." She curtsied as the Duchess of Hawksford came to join them.

"There is no need with all that formality, Miss Bailey." She reached for her hand and gave it an affectionate squeeze. "I feel we are to be good friends after all. I have a way of knowing these things." She looked over and gave her sister-in-law a subtle wink.

Cam continued to observe Miss Bailey as she stood with the other ladies on the opposite side of the formal drawing room.

"Miss Bailey made quite the transformation."

Cam narrowed his eyes at Ian McDonough. "I'm glad Emma could see her outfitted decently. The dress she wore here was worn and tattered. Burn it. It doesn't suit her."

Ian laughed. "I'm sure Emma has already seen to it. She has mentioned many times that Miss Bailey would need a new wardrobe for London, and it will give Emma great pleasure to provide it. She is determined to see her successful."

Cam nodded as he glanced back to where Miss Bailey stood. She had indeed transformed. After seeing her at the inn, he had suspected that she would be pretty dressed in the more updated fashions of London, but he had never expected her to look as she does now. She was a vision of exquisite loveliness, and he couldn't help but stare. Her light blonde hair seemed to reflect the light from the candles around the room and the pink on her cheeks nearly matched the color of her dress. There was no doubt in his mind that she would be a success in London, especially with the backing of her influential friends.

"How long are you planning on staying before returning to London?" Ian asked, drawing his attention back to him.

"It depends on what Cavendish discovers at the inn. He should arrive by tomorrow, if not, I will go back for him."

Ian grunted. "Of course, you know that you are welcome to stay for as long as you like. And if you have to return to the inn, I will go with you. I don't think you should go alone."

Cam turned his head quickly. "And leave your beautiful duchess and friends behind? No, it is better that you remain here."

Ian frowned. "I owe you a great deal, Davenport. I am indebted to you."

"And you wish to pay off that debt." His lips turned up on one corner in a crooked smile. "Never fear, I'm certain there will be a time for you to return the favor, although this is not it."

Ian nodded in understanding.

Abigail found herself conversing with the duchesses rather easily and was even beginning to look forward to the start of the London season. They made London seem like one giant ball, and it would be an experience like no other. She could only imagine the acrobats performing under the many twinkling lights of Vauxhall Gardens and the opulence of the theater. All things she never imagined she would ever be able to see.

When dinner was announced, she found the Duke of Hawksford by her side. She had learned that his friends called him Hawk, and he was exactly what you would imagine a duke to be. He was tall with dark eyes and an aristocratic nose. Handsome yes, but with an aura of authority about him. She imagined him a force to be reckoned with and seldom had anyone go against his wishes.

"Miss Bailey, might I escort you into the dining room?"

She looked around seeing all the other ladies on the arms of the gentlemen, her friend Emma laughing at something Davenport had said to her. She looked up at the duke. "Thank you, your grace."

They followed the other couples from the drawing room and down the hall. Just as she was being seated at the table, Duncan, Ian's butler, rushed forward and whispered something to Davenport who in turn looked to Ian before excusing himself from the room.

"Pardon me, ladies. Something has been brought to my attention that I must see to immediately. Please do not wait for me, I am not sure how long I will be."

Abigail watched him as he rushed from the room. Once the doors closed behind him, the servants began serving the first course. Abigail looked to Emma who was speaking to her husband quietly. She wondered if Mr. Cavendish had returned, and if so, what information had he discovered.

"You must eat, Miss Bailey. I'm sure we will all find out soon enough why Davenport had to rush off so quickly," Catherine said as she raised her spoon to her lips to taste the soup.

Abigail hated that her facial expressions were so easy to read, but the duchess was right, and it was none of her concern anyway. She picked up her spoon and took a sip of the soup. It was delicious, probably the best thing she had eaten in years, but her mind could not concentrate on the meal, and her eyes kept watch on the door anxiously waiting for Davenport to reappear.

Cam had expected Cavendish tonight or in the morning so when Duncan informed him of his friend's arrival it did not come as a shock. It was unfortunate, however, that he showed up right at dinner. Ian's chef was superb, and he had been looking forward to the roast beef they would be serving all day.

Duncan showed him into the library where he found Cavendish standing by the big double windows looking out toward the gardens. "I'm glad to see you, John. Were you successful in finding out if what Miss Bailey heard was the truth?"

"Aye, I did. The lady was speaking the truth."

Cam walked over to a decanter of brandy and poured his friend a glass before walking across the room to give it to him.

Cavendish took a long slow sip closing his eyes tightly as the liquor burned his throat. "This is much better than that piss they called ale we had at the inn." He took another sip. "You aren't going to like what I found out, your grace."

Cam crossed his arms over his chest waiting for his friend and longtime partner to continue.

Cavendish sat down the empty glass. "After you and the lady left, I waited until almost dawn to question the innkeeper. I wanted to make certain that you had put some distance between yourself and the bastards trying to kill you." He took a few steps forward. "The inn keeper was not cooperative at first, I had to be a bit...persuasive." He tapped his fingers on the hilt of the knife he had sheathed through his belt leaving Cam no doubt about what had occurred.

"The men at the inn were people he knew from the village. There were three of them and he said they were always looking for a way to make extra blunt. When they approached him and asked about you, he told them about you giving your room up to the lady. They became angry and very nervous when they couldn't locate you." He shook his head as he stared down into his almost empty glass. "They weren't very bright either. You would have thought they would have ventured out to the stables to see if we were there, but thankfully their stupidity might have saved our lives."

"Why would three men from a small village in Scotland want to kill me, how would they even know who I was? Did they think to rob me?"

Cavendish shook his head. "I was thinking the same thing, then the innkeeper said a fourth man was with them, a man with a limp who spoke French."

"Toussaint." Cam breathed the name in a menacing soft tone. A name synonymous with evil and death.

Cavendish nodded.

"We need to find the men from the inn and question them. I need to know where Toussaint is and deal with him. The fact that he is on English soil is troubling," Cam said his expression darkening at the thought of a madman traipsing about trying to kill him.

"No need. I already found them. Toussaint doesn't leave loose ends."

"Damn it!" Cam raked a hand through his hair frustrated that Toussaint was still a concern for him even after Napoleon surrendered.

"Their murders were brutal. One of the men was still alive when I found them. His throat was slit, but the artery wasn't severed. Sloppy for a man like Toussaint. When I went over to him, he kept repeating, '*I don't know her name*'. He said it over and over while the rest of his lifeblood slipped away."

"Miss Bailey," Cam said her name in a low whisper. "He is trying to find out about Miss Bailey's identity."

Cavendish once again nodded as he had come to the same conclusion. "That's what I think too. When you gave her your room, it led Toussaint to think you are linked and irrevocably now you are, whether you wish to be or not."

Cam pounded his fist against the table. "Son of a bitch! I should have killed him. I should have set sail for France and killed him the minute Napoleon surrendered." He began pacing back and forth. "There is still something that is bothering me, something I do not understand. I don't understand why Toussaint, an experienced assassin would have hired three inexperienced men from the village to kill me. He would have known they would be no match for my skills."

"You can believe that there is a purpose behind everything that madman does. He knew they wouldn't be successful. He wants you to know. It's all a game to him. He wants you to be aware that he is coming for you, and he will not stop until one of you are dead."

Cam clenched his hands into fists. "We leave for London at first light."

"What of the girl?"

"I can't leave her here. It's too dangerous. I would not want to bring trouble to McDonough, and he is not capable of protecting her as I am."

Cavendish put his arms on his hips. "You plan on dragging a lady with you all the way to London? It will slow us down, not to mention, I'm sure it will not be a pleasant trip for her."

"I need to talk to Hawk and Ian. I will explain everything, but I know she will not be safe as long as Toussaint seeks her."

Cam sat with Cavendish and did not rejoin the others in the dining room. He saw no reason to disturb their meal with the news he would have to share with them, and he was certain his plan would be met with opposition. He knew that Ian and the other men would stay in the dining room after the ladies left them to enjoy their port, so when he heard the doors open and the ladies' voices drift down the hall as they made their way to the drawing room, he and Cavendish decided it was time to join the other gentlemen and let them know of their plans.

When Ian saw them both, he motioned for them to take a seat and instructed the footmen in attendance to serve them.

Mr. Cavendish bowed deeply as he made his way to the chair Davenport indicated for him to take.

"It is good to see you again, Mr. Cavendish. I hope all is well," Hawk said as he raised his glass toward them.

Cavendish nodded to both him and Leicester. "Things could be better, your grace."

"I assume you are speaking of the incident that occurred at the inn," Ian said leaning forward most interested in hearing what, if anything, had been discovered.

Cam took a seat and looked across the table to meet Ian's eyes. "While doing what needed to be done for the good of England, I was in the company of some unsavory individuals. One of whom was a French spy named Toussaint." He paused long enough to see that all three men were listening intently. "Toussaint has no scruples. He kills without conscious anyone that gets in his way. He is well known for his brutal tactics and the barbaric way he tortures his victims."

"And this Toussaint has something to do with what happened at the Rose and Thistle?" Leicester asked almost as if he were bored with the story already.

"One night, several years ago, I was to meet Toussaint. At the time we thought he might be beneficial to us. Perhaps he was working for both sides. I discovered that was not the case when he tried to kill me. I bear a long scar across my chest from his saber. In return, I shot him in the leg. He has a permanent limp and because of it, he bears me ill will." He looked at Leicester. "Toussaint was responsible for my injury in Dover. He sent the man that attacked me and your duchess that night."

At that, Leicester sat up and leaned closer. "Do go on."

"Toussaint sent the men that Miss Bailey heard outside her door at the Rose and Thistle, inexperienced men knowing they would be unsuccessful in their mission. It was a message; he wants me to know that he is coming for me."

Ian stood from his seat. "We need to get word to your contacts in London."

"The men that were at the inn, did they positively identify this Toussaint?" Hawk asked.

Mr. Cavendish looked down at his plate before answering. "The innkeeper said there was a French speaking man with a limp with the three men who were waiting for 'his grace' that night."

"Have you located the other men?" Leicester asked, becoming more agitated.

"I did, your grace. They were dead. All tortured and then had their throats slit."

Hawk stood from his seat joining Ian as they spoke in unison together, "Bloody hell!"

Cam stood as well. "One of the men was still alive when Cavendish found them. "He made reference to Miss Bailey."

Ian moved toward him. "What?! How the hell did she get mixed up in all this?"

Cam knew his friend was not going to like what he had to say next. "When I gave up my room to her because the inn was full, the men must have thought that we were connected in some way. They must have told Toussaint that bit of information under torture mistakenly thinking he would let them live. But that is not his way, he must have continued with his torture trying to discover what he could about her. Of course, they knew nothing, but that will not stop him. He will stop at nothing to get to her thinking it will hurt me. He will see her as my weakness, a way to draw me out."

"I will double the guards around the castle and make sure she stays within these walls at all times," Ian stated in a firm deep voice.

Cam shook his head. "It's not safe for her here. None of you are safe as long as she and I are in residence. We will leave at first light tomorrow."

"By God man, are you seriously thinking of dragging a lady, an unmarried lady I might add, with you while you are on the run from a killer? This is preposterous!" Leicester shouted. "Surely she would be safer behind the safety of these walls than out in the open with you."

Cam sat down the glass he was holding. "Toussaint is a killer, an experienced assassin. It would be easy for him to sneak inside the castle and kill whomever he wished. Do you really want to put your wives and children in that kind of danger?" He saw their faces pale. "Regardless of what you think of me, I am trained to kill. I spent the last eight years living in hell with all manner of evil around me. None of you have seen what I have seen, and none of you are capable of doing what I am. She is safer with me!"

Ian began pacing back and forth. "Where will you go?"

Cam kept his eyes on Leicester. "London. I have places there where she can be safe, and I will be closer to my connections."

"Will you take my carriage?" Ian asked, obviously worried.

Cam shook his head. "We will travel by horseback. A carriage is too easily noticed, and an easier target if he decides to attack on the roads."

"Bloody hell! You can't drag her to London by horseback, it will take at least two weeks if not more. The weather alone would be miserable. It would be a brutal trip for anyone, let alone a lady," Hawk replied.

"Hawk is right. Travel to Edinburgh to the Forth of Firth and take my yacht at Leith. I will send with you a letter of introduction and instructions to the captain. The ship can be made to sail within a few hours. There is always a small crew available."

Cam nodded his thanks to his friend. "I must go talk to Miss Bailey and inform her of what must be done."

Ian laughed, but it was not one of mirth. "We better go with you. We might not be able to protect you from Toussaint, but we might be able to help with our wives."

Cam followed them out of the room but paused long enough to look over his shoulder at Cavendish. "Will you be joining us?"

"No, I'll help you fight the French, I'll face off against Toussaint, but you will have to deal with the wrath of those ladies on your own." He grinned as a plate of roast beef was set before him. "Besides, I can't let good food go to waste."

Cam frowned as he left the room wishing there was another way, but knowing there was not, he accepted his fate.

Chapter Four

"This is just like our husbands to keep us waiting. They should know we would be just as anxious as they are to hear what Mr. Cavendish has to say," Catherine said as she narrowed her eyes at the closed drawing room door.

Persephone was sitting in a chair beside her sister-in-law. "Now Catherine, we are not even certain what business Davenport had to see to before dinner. It may not even concern Mr. Cavendish or what happened at the inn. You are letting your natural inquisitiveness take over your rational thoughts again, my dear."

Catherine frowned. "You are the one who is not thinking rationally. Can you tell me any other reason Davenport would have for rushing off right as dinner was being served?" She tapped her foot in annoyance waiting to see if her friends had anything to say. "I didn't think so."

Persephone giggled. "For the life of me, I have not figured out why you are so interested in this matter. It doesn't concern you one bit." Her hand suddenly flew to cover her mouth as her eyes widened in surprise. "That's it! You are jealous."

Catherine's eyes opened wider. "Don't be ridiculous, Persephone. Jealous of what?"

"It's true! You can't stand the fact that Miss Bailey is involved in an adventure with the dashingly handsome ex-spy, Camden Davenport." Persephone laughed louder. "This is too much. You will no longer be the only woman to participate in his shadowy intrigues."

Catherine crossed her arms over her chest and huffed in annoyance. "You are absolutely ridiculous, Persephone." She looked over at Abigail and Emma. "I must apologize for my sister-in-law; it appears she has lost her mind."

Emma giggled. "I think we are all getting ahead of ourselves. We don't know what Mr. Cavendish has discovered, if anything at all, and Abigail's involvement ended when she went to warn him."

Listening to the conversation swirl around her was almost enough to make her dizzy. Abigail kept her eyes on the door anxiously waiting for the gentlemen to rejoin them. After waiting for what seemed like an eternity the door finally cracked open, and she surged to her feet as did the other ladies. From the looks on the faces of the gentlemen, the news was not good. Abigail looked past the others until her eyes met Davenport's. It was strange that she instantly sought him out and as soon as their eyes locked, she knew the information he had received from Mr. Cavendish could not be good. Davenport didn't approach her but rather stood off to the side as Ian moved to the center of the group.

"Ladies, please sit, I'm afraid that what we have to say is not going to be welcome news." He moved to take Emma's hand and raised it to his lips affectionately as if preparing her for what was about to be said.

Abigail watched as the other men approached their wives as well. She clasped her hands tightly in her lap and chewed her bottom lip anxiously. Davenport's face was unreadable so she turned to Ian hoping he wouldn't make her wait much longer.

"Well, what is it?" Catherine said abruptly not being one to beat around the bush.

"Abigail did indeed overhear a plot on Davenport's life. Mr. Cavendish discovered that much out at the inn," Ian said as he looked down at his wife.

Catherine looked to Davenport. "Do you know who it is?"

He nodded. "I do, it's Toussaint."

Catherine's eyes grew wider. "Well, that certainly increases the danger."

Abigail looked at him noting how calm he outwardly appeared despite the fact someone was trying to kill him. As if this was just something he dealt with every day.

"What are we going to do?" Persephone asked looking to her husband.

"We are not going to do anything...yet. Davenport will be leaving tomorrow. It is too dangerous for him to remain here," Hawk replied as he looked down at his wife.

Emma frowned as she gripped her husband's hand tighter. "Is there nothing we can do to help keep him safe?"

Ian shook his head.

"Thank goodness you got Abigail here safely. I am glad you didn't leave her behind especially knowing dangerous men were about." Emma smiled at her friend and patted her hand.

"Miss Bailey will be leaving with me tomorrow." Davenport's voice was deep and firm, and his words held a touch of finality to them as if there was to be no discussion or argument.

Abigail gasped when what he said sank in but didn't speak. All the other ladies had decided to do that for her.

"What do you mean, she will be leaving with you?!" Emma asked as she surged to her feet not happy at all with this turn of events.

Davenport stepped closer to the group. "When I gave up my room to Miss Bailey, she became a target. The man who wants to kill me will be looking for her. He may believe there is some sort of connection between us and could very well come for her. He could have every intention of using her to get to me. She will not be safe here."

"My goodness, that is not a very positive outlook," Persephone said looking concerned. "Are you quite certain there is no other alternative?"

He sighed heavily and searched for patience as he was not accustomed to having his plans questioned, especially by three ladies that had no idea about the danger involved. "I know this is not an ideal situation, but there really is no other way. If she stays, it puts all of you in danger. I am the only one here capable of keeping her safe."

Catherine stepped forward. "Where will you go?"

"We will leave here at first light and travel by horseback to Leith, from there Ian has offered us use of his yacht to travel the remainder of the way to London." Cam turned his eyes to study Miss Bailey's face as he laid out the plan. He was more than thankful not to see her burst forth into tears. This would be difficult enough without the hysterics. Although, after spending time in the company of the lady, he discovered she was much more sensible and stronger than any of the others suspected.

Emma looked from Abigail back to Davenport. "I wouldn't think London would be any safer than here. Where will you go once you have reached the city?"

"The Devil's Lair. Kingston will be able to help as will the Duke of Avanley, and it will be easier to protect her there."

"The Lair! You are taking her to the Lair?" Catherine asked with a bit of a gleam in her eyes that Persephone didn't miss.

"I still don't think this is a good idea. She is a young unmarried lady, who has the opportunity to have a season this year and perhaps find a husband. This could ruin her," Emma said as she looked to her husband hoping to gain his support.

Cam walked forward and took both of Emma's hands in his and spoke very gently. "This is not a garden party, your grace. This is a matter of keeping your friend alive. Toussaint is an extremely dangerous man, and you would not want Miss Bailey to become his prey. I will keep her safe, it's her life I am concerned with more than her reputation."

Ian frowned at him as he watched the color drain away from his wife's face and wished Cam had not been so direct. "She will be in very capable hands, Emma. There is little chance of anyone finding out about this."

Catherine crossed her arms over her chest. "Even so, perhaps one of us should go along with her."

"No!" was spoken in unison by all the men in the room.

Abigail continued to listen as everyone debated the situation around her, but she had heard enough. She stood from her seat causing all eyes to turn in her direction.

"I know all of you have my best interests at heart, but if his grace believes I am not safe here, I trust him. Besides the fact that I would never wish to see anyone else get hurt because of me." She turned to Davenport. "I believe you mentioned that we were to leave at first light."

He nodded.

"If that is the case, I should begin gathering my things."

Cam's admiration for her just went up another notch. "One small bag is all you can carry. We will be traveling fast. Once in London, I will see that you have anything you require but for the journey just one change of clothes. And dress warmly."

Abigail nodded in understanding then turned back to Emma. "I hate to ask this, but do you have something warm I can wear?"

Emma moved to her and quickly wrapped her arms around her in an embrace. "Oh Abigail, I am so sorry." Her voice broke on the words.

Abigail gave her friend a reassuring smile. "I'm sure everything will be fine. Davenport is more than capable of thwarting this villain Toussaint, and I will see you again when the season begins in London." She could see that her friend was still not convinced. "You had your adventure, Emma. Now it is time for me to have mine."

Both Catherine and Persephone came forward.

"Let's go see about gathering some things for you. I have a very warm wool cloak you can wear. It is quite heavy and will offer protection from both the rain and the wind." Persephone offered helpfully.

"And I have a riding habit as well that will be quite warm," Catherine added.

Davenport watched as the ladies left the room, all of them coddling Miss Bailey.

"That went better than expected," Hawk remarked in a low deep voice once the ladies had left the room leaving the men alone again.

"Hmm, I'm not so certain we have heard the last from our wives on this matter," Leicester said as he took the seat his wife had just vacated.

Ian looked at Cam. "What do you need from me for this journey? I will supply Miss Bailey with a horse, and I'm certain Cavendish could use a fresh mount as well. I will have the kitchen staff prepare some bread and some things to pack to eat along the way. I know you intend to travel light and fast, but you can't starve the lass. She already looks as if a good wind would blow her away. Is there anything else I can do?"

Davenport grinned slightly. "Yes, keep your wives away from London no matter how much they try to persuade you otherwise. They do not need to try and get involved. Toussaint is dangerous, and I would not like them to be hurt."

He saw their eyes narrow.

"I'm going to see if Cavendish left any of your cook's roast beef."

Ian stood and moved toward the door. "When you are done, come to my study. I will give you the letters and instructions for the captain of my yacht, and we will determine the best route to take to Leith."

Cam nodded before leaving the drawing room. He knew how Toussaint worked and he would have to make certain that he did not follow them. He wanted to get Miss Bailey to the safety of *The Devil's Lair* before facing the man that was responsible for the deaths of so many innocent people.

Cam spent a few hours with Ian in his study going over the best route to take to Leith. Keeping Miss Bailey in mind, as well as the need to keep off any main roads, they had finally decided upon the best roads to take. The way was not treacherous, but it would extend the trip by at least a day. Once the route was decided, Ian wrote letters of introduction as well as instructions to the captain of his yacht the *Fascination*, which was docked in the harbor at Leith. Mr. Cavendish was getting their gear together as well as supplies from Ian's kitchen.

The castle was now quiet and the hallways dark. As he made his way to his room, the heels of his boots clicking against the stone floor were the only sound to be heard, he caught sight of a light shining under the door of the room Miss Bailey had been given for the night. Perhaps she had fallen asleep with her candles burning. He tapped lightly on the door before opening it just a crack to see inside.

Abigail heard the creak of the door from where she sat on the bed and turned her head just as Camden Davenport poked his head inside. She put down the book she had been reading and looked at him curiously.

"Was there something you needed, your grace?"

Cam moved further into the room, closing the door behind him but not moving away from it. Being in Miss Bailey's room was certainly not the proper thing to do, but as they were about to embark on a journey where they would be in several improper situations, he didn't see the need to observe propriety at this point.

"I saw the light from the candles underneath the door as I was passing by. I thought you might have gone to sleep with them still burning." He put his hand back on the doorknob but hesitated in leaving. Her hair was hanging loose around her shoulders, and she looked the perfect picture of loveliness sitting up in the bed among the bright white sheets, propped up against the large thick pillows.

Abigail lowered her lashes. "I couldn't sleep and thought if I read a bit it might help."

Cam resisted the urge to walk closer to the bed. "You should at least try to rest. Tomorrow will be a long day."

She nodded and set her book on the table beside her bed before asking, "Once we get to London, will you go after this Toussaint by yourself?"

"I intend to do just that. It's better that way."

She pushed her covers back and stood from the bed. "How can that be better? You could be ambushed and what if he injured you? There will be no one to give you aid."

He tried to focus on her face rather than the fact that she was standing before him wearing a robe concealing what was probably a thin cotton nightgown, her bare toes peeking out from beneath the hem. "Miss Bailey, I have no intention of being ambushed or injured. You do have quite the imagination, don't you?"

She scoffed and stepped closer to him. "I don't imagine that people plan on being injured, your grace. No one ever says, you know I think I will go out and perhaps be set upon by brigands or mayhap I will get wounded and incapacitated, don't expect me home for dinner."

God, he loved her cheekiness.

"Miss Bailey, I assure you I can handle myself." He put both hands on her shoulders and faced her. Her eyes narrowed and her lips were set in a firm line. *What was it about this woman that made him want her so?* "We both need to get some rest. It will be a long journey and unless you would like for me to crawl in that bed with you, I should probably leave and return to my room."

She crossed her arms over her chest. "There is no need in you trying to frighten me with such talk, your grace. I just don't see why you must take such chances with your safety. Couldn't Mr. Cavendish or your friend Kingston go after Toussaint with you?"

Cam stepped closer and took her chin in his hand forcing her gaze up to his. "Abigail, I am perfectly capable of handling any threat that comes my way. Cavendish will certainly be ready to assist me, but Kingston will be entrusted with watching over you. I will not take any chances with your safety."

Her lips slightly parted as if she wished to say something else but thought better if it. *Damn, he wanted to kiss her, to taste her sweetness, to feel her yield to his desires.*

He backed away quickly and moved toward the door. "Get some sleep. Tomorrow will come sooner than you wish."

She nodded and got back into her bed before blowing out the candle.

Cam closed the door and leaned his back against it as he tried to purge her from his mind. The way she had looked sitting against those pillows would make any man long to have her in his bed every night, to think about a future, but that was not for him. He shook the thought from his head. Toussaint was much too dangerous for him to allow the lovely Miss Bailey to distract him. Remaining focused would be the only way he could outsmart the butcher, and once he faced him again, he would finish the job he started years ago.

Cam had been correct on one thing; morning had come sooner than she wished, and Abigail had spent the last hour trying to soothe Emma. Her friend had tried to think of a way to avoid her having to leave McDonough Castle, but after much argument, she finally gave up. Abigail had never known her friend to be afraid of anything, so to see tears shining in her eyes when she told Davenport that when she got back to London, she would expect to find Abigail safe and sound, surprised her.

Abigail sat on the horse Ian had loaned her with Mr. Cavendish mounted on his horse beside her. The sky was bathed in pink and purple light as the sun began to peek over the Scottish Highlands. A thin mist covered the ground making everything it covered look otherworldly. She watched as Davenport talked to Ian and then after shaking hands with him, mounted his horse and proceeded to walk on, leaving her behind.

"We best be following him, miss," Cavendish said as he looked over and gave her a small smile.

Abigail turned to wave at Emma one more time, then nudged her horse forward following behind Davenport. "Is he not going to wait for us?"

Mr. Cavendish's grin grew wider, "He never waits, miss."

Abigail looked to where Davenport rode ahead of them. "Have you known him for very long, Mr. Cavendish?"

"Aye lass, we have been through hell together."

Abigail turned to look at him. "The war?" when he nodded, she continued, "Did the two of you fight alongside the British army?"

"Davenport and I operated behind enemy lines. Most everything we did was in secret. For most of the war, only one man in the war department knew about his grace and what he was doing. Of course, he wasn't a duke at that time, nor did he ever think to be."

Abigail listened intently. "Why is this Toussaint trying to kill him?"

Cavendish narrowed his eyes. "Toussaint is an indiscriminate killer. He enjoys it. Davenport only did what had to be done. He did not take pleasure in taking lives. There was a meeting arranged between the two before anyone knew the kind of man Toussaint was, and both men were injured. Toussaint has been obsessed with killing him ever since."

"Is the man really so dangerous?"

Abigail suppressed a shiver at the look in Mr. Cavendish's eyes when he responded to her question.

"Both of them are."

Abigail pondered his words as they rode along, but as Mr. Cavendish did not seem inclined to answer any more questions, she continued riding in silence.

The sun was still low in the sky and a gust of wind whipped around her causing a shiver to travel up her spine. Spring was much colder in the Highlands than it was in Somerset. Abigail peered forward and noted that Davenport had not slowed his pace. Evidently, he was not concerned with whether she could keep up or not and had no intention of talking to her. She pulled the hood of her cloak over her head to ward off the chill. Mr. Cavendish remained by her side as she guessed he had been ordered to do. Emma had mentioned that it would take several days to get to Leith, she could only hope time would pass quickly.

Cam was pleased with the progress they had made today, and even more glad that Miss Bailey had been efficient at keeping up with the pace that he set, as well as keeping any complaints or grumblings she might have to herself. They had stopped midday for a brief break, but while she stayed close to Cavendish, he had kept his distance. Now that the sun had lowered behind the hills, the wind was decidedly colder. He knew they would need to stop soon, but he wanted to push as far as possible before making camp.

"Cam, we need to stop. The lady isn't going to last much longer. She is teetering in her saddle as it is," Cavendish said as he rode up beside him.

Cam turned to look behind him and saw that Miss Bailey's head was lowered. "She is keeping up."

"Aye, she has done admirable, much better than I expected, but she isn't used to this and while she hasn't protested, I can see the exhaustion in her face and body movements."

Cam sighed heavily before pulling his horse to a stop. "Damn it." He looked around. "There appears to be a grove of trees just up ahead. We can make camp there for the night. It will give her a few hours of respite. The horses could use the rest as well."

They rode on and when they reached the grove Cam dismounted and moved to stand beside Miss Bailey's horse. As he reached her, he said, "We will camp here…." But before he could get the words from his mouth, he saw her tetter and reached up to catch her just as she slid from the saddle.

He held her in his arms as her eyes fluttered open. He waited until he was certain she was alert before setting her back on her feet.

Abigail wrapped her arms around herself as she shivered. "I'm sorry, I was just going to close my eyes for just a minute. I suppose I was more tired than I realized." Her voice was soft and shaky.

Cam frowned as he stared into her face. "I should have been more considerate of you. I apologize for pushing you at such a punishing pace."

She accepted what she felt was a hesitant apology. "We are stopping for the night?"

He took her arm and led her closer to the trees. "We are. Cavendish will see to the horses, and I will get us something to eat."

Abigail turned to look up at him. "What should I do?"

He gave her a small smile. "Just rest."

Abigail didn't argue with him. She would never complain, but every part of her body ached, and she was exhausted. She had never spent more than an hour or two on a horse, so after an entire day and evening horseback, she hurt and ached everywhere. All she wanted to do was sleep.

She gingerly sat down and leaned back against a tree stretching out her legs and stretching her back. It was going to be a cold night and she hoped they would build a fire soon.

Cam went to his horse and pulled out some bread and cheese that Ian's cook had prepared for them. When he got back to where Abigail was sitting against the tree, her eyes were closed and he wondered if she had already fallen asleep, but when he knelt in front of her, her eyes fluttered open, and she pressed her hand over her mouth to cover a yawn.

"Are you hungry?" Cam held out some bread.

"Not very, I am tired and cold. Will you build a fire?"

Cam shook his head. "I'm afraid we can't do that. We don't want to draw any attention to where we are, and a fire would be too easy to spot."

Abigail pulled her cloak closer around her. "I see." She took the bread and cheese he offered her.

She watched as they made camp and couldn't shake the feeling of guilt at not helping. Mr. Cavendish had walked over and given her a thick wool blanket to spread on the ground and another to cover herself up with. She was in the process of getting her makeshift bed ready when Davenport came up behind her. His soft deep voice caused her to jump.

"Get some sleep, Miss Bailey. You will be safe here. I will take the first watch and Cavendish will relieve me in a few hours."

Abigail pushed her hair back from where it had fallen across her face. "Do you think Toussaint is out there somewhere ready to attack us as we sleep?"

Cam shook his head. "Cavendish made it known in the village that we were traveling north toward Inverness and the islands beyond. It will throw Toussaint off our trail long enough for us to reach Leith. By the time he discovers that he has been duped, we will hopefully be sailing to London."

"Thank goodness. It was very clever of you to do that."

Cam reached for her, griping her upper arms lightly and then rubbing up and down to warm her. "Paying me compliments again, Miss Bailey, if you aren't careful, I will begin to think you are developing an affection for me."

He saw her roll her eyes even if he did detect a hint of a grin on her pretty face, then he said more seriously. "I will protect you, Abigail. There is no need for you to worry."

Just the feel of his touch, even if it was through the thick wool of her cloak, seemed to make her feel more secure. It was dark with only the moon to give them light, but he was close enough that she could still see his eyes, and they seemed to hold her captive. Then just as suddenly as he touched her, did he step away.

"Go to sleep, we have another long day tomorrow." He had not meant for his voice to sound so abrupt and from the way her eyes widened, she had not expected it either. There was something about her that drew him, and that distraction could be dangerous.

He walked toward where Cavendish was standing. "I'll stand watch." He didn't wait for his friend to answer before walking away.

He moved along the perimeter of the camp wondering how in the hell he ended up in this situation. This is what he gets for trying to do a good deed. Now he was stuck with the desirable and altogether too cheeky Miss Bailey for God only knows how long. At least, once he got to London, he could leave her in the care of Kingston at the Lair while he settled things with Toussaint.

It was three hours later when Cavendish walked up behind him. "Go get some sleep and go take care of the lady. I'll keep watch for the rest of the night. Her teeth are chattering so loud if Toussaint was out there, the sound would draw him right to us."

Cam frowned. The night had been much colder than he had expected. He didn't know what else he could do to make this more comfortable for her. This was not a journey for a lady. Sleeping on the cold ground without even the warmth of a fire and just bread and cheese to eat until they reached Leith.

As he walked back to the camp, he tried to think of any way he could to make this more bearable for her. He walked over to where she was lying near the tree, on the heavy wool blanket he had given her. She had pulled the blanket up over her head, but even in the darkness of night, he could still see her shaking and shivering underneath.

He blew out a heavy breath, the warm air forming a vapor cloud as it met the cold. He knew what he had to do, and while Ian would probably call him out for it, there was no other way to keep her warm. He grabbed his blanket and moved over toward her. As he laid down beside her, he pulled her into his arms letting the heat from his body warm her as he covered them both in his own banket. She stirred but instead of pulling away, she only snuggled closer against him. Her shivering ceased and while he knew he should try to get some rest, the feel of her warm feminine curves pressed against him was not making it easy.

Abigail finally felt warmth. After shivering and shaking until her teeth rattled, she finally succumbed to warmth. She rolled over trying to get closer to the heat and her eyes flew open as she felt the strong firm chest of the man beside her. She placed her hands against him feeling the rise and fall of his chest as he breathed and a sense of panic overcame her.

"Go back to sleep, Abigail," he said quietly but firmly.

She paused. "We can't…"

"You were shivering. I am only keeping you warm, you may rest assured your virtue is safe from me. Besides, do you see anyone around that would report this indiscretion to the scandal sheets in London?"

He never opened his eyes as he spoke and Abigail frowned. She supposed she was being a trifle bit ridiculous. Just her being with him on this trip meant she was compromised beyond redemption from the start, especially if any of this was discovered.

"Would it make you feel better if I moved away?" he finally asked her.

Abigail looked up to see one eye open and a smirk on his face. She could either stay beside him or freeze. As much as she knew she should insist that he move away from her, the warmth from his body felt good, too good to relinquish. "No, I'm sorry I woke you."

He didn't reply only pulled her closer so that her head rested under his chin and went back to sleep. Abigail kept very still listening to his slow even breathing. Her face was turned toward him and her hands rested on his chest. She closed her eyes secretly letting herself relish in the way it felt to be held in his arms and glad he could not read the thoughts going through her mind.

Chapter Five

T he next morning when Abigail opened her eyes, she found herself alone again and for a moment she wondered if something terrible might have happened while she slept. She frantically began looking around and was relieved to see Mr. Cavendish walking towards her leading her horse.

"We need to get moving, Miss Bailey."

She stood and grabbed the blankets. "I hope you have not been waiting for me."

"Davenport said to let you sleep." He took the blankets from her hands. "There is a small stream a few yards through those trees." He raised his arm pointing in the direction she should go. "You can take a few minutes to freshen up and see to your needs. We will leave as soon as you are ready."

Abigail walked a few yards through the trees and followed the sound of running water to the stream. She took a few minutes to freshen up, splashing some cold water on her face and trying to mentally prepare herself for another full day on horseback. She was in the process of pulling up her hair when she was suddenly startled by the sound of a limb breaking behind her and jumped to her feet. Different scenarios began to play through her mind. Could there be a wild animal watching her through the brush waiting to attack, or highway men planning to ambush their group, or worse, the killer Toussaint had discovered their deceit and had found them? She picked up a large branch that was lying at her feet and made herself ready in case of an attack.

"It's just me, no need to run in fright, Miss Bailey," Davenport said with a grin on his face as he approached.

Abigail threw down the stick, picked up her skirt, and moved toward him. "I was not about to run, your grace. You simply startled me."

He moved out of the trees and when the light from the first morning rays of the sun hit his face, she was reminded once again of how handsome he was.

"I don't think it necessary for you to continue to address me as, 'your grace'. I must confess it does get tedious after a while."

Abigail raised her face to his noting the deep rich brown of his eyes and the way the corners of his lips were turned up slightly in a half grin. His nose had a slight bump on it as if it had been broken at one time, but it certainly didn't detract from his looks. If anything, it made him look more dashing, especially with the stubble of a day's growth of whiskers on his face. "I don't think it is proper for me to address you as anything else, your grace."

He reached for her hand to help her walk over the fallen log in front of her. "After last night, I think we can forget about being proper, at least until we arrive in London."

Abigail felt her cheeks flame. She knew he was referring to the fact that she had slept quite peacefully wrapped in his arms last night and regardless of the reason for it, she couldn't deny that it had felt good for him to hold her. "That was simply a matter of survival, your grace."

Cam liked her sharp tongue and the way her cheeks pinkened at the reminder of how she had slept curled against him. Whether he liked to admit it or not, he had enjoyed holding her. He clenched his fists at his sides thinking of the way her body had curved against his as if she had been created for him. If not for the fact that a madman was trying to kill him, he might take the time to appreciate her curves all the more, but alas, now was not the time.

He led her back to camp and lifted her into the saddle. He had asked Cavendish to ride out front this morning so he could stay behind with her and was met with a knowing look from his long-time friend.

"Might I ask a question, your grace?" Abigail asked looking over toward him as they rode on.

He narrowed his eyes, annoyed that she continued to address him by his title. "Are you going to continue to persist with the 'your grace' nonsense?" He sighed in annoyance. "What is your question?"

"When we arrive in London, what is it that you will do with me?"

There was quite a bit he would like to do with her, but he was certain that was not what she meant. "Once we reach *The Devil's Lair*, I will leave you in the care of my friend Benedict Kingston. He will protect you while I seek out Toussaint."

"You are going to leave me? But I thought you had said that you would protect me."

Cam was surprised to see the concern on her face, and he did not miss the panic in her voice. The thought that she felt safe with him pleased him more than he cared to admit. "You will be well protected, Abigail. I will see to it. I wouldn't leave you if I wasn't completely confident in Kingston's abilities and sure of your safety."

She sighed heavily, her hands gripping the reins tighter. "This isn't what I expected."

He chuckled softly. "I don't imagine it is, but Kingston will be able to keep you safe. I have other friends in London as well that are capable of looking out for you."

"I would much rather stay with you." Her words were spoken softly, but she knew he had heard her from the intense frown on his face.

The next several days were very much the same. They rode through the day with Davenport speaking very little to her. Every day her body ached in a new area. It was not a pleasant journey, and if she never rode a horse again, she would be content with that. At night when they would stop, she would help Mr. Cavendish get the camp ready while Cam disappeared to do whatever he did to make them safe. Without fail, after she would fall asleep, she would be awakened sometime during the night as he lay beside her and wrapped her in his arms to ward off the chill of the night air. She had grown accustomed to sleeping beside him and missed the warmth of his body when she would awaken in the morning to find him gone.

This morning, however, she found that the sun had risen much higher in the sky before she opened her eyes. She sat up startled that she had slept so late.

"Good morning," his deep voice said from where he stood along the tree line.

She stood up quickly grabbing the blankets from the ground. "I'm sorry I slept so late. I can get ready quickly."

He moved closer to her and took the blankets from her hands. "There is no need to rush. Cavendish has already ridden into Leith. He has the letters for the captain of the *Fascination* and will make the arrangements for our departure. I thought you would like to take some time to freshen up before we go to the port."

Abigail self-consciously put a hand to her hair and looked down at the riding habit she had worn for the past few days. It had definitely seen better days. She brushed her hands over the skirt knowing she must look a mess. "Is there somewhere close by where I can change into the extra dress I brought with me?"

"There is a secluded cove with a small lake where you can bathe and change your clothes. I will keep watch." He tossed her a bar of soap and smiled when her eyes widened. "Don't worry, I won't peek… unless you want me to."

Abigail felt her cheeks flush even though she was growing accustomed to his rakish comments and manners. "Are you certain it is safe?"

He gave her a wink. "Positive."

After grabbing her bag that held her extra change of clothes, he took her hand and led her down a hill and through some thick brush and trees to a secluded area.

She wrapped her arms around herself. She knew the water would be frigid, but she was beginning to smell more like her horse than a lady, so it was prudent that she bathe before they travel into the port.

"I will wait on the other side of the trees close enough to hear if you need assistance… or if you decide you would like some company."

Abigail couldn't help but laugh. "Does that type of flattery usually work for the ladies you typically consort with?"

"Usually, although some ladies are more easily swayed than others." He gave her a wink before turning and walking back the way they had come to give her privacy.

Abigail waited a few minutes before removing her clothes, she had never been naked outdoors and the thought of being so exposed was a little frightening. Her fingers trembled slightly as she removed her riding habit and the chemise beneath it leaving her standing nude. A chilly wind whipped around her causing goosebumps to appear on her arms. She hurried into the water sucking in her breath as the cold consumed her. It was like ice. She went out in the water until it was halfway up her thighs. There was no way she could linger in the frigid temperatures, so she dunked her head quickly to wet her hair and vigorously began rubbing the soap over her body as she fought to keep her teeth from chattering. She scrubbed until she felt like she had finally been successful in cleaning the past few days' dirt and grime off her skin. She then began washing her hair hoping she would be able to brush out the tangles without too much trouble. She dunked her head back in the water to rinse the soap when she felt something rather large swim through her legs. She let out a shrill shriek as she raced back to the bank to get away from whatever creature was in the water with her.

Cam had left Abigail to allow her the privacy she would need to wash, but he didn't go far. He could hear her splashing in the water. After holding her in his arms for the past four nights, his mind couldn't help but imagine her as she swam naked in the loch. He leaned back against the tree and closed his eyes briefly. He needed to turn her over to Kingston as soon as possible so he could concentrate on finding and killing Toussaint. Unfortunately, the longer he remained in her company, the more he found himself thinking about her and looking forward to the nights when he could hold her. He reached down and plucked a piece of grass from the ground and twirled it between his fingers when he heard a scream, her scream. He raced back to where he had left her not thinking of anything except killing whoever had dared to harm her. He moved through the trees stopping dead in his tracks when he came through the clearing to see Abigail rushing from the water, gloriously naked. For a moment it seemed as if the breath had been knocked out of him.

"Something is in the water!" she yelped as she came onto dry land and then as she remembered her unclothed state, blushed furiously and rushed over and grabbed her bag and held it against herself trying unsuccessfully to hide her nudity behind it.

Cam tore his eyes away from the vision before him and looked around quickly for any dangers. He turned back to her. She was standing with her arm crossed over her breasts and the bag hiding the triangle of curls at the apex of her thighs.

"Something swam between my legs." Her breath was coming quickly through her lips.

He raked a hand through his hair as he turned his back to her. "Christ woman! It was probably an eel." He closed his eyes trying to push the image of her curves glistening from the water, her nipples hardened into tiny nubs from the cold, her flat belly, and her long slender legs from his mind.

He heard her moving behind him and he thought this must be some sort of punishment for the sins he had committed in his life, to desire a woman he had no business wanting, a woman he could never have.

If anyone could die from embarrassment, she would be standing at the gates of St. Peter right now. Abigail didn't know how she would face him again. He had seen her, all of her, when she frantically ran from the water. It was completely her fault, so she had no reason to be upset with him, but that fact didn't make the situation any less humiliating.

She rummaged through the bag and found the linen Emma had packed for her along with a fresh chemise and dress. She hastily dried herself off keeping her eyes on Davenport's back in case he decided to turn around. When she had the dress on, she nervously cleared her throat. "I'm dressed, you may turn around now."

She knew her face had to be bright red, and she couldn't look directly into his eyes.

Cam watched as she nervously clutched the bag in front of her. She was dressed and a part of him despised the muslin fabric that was now covering her body from his sight. "Come with me, I built a fire earlier this morning. You must be cold."

"It's alright, I'm fine, besides I thought we couldn't have a fire," she said hesitantly as she followed a good distance behind him.

"I can hear your teeth chattering from here, and we are not that far from Leith. It was safe to do so, besides I knew you would need to warm up after being in the water." He didn't tell her that if he took her into his arms right now to warm her as he wished to do and as he had the past few nights, he would not be able to hide the evidence of his desire for her.

He led the way back to where they made camp and went about the business of getting things ready to move into town when he noticed that she was twisting her arms behind her back still trying to reach the buttons on the dress Emma had sent with her. He threw down the armload of blankets and supplies he was about to put in his bag and moved toward her. He grabbed her shoulders and turned her around moving her long wet tresses aside so he could button up the back of her dress. Her skin was still damp, and he could see her shiver when his fingers grazed the skin down her back as he tried to do up the dress.

Damn it all to hell. He was not supposed to feel desire for this woman, to want to pull her into his arms and kiss her, to want to kiss his way down her spine. "Damn dress must have a hundred buttons." The irritation he was feeling at himself must have carried over into his tone of voice because her body tensed.

"I'm sorry, I tried to do it myself," her voice sounded equally irritated.

He heaved a heavy sigh regretting the harshness of his voice. He finished the last of the buttons and went over to see to his horse.

Abigail put on her heavy cloak and wrapped the wool blanket around her shoulders. As if this trip needed to be any more uncomfortable, now she was mortified that he had seen her naked. Not only that, but he seemed angry at her because of it. She walked over to her bag and took out her brush so she could try to run it through her wet hair. She could feel the tears gathering in her eyes. The trip had been hard, she hurt everywhere, she had not eaten a decent meal in days, and through it all, she had not complained. All she had wanted to do was leave Somerset, visit her friend Emma, and have her own grand adventure in London. She was getting a bit more than she bargained for, however. She did not want to be seen as a burden, she wanted to help but now because of her foolishness, Davenport was angry with her. She closed her eyes to fight back the tears that threatened to fall and continued raking the brush through her hair savagely pulling at the tangles.

"If you keep that up, you won't have any hair left."

She had not heard him come up behind her and was startled when he took the brush from her hand.

"Come warm yourself by the fire."

Abigail still couldn't face him, but she nodded her head and moved to stand before the flames. The heat felt good, and she held out her hands to warm them.

"Once Cavendish returns, we will head straight to the *Fascination* and sail as soon as she has been made ready. We will be in London in a day or two, and then we will see about getting you some more clothes."

Abigail simply nodded as she held her hands closer to the fire, pleased he had not chosen this moment to make a jest or comment on what he had just seen.

He watched her as she stared into the flames and the urge to take her into his arms was almost overwhelming. "I know this trip has been difficult, Abigail, and I wish I could have spared you all of this."

She looked up and her violet eyes were shining. "I haven't complained."

"I know you haven't and because of that you have earned my respect."

She gave him a small smile. He moved closer and took her hand in his. When her fingers closed over his, he pulled her closer wrapping his arm around her waist. He lifted her chin higher so he could look into her eyes. When she nervously ran her tongue over her lips, that sealed her fate.

He leaned down slowly giving her every opportunity to pull away, but when her eyes fluttered closed, he pressed his lips to hers and a jolt went through him at the contact. He had only meant for it to be a quick kiss, just a taste, a taste that would purge her from his system, but no, the feel of her lips against his only made him want her more. He ran his tongue along the seam of her lips urging her to open for him and when she did, he took advantage, pulling her closer letting his tongue delve deep mingling with hers. Reaching up, he wrapped a hand in her wet mass of curls. He swallowed the small gasp she made when he tilted her back giving him better access to plunder her mouth. His arm tightened around her waist, and he lifted his lips so he could press kisses down her neck when he heard a loud cough behind them. He instinctively pushed Abigail behind him to shield her from whatever danger there might be.

"I found the captain of the *Fascination*. He said he will have her ready to sail on the afternoon tide, so we should hurry and make our way to the port," Mr. Cavendish said with a look of strong disapproval on his face and Cam felt like a schoolboy about to be chastised by his headmaster.

Abigail reached down to pick up the blanket that had fallen away from her shoulders during their embrace and moved to stand away from him. "I will go see to my horse and pack up the rest of my things."

Cam nodded and watched the gentle sway of her hips as she walked away and cursed the fact that Cavendish had returned when he did. He turned back around to talk to his longtime friend only to be met with a hard punch to his shoulder.

"What the hell do you think you are doing?!"

Cam rubbed the spot on his arm that was sure to bruise and narrowed his eyes. "If you don't know, then you have been without a woman longer than I suspected."

"Don't spout that codswallop to me. Miss Bailey is a lady, a lady that has been through a hell of a lot the past few days and may not have all her wits about her to fight off a rogue like you."

Cam kicked dirt over the fire. "It was just a kiss. I didn't tup her for heaven's sake."

"A kiss that looked a few minutes away from stripping her of her clothing. If that wasn't bad enough, you were so caught up in your desire that you didn't even hear my approach. I didn't come this far with you to see Toussaint kill you because your cock was overpowering your brain."

Cam clenched his fists tightly at his side. If it was anyone else speaking to him like that, he would have knocked several of their teeth out by now, but what frustrated him the most was that he knew Cavendish was speaking the truth. He had let his desires interfere with getting her to safety, and he wouldn't let it happen again. He would have to cast out the beautiful Miss Bailey from his mind, at least until he had taken care of Toussaint. But once he had put Toussaint in the ground, he would be taking Miss Bailey to his bed, of that he was certain.

Abigail should feel relieved that Mr. Cavendish had interrupted her kiss with Davenport, but instead, she felt frustrated, as if she were on the edge of something wonderful only to have been pulled away abruptly. She had never been kissed like that before. Of course, at the age of twenty and one, this was not her first kiss, but the young men from the village that had dared to steal a kiss from the vicar's daughter were inexperienced, and their kisses were rushed and awkward. This kiss was nothing of the sort. When Cam had wrapped his arms around her, it felt as if a force was pulling her to him. His touch seemed to erase all the humiliation she had felt earlier when he had seen her naked by the water. The contact had been tender, yet possessive. Foolish is what it was. This was not a morning ride through Hyde Park, there was a very dangerous man wanting to see Davenport dead, and if he is to be believed, she was now a target as well.

She busied herself with packing things up so they could continue traveling to Leith where they would take Ian's yacht on to London. She had never sailed before. This journey was filled with many firsts for her. She had never been more than twenty miles from Somerset, she had never seen Scotland, she had never ridden horseback for hours and hours a day, and she had never been hunted by a killer. Now she could add sailing the channel to her list of firsts.

It was quite daunting to think of the dangers of sailing. She had heard stories of ships that had gone down in the rough storms off the coast of England. There was an older couple from the village that had sailed from Dover when she was a young girl, and she had heard her father telling her mother how their ship had sunk with no survivors. The thought of drowning in the deep cold water of the

English Channel was terrifying but riding all the way to London on horseback was beginning to seem an even worse fate. She would have to pray that they had fair weather and that she would be a good sailor not succumbing to the sickness that plagued many people on the water. Although right now the biggest peril she had to face was her inability to resist her attraction to Camden Davenport. That man was becoming increasingly more dangerous by the day.

Chapter Six

When they had entered the port at Leith, Abigail excitedly observed everything that was going on around her. She loved seeing the tall, masted ships and all the activity bustling about the port. The sailors hurrying around carrying freight to the ships bound for all parts of the world and the sounds and smells of the port added to her excitement. For a girl that had never been far from home, it was all so thrilling. She was just about to follow Mr. Cavendish up the gangway when Davenport grabbed her arm and pulled her close.

"Because of the circumstances surrounding us and the reasons you are traveling with me without a chaperone, it was necessary to concoct a story to tell the captain and the crew onboard the yacht."

Abigail looked at him curiously. "A story? What sort of story?" she asked, almost afraid to hear what he had come up with, especially with the way his grin widened.

"They have been told that you are my wife."

"Your wife! Was that really necessary?" Abigail replied, her voice rising with the shock of what he had said.

He wrapped an arm around her waist and pulled her closer. "Now, now, darling you wouldn't want to draw attention. Besides, this was the only way we could think of to protect your reputation as well as keep you safe onboard ship."

"Safe? Is the captain not trustworthy?" She asked, forcing a smile to her face when she noticed some of the crew staring at them from the deck of the ship.

Cam took her hand and lifted it to his lips as he eyed the men staring at them. "The captain, yes, but I can't vouch for the other members of the crew. Ian thought it would be best if we just played the part. The letter of introduction he sent the captain mentioned that we were recently married. He saw no reason to add anything else about our debacle."

"Why was I not told?"

Cam ushered her forward toward the waiting ship. "We thought it might be upsetting and from the lack of color on your face, it seems we were right. It does prick my pride a bit that the thought of being my wife is so troubling to you, I am almost offended." He gave her a wink. "It is just while we are onboard the ship. Once we get to London there will be no need for the farce, and you will return to being Miss Abigail Bailey." He leaned closer and spoke softly near her ear, "But for right now you are my wife, Abigail Davenport, Duchess of Stafford." Before she could protest further, he handed her off to Mr. Cavendish, who quickly ushered her up the gangplank of *The Fascination*.

The yacht was white and gleamed in the sun and was more impressive than she had expected. If it were not for the shocking turn of events that she had just been made aware of, she would have wanted to take more time admiring it. The captain was standing on deck dressed in his finest naval attire, rolling the ends of his long mustache between his fingers as he welcomed them onboard with a bright smile and a deep bow.

"Your grace, it is an honor to have you on board *The Fascination*. We all will endeavor to make your journey to London as pleasant as possible. Please allow me to show you to your cabin."

Abigail pasted a smile on her face, but she wished Davenport had given her more time to prepare. When the captain referred to her as, your grace, she was in such shock that she almost curtsied. She followed the captain below deck and was surprised at how spacious the cabin was and for a moment she wondered if she would be expected to share it with Davenport since the crew believed her to be his wife. She shrugged off her concerns, she was much too excited to be on a ship about to set sail for London to worry over something that could not be helped. After the captain left her, she opened the cabin door to see Mr. Cavendish waiting for her outside in the passageway.

"Are you angry enough to bash in my skull for deceiving you, lass?"

She crossed her arms over her chest and tried to appear incensed, but she was not successful. "You knew about this deception before today?

He nodded. "Aye"

"It would have been nice to have known before I was about to walk onboard the ship. I would have attempted to play the part better."

"Davenport has his reasons even if they only make sense to him at times." He gave her a smile and offered her his arm. "Would you like to go on deck, your grace, and watch as we set sail?"

"Can we please? I would love to." Abigail eagerly wrapped her arm through his and together they walked up to the deck. She wondered where Davenport had disappeared, but she was sure he was around somewhere.

Cam knew he didn't have a lot of time before the ship sailed, but with Abigail safely onboard *The Fascination* with Mr. Cavendish to look out for her, he thought it would be the perfect opportunity to ask questions around the seedier side of the docks. He moved through the dark and dirty dockside tavern ignoring the half-naked woman trying to get his attention. A drunken sailor moved toward her, and he saw the man place some coins in her hand before they both disappeared into a darkened corner. He moved toward the bar intending to speak to the man pouring grog to the patrons of the establishment.

He was almost there when an overly large man stepped in front of him wearing torn pants and no shirt. His bald head had a few lumps on it, and Cam imagined he had been in more than a few scuffles. "What's a nob like you doing 'ere?"

Cam held up both his hands. "I'm not here for trouble. Just step aside and you won't get hurt."

The man's boisterous laughter drew others' attention their way, and Cam sighed knowing this was not going to be as easy or uneventful as he had hoped.

When the man finished laughing, he curled his hand into a fist and leaned close enough that Cam could smell his foul breath undoubtedly caused by the rotten teeth in his mouth. "Why don't you give me all ye blunt and that fine coat ye be wearing, and I might let ye leave 'ere under your own power."

Cam watched as the man smiled and looked around at the others in the room thinking he was being clever, that is when he decided to strike.

Before the man knew what happened, Cam struck out with his fist breaking the man's nose, then kicked his knees causing the giant to buckle and fall to the ground. He knew the others would join in the fray and was ready for them. A man moved in from the right and he hit him before twisting his arm at an unnatural angle till he heard the sharp pop and the man's screams. The man that was foolish enough to approach from behind received an elbow to the temple that dropped him immediately. Cam then swiftly pulled his knife from the inside of his coat and moved back to the first man who mistook him to be an easy mark. He placed the blade at his throat pressing the metal into his skin causing blood to begin to ooze from the superficial cuts.

"Stand up!"

He pulled the man up keeping the knife pressed tight to his throat, if need be, he would not hesitate to slit his throat and let him bleed all over the floor.

"Now that I have your attention, you will answer a few questions. If I am satisfied with the answers I receive, I will let you live."

He heard the man blubbering as one hand cupped his nose as it continued to gush blood through his fingers.

"I want to know if a Frenchman has come through here. He is tall, thin, and has a distinct limp and at times he has been known to use a cane. Have any of you seen him here or anywhere else in port?"

None of the men made a move, and the man he was holding a knife to was beginning to cry. Just when Cam thought his efforts had been wasted, the half-naked prostitute he had seen when he first entered the tavern came forward.

"I seen 'im."

Cam arched his eyebrows higher waiting for more information. When none was forthcoming, he pressed the knife tighter against the man's throat causing him to cry louder as a stream of blood began to flow down his neck.

"Go ahead and slit his throat. I ain't no friend of his, the skinflint tupped me two weeks ago and didn't pay up. Serves 'im right if you slice 'is head from 'is body."

Cam smiled at the woman's comments. "Hmm, maybe I should do just that." The big man started pleading with him, but Cam ignored him and turned to the woman.

"Give me some useful information and I will pay."

She reached up and scratched her exposed left breast. "'Ow much?"

"Enough that you won't have to spread your legs for the likes of this man, for a few days anyway."

The woman nodded. "He came in 'ere about a month ago, asked for one of the other girls. When he was done with 'er, we weren't sure she would live." She spit on the floor in disgust before continuing her story. "Said he was looking for a friend, an Englishman. You be the man he is looking for?"

"I wouldn't know." Cam slid the knife slowly across the man's throat slicing it from ear to ear but not deep enough to cause any permanent damage. He dropped to the ground crying and holding his throat as if an artery had been severed. Cam rolled his eyes at the theatrics and tossed the woman a pouch filled with coins.

She nodded as she stuffed the pouch down her bodice between her breasts. The rest of the people in the tavern parted for him as he made his way out the door. He looked down at his coat and frowned at the amount of blood that had gotten on it from his little incident. Thankfully, he and Ian were the same size and the cabin on the yacht would have something for him to change into. As he walked back toward the pier where *The Fascination* was docked, he thought about his pretend wife. Her face had been shocked when he told her of the deception he and Ian had conjured up. It was just a farce put in place to protect her, but the thought of possessing her, of making her his, was becoming stronger, regardless of the danger.

Abigail stood on deck with her hands gripping the railing as the yacht moved away from port, the fresh salty sea air swirled around her blowing her long blonde hair away from her face. She thought that even with the duplicity of pretending to be Davenport's wife, this was the first time in several days that she felt at ease, as if everything was going to be alright. Her lips turned up into a smile as a dolphin breached the surface of the water and swam alongside the ship. Time slipped away from her as the crewmen continued about their tasks while the ship continued further out to sea.

"Your grace, the captain and Davenport request that you join them in the dining room," Mr. Cavendish said as he came up behind her.

Abigail smiled but was reluctant to leave the fresh sea air to go below deck. "You don't have to call me that when no one is around, Mr. Cavendish."

He grinned. "It's best in case someone is listening, miss."

Abigail nodded slightly in understanding. "I have so loved being on deck as we sailed away from the port. Have you sailed often before, Mr. Cavendish?"

The older man shielded his eyes from the sun as he looked out over the horizon. "Davenport and I have made several trips across the channel during the war and on those times, we didn't sail on such a fine vessel as this." He gave her a fatherly grin. "We were also at war, so that takes a bit of the enjoyment out of it too."

Abigail liked Mr. Cavendish but sometimes she could detect a trace of sadness in his eyes, and it made her wonder if there was something in his past that haunted him. He held out his arm to her and she linked her arm through his as he led her across the deck of the ship. As they went below deck, he led her down a passageway toward a dining room. The table had been set and two large silver candelabras were on either side of the table, the light from the candles illuminated the interior. The captain was standing on the far side of the room talking to Davenport. Both men turned to her as she entered. She immediately dropped into a curtsey and then reluctantly remembered that she was supposed to be a duchess.

"Your grace, it isn't often I have the privilege of dining with such a beautiful lady," the captain said as he took her hand and brought it to his lips for a brief kiss.

Abigail blushed. "It isn't often that I have the privilege of dining on a yacht with a capable man as yourself, captain." She cast a quick glance at Davenport. "Other than my husband, of course." He offered her his hand and led her to a seat at the table. Davenport sat at the head of the table and she to his right while the captain took the seat across from her.

Davenport took a minute to simply admire her. From the moment she entered the room, he had been entranced. The gown she was wearing was very simple, but the color suited her. Her hair had been blown by the wind and was hanging loose down her back, a few tendrils hung down in her eyes. Her cheeks were flushed pink from the wind where she had stayed too long on deck, and he couldn't help but think that she looked more beautiful than any woman he had ever seen grace a London ballroom.

Abigail smiled as one of the crew came forward and filled her glass with Madeira. She took a small sip. "How long do you anticipate the trip to London, captain?"

The captain was an older man, but he seemed utterly captivated by Abigail. Cam tightened his grip on the stem of the wineglass as he continued to watch the exchange between the captain and his wife, well his pretend wife.

"If the weather and wind are on our side, we should reach London in three maybe four days. This time of year, the weather can be unpredictable."

Cam looked over and saw Abigail bite her bottom lip. He reached under the table and placed his hand on her knee and felt her body tense. He told himself that he did so because he wanted to reassure her, but in truth, he just wanted to touch her. When she gave the captain another bright smile, he removed his hand.

He continued to watch throughout dinner as Abigail charmed the captain. He told her stories of crossing the channel, of pirates, and Cam couldn't help but grin at the expressions that crossed Abigail's face. She was listening intently to the stories that were more than likely exaggerated just for her sake, but he would not spoil it for her. If she wanted to imagine pirates storming over the side of the ship, he would let her.

They were interrupted when one of the crewmen came in and whispered into the captain's ear. He took his napkin and wiped his mouth before standing from the table.

"As I said earlier, the weather can be unpredictable. Unfortunately, I must call it an evening." He walked over and took Abigail's hand. "It has been my pleasure, your grace." With that, he left the room, closing the door behind him.

Abigail nervously fidgeted with the food on her plate. "I suppose that means the weather has changed."

"I'm sure it is nothing to be concerned with."

Abigail cocked her head to the side. "You changed clothes from earlier?"

Cam nodded before turning up his glass and finishing the brandy. "There was an unfortunate incident before I boarded, and my coat was ruined."

He hoped she accepted that explanation because there was no way he would tell her what happened back at the tavern. She wrinkled her brow and made a small noise as if she were about to question him further but then thought better of it.

"Would you like for me to escort you back to the cabin?"

At this, her eyes widened. "Is it to be…I mean are we…oh dear."

He narrowed his eyes even as his lips turned up in a wicked grin. "Are you asking me if I am sharing the cabin with you, Abigail?" He once again found the way her cheeks flamed when she was embarrassed to be utterly desirable.

"Well, you did tell the captain and everyone onboard this ship that we are married. I was simply wondering how far you expected to take this ruse."

He continued to watch her. "I'm not planning on bedding you if that is what you are afraid of. At least not unless you wish it."

Abigail stood up quickly. She hated when people tried to make her appear foolish and Davenport was taking advantage of her ignorance and it infuriated her. "That will not happen, your grace. Please don't bother yourself. I can find the cabin on my own."

Before she could reach the door, he was upon her. He spun her around and pressed her body against the door caging her in with a hand on either side of her head. "Am I right to think that you are insulted that I am planning on behaving like a gentleman? Were you hoping I would take you to my bed, Abigail?"

She sucked in a deep breath at his accusation. "Of course not! As if I would allow you in my bed. But there was no need in you making me feel stupid for asking a question and you shouldn't say things like, '*unless you wish it*'."

Her chin was raised defiantly, and he wanted to kiss her badly but resisted the urge. "I apologize. While for all intents and purposes, we will give the appearance of me staying with you, I will bunk with Cavendish."

Abigail let out a slow breath as he stepped away. "I see. Instead of the cabin, I would like to go back up on the deck."

Cam shook his head. "I'm afraid I can't let you do that. The captain was called on deck because the weather was worsening. It will be much too dangerous for you on deck. I can't have a wave wash my wife overboard. What would the gossips say about that?" He gave her a smile hoping to ease her mind and offered her his hand. She laughed softly, and it made him feel good to be the one to put a bright smile back on her face.

"Will you come to get me if the weather subsides?"

"If it is safe for you to come on deck, I will come for you." He opened the door to the cabin and allowed her to walk inside. "Don't leave the cabin, Abigail."

She nodded but before he closed the door she reached out and placed her hand on his sleeve. "Where will you be?"

"I'll be on deck lending a hand if I can."

He felt her hand gently squeeze his arm. "Please be careful."

Abigail saw the way he stared at her hand as it lay on his arm. She quickly pulled her hand away, and he left without another word. Abigail moved about the cabin and found a stack of books on a desk. She moved over and selected one and took a seat on the bed just as the ship tilted a bit to the right. She put a hand on her stomach hoping she would be able to go back up on deck soon.

An hour later Abigail was on the floor clinging to the chamber pot in the cabin. She had expelled everything in her stomach and was now just heaving with every pitch of the ship. She had prayed it would pass after the ship tossed the book she had been reading across the room, the table had been nailed to the floor to keep it from moving, but everything else was shifting from side to side. She desperately needed air, but when she made it to the door and wrenched it open, a spray of seawater rushed down the passageway and she quickly closed the door falling to her knees and crawling back to the bed. When she tried to get back on the bed, the ship pitched again and so did her stomach. She stripped out of her soiled dress and lay on the floor wearing only her chemise and prayed for the water to still, or death to take her.

Chapter Seven

C am had been on deck for over an hour as the ship rocked and pitched on the rough seas. The storm was much worse than he expected, especially for this time of year. The waves had repeatedly washed over the deck of the ship knocking many of the crew off their feet. One of the more inexperienced men had almost been swept overboard. Had it not been for the quick reaction of some of the other crew, he surely would have been lost. The storm would not be relenting anytime soon and while he could be of help on deck, he had the urge to check on Abigail. This was her first time sailing, and he was certain she would be nervous with the way the ship was being tossed about.

He struggled to move down the stairs going below deck as another wave washed some water below and his shoulder slammed against the wall. He continued toward the cabin Abigail had been given and was thankful she had stayed below deck as he had instructed. He opened the door to the cabin just as the ship pitched to the side again and his heart fell into his stomach. Abigail was lying on the floor on her belly. Her face was turned away from him but with the half-filled chamber pot lying beside her, he knew what had happened. He hurried over to her dropping to his knees beside her. He reached down and scooped her into his arms heedless of his soaking wet clothes and carried her to the bed. Her eyes flew open and she groaned as if she were in pain.

He laid her on the bed and moved to the washstand to wet a cloth for her head and silently chastised himself for not coming to check on her sooner when the storm worsened. He sat beside her on the edge of the bed, and she closed her eyes and grimaced from the movement.

"Tell me that you have come to kill me," she replied in a pitiful whisper as she threw an arm over her eyes.

He pressed the wet cloth to her forehead. "I'm sorry, darling. I know you may feel as if you are going to die, but it will pass as soon as the sea calms."

The ship rolled again, and he watched as she pressed her eyes closed, as if the tighter she closed them, it would make the motion go away. He took the cloth and began bathing her neck and her chest above her chemise. If she could see the way her chemise did little to hide the rosy tips of her nipples, he knew she would be mortified. However, she was much too sick to be concerned with modesty, and he was much too concerned for her well-being to be affected by her scantily clad body.

"I need to get out of these wet clothes, sweetheart. I'll be right back."

He moved toward Ian's closet and swiftly removed the wet clothes he was wearing and changed into a dry shirt and trousers.

Once changed, he moved back over to the bed to find Abigail with one arm covering her eyes and another wrapped around her belly.

"Are we going to sink? And please tell me the truth, don't try to spare my feelings." She asked the question almost as if she was hoping something would end her torment.

"No, sweetheart. We aren't going to sink. The storm is bad, but it will be over in a few hours. As soon as the weather subsides, and you are feeling better, I will take you on deck for some fresh air."

She shook her head slightly and removed her arm from across her eyes but didn't open them. "I won't live that long."

He couldn't help but smile at her comment. "I know you feel miserable right now, love, but I can't let anything happen to you. If I did, Toussaint would not be the only one hunting me down, Emma would surely be a worse threat." He saw one corner of her lips turn up slightly. "Besides, you're my pretend wife and what kind of a man would I be if I let something happen to you? Especially, when I haven't even had a chance to bed you yet."

She threw her arm back over her eyes. "Even as I am on the verge of death, you say the most ridiculous and most inappropriate things." The ship tossed again. "With the way I am feeling now, you won't have to pretend to be my husband for much longer, you will be a pretend widower before this journey is over."

He chuckled softly at her wit knowing that if she could still find humor in her situation, she would be alright.

"Would you like to try a few sips of water?"

She shook her head, and the motion made her groan softly. "No, I don't think I can hold anything down." She moved her arm and opened her eyes. "You know I was so excited not to be on a horse anymore, now I would give anything if we had just ridden all the way to London."

Cam wished he could make her feel better, but he knew seasickness was something there was little he could do for her.

He stood from the bed and moved back toward the washstand. He poured fresh water over the cloth then moved back toward the bed and placed the cloth over her forehead.

"Please don't leave me."

He sat back down beside her. She had lost all the coloring in her face and her eyes were not as bright as they had been earlier in the day. He reached out and moved a stray curl from her cheek. "I will stay as long as you need me, Abigail."

His words seemed to comfort her, and she closed her eyes as another wave caused the boat to tilt onto its side. She reached out and grabbed his hand. Cam could tell she was frightened, so he did the only thing he thought would make her feel more secure. He crawled into the bed beside her and wrapped his arms around her pulling her into his chest much like he had done on the journey to Leith to protect her from the cold. While he couldn't take away her sickness, he would offer her any comfort he could. As he lay there listening to the storm rage outside, feeling her cringe with each movement, he knew he would do anything he could to protect this woman, anything he could to make her comfortable and bring her joy. And that thought scared the hell out of him because he knew when this was over and Toussaint was dead, he wouldn't want to let her go.

Abigail spent the next two days in bed feeling as wretched as anyone could feel. Davenport had been extremely attentive, and she was grateful for the care he had given her. The night of the storm, he had slept in the bed beside her, but after the danger had passed, he had moved into Mr. Cavendish's quarters. Mr. Cavendish had stopped in to check on her the morning after the storm and the captain had also come by to wish her well. Davenport had tried to get her to eat several times, but the thought of food was not appealing. She had managed to drink some tea. The dress she had been wearing onboard the ship had been cleaned and while it was wrinkled, she thankfully she had removed it before it became completely ruined.

A loud knock at the door of her cabin caused her to jump. She moved across the room and opened it to find Mr. Cavendish holding a tray of some bread and butter along with a pot of tea.

"Good morning, miss. Davenport said you were feeling better but had not eaten anything. I thought you might try to put some food in your belly this morning. You are already so light I'm afraid a stiff wind will blow you overboard when you go on deck."

Abigail giggled and moved to the side so Mr. Cavendish could set the tray down beside her bed. "Thank you. I will try to eat something today."

He nodded and turned back toward the door.

"Mr. Cavendish, how much longer before we reach London?"

"We should start moving up the Thames before sunup tomorrow. So tonight, should be your last night onboard ship."

Abigail clasped her hands before her. "Have you seen Davenport this morning?"

Mr. Cavendish narrowed his eyes slightly. "He is on deck talking to the captain."

Abigail nodded and he moved through the door leaving her alone in the cabin, but she did not miss the way his expression changed when she asked about Davenport. It made her wonder if Mr. Cavendish was somehow displeased with her or if maybe Davenport had expressed something to that effect. While he was caring and attentive to her when she was so sick, it could not have been an enjoyable experience for him. Perhaps he was glad they would reach London, and he could be rid of her giving the responsibility of her protection to someone else. The thought was frightening. She had become accustomed to him and the thought of being dependent on a total stranger for protection was unnerving.

Cam had spent the morning talking to the captain and staying on deck to avoid the temptation to return to Abigail's cabin. The morning after the storm, he had been met with Cavendish's censure because he had stayed the night in her cabin and had gotten a lecture about the difference between a lady and a common trollop. His friend was becoming more protective of Abigail and her virtue by the day, and it was beginning to annoy him. He had tried unsuccessfully to convince Cavendish that the only reason he had stayed with her was because of her violent seasickness, and while that certainly was true, a part of him couldn't deny the fact that he was becoming increasingly drawn to Miss Bailey.

"I took the girl some food and tea. She looks like a walking skeleton and needs to eat," Cavendish said as he came up to stand alongside him.

"She will recover."

"Aye, that she will…from the seasickness."

Cam turned toward his friend hoping he was not about to launch into another lecture on the importance of a lady's reputation. "I'm not in the mood for this right now."

"I'm going to say it anyway. You need to leave the girl alone. I can tell she is right on the verge of falling for your charms."

"Have you been in the captain's rum? What the devil are you talking about?" He shook his head and turned back to look out over the horizon.

"She asked about you when I brought her breakfast and had that dreamy look in her eyes that women get when they are interested in a man. You are already spending more time with her than is necessary. If you are not careful, you will break her heart. Not to mention that if any of this gets out, she will be ruined beyond repair. She is a sweet lady, and I don't want to see anything bad happen to her."

"She is not a London debutante, John. She is the daughter of a poor vicar from Somerset. No one in London will be concerned with her or her situation."

John shook his head. "You know that isn't true. This could ruin her life, Cam. The way I see it, you have two choices, stay away from her, or marry her."

Cam pushed his hands off the railing angrily. "This entire conversation is ridiculous. I can't figure out if you are playing matchmaking dowager or overprotective father." He saw his friend start to say something else, but he was not about to discuss this further. He walked off leaving Cavendish behind.

He was angry, not because of what Cavendish said, but because his words had a ring of truth to them. He didn't like having people telling him what he should do. Abigail was the most beautiful woman he had ever seen. Her sharp wit and cheeky tongue made him desire her all the more, and while he knew he should leave her alone and stay out of her bed, he didn't have the restraint. She deserved a nice peaceful quiet life, raising children with a husband that did not have a past that could come back to haunt him at any time. She was worthy of more than a man that wasn't certain if he was capable of staying faithful to the woman he married. Sure, he could offer her passion in his bed, a title, and wealth, but he knew Abigail would want more than just to be a duchess. She was not the kind of woman that would be satisfied with a coronet and a place in society. She would want love and commitment, and he wasn't the man to give her that.

Yes, it would be for the best if he just did what he originally set out to do, deliver her to Kingston at the Lair where she would be protected while he found Toussaint. Then when the danger had passed, he would turn her back over to Emma and Ian. He was certain Emma would be able to secure her a future with a man that deserved the happiness she would bring to him. He just wasn't that man.

Abigail paced the length of her cabin hoping Davenport would come to escort her above deck, but after waiting for most of the day, she decided to take matters into her own hands and venture up on deck herself. If she stayed below much longer, she would go mad. She wrapped a cotton shawl around her shoulders and made her way top-side. The fresh sea air and the sun on her face instantly made her feel better. She moved over to the rail and looked out at the horizon. The sun was high in the sky and made the tops of the waves glisten as they rolled by. The ocean was calm today, thankfully, and the queasiness she had been experiencing since the storm was beginning to subside.

She leaned over letting her arms rest on the railing as she watched small fish jumping up out of the water alongside the ship.

"Some people call them flying fish."

Abigail stood up abruptly and spun around at the sound of the masculine voice she did not recognize.

"Don't be alarmed, your grace. I was only coming to see if you need assistance. My name is Thomas Miller. I'm the first mate on the *Fascination.*" He removed his hat and bowed deeply.

Abigail was still uncomfortable with the deception of posing as the Duchess of Stafford, but she smiled at the young handsome first mate, putting him at ease. "It is very nice to meet you, Mr. Miller. I was just taking some air and admiring the view. This is the first time I have ever sailed and after the storm we experienced, it may be my last sailing. This is the first day I have ventured out of my cabin since the storm." She watched as he looked around, perhaps looking to see if Davenport was nearby.

He offered his arm. "If you would like to take a stroll around the ship, I would be happy to be your escort. Unless you were waiting for the duke, if that is the case, I will make myself scarce."

Abigail had not seen or heard from Davenport all day, and she was certain he would not mind if the young first mate escorted her. "I would love to take a turn around the deck, Mr. Miller." She smiled and placed her hand on his arm.

Davenport and Cavendish had spent the past hour below deck in one of the lounges playing cards. After losing more to the captain and Cavendish than he would have liked, he decided he should go check on Abigail. He should have done so long before now, but he was trying to follow his friend's advice and stay away from her as much as possible.

He maneuvered down the passageway toward her cabin and hoped she was not overly upset with him for leaving her there for most of the day. He knocked a few times, but she never came to open the door. He turned and started to walk away thinking that perhaps she was napping and didn't want to be disturbed, but something in his gut said that wasn't the case. He opened the door as quietly as he could, but the cabin was empty.

"Abigail?" He called her name knowing he would not get an answer.

He left the cabin and moved down the passageway toward the stairs that led to the deck. The weather was calm and while it should be perfectly safe for her, especially since all the crew believed her to be his duchess, he still didn't like the thought of her not having an escort. He squinted his eyes against the sun as he scanned the deck for her. As he walked around to the other side of the ship, he heard her laughter drift to his ears on the breeze. He squinted his eyes against the sun and saw her standing on the bow. The wind blew her skirts back as the captain's first mate Thomas Miller had an arm wrapped around her holding a spyglass up for her to look through. He watched as she held out her other hand as if trying to touch what she was seeing through the glass. Mr. Miller said something to her, and he watched as she laughed again, the sound making him clench his hands into fists at his side.

Abigail looked through Mr. Miller's spyglass again. "Oh my, I can just imagine what it would be like to look through this and see a pirate ship headed our way." She handed the glass back to Mr. Miller. "Tell me, what is the most exciting thing you have seen while peering through your glass over the ocean waves?"

Mr. Miller took a deep breath, and she got the distinct impression he was trying to make himself appear taller, more impressive.

"I have seen whales, of course, and occasionally seals, but the most exciting thing I have seen was a French frigate, and another time we saw a band of smugglers crossing the channel."

"So, no pirates then?"

He shook his head and smiled. "No, I suppose I should be thankful for that."

"I suppose the smugglers could be counted as pirates if you wanted to make your story more exciting."

Cam moved to stand behind them, his irritation growing with how close Mr. Miller continued to stand near her and at the way Abigail smiled up at him. "I'm sure Mr. Miller has more important things to do than regale you with stories of his naval adventures, my love."

Abigail spun around quickly, and Mr. Miller seemed to jump a foot away from her as Davenport approached. Cam reached out and took her arm and pulled her to his side. "I was surprised to not find you in our cabin, darling."

Abigail tilted her head to the side confused at the tone of voice he used. "I thought some fresh air would do me good." She couldn't help but notice how he kept his eyes on Mr. Miller. "I was tired of being cooped up and decided to come on deck. Mr. Miller was kind enough to escort me and even show me some parts of the ship."

Abigail turned back to Mr. Miller and gave him another bright smile. "Thank you again for keeping me company. I look forward to tonight."

Mr. Miller bowed at the waist. "I am looking forward to it as well. Of course, you are welcome to join us, if you wish, your grace."

Abigail felt Davenport's arm tense and she thought she should explain. "Mr. Miller has promised to point out some of the constellations tonight. He says there is nothing like seeing the stars from the deck of the ship on the open ocean."

"Indeed, perhaps I will join you. Mr. Miller, if you will excuse us, I'm sure my wife has kept you from your duties long enough, and we certainly don't want the captain to be cross with us."

Mr. Miller bowed his head before turning back to Abigail. "Be sure to enjoy the sunset, your grace."

She watched as Mr. Miller walked away and made certain he was out of earshot when she turned back to face Davenport. She was not happy with the way he had treated the young man.

"Why are you so cross? Poor Mr. Miller has done nothing wrong. He was very pleasant to me." She reached out and gripped the railing as a strong gust of wind caused her to nearly lose her footing.

Cam reached out and wrapped an arm around her waist to steady her and prevent her from falling. "Yes, he seemed very attentive to you."

Abigail narrowed her eyes. "At least he was here to escort me on deck. Are you angry with me?"

Cam took a step closer not wanting any of the crew members working on deck to hear their conversation. "Of course not."

He spoke the truth, he wasn't angry at her, but seeing Mr. Miller standing so close to her and watching as she smiled back at him just didn't sit well with him. Cavendish was right, he was allowing her to be a distraction, and distractions could get you killed. He had to distance himself from her and concentrate on Toussaint. Once he handed her over to Kingston, he could do just that knowing she would be safe. But he still couldn't shake the feeling of intense jealousy at seeing Mr. Miller standing so close to her.

"Mr. Cavendish said we would reach London tomorrow morning if everything went as expected. Are you certain your friend Mr. Kingston will be willing to protect me?"

Cam allowed her to step away from him and move back toward the railing. The wind was whipping through her hair and blowing her skirts back and she looked incredibly beautiful.

"Kingston and I have worked together in the past. There won't be a problem."

She sighed and turned back to face him. "Once you have deposited me over into Mr. Kingston's care, will I see you again?"

"I don't know." He gave her an honest answer, but when he saw the way her smile fell, and the look of worry enter her eyes, he wished he could tell her something different. But Cavendish was right, the best thing he could do for Abigail was to keep his distance.

Abigail felt her heart drop in her stomach at his words. They sounded so final. She turned back to look out over the horizon hoping he wouldn't see the anxiety on her face. "I'm going to go back to my cabin. I would like to freshen up before dinner."

"I'll walk with you."

She smiled and shook her head. "That won't be necessary. I'm sure you have other things you need to do."

Cam nodded and watched as she made her way back to the stairs that led to the cabins below. Hopefully, he could dispatch Toussaint quickly and put this bloody nightmare behind him. He was certain that once he was no longer around Abigail every day, his life would go back to normal.

But first, he needed to speak to the captain and make certain that Mr. Miller received some additional duties tonight that would prevent him from spending any time with Abigail. Constellations indeed.

Chapter Eight

London, The Devil's Lair

Abigail eagerly looked out the window of the hired hack that she and Cam had taken from the dock after they left the *Fascination*. London was everything she had imagined it to be. There were people everywhere, fine carriages taking people back and forth around the city, while others walked where they wished to go. The streets were crowded with all manner of people, and she thought how easy it would be to disappear in a city this size.

When Emma was in London for the season, she had written letters and sent them to her in Somerset extolling all her adventures and the excitement London had to offer. Abigail had always hoped she would get a chance to do some of the things Emma had written to her about, but she never imagined that she would be forced to hide out in a gaming hell because a madman might wish to kill her.

She looked across the conveyance at Davenport. He had not said very much to her since their brief exchange on the deck of the ship the day before, and now he sat stoically, his eyes closed as he leaned back. She wondered if he was sleeping or simply faking sleep so he would not have to talk to her.

Mr. Cavendish had taken a separate hack at Davenport's instruction to go gather items she might need and to inform Charles Newberg, Duke of Avanley about their dilemma. She had listened to their conversation from a distance and from what she could decipher, Avanley had worked with Davenport at one time and had been a spy himself. Cavendish had alluded to the fact that he might be of some help to them in the search for Toussaint.

The hack came to a stop, and she saw Davenport's eyes fly open before he opened the carriage door and stepped out onto the street. He held his hand out for her and she took it grateful for his assistance. They had stopped in front of a large building with huge white columns along the front portico. Large windows were on either side of the oak door.

"Where are we?" Abigail asked as she looked to Davenport.

He held out his arm for her. "Welcome to *The Devil's Lair*, Miss Bailey."

Abigail took a second look at the building. "This is the infamous gaming hell everyone talks about? It looks more like a bank or a museum. I was expecting something more... seedy."

Davenport arched an eyebrow at her comments. "Looks can be deceiving. Although I would venture to say that more money is exchanged within these walls on a daily basis than the Bank of England." He began walking toward the alley that was alongside the building. "We will enter through the back and go straight to Kingston's apartments. There will be no need for you to mingle in the gaming rooms with the patrons."

Abigail pushed down her nerves and followed Cam to the back door of the building. He knocked three times and a huge man with a scar down the right side of his face opened the door. She instantly took a step closer to Davenport when the man looked over at her.

"Sam!" Cam greeted the man enthusiastically. "I didn't know you were back working for Kingston. Last I heard you had met a little lady and had decided to start farming."

The man shrugged his shoulders. "Farming didn't suit me, and marriage didn't suit my wife. She ran off with one of those traveling performing groups, so I came back to work at *The Lair.*"

Cam put a hand on the man's shoulder. "I hate to hear that, Sam, but I am glad to see you again." He reached behind him and gripped Abigail's hand pulling her forward. "This is Miss Abigail Bailey. She and I have found ourselves in an unfortunate position, and I need to speak to Kingston, is he here?"

The man shook his head. He left out about an hour ago. I don't know when I can expect him to return, but you and the lady are welcome to come inside, your grace."

He stepped to the side and Cam, still holding Abigail's hand, pulled her in behind him. Once inside, Abigail gasp at the opulence surrounding her. "Oh my! It's beautiful."

She saw the large man Cam had called Sam puff up a bit at her words. "Mr. Kingston runs a first-class establishment, Miss. *The Lair* has the best of everything and spares no expense."

Cam chuckled slightly. "He can afford to spare no expense because his patrons lose thousands of pounds here a night."

"Mr. Kingston doesn't cheat people. He runs a fair game," Sam said in defense of his boss.

Cam slapped him on his shoulder. "You don't have to convince me, Sam. I am fully aware of the way Kingston conducts business."

Abigail took in everything as they made their way down the hall to a set of apartments. When Cam opened the door, she found herself in amazement again. The rooms looked like something from a palace. The front room was a large parlor with several couches and chaise lounges, plush Axminster rugs, red velvet draperies, crystal chandeliers, and gilt everywhere. She walked around the room admiring the furnishings.

"My goodness, everything is so luxurious."

Cam took her hand and led her through a set of doors into an equally opulent bedchamber. He watched as she looked around in wonderment.

Abigail walked over to the massive bed. She had never seen anything like it in her life. It looked as if ten people could sleep in it comfortably. Then she looked up at the ceiling and gasped loudly at the scene depicted. A beautiful fresco was painted over the entirety of the ceiling depicting a scene where young scantily clad women wearing sheer white robes were being chased by ardent admirers wearing nothing at all. She had never seen anything so vulgar before, and try as she may, she just couldn't seem to pull her eyes away from it.

Cam smiled at the stunned look of innocence on her face and the way her cheeks pinkened at the sight of naked men and women. Kingston had always taken pride in the fresco saying it was a work of art, of course, Kingston didn't normally entertain innocent virgins in his apartments.

"I have some things to take care of, and I am going to try to find Kingston and explain everything to him. I will talk to Sam and make certain he stays close by in case you need anything. Stay in these rooms, Abigail. I don't want you wandering around the gaming rooms once the patrons arrive."

Abigail finally managed to pull her eyes away from the fresco. "You are leaving me here…. alone?"

"You will not be completely alone. I have wasted enough time already." He saw the way her eyes narrowed, and he cursed himself for not thinking before he spoke. "I must see what I can discover about Toussaint."

Abigail turned away. "I understand. Will I see you again?"

Cam wanted to reassure her, to kiss her senseless before leaving so that he was the only thing she had to think about while he was gone. "I will be back later tonight, Abigail. I will introduce you to Kingston. I wouldn't just abandon you here to explain everything to him yourself."

"I understand." She moved toward the bed letting her hand slide across the red coverlet to the thick white pillows. "Do you think Mr. Kingston would be upset if I perhaps took a nap?"

Cam huffed out a sigh. Thinking of her in Kingston's bed was not helping him at the moment. "Certainly not, and I will have Sam bring you something to eat, but don't let anyone else enter this room, Abigail. Do you understand?"

She nodded as she plumped up one of the pillows with her hands. "Please don't worry about me. I'm sure I will be fine."

Cam hesitated. He didn't like the idea of leaving her alone. Hopefully, he would be able to find Kingston sooner rather than later. He was certain that once he introduced them it would ease Abigail's fears and he could begin his search for Toussaint.

He walked back to the door. "Get some rest and eat something. I'll return as soon as I can."

After leaving Abigail in Kingston's chambers, he went to find Sam, he was reliable and could be trusted to protect her until he returned. Once he had everything settled at *The Lair*, he could go in search of Kingston.

Cam had been true to his word and about an hour after he left, Sam had brought her a tray of sandwiches and a bowl of soup. She had eaten her fill and then climbed into the large bed and quickly fell asleep. She didn't know how long she had slept before she heard a noise outside the bedroom in the parlor.

She quickly jumped from the bed thinking Cam had returned, but it wasn't his voice she heard, but rather two men arguing quite vehemently in the parlor outside. She looked around frantically wondering what she should do. Cam had told her not to allow anyone in the rooms, and he certainly would have told Mr. Kingston about her presence by now.

Footsteps grew louder as they approached the door and the voices sounded angrier. She reached for a porcelain vase that was sitting on a side table near the door. What if it were Toussaint or the men from the inn? What if they had followed them to London and had discovered where she was hiding already?

She stepped off to the side and watched as the handle of the door turned. She didn't stop to think, when a man walked inside, she crashed the vase down on his head with as much force as she could muster and watched as he crumbled to the floor clutching his head just as Sam, the man from earlier, rushed in behind him.

"Bloody hell, Miss Bailey! You just clobbered Mr. Kingston!"

Abigail put both her hands over her mouth as she looked down at the man laying at her feet. She immediately bent down beside him cradling his head in her lap. She looked at his chest and was relieved to see that he was breathing.

"Thank heavens he isn't dead, although I'm sure once he wakes, he will not be too pleased with me. Go fetch me a basin of cool water and a cloth."

She raked the hair from the man's face and noticed that he and Davenport were about the same age. He was also a very handsome man with a large lump growing on the side of his head where the vase had bashed into his skull. She had a rush of guilt go through her and hoped he didn't kick her out of his establishment once he woke and realized what she had done.

Sam didn't waste any time getting the water she asked for and she immediately started bathing his forehead and the lump on his head. She leaned closer speaking softly to him.

"I'm so sorry, Mr. Kingston. I hope you will forgive me."

She watched as he opened one eye and grinned up at her. "Darling, waking up with my head in your lap and you speaking so sweetly as you care for me is worth the lump on the head."

Abigail felt a rush of relief wash over her. "Oh, I'm so happy you are awake. I truly do apologize for hitting you. I panicked."

Kingston moved to sit up, but the action caused his head to ache and he closed his eyes as a pain shot across his forehead.

Abigail put a hand on his shoulder. "Please don't try to get up yet." She placed the wet cloth on his head. "I guess you are wondering who I am and what I am doing in your bedchambers."

He lay still on her lap enjoying the way her fingers felt as she moved his hair back away from his face. "Sam gave me a brief synopsis of your situation. I was coming to introduce myself when you decided it would be a better idea to bash in my skull."

Abigail felt her cheeks burn. Perhaps he was angry with her after all. "I'm sorry. I heard voices I didn't recognize and you were arguing. I can't tell you how sorry I am."

He reached up and took her hand. "It is I who should apologize. Sam had told me of your predicament, and while I have not spoken with Davenport yet, I wanted to meet you. We were arguing over something that happened upstairs on the gaming floor. I should have realized that after the ordeal you have been through you would be nervous."

She smiled. "I should clean up the mess I made. I was taking a nap in your bed. I hope you don't mind."

He sat up a bit slower this time and gave her a mischievous grin. "My dear Miss Bailey, you are welcome in my bed anytime you wish."

Abigail tilted her head to the side thinking that this man was quite cheeky for someone that had just been hit on the head. "Let me help you to the bed. You should lie down. That bump on your head looks terrible." She stood up and helped him to his feet even though he didn't need much help. He was quite tall, not as tall as Davenport but close. He was dressed elegantly and looked very much like he belonged among the beau monde. He walked over to the bed and lay down on top of the covers. She took some of the pillows and fluffed them up then placed them under his head.

"Shall I go get you something to drink?"

"No, if you will just sit with me. I find your presence to be calming. Perhaps you could hold my hand as I rest."

Abigail narrowed her eyes wondering if Mr. Kingston was up to something, but since she did whack him over the head with his own vase, she supposed the least she could do was sit with him. "Let me pull a chair up closer."

He reached out and grabbed her hand. "There is no need, you can sit beside me on the bed. I assure you that in my current condition, I am unable to cause you any harm."

"I'm not sure that is a wise idea." She watched as he closed his eyes tightly as if trying to overcome a wave of pain and decided what could it hurt. "Alright, but just until you feel better."

She moved onto the edge of the bed beside him and took the cloth and placed it over his eyes. "Is there anything else I can do for you?"

He reached up and ran a finger over her cheek. "Well, you could give me a kiss. A kiss from an angel like you could cure any ailment."

Abigail sucked in a breath at his words and was about to tell him that if he didn't behave, she would hit him over the head again, but before she had a chance to find her voice, she heard Cam's deep booming voice from the doorway.

"What the hell are you doing, Kingston?!" Cam walked forward wanting very much to strangle his friend. "Get off the bed, Abigail, and come here."

Abigail watched in shock as the man beside her sat up as if nothing had happened to him at all. "Oh, come on Davenport. You can't fault me for trying to get a kiss from this beautiful angel."

Kingston grinned as he looked over at her. "I'm sorry sweetheart. I just couldn't seem to help myself."

Abigail stood from the bed and put her hands on her hips as she gave Mr. Kingston a fierce look. "You aren't really hurt at all, are you?

He jumped from the bed to stand before her. "Oh, I am wounded." He placed a hand over his heart. "You did give me quite the headache, my dear. But like I said, it's nothing that a little attention from you might cure."

He gave her a wink and a smile. She finally figured out that he was teasing her. "You are being terribly wicked, Mr. Kingston, and you should be ashamed for giving me such a fright."

"I apologize, Miss Bailey. You will have to allow me to make it up to you. Perhaps we can have dinner this evening and get better acquainted."

Cam stood there in disbelief as Kingston flirted shamelessly with Abigail. "Kingston, if I might have a word with you. I think we should discuss the reason we are here."

Kingston pulled his eyes away from Abigail and turned to his friend. "Sam has already given me a quick explanation, but I am certain there is more to it. Let's take a walk around the gaming rooms. I am most interested in hearing how a rogue such as yourself ended up with such a beauty in your care."

Cam saw Abigail's cheeks flush, and he frowned wondering if it was a mistake to bring her here to *The Lair*.

Abigail moved closer to him. "If this is about me, I think I should be present."

Kingston stepped closer to her. "While I would usually agree with you, my dear. I do think it would be wiser to stay here until I have had a chance to hear what our mutual friend has to say." He took her hand and raised it to his lips. "I promise that once we have a plan set, we will be certain to explain everything to you."

Cam took a step forward ready to pull Abigail away from Kingston's lecherous grasp and tell his friend to go to the devil when there was a sharp knock on the door that caused him to stop in his tracks. "That should be Cavendish. I sent him to Avanley's to ask for his assistance. His experience as well as his connections will be beneficial."

Cam opened the door and just barely got out of the way as a flurry of silk and lace swept into the room.

"Bella! What are you doing here?" Cam asked, surprised to see the Duchess of Avanley. He looked behind her to where her husband and Cavendish stood back as if none of what was about to occur was under their control.

Kingston took a step toward her and raised her hand to his lips. "It is good to see you again, duchess."

Isobel Newberg, Duchess of Avanley looked around the room until her eyes fell upon Abigail then back to Davenport. "Surely you are going to introduce us, Davenport."

Cam walked over to stand beside Abigail whose eyes had widened at the duchess' arrival. "Abigail Bailey, may I introduce the lovely Isobel Newberg, Duchess of Avanley."

Abigail sank into a deep curtsey. "I am pleased to meet you, your grace."

Cam stepped off to the side as Bella moved forward taking both Abigail's hands in hers. "I am so glad that I am finally getting to meet you, Miss Bailey. Emma spoke so highly of you when she was in London. I have been most anxious to meet you." She looked around the room at the men standing around watching them. "Mr.

Cavendish told my husband and me of your troubles and how you came to be here. I am so sorry, but there is no need to worry." Bella linked her arms through Abigail's and turned to face the gentlemen in the room. "I am certain the four of you have things to discuss, as do we. Would you like for us to leave the room, or will you?"

Kingston was the first to answer. "Oh no, duchess, I don't want you anywhere near the gaming rooms." He looked over at Abigail before giving Bella a grin. "The duchess has an unnatural ability to win at any game I or her husband has taught her. It really is unfair to play against her, that is why we decided that it would be best for our friendship as well as my pocketbook if she never gambled here at *The Lair*. I would be bankrupt in a night."

Bella laughed and gave Abigail a wink. "That is not entirely true, but it is probably best if I keep my games private." She gave her husband a sultry grin.

Cam was growing increasingly agitated. "Can we please focus on the reason we are here? We will be back shortly, Abigail."

"There is no need to rush. Miss Bailey and I are going to become good friends," Bella said as she took her hands and shooed the men toward the door.

Charles, Duke of Avanley was leaning against the door frame. "I promise she will not spirit her away, Davenport."

Cam frowned at his friends, but after seeing Bella walk away chatting happily with Abigail, he relented and followed the other men out of the room.

"Why is she here, Charles?" Davenport asked as soon as the door was closed.

Avanley shrugged his shoulders. "When Cavendish came to tell us of your predicament and ask for my help, she insisted that she come along as well. She said it wasn't right for Miss Bailey to have her fate rest in the hands of a group of men that didn't know the first thing about what a woman needs. I argued against it, but as you can see, she was most persuasive."

Kingston laughed. "I can certainly see where it would be hard to deny the duchess anything. How are the babies, by the way? I heard that she has given you twins."

Charles' face instantly transformed. "Indeed, a boy and a girl. They are very healthy and growing faster than I anticipated. Already at two months old, they know how to command the household."

Cam shook his head and narrowed his eyes slightly as he regarded the two men with him. "I hate to break up this little reunion, but this is a serious situation that could put us all in danger. Charles, you of all people know how dangerous Toussaint can be, and if my guess is correct, he will come after me while I am here in London."

Kingston became instantly more alert at the mention of the French assassin. "That butcher is still alive? I had no idea he was the one involved in this. One would have hoped that someone would have already sent him to hell by now."

"Now you realize the seriousness of the situation and why I had to get Miss Bailey here to London so she would be better protected."

Charles nodded. "Toussaint is a deadly adversary for certain, but do you truly feel she would be safer here at *The Lair?*"

Cam cocked his head to the side wondering what his friend was about to suggest. "I can't think of anywhere else. Kingston and his men will not allow anyone near her."

"Why don't you allow her to come home with Bella and me? I will contact Harrison at the War Department and ask for additional security. He will be as anxious to catch Toussaint as much as anyone.

You can't truly mean to lock her away here in Kingston's apartments. It might take months to catch Toussaint, and that is if he doesn't give up and return to France now that he has lost the element of surprise."

Cam did not like the idea at all. It would put more people at risk. "Do you really want her under your roof? What if Toussaint comes for her there? Bella and your children could be harmed."

Charles' narrowed his eyes and his expression darkened. "He will not get into my house, Cam. I promise you that I can protect her far better than Kingston here. Besides the fact that Isobel has already decided that *The Lair* isn't the ideal place for a lady like Miss Bailey."

"It may not be ideal, but it is safe."

Kingston stepped forward. "While I am more than willing to take the beautiful Miss Bailey off your hands, Cam. I must agree with Avanley on this." He grinned. "Besides, Avanley's house might be the better spot for paying my addresses to the young lady."

Davenport closed his eyes and hung his head while Charles chuckled at Kingston's remarks. "Cavendish, you have been quiet while these two shared their ideas of how we should proceed. I am curious as to what you think," Cam asked hoping he would at least have at least one ally on his side.

His long-time friend and second-in-command stood along the wall, his arms crossed over his chest. "I agree with Avanley. This ain't no place for a lady to be. Besides the fact that you have no idea how long this will take. She can't stay hold up here with Kingston for months."

Kingston cleared his throat. "Well let's not be too hasty. Me being hold up for months with a beautiful woman does have its appeal."

Charles laughed at the remark while Cam chose to ignore it.

Cam looked away hating to admit it, but they were right. "I'll agree to her going with you as long as you get the extra security from Harrison."

Charles nodded, not entirely surprised that he had gotten his way.

Cam huffed out a breath hoping he was doing the right thing in letting Abigail go with Bella. "Charles, one of the reasons I didn't leave her with McDonough was that I was afraid Toussaint would hurt the others there. You must protect your family. I have a feeling Bella will want to take Abigail about London. That will be much too dangerous. If she does leave the safety of Avanley House, you must accompany them, or send for Cavendish or myself. I don't want to see anyone else hurt at the hands of Toussaint. Once I find him, I will end this nightmare for everyone that has ever come in contact with the man."

Charles nodded. "I understand and I wish you luck in finding the madman, but who better to hunt down and destroy Toussaint than *Ange De La Mort.*"

Chapter Nine

Abigail thought the Duchess of Avanley was just lovely. She was very petite with dark hair the color of mahogany, and her skin was flawless and creamy. She looked very regal and exceptionally beautiful. But she was also very kind and understanding. She had listened intently to Abigail as she told the story of how she had heard the men arguing about killing Davenport at the inn, the journey to McDonough Castle, the ride to Leith, and even the horrible storm and bout of seasickness she experienced while on *The Fascination*. All while the duchess looked at her with sympathy.

"And Davenport expects you to stay here at *The Devil's Lair* while he goes in search of Toussaint?" Bella asked finally.

Abigail sighed heavily and took a sip of the tea that Kingston's man Sam had brought in for them. "Yes, he thinks Mr. Kingston will be better able to protect me in the event that this Toussaint tries to hurt me in order to draw out Davenport."

The duchess shook her head slowly from side to side. "Hmm, isn't that just like a man thinking they know what is best? I'm sure he never took anything else into consideration. A woman can't be happy staying here, cooped up and shut away from the rest of the world. While Kingston's apartments here at the Lair are very luxurious, they are also a bit scandalous. I can't let Emma's best friend sleep under that." She pointed up at the mural of naked ladies above Kingston's bed.

Abigail giggled softly. "It is not exactly what I expected, I'll admit that, but I'm not sure Davenport will consider anywhere else for me."

Bella put a hand to her hair and tucked a stray curl back up in its pin. "I will handle Davenport. Charles and I have already discussed it, and he agrees with me that you can't stay here." She held up her hand. "Does he really think it would be best to keep you here as a prisoner, bringing you food but never letting you leave these rooms? You would go mad within a week. Not to mention the fact that it is entirely improper. It would cause quite a sensation if it were discovered that you were staying here."

Abigail furrowed her brows. The duchess was right. She would hate being kept indoors and once Davenport was gone and Kingston was working, she would be all alone, stuck here. Not to mention the fact that she was unmarried, staying in a gaming hell, with unmarried men and no lady for a chaperone. Her father would have been appalled at the situation she found herself to be in. "Where do you think I should go?"

The duchess' smile widened. "To Avanley House, of course. You can stay with me there. I would love the company and could certainly use the help with the twins. Charles can add extra security around the house, and while we may not have the usual freedoms we would under other circumstances, it will still be better than staying here."

Abigail thought on the matter for just a minute before she finally agreed that the duchess' plan did sound more appealing than staying with Mr. Kingston, a man she just met, and who by all accounts was more of a rake than Davenport.

"I am not sure how Davenport will feel about it. What if he refuses?"

Bella gave her an encouraging wink. "Darling, Charles is at this very moment speaking with him about it. I'm sure once he explains how much better it will be for you, he will agree without any hesitation."

Abigail was hopeful. She liked the duchess very much.

"I hope you don't find this next question too meddlesome but are you and Davenport…."

Abigail blushed. "Oh, my goodness no. He teases me sometimes, but I think it is just to relieve my nervousness about this entire situation."

"So, he hasn't kissed you then?"

Abigail bit the bottom of her lip not sure of what she should say, but thankfully she was saved from answering the question when the door swung open, and the gentlemen returned to the room. She looked towards Cam and then back to the duchess to see her hiding a grin behind her cup of tea. Abigail stood from her seat and clasped her hands nervously in front of her.

"There has been a change in plans," Davenport said as his eyes met hers across the room. "I think it will be better if you return to Avanley House with the duke and duchess. Avanley will arrange for more security, and I think you will be better protected there than you are here." He gave Kingston a pointed look then.

Bella shot to her feet. "Excellent idea, your grace. I think you have made a wise decision. Miss Bailey will be a great company to me while we await the rest of London to return for the season, and I can certainly use help with the twins." She looked over to Abigail. "I truly have been lonely since Persephone and Catherine left to join Emma in Scotland. We will have such fun."

Cam stepped forward. "This isn't about having fun, Bella. It's about keeping her safe."

The duchess waved his comment off. "Everything will be fine. I think you are worrying too much, Cam." She walked over and linked arms with her husband who was looking down at her upturned face with complete devotion.

"Miss Bailey, if you would join us, we can make our way home. We already have had the servants make a room up for you, and I'm sure you would like to rest before we have dinner tonight," Avanley said before turning to Kingston. "Will you still be joining us for dinner tonight?"

Kingston walked over to take Miss Bailey's hand. "With a lady like this present at your dinner table, you may be certain of it." He raised her hand to his lips. "Might I escort you to Avanley's carriage, Miss Bailey?"

Before Abigail had a chance to open her mouth to answer, Cam was at her side and removing her hand from Kingston's grip. "Keep your hands off her, Kingston. You have done enough today."

Kingston rubbed the knot on his head. "Don't you think I deserve some sort of compensation for my injury?"

Abigail was afraid this was about to escalate, but then she heard Bella's soft laughter. "I think this is a story you will have to tell me on our way home. Now will one of you escort her, or shall I do so myself? I have babies I need to get home to." She sailed past them both and walked out the door.

Davenport looked over at Charles who was grinning like a lovesick fool after his wife. "Your wife is sounding more and more like Persephone." He took Abigail's hand and led her out to Avanley's carriage.

Once outside, Cam felt the tension in Abigail's body, and her hesitation before they reached the carriage. "It is going to be alright, Abigail. I have some things to do tonight, but I will come by tomorrow and check on you. If you need me at any time, send word to the Lair." He raised her hand to his lips and felt her tremble.

Abigail gave him a small smile. She would never admit it, especially in front of the others, she wanted so very badly to appear brave, but it was a bit unnerving leaving Davenport behind. He had taken care of her through so much since they left the inn together that fateful night. "Thank you for everything, your grace. I'm sure everything will work out." She leaned forward and whispered softly. "Please be careful."

He handed her into the carriage to sit beside Bella. Charles gave him a nod before climbing in after the ladies. As soon as the door closed, the carriage started down the street.

John Cavendish walked up behind him. "It's for the best. Avanley will keep her safe and now that she is no longer your responsibility, you can concentrate on what needs to be done to take care of Toussaint."

Cam gave his friend a harsh look. "She is still my responsibility." It was an odd feeling, but he knew he meant every word, and once this was over, he would make certain that Abigail knew it too.

Later that night, Cheapside, London

This was familiar, this was what he had done for eight years while the British fought with Napoleon, slinking in the shadows, amongst some of the vilest members of society, in the seediest places. This was what he excelled in, and if anyone in this area of London had seen or had news of Toussaint, he would discover it.

There was one man in particular that called this part of London home, and he knew everything that happened within his realm. Peter Gaston was a retired smuggler, some call him an old pirate, but whatever he was in the past, he now was the leader of one of the largest rings of thieves in London. Cam had met him a few years back when he was spying for the crown under the disguise of being a smuggler. While Peter might be a criminal, at least he was a patriotic one and had no love for the French. He had set out with Cam on a few missions, captaining a ship and helping him bring contraband across the channel. The two of them formed a friendship of sorts, and while they lived two different kinds of lives, Cam knew that he could count on Peter to keep his eyes and ears open for word on Toussaint.

As he sat in the dark filthy tavern waiting on Peter, he took time to study his surroundings. It was a habit to search for all exits and make note of the people around him. Two large men standing across the room by the hearth were watching him warily. He had not brought Cavendish with him tonight thinking that if he got finished with his business early enough, he would stop by Avanley House and see how Abigail was adjusting, and he didn't want to listen to another lecture on why he should leave her alone so she could find a proper husband.

He took a drink of the ale the barmaid had brought him and wondered if perhaps he had been too quick in thinking it was safe to come here alone.

"Davenport, while I'm surprised to find you in a place like this, it's good to see you old friend." The deep voice crackled as an older man stepped out of the shadows.

Cam stood and shook hands with the man before him. It had been a few years since he saw Peter and in that time the man had aged quite a bit. He still wore his hair long, but it was much whiter than it had once been, and he still wore a gold hoop in his ear. Cam thought he looked more like a pirate than he remembered.

"Peter, I was hoping you would be able to meet with me. It was short notice so I wasn't sure."

The older man took a seat across from him and motioned for the barmaid to bring him a drink. "I am not nearly as busy as I have been in the past. Age is catching up to me, and I'm slowing down. But when I received your note, I thought it might be interesting to see what trouble you have gotten into this time."

Cam chuckled before his expression turned serious. "It's Toussaint. He hired men to kill me when I was in Scotland. Obviously, he wasn't successful."

"Argh, that villainous frog is here in England? Someone should have gutted him long before now," Peter said as he slammed his fist down hard on the table drawing every eye in the place to them.

"I came to London knowing he would seek me out. I would ask you to let me know if anyone in your organization hears of a Frenchman with a limp here in London, or if any other information you think pertinent comes to your attention."

The man grinned at the barmaid as she turned to walk away and slapped her arse laughing loudly before turning back to face Davenport. "I will do what I can, but as I said earlier, I am not as busy as I once was."

"I understand and am appreciative of any help you can give. You can find me at *The Devil's Lair* if you need to reach me."

Peter grinned before taking a sip of his ale. "Kingston still running the place, is he?"

Cam frowned slightly as he thought about the fact that Kingston was at this very moment at Avanley House in Mayfair having dinner and more than likely using his charms on Abigail. "Yes, he is still there. He as well as Avanley will also be helping me to find Toussaint."

"I wish you luck, my friend. Toussaint is cunning as well as tricky. It will be difficult to catch him, especially if he is hunting you."

Cam sighed heavily. "I realize that."

Peter clapped his hands together loudly and four scantily clad women appeared at the table. "Why don't you choose one of these lovelies and relieve some tension? They are fairly new here and most eager to please, especially a young handsome man like you."

Cam glanced over at the young women and felt a sense of pity for them. These women were not working in the fashionable pleasure houses of the ton. Circumstances had brought them here to the seedier side of London where fate played them a cruel hand.

"I think I will pass tonight." He reached in his pocket and gave each one enough coin that they could take a few nights off if they wished.

The old man frowned. "Ahh, why did you have to go and do that? I had been hoping for a good tupping tonight and now they won't lift their skirts for a week."

Cam smiled as he stood from his seat. "Thanks for your help, Peter."

The old man didn't rise but continued to grumble about his loss for the night as Cam made his way to the door. He had a few more places he wanted to search out tonight and then he would return to the Lair. As he moved through the alleys and streets his thoughts kept drifting to Abigail, and he wondered how she was adjusting to Avanley House and if Kingston was keeping his hands to himself.

Avanley House

Ever since arriving at the London home of the Duke and Duchess of Avanley, Abigail felt as if she had been swept up in a whirlwind. After a quick tour of the enormous mansion, Bella had taken her to the nursery where she had a chance to meet the duke and duchess's twins Caroline and William. They were only two months old and despite their age had both their mother and father securely wrapped around their tiny fingers.

After they visited the nursery, the duchess sent for a seamstress from Madame LaCroix's dress shop to take measurements for a wardrobe for Abigail. While Abigail insisted that she didn't need very much, the duchess was most persistent and now Abigail worried about how she would pay for everything once it was delivered.

The seamstress had brought three gowns with her and after a few minimal alterations, they fit her perfectly. The duchess had assigned her a lady's maid who had helped her dress and styled her hair for dinner. After a quick look in the mirror, she barely recognized the image staring back at her. Her old wardrobe had consisted of three dresses, all of which buttoned up to the neck and were at least twenty years out of style. Two of them were brown while she had one dark gray dress that she would wear for church or special town assemblies.

She had never owned anything as fine as this and while she had borrowed a few of Emma's dresses, she never imagined owning anything so lovely for herself.

The room she was given was very beautiful and quite larger than anything she had stayed in before. There was a large four-poster bed in the center of the room with a deep burgundy canopy top that matched the burgundy coverlet. A chaise lounge of the same color was by the window and Abigail imagined herself reading a book or resting while she watched the comings and goings on the street below. Oh, what it must be like to belong to one of these grand houses, for it to be your home. She shook her head slightly, reminding herself that this was all a dream that she would be forced to leave one day. She could not stay with her friend Emma or be a burden to any of the nice people she had met forever. Eventually, she would have to decide on a path for her future.

Bella had told her that they would dine around eight and as she looked at the clock on the wall, she realized she was already ten minutes late. She hurriedly put on the slippers that matched the blue dress she was wearing and left her room. Once in the hallway, she had a brief moment where she wondered if she could find her way to the dining room. She hurried down the hall to the stairs but stopped when she noticed Mr. Kingston waiting on the bottom landing for her. She slowed her pace, ladies didn't run down stairways, ladies didn't run at all. She nervously placed a hand to her elegantly styled coiffure and slowly descended the stairs to join him.

Kingston held out his hand to take hers. "I must tell you, Miss Bailey. Until this moment I never believed in a heaven, but upon seeing you tonight, I know there must be one. Because a lady as lovely as you must be an angel." He raised her hand to his lips for a lingering kiss.

Abigail wasn't quite comfortable with such flattery and attention. "Thank you, Mr. Kingston, but I assure you I am no angel." She saw his eyes flicker with something she didn't recognize.

"Miss Bailey, you are so very tempting. How did Davenport manage to keep his hands off you?"

Abigail found herself flustered at such talk and did not know exactly how to respond.

"Mr. Kingston is quite the character but don't let him tease you, Abigail," Bella said as she came out of the drawing room followed by her husband to join them. "Once the season starts you will be beleaguered with gentleman paying their addresses and being around Kingston will give you the practice to wade through their nonsense."

Kingston still held her hand and moved to place it on his arm to escort her to the dining room behind Avanley and Bella. "I'm not so certain that the lady will not already be spoken for before the start of the season."

Abigail turned her head to look at the man beside her. He was giving her a warm smile, and she wondered if he was flirting with her.

"My goodness, Kingston, I don't believe I have ever seen you so flirtatious. Let Abigail enjoy London and the season before you have her traipsing off down the aisle to the altar," Bella said as they entered the dining room.

Kingston held the chair out for her and took the seat to her left. "My apologies, Miss Bailey. I am not accustomed to the rules of polite society. I sometimes need a guiding hand in such matters."

Abigail couldn't help but like Mr. Kingston. He was so kind and his sense of humor made her laugh. "As I am also not accustomed to the rules of London society, I'm not certain I will be the best one to help you."

"Then we shall endeavor to maneuver through the mire together, Miss Bailey."

The Duke of Avanley rolled his eyes and cleared his throat loudly. "For the love of God, Kingston, I'm not certain how much more of this sickening sweetness you are sprouting from your mouth I can take. I apologize as well, Miss Bailey. I have never known him to behave this way."

Abigail laughed softly. "There is no need to apologize, your grace. I'm sure Mr. Kingston means no harm, and I find him rather amusing."

Kingston put a hand over his heart. "Amusing? Not charming or handsome? Perhaps swoon-worthy?"

At this both Bella and Abigail laughed.

"Swoon-worthy? Where do you come up with such things, Mr. Kingston?" Bella asked as she wiped a tear from her eye.

He gave Abigail a wicked grin. "I will have you know; I have been called many things by a great many women, but this is the first time I have been called amusing."

Avanley once again cleared his throat rather loudly. "There are a great many things I would like to call you right now, but with ladies present, I will refrain. Can we please eat before I lose my appetite listening to Kingston's nonsense?"

He rang the small bell on the table and the servants came in with the first course of the night. Abigail enjoyed chatting with the Duke and Duchess of Avanley as well as Benedict Kingston throughout dinner, but in the back of her mind, she couldn't stop thinking about Davenport and what he was doing. He had told her that he would come by to check on her, but now that he had seen to her safety, she wondered if she would see him again.

Cam hesitated outside Avanley House. The extra security that Avanley had boasted about had been easy to sneak past, and he found his way to the gardens at the back of the house with no problem or interference. From where he stood, he could see Avanley and his duchess sitting on the settee in the drawing room, but Abigail wasn't in the room nor was Kingston, and since his carriage was still outside, he knew that he was still there. He moved around the garden back toward the front doors intending on going inside when he heard voices coming from the terrace to the right of the rose arbor where he had been standing earlier. He moved silently toward the sound of laughter, Abigail's laughter. He stood well out of sight and listened as Kingston regaled Abigail with stories of how *The Lair* got its name. He could see her smile and the way her eyes twinkled in the moonlight when she laughed at something Kingston said. She seemed as if she were truly enjoying his company, and that didn't sit well with him at all.

Abigail couldn't remember the last time she had laughed so much. The stories Mr. Kingston told her of when the three dukes were younger were quite scandalous but hilarious. As she thought of the Duke of Avanley, she couldn't imagine him dressing up in women's clothing and performing with a troupe of actors in Vauxhall after a night of drinking and carousing, as Kingston had put it. She would have liked to have seen that performance.

"Your stories have been most entertaining, Mr. Kingston."

He reached for her hand. "I would tell you stories every day, my dear, if I could see that beautiful bright smile."

Cam rolled his eyes and felt his temper begin to flare as Kingston continued trying to charm Abigail.

"Are all men in London so practiced with their flattery, Mr. Kingston? I'm afraid it will take some time for me to get used to it. The young men in Somerset are not nearly as outspoken. If you don't mind, I think we should rejoin the duke and duchess."

"Of course, I'm sure you are exhausted from everything that has happened, and I'm certain you are looking forward to a comfortable night's sleep. I should head back to *The Liar* anyway. Sam does a good job of taking care of things for me while I'm away, but I do like to make myself seen around the gaming rooms to let everyone know I am present and very much in charge. Do you still wish to go for a carriage ride through the park tomorrow morning?"

Abigail's eyes lit up at the idea. "Oh, I would love that. I wasn't sure you were being serious earlier when you asked. I thought I was to stay hidden here at Avanley House."

Kingston clucked his tongue. "My dear, I would never jest about spending time with a lady as lovely as yourself." He raised her hand to his lips.

"Well, if you are certain Davenport will not mind. He has been quite concerned with my safety, and I wouldn't want to do anything to make him upset with me."

"Davenport will be much too busy with finding Toussaint to worry about something so innocent. Who knows where this investigation will take him? He may even have to leave London to find Toussaint. I assure you he will not mind. Come, I will escort you back inside before I take my leave."

Abigail felt her heart drop a little into her stomach. She knew it was entirely possible that she might not see Davenport again, or that he would become so entrenched in finding the French assassin that he would not have time for her now that he had seen her safely ensconced at Avanley House, but to hear it from Mr. Kingston was an altogether different matter.

He took her hand and gave it a light squeeze and she nodded as he led her back inside the house.

Cam watched from behind the shrubbery as Kingston escorted Abigail back inside. He wasn't sure exactly how he was going to kill his long-time friend but the urge to strangle him was strong. He did know that Kingston would be explaining himself very soon. He moved back toward the front of the house, still concerned with Avanley's obvious lack of security, and made his way to Kingston's waiting carriage. Now was as good a time as any to face his friend and get the answers he wanted.

Chapter Ten

Cam waited inside Kingston's carriage for at least half an hour, if not more, and was just about to go inside Avanley House and drag him out by his coat when he heard the front doors open and Kingston and Charles speaking as they stood on the front steps. He sat back against the cushions, his body hidden in the darkness, and waited for his friend. The door to the carriage opened and Kingston stepped inside.

"I was wondering when you would decide to make an appearance," Kingston said completely aware that Davenport was waiting for him. He tapped on the roof of his carriage and it started moving.

Davenport leaned forward just enough that his friend could see his face. "What the hell are you doing? I brought her here to keep her safe, not to attend parties and balls, or go on carriage rides in the park. Avanley's security is shite and you are behaving as if you are her suitor, not her protector. I can't find and kill Toussaint if I must keep watch over Abigail because you can't keep your hands to yourself."

Kingston chuckled and Cam clenched his fists wanting very much to break his nose. "If you must know, Avanley knew you would show up tonight. He had already warned the guards stationed around the house should you come lurking about. And before you decide to chastise me about being in the garden with the lovely Abigail Bailey, I will inform you that I also knew you were there, prowling in the shrubbery like some peeping Tom."

Cam leaned back about the cushions no less angry but feeling a bit less murderous. "Why are you taking her to the park? I think it best to keep her hidden."

Kingston shook his head. "I don't agree. You say that Toussaint could have the idea that she is somehow connected to you. What better way to disavow that notion than to have her linked to someone else? If she is seen in my company rather than yours, it could deter him. Of course, he will still seek to kill you, but at least Abigail will be safe."

Cam growled his annoyance and was not convinced that his friend had Abigail's best interests at heart. "So, this plan I assume has been concocted by you and Avanley without my input or consent. Why was I not consulted?"

"Because your judgement is clouded by your desires for the lady."

"Ridiculous! From where I stood in the garden, it looked like you were the one who had desires for her." The denial he expected was not forthcoming from his friend.

"I find Abigail most attractive, and her innocence is very appealing. Moreover, she can converse with you. Not one time tonight did she mention the weather, ribbons, dresses, or upcoming parties she wished to attend. It was refreshing to be around a woman who is educated and well-spoken. The fact that she looks like an angel is an added benefit."

Cam was feeling murderous again. "Keep your hands off her, Kingston. She is not the type of lady you are familiar with. You can't just play with her and then cast her aside. She will need to find a husband this season and being in your company will not help her to do that."

Kingston leaned forward. "Have you claimed her for your own then, Davenport? If so, speak now, and I will gladly stand aside."

Cam nervously shifted in his seat. "I am responsible for her safety, nothing more."

"Is that all then?" Kingston said as a smirk appeared on his face.

"Yes, damn it!"

"Then there is nothing more to say. I am more than capable of keeping her safe. If you stay away from her and are not seen with her in public, Toussaint will not develop the idea that she is yours. Which by your own mouth you have admitted that she is not. If you will try to overcome your blatant jealousy, you will see this is a good plan."

Cam tried to see the logic in what Kingston was saying but Abigail, being in the company of Kingston, a known rake, did not sit well with him. As the carriage continued toward *The Devil's Lair*, his anger didn't dissipate.

"Did you find out anything about Toussaint tonight?"

Cam sighed heavily. "I visited Peter Gaston; he will let me know if he hears anything or if anyone catches sight of Toussaint. Other than that, I know nothing more."

"I'm certain that if Toussaint sets foot in London, you will be informed. Let's go back to *The Lair* and have a few drinks before I make my rounds about the gaming rooms. If you listen carefully as we make our way around the tables, you might be lucky to hear of something that could prove to be beneficial."

Cam didn't speak and as the carriage came to a stop, Kingston climbed out and Cam followed behind him, but this was not where he wanted to be. He wanted to see Abigail, to tell her of his search and warn her of the dangers of London and the so-called gentlemen that lurked there.

Kingston walked in through the back door and Cam followed behind. Sam was waiting for them as they entered.

"Everything going well tonight, Sam?" Kingston asked before handing off his greatcoat.

"Aye, no trouble other than a young lord who seems intent on losing his shirt tonight."

Kingston's eyes narrowed slightly. "A young lord you say? Who is this young lord?"

"Lord Pettigrew, I believe. New to his title no doubt and wanting to show everyone in London how big his cock is."

Kingston nodded. "Keep an eye on him, Sam. Let me know if things get out of control."

"Afraid you will take too much money from the young pup?" Cam commented as he reached for a bottle of brandy.

Kingston's eyes narrowed. "Young fools come in here all the time losing fortunes. I try to steer some of them down a better path. Unfortunately, some do not want any advice or assistance. If they are foolish enough to lose their fortunes after that, then I am more than willing to oblige them."

Cam poured a glass full of brandy, then asked, "When did you become such a saint?"

"Don't be an arse, my friend. You know I have always had a soft spot for the young fools that come here trying to lose everything their family owns."

Cam didn't answer but turned up his glass and drank the remainder of his brandy.

"If you want the girl, Davenport, it would be best if you would say so now," Kingston said as he watched his friend down his drink.

Cam slammed the glass down on the table. "I never said I wanted her. She is my responsibility. I am the reason she is here. She risked her life to tell me that men were waiting to kill me. I owe her my protection."

Kingston casually leaned against his desk, unperturbed by his friend's anger. "And how are you going to give her that protection, by restricting her every move, keeping her under lock and key? Or did you have something more permanent in mind, such as giving her your name?"

"You know I can't do that. After the life I have led, what could I offer her? No, that's not possible," his voice a bit softer than before.

Kingston walked toward the door that led to the gaming rooms, but before he left, he turned and gave Cam a hard look. "Then don't be angry at the man that can."

Cam stared after his long-time friend well after he had left the room wondering what message he was trying to convey to him. The thought of Abigail in the company of any other man was enough to make him want to drink himself blind, and the image of her being held as she slept in the arms of another was more disturbing than he cared to admit. He poured himself another drink. Toussaint should be his biggest concern, catching him and killing him, his top priority, Instead, he was drinking himself into oblivion over a woman. A woman he had no business desiring and wanting for himself. One thing he was sure of was that if he had to sit back and watch Abigail Bailey be pursued by another, he was going to need more brandy.

The next morning at Avanley House

Abigail sat at the dining room table picking at the eggs on her plate with her fork and taking a few bites here and there of her pastry. She had hoped to have had some word from Cam, but he had not stopped by last night as she had hoped, nor had he sent word this morning. She chastised herself for being foolish. He certainly had more important things occupying his mind and time than her.

"Is something wrong, Abigail?"

Abigail jumped slightly at the duchess's words. "I'm sorry, my mind was wandering." She looked up and saw the duchess grinning at her.

"No doubt. Is it Camden that has your mind drifting elsewhere this morning? I know you were hoping to see him last night."

Abigail pushed her plate away. "I was just speculating on whether or not he had found out any useful information, anything concerning Toussaint."

"I don't know exactly what Cam does or exactly what he has done in the past, but my husband assures me that he was one of the best spies the British had during the war and that a good many lives were saved because of the information he brought across the lines. I feel confident that this Toussaint will be no match for him."

Abigail sighed and forced a smile to her face. "I'm sure you are right."

She took another bite of her breakfast but didn't get a chance to finish when Avanley's butler came into the dining room.

"Your grace, Mr. Kingston is requesting an audience with Miss Bailey."

Bella looked over at Abigail and gave her a soft smile and a wink. "I believe your suitor has arrived for your ride through Hyde Park."

Abigail blushed. "Oh no, Mr. Kingston is not my suitor. He was simply telling me how lovely the park was and since Emma had written to me often about it, I had mentioned my longing to go there. He is just humoring me."

Bella laughed softly. "Darling, men like Kingston and my husband don't do things on a whim just to humor people. They are much too powerful for that. If he didn't wish to be with you, I assure you he would not be here."

Abigail sputtered a bit not knowing what to say when Kingston came through the door. "Your grace, you are looking more beautiful every time I see you. Charles is lucky to have married you before your arrival to London, or I would have swept you off your feet myself." He bowed deeply over her hand before raising it to his lips.

"Kingston, save your flattery for Miss Bailey."

Abigail smiled as Mr. Kingston turned to her. "Ah, an angel indeed. You are so very lovely, my dear."

Abigail felt herself growing warmer and her cheeks blushed at the compliment. Mr. Kingston was an incredibly handsome man, tall, broad shoulders, dark hair, and ice blue eyes. He was what most women dreamed of in a suitor.

"Good morning, Mr. Kingston."

He took her hand and raised it to his lips. "Am I too early? I confess I was most eager to see you again, my dear."

Abigail lowered her lashes at the intensity in his eyes.

"You are not early at all, Kingston. I think you and Abigail should make the most of the day. Of course, you will take the lady's maid I assigned for her. Now that she is in London, we must make certain everything is proper, and she is well chaperoned."

Abigail thought she saw a trace of annoyance cross his face, but he simply nodded his agreement as he offered her his hand to help her rise from where she was seated.

"I will gather my gloves and cloak. I will not be long."

"There is no rush. I would wait an eternity for you, my dear."

Abigail caught herself before she could roll her eyes at his comments, then hurried from the room.

"You and Charles still think this is a good idea?" Bella asked as Kingston took the seat Abigail had just vacated.

"What? Having Miss Bailey seen in public with someone other than Davenport? Yes, it's a good plan."

"Do you not think that he should have been consulted? I'm sure he will be angry once he discovers what you are doing."

Kingston grinned. "Oh, he was very angry." He looked over to see the duchess eyeing him warily. "He was waiting for me in my carriage when I left here last night. He also was snooping around the house spying on Abigail and me while we were on the garden terrace. He overheard me asking her to take a ride this morning through the park."

Bella's eyes widened. "And he was against the idea, no doubt."

Kingston nodded. "Very much so. I honestly thought he was going to want to fight me at one point." He chuckled as if the thought amused him.

Bella clucked her tongue. "Are you and Charles doing this deliberately to torment him or make him jealous?"

Kingston put a hand over his heart. "My dear duchess, we are doing this solely to help Miss Bailey. If our actions provoke Davenport or annoy him in the process, then that is just an added benefit to the plan. Never hurts a man to be a little jealous over a woman."

Bella stood from her seat. "As usual you and my husband have forgotten one important detail to this brilliant scheme of yours."

Kingston raised his brows at her in astonishment. "And what would that be, your grace?"

"Abigail. What happens to her if she falls for your flowery words and sweet sentiments? How do you plan to deal with that if she chooses you over Davenport? Will you be willing to marry her, or will you find it satisfying to break her heart? I don't like the idea of her being used as sport, but at least the two of you will have gotten a good laugh at putting Davenport through the paces."

She put down her napkin and moved from the room just as Charles came into the dining room.

"Good morning, my love," he said to his wife as she sailed past him.

He turned back to Kingston when he received no answer. "What the hell did you do?"

"Bella is unhappy with our plan and is afraid that Abigail might develop affections for me which in turn would break her heart."

Charles leaned against the doorframe. "Hmm, the idea is ridiculous. How could a lady as lovely as Miss Bailey find herself attracted to a rakehell like you?"

Kingston stood from his seat. "I am no more of a rakehell than you were yourself, and you managed to marry a lady that you certainly don't deserve. Why would the idea of me with Miss Bailey be ridiculous? I have my own fortune, and I have been told by several ladies, your wife included, that I am rather handsome. I do plan on marrying one day."

Charles grinned as he placed a hand over his heart. "My apologies, if I have offended you."

Kingston frowned and moved to the door. "You are trying to rile me. I can see it in your eyes. I suppose a devil never truly seeks redemption."

Before either of them could comment further, Abigail had returned and was waiting along with her lady's maid.

"I am ready, Mr. Kingston."

Kingston turned at the soft sound of her voice. She looked very pretty dressed in a light pink day dress with a matching bonnet and white gloves. He smiled and reached for her hand, but inside he thought that if Davenport didn't make his intentions known soon, he just might find himself tempted to take the lady for himself, and damn Avanley for putting the thought in his head.

Office of Thomas Harrison
War Department

Davenport did not have an appointment to meet with Harrison and was unperturbed when his secretary said he would have to come back another day. He simply ignored the small man that tried to bar the door and pushed him aside, shoving the door open to see Harrison sitting behind his desk. The man did rise but didn't seem surprised to see him either.

"Harrison, I need a few minutes of your time." Cam moved further into the room after shutting the door in the face of Mr. Brown, Harrison's secretary that had just risen from the floor where Cam had deposited him earlier.

Harrison tilted his chin down a notch. "By all means, do come in, your grace."

Cam took a seat in front of Harrison's desk.

"Is this about Toussaint?"

"Avanley has already told you then."

"He has reached out to me, yes, but I already knew Toussaint had crossed into England."

Cam leaned forward in the chair he occupied and narrowed his eyes at the man sitting across from him. "You knew? How?"

Harrison opened a box on his desk and took out a cigar before offering the box to him. "It is my business to know."

"Why was I not contacted?"

"The department had our reasons. Besides, we are most confident in your abilities."

Cam stood up and began pacing the room. "You knew he was coming to kill me and gave me no warning. Now there is an innocent lady involved, and if I had been made aware, that could have been avoided."

"That was unfortunate. We do regret that Miss Bailey became embroiled in something so unpleasant, but I don't believe Toussaint will come after her, especially if Avanley and Kingston are successful."

Cam didn't like that answer. "I am not nearly as confident as the three of you in that matter. I would request extra security for Avanley House."

Harrison nodded. "It has already been seen to."

"And damn it, Harrison, I want to know everything you know about Toussaint, and why he is in England. The man had a vendetta no doubt, but there is something more. Something that has brought him to our shores."

"You are very astute, your grace, another reason you have been so successful over the years. There are rumors that there are those still sympathetic to Napoleon's cause here in England. We believe he might have been sent to see if their support might be swayed to another's cause or even a way to help Napoleon escape St. Helena."

Cam scrunched up his forehead in disbelief. "Napoleon is defeated, soundly defeated. How can he still pose a threat?"

"Napoleon is not the threat. The threat comes from those that are like-minded, that shared his vision. We believe Toussaint is seeking those out here in England who might still believe in the cause. His hatred for you and seeking his revenge against you was a bonus."

"You do know I must kill him."

Harrison rose from his seat for the first time. "I am aware of that and let me assure you that you will be working with the full authority of the Prince Regent and this office. We are convinced you will succeed."

"And Miss Bailey?"

"As I said, I don't believe Miss Bailey is any concern to Toussaint, but she will have our protection."

Cam nodded. "Very well, but once this is done, I will be done with this work."

Harrison offered his hand. "That is fair. I wish you well, your grace, and hope Toussaint shows his face soon so this madness can be concluded without haste. Many men, including yourself and those in this office, have wasted too much of their lives with war and death."

Cam agreed but kept his words to himself. He turned and left Harrison's office narrowly avoiding another collision with Mr. Brown on his way out the door. Now that he knew Toussaint had other business in England, other than seeking him out, he felt that Abigail might be in less danger than he first thought. Oddly enough, that didn't take the weight of worry from his shoulders, because of his fear of Toussaint harming her, he had brought her to London and now she may be facing an even greater danger from a man who was just as crafty as Toussaint.

Hyde Park

Abigail thought the park was much lovelier than Emma described it in her letters, and although the season was not upon them, there were still a few other people out and about in their carriages or riding horses down Rotten Row.

"The park is quiet this morning. When the season is in session these paths are filled with people. Carriages driven by London's most fashionable, and ladies wearing their best hoping to catch the attention of any gentleman with a title," Kingston said as he tooled the horses along the carriage path through the park.

Abigail smiled brightly. "I do hope I am still in London for the season. Emma said she would be coming back to London, and I could stay with her, but now with the mess I have found myself in, I'm not sure if I will still be here to enjoy it."

"I wouldn't worry about that, my dear. You are destined to be a sensation this season."

Abigail laughed. "Mr. Kingston, you are quite possibly the biggest flirt I have ever met. I am well aware, that the only reason I can even attend the events of the season is because of my relationship with Emma, who is now a duchess. I am a poor vicar's daughter with no prospects, no money, and no connections. I am living off the charity of my best friend, and the new friends she has made since her marriage. Please don't try to make me believe that I could be anything more than what I am."

Kingston slowed the horses astonished at the frankness of her words. "My dear, you must know that you are an extremely beautiful woman, and from what I can tell from our conversations, you are also intelligent. The fact that you have come to London with Davenport knowing a madman might be trying to kill you only speaks to your character and tells me you are also a strong brave woman. Not every man in London is seeking a woman of means or one that comes from a grand aristocratic family."

Abigail laughed softly. "I am from a small village and up until recently, I have never been to London. There is no way I can compete with the sophisticated ladies of the ton. I don't think men will be lining up to pay their addresses to me. Eventually, when Davenport finds Toussaint, I will have to leave all of this and return to my life." Her smile slipped a little. "Mr. Kingston, have you seen Davenport? I was hoping he would come by Avanley House last night. I was curious if he had discovered any new information."

Kingston steered the horses off to the side. "I saw him last night after leaving Avanley House. He had been out combing the seedier sides of London seeking information on Toussaint."

Abigail perked up. "So, he is alright?"

Kingston pulled the horses to a stop. "He was last night when I saw him." Kingston stepped down from the carriage, then assisted her to the ground. "Why don't we take a walk by the Serpentine? The weather is very nice today, a rarity for this time of year in London, and I can't remember the last time I had such a lovely lady on my arm." He gave her lady's maid a pointed glance that communicated silently that she was to stay with the carriage.

He placed Abigail's hand on his arm and led her down the path. They had not strolled very far from the carriage when he saw Davenport riding toward them. "It looks like you will have the reunion you have been seeking very soon, my dear."

Abigail tilted her head up and shaded her eyes from the sun with her hand. "He doesn't look very happy, does he? I hope something bad hasn't happened."

Kingston placed his hand over hers as it rested on his arm. "We are about to find out, I'm afraid."

Cam knew there were other places he needed to be. Cavendish would be waiting for him back at *The Lair*, and after meeting with Thomas Harrison, he wanted to delve deeper into his idea that Toussaint was here to meet others that were sympathetic to the French cause. As he rode back toward *The Lair*, he couldn't get over the urge to seek out Abigail. He knew Kingston was to take her for a carriage ride through the park this morning, so instead of heading toward Bond Street, he urged his horse toward Hyde Park. After riding along the carriage paths and not seeing them, he finally caught sight of a couple walking along the banks of the Serpentine. Abigail was not hard to recognize, her light hair catching the rays of the sun, her slight figure moving gracefully as she walked, and her smile was something he could long to see every day. Only today, she was giving her attention to Kingston, the blackguard, who was holding her hand and leaning in close enough to steal a kiss, if he wished. Cam spurred his horse toward them and by the time he reached them, his irritation had grown significantly. He pulled his horse to a hard stop and slid to the ground.

"Davenport, what the devil? You are riding as if Lucifer himself is chasing your tail. Is it safe to assume you are not having the best day?" Kingston said purposely mocking him.

Cam held tight to the reins of his horse and glared at both Kingston and Abigail. "Apparently, not as nice of a day as you are having."

Abigail stepped forward. "Whatever is the matter? Is it Toussaint?"

Cam narrowed his eyes a fraction. "I did discover that Toussaint may not be the threat to your safety as I first thought, but it looks as if you have not made the trip to London for nothing." His glare slid from Abigail to Kingston. "You seem to be having no trouble gathering ardent admirers. I suppose I should be thankful the season is not in session."

Abigail inhaled sharply and Kingston took a step forward. "Careful Davenport, abuse me all you wish, but don't bring the lady into this."

Cam took a menacing step forward, ready to knock Kingston to the ground when Abigail's voice cut through to him. "Mr. Kingston, while I appreciate your interference, I believe I can speak for myself in this instance. Do you mind giving his grace and me some privacy?"

Kingston frowned at Davenport then looked back over to Abigail. "Certainly, but if you need me, I will not be far."

Abigail turned and watched as Kingston turned back toward the carriage, once she was sure he was out of hearing, she turned back to Davenport. "Do you have a problem with me being here in London?" Her hands were firmly set on her hips. "If you do, let me remind you of the circumstances that brought me here. It was your decision that I travel to London, I was perfectly content to stay at McDonough Castle, but when you adamantly declared it would be safer for me in London, I trusted you and followed you willfully. I rode a horse for days, stopping only briefly, and froze at night. I almost died of sea-sickness, and when you deposited me at a notorious gaming hell, with a man I had never met, I accepted that decision without argument."

Cam knew she spoke the truth and it was his anger at himself for misjudging the situation that was fueling his actions now. He gripped her arm and pulled her closer. "Let me remind you a bit about our journey, in case you have forgotten. At night, when you were cold and shivering, I lay beside you and held you close in my arms. On the ship when you were seasick, wearing nothing but your sheer chemise, it was I that bathed your face and neck." He stepped closer and tilted her chin up so he could look down into her eyes. "I picked you up from the floor and carried you to the bed, trying to ignore your rosy, pink nipples peeking through your sheer chemise." He should have stopped when he saw the shocked expression on her face. "When you changed and bathed by the loch, it was I that ran to your aide when you screamed, and it was I that saw you naked." His grip tightened on her arm. "I was the one that kissed you afterward." He leaned closer, his lips next to her ear. "Tell me, do you remember that part of your journey to London?"

Abigail sucked in a breath as her cheeks flamed. "I remember." Her voice was soft and breathy. "What are you implying, your grace?"

Cam tilted his head toward where Kingston was standing. "I'm not implying anything. Just taking note of how quickly you adjust to the situations around you. Tell me, did you have any qualms about leaving the safety of my arms for the safety of his."

He was not prepared for the hard smack as her hand cracked across his cheek. "You are the biggest fool and most hateful man I have ever met. To think that I lost sleep last night worrying for your safety, and the time I have spent hoping you had found something that would help you with your search for Toussaint. That is a mistake I will not make again." She angrily swiped at a stray tear that slid down her cheek. "No, I must amend that statement, I am the fool, you are simply an arrogant arse. It is no wonder you have people trying to kill you." She raised her chin a notch higher. "I hereby relieve you of all responsibility you may feel for me, your grace. I no longer wish to see you or hear your name. I do not wish for Toussaint to do you harm, however, I will no longer lose sleep worrying about it."

She turned and tried to move away, but Cam gripped her arm and stopped her. "Oh no, you don't get to dismiss me, Abigail. You are my responsibility in more ways than one. I..."

"Please remove your hand, your grace."

Cam let go of her arm, her voice was cold enough to form icicles. He watched as she made her way back to the waiting carriage. Her head was held high and her back rigid. Kingston lifted her into the seat, then moved toward him. Cam was not in the mood for a fight, but if Kingston wanted one, he would give it to him.

Kingston stopped a few feet away. "Bloody idiot!"

Cam squared his shoulders.

Kingston glared at his friend. "Just what did you think to accomplish with that display? Did you think she would fall on her knees, thankful that you deemed her worthy of your affections? The girl very well could have been in love with you, but after that show of arrogance and ignorance I'm not certain she will ever talk to you again."

Cam stepped forward. "I suppose that makes you happy."

Kingston huffed out an angry breath. "Believe what you wish. If I did have designs on the lady, you certainly made it easier for me."

Cam was beginning to calm down. He had never let his temper get away from him like this before, and he had never cared enough about a woman to feel the jealousy that had been coursing through his veins. He looked back over at the carriage where Abigail sat stiffly waiting for Kingston to return. "I feel as if I am going mad. I don't know what I'm doing anymore. It's like being lost or stuck in a fog. I need to speak with her."

Kingston gripped his arm. "Not now, let her calm down. Besides, the apology she deserves will require more than words."

He turned and walked back to the carriage. Cam took a few steps forward, but Abigail never looked in his direction. As the carriage turned away, he kicked the ground causing a cloud of dust to fly into the air. What was happening to him? What was it about the woman that made him lose his mind? He moved back to his horse, he needed to go meet with Cavendish, then he was going to Avanley House. He needed to apologize, and if Kingston was correct, he needed to buy the biggest floral arrangement in London to go along with it.

Chapter Eleven

A bigail didn't think she had ever been so furious. She had been completely unprepared for Davenport's anger. She just didn't understand it. Where had his anger toward her even come from? What had caused Cam to behave so irrationally?

"Miss Bailey, I apologize for Davenport's behavior," Mr. Kingston said obviously unhappy with his friend's comments and behavior as well.

Abigail turned to face him and the sympathetic look he was giving her made her even more angry at Davenport. "It is not for you to apologize, Mr. Kingston. You did nothing wrong and certainly didn't make him say the things he did." She reached for her parasol and flipped it open and angrily began twirling it with her fingers. "I am so angry, I could…I could…punch him right in the nose."

Kingston guffawed loudly at her remark. "Oh, Miss Bailey, you have no idea how much money I would pay to see you do just that. In fact, I will turn the carriage around right now if you wish."

Abigail closed the parasol again and put it aside. "That's alright, in order to punch him, I would have to see him again, and that is something I have no wish to do."

Kingston blew out a long slow breath as a look of guilt came over his face. "Well, don't be too hasty, my dear. This might be just a bit my fault as well. I didn't force the words from his mouth, but I might have encouraged his behavior just a little."

Abigail narrowed her eyes. "I don't understand."

"Miss Bailey, you are exceptionally beautiful, and I believe that Davenport may have developed feelings for you other than those of responsibility for your safety. Because of that, I might have stoked the fires of jealousy with the attention I have been showing you. A man like Davenport has likely never felt those types of feelings before, and while I am not making excuses to justify the things he said, I do believe there is a reason behind it."

Abigail rolled her eyes, his words not easing the anger she was feeling. "I appreciate that you have been so kind to me since my arrival, especially after I so ungraciously broke a vase over your head upon our first meeting, but the assumption that Davenport is jealous is just ridiculous. Even if it were true, I don't know if I could ever forgive him for the things he said. I do not wish him ill will, but I hope I have seen the last of the Duke of Stafford." The words tasted of a lie as they passed through her lips.

Kingston leaned over a bit closer. "If I believed that to be the truth, my dear, you have no idea how happy it would make me."

Abigail gave him a sharp look. "Whatever do you mean?"

Kingston grinned but didn't offer an explanation and before she realized it, they were already in front of Avanley House. Mr. Kingston pulled the horses to a stop, then walked around and lifted her to the ground. He escorted her inside where Bella was waiting for her.

Abigail saw the duchess' smile fade and hated that her emotions were so evident on her face.

"Oh my, what has happened?"

"Davenport showed up at the park and made an utter fool of himself. He said some things that Miss Bailey found offensive, and rightly so," Kingston helpfully answered for her causing Abigail to frown in his direction.

Bella stepped closer. "Oh no! Abigail, are you alright?"

"I'm fine, thank you. Just a bit shocked at his behavior."

Bella frowned at Kingston. "I knew something like this would happen."

Abigail turned sharply at the duchess's words.

"Never mind, dear. I'm sure Davenport didn't mean what he said and will come to his senses soon if he has not already. Men can be rather dense at times, especially in matters concerning women. I do have something that might make you feel better. Madam Lacroix sent over a beautiful gown and tonight we will attend dinner with the Countess of Mulford, or as most of us fondly know her, Aunt Louisa."

The only thing Abigail wanted to do was go to her room and be alone, where she could feel miserable in peace and solitude. She certainly didn't feel like dressing up and going to have dinner with the Countess of Mulford, but it would be rude to refuse, and the duke and duchess had been so kind to her, she did not want them to be disappointed.

She turned to Mr. Kingston. "Thank you so much for the ride through the park this morning. I'm sorry it was ruined."

"I wouldn't say it was ruined, just interrupted. Have a good evening, ladies, and Miss Bailey, do consider what I said. I am not trying to plead Davenport's cause, just offering insight into his reasons." He bowed deeply at the waist before turning back toward the carriage.

Bella came to stand beside her. "While I am curious as to what happened at the park, I will not push you to tell me anything until you wish it."

Abigail breathed deeply, thankful that she was not having to endure an interrogation at the moment. "I suppose we should take a look at this gown I am to wear tonight."

Bella gave her a soft, if not sad smile. "I suppose we should."

Abigail followed the duchess up the stairs to her bedchamber hoping that the evening's festivities would take away the hurt and anger she was feeling. Now that the danger had passed with Toussaint, she wanted to put all of this behind her. Perhaps even rejoin Emma in Scotland at the end of the season. There were so many things that were uncertain in her life, but one thing she was sure of was that if she ever saw Camden Davenport, Duke of Stafford again, it would be too soon.

Much later that Night

Abigail took a heavy breath as her lady's maid began brushing out her hair for the night. It has been a long exhausting day after her fight with Davenport in the park. Bella had tried to help take her mind off what had occurred, but Abigail was still angry and hurt by Davenport's accusations. The dinner party at the Countess of Mulford's townhouse had been pleasant. The countess was an older lady, but Abigail imagined that she had been quite the handful in her youth. She had regaled them of stories from when she was younger as well as some from when the dukes, Hawksford, Leicester, and Avanley had been young. She had managed to enjoy the evening despite the lingering anger and confusion she felt over Davenport's outburst.

"Is there anything more I can do for you, miss?"

Abigail gave the shy young woman that had been assigned to be her maid a tired smile. "No, I have everything I could ever need. You have been most helpful, Jenny."

The small amount of praise caused the young woman's eyes to light up.

"Thank you, miss. If you need anything throughout the night just ring the bell."

Abigail nodded and watched as Jenny left the room. Once she was alone, she walked over to the window and opened it to let in some fresh air before moving to the writing desk. It was very late, but she did not feel like sleeping, and she had forgotten to grab a book from the library before she came upstairs. She sat down and reached for a piece of paper. This would be a good time to write to Emma, and if she could get the duke to frank her letter and send it out tomorrow, perhaps Emma would get it before she left Scotland to return to London.

There was quite a lot to tell her, and she didn't know where to begin. Should she recant everything that happened on the way to London, or simply tell her that she arrived safely and was now staying with the Duke and Duchess of Avanley? It would ease Emma's mind to know she was not staying at *The Devil's Lair*. She wanted to tell her about Davenport and how he had behaved in the park, but she knew he was a good friend of Emma's husband, and she would never wish to cause a rift between her friend and the man she married. Perhaps it would be best to tell Emma once she arrived in London.

So much had happened since she had left McDonough Castle, that she finished the first page quickly. She took out a second sheet of paper and dipped her quill in the ink pot when a noise behind her made her drop the quill and spin around quickly in her seat.

"What the devil are you doing here?!"

"Why the hell do you have your window open?! Just because the others feel that Toussaint is no longer a danger to you, doesn't mean I want you to take chances with your safety. He isn't the only dangerous man lurking about London at night, and I don't want any other lecherous bastard thinking you are easy prey," Davenport said as he leisurely leaned against the wall beside the window.

She jumped up from her seat and moved quickly over to the bed where her robe lay draped over the footboard.

"That is certainly obvious, but might I remind you, my safety is no longer your concern. You made that clear this morning. Why are you lurking about climbing through my window and what on Earth are you carrying?"

He glanced down at the wilted, tattered, and destroyed bouquet of flowers he had gripped in his hand. "Well, this afternoon it was the loveliest and largest bouquet in London. I have been trying to deliver it all bloody day, but I kept being turned away at the door. Unfortunately, it did not survive the climb up the trellis as well as I had hoped."

Abigail fumbled with getting her arms into the sleeves of her robe even as Davenport came further into the room and removed his coat tossing it on the chaise beneath the window.

"Being turned away from the door should have given you the hint that you were not wanted. I never imagined you would have had such a difficult time understanding. I said in the park that I had no desire to see you, and I meant it. That was not an invitation to climb through my window and sneak into my bedchamber. Since the household is all abed, I suggest you leave the same way you entered."

She took a backward step as he grinned and stalked toward her, still carrying the tattered remains of the bouquet in his hand. "I'm not leaving until we have talked, Abigail. If you feel the need to scream, go ahead."

Abigail narrowed her eyes and closed her mouth tighter forming a hard straight line. "Go ahead then, say what you will and get out."

Davenport was within arm's reach but did not move to touch her. He thrust the ragged remnants of the bouquet into her hands and smiled when her nose wrinkled up upon closer inspection of the specimen. "You have bewitched me, Abigail Bailey, there is no other logical explanation I can come up with for my poor behavior."

She opened her mouth to speak, but he held up his hand to silence her.

"You are constantly in my thoughts. I can't eat, I can't sleep, I'm ready to fight anyone that looks in your direction, and I can't focus. You are dangerous, my dear."

Abigail blinked a few times stunned at his words. "If I am so dangerous, don't you think it wise to stay away from me."

A deep laugh rumbled in his chest. "Oh, if it were that easy."

He stepped forward quickly wrapping an arm around her waist and pulling her into his chest. She squirmed in his arms dropping the pitiful remnants of the floral bouquet on the floor between them.

"What the devil has gotten into you? Let me go."

"If I could do that, I wouldn't have risked life and limb climbing the side of Avanley's damn house."

Abigail pushed against his chest. "This is ridiculous. You need to leave. For heaven's sake, stop looking at me like that."

Cam leaned a bit closer. "Like what? Like a starving man that has a feast set before him but knows he shouldn't partake of it."

Abigail blinked in astonishment. "My goodness, what a terribly inappropriate thing to say. It sounds as if you want to…"

"Devour you? That is exactly what I want to do."

Before Abigail could protest further Cam's lips descended upon hers. At first, she was so shocked that she felt frozen, but as his lips claimed hers, and the way his arms held her close to his body, she slowly began melting against him.

Cam felt her rigid body soften as he held her. He pulled back to look down at her face. She was extraordinarily beautiful and no matter what anyone said, or the fact that he knew he should stay away from her, he knew she belonged to him.

He leaned closer again. "I love the way you smell of lavender." He ran his fingers along the length of her arm. "Your skin is soft like silk." He pressed a kiss to her cheek. He lifted her hair and ran his fingers through the silky strands. He grinned as he leaned in again for another kiss but was taken off guard when she shoved him hard causing him to stumble backward. He was barely able to catch himself before his arse hit the floor.

"What the hell, woman?!"

Abigail put her hands on her hips. "After what you said to me in the park this morning, did you really think that you could show up here with those flowers, pitiful as they are, and think I would fall on my knees thankful for your attention?"

Cam grinned and arched one eyebrow as he regarded her standing before him like an avenging angel. She looked even more spectacular in her anger. "Well, I had hoped."

Abigail took a deep breath as she picked up the ragged remains of what must have been a beautiful arrangement of flowers off the floor. She took a few steps to reach him and placed the bouquet in his hands. "I am not so easily swayed, your grace, and my forgiveness must be earned. Now, kindly leave my room." She pointed to the window. "By the same way you entered."

Cam shrugged his shoulders as he strolled back toward the window. "If I fall to my death, will you weep over my crumpled corpse?"

For a moment, he saw a trace of fear in her eyes quickly replaced by resolute determination. "There are bushes below the window, I'm certain they will break your fall."

Cam threw one leg over the edge.

"Wait!" Abigail rushed forward. "Have you heard anything more about Toussaint? Not that I am overly concerned with your safety. I am merely curious as to if he will do you in before I have to do so myself."

Cam laughed at her cheeky comment. "Only what I learned from Thomas Harrison at the War Department yesterday."

Abigail took another step closer. "Will you share with me what you know?"

Cam grinned. "Perhaps tomorrow, if you will see that I am allowed admittance, I could pay you a visit and share with you exactly what I have learned."

Abigail nodded and rolled her eyes. "Very well, but you better show up with a better bouquet of flowers than the ones you had tonight."

Before she could move away, he grabbed her hand and tugged her close enough to plant another quick kiss to her lips. "Close and lock the window after I leave. I wouldn't want any other man thinking to claim what is mine."

Abigail was too stunned to speak as she watched him disappear out the window. She quickly moved forward and did as he suggested securely locking the window after his departure. She moved back toward her bed and pulled back the covers before grabbing the pillows and punching them a few times to fluff them up before she climbed into bed to lie back against them. She stared up at the ceiling wondering how long it would take her to go to sleep after her encounter with Davenport. The man was just exasperating. So why did her skin warm to his touch and why did she find herself thinking of him? She punched the pillow again and sank down lower into the bed. She hoped it would not be a mistake to see him again tomorrow, but her curiosity was getting the best of her. She simply had to know what he had discovered about Toussaint.

The Devil's Lair

It was well past midnight when Davenport made his way back to *The Devil's Lair*. This time of night it was packed with patrons and Kingston would be moving about the gaming rooms. Sam was waiting at the back door to admit him and leaning up against the back wall with his arms crossed over his chest wearing a disapproving, if not fatherly, look on his face, was John Cavendish.

"Evening, Sam. Kingston having a busy night?"

Sam shut and barred the door behind him. "Not as busy as it gets during the height of the season, but there are enough nobs in town now to make it a profitable evening."

Davenport knew exactly how busy London became during the season and *The Devil's Lair*, being the most reputable and high-class gaming establishment in London, people were usually waiting to get inside. He moved over to stand in front of Cavendish.

"Any word on Toussaint or anyone that might be connected to him?"

Cavendish pushed away from the wall. "It has only been a few hours since you told me what I needed to be looking for, and no, I have not discovered anything of importance." He reached out and grabbed a wilted flower from the ragged bouquet Davenport still clutched in his hand. "Is this a different plan you have for finding Toussaint?"

Davenport frowned as he looked down at the bouquet. He threw the pile on a table nearby. "They were for Abigail."

"If what Kingston told me about what you said to her in the park is the truth, you are going to have to do better than that."

Davenport narrowed his eyes. Damn Kingston for not being able to keep his mouth shut. "She turned me away and is not nearly as eager to forgive me as I had hoped, that should make you happy."

"Aye, it does make me glad to see that Miss Bailey has some sense about her, but since you seem determined to have the girl, I would give you a bit of advice."

Davenport sighed, not really in the mood for his friend's advice but knew he was going to hear it anyway. "What do you suggest then?"

Cavendish grinned. "Buy a nicer bouquet of flowers. That shouldn't be too difficult for a man of your means."

Davenport growled as his friend walked away. "I'm going to find Kingston."

He made his way up the stairs to the gaming rooms. It was busy but at least a person could move freely without bumping into others. He searched the crowd for Kingston. It didn't take long to find him. He was standing off to the side in the shadows watching a group of young men playing a game of hazard.

Kingston turned and nodded his head in acknowledgement as Davenport came to stand beside him. "How did you fair with the lovely Miss Bailey?"

Davenport stared straight ahead. "I was not admitted through the front door, so I had to climb through her window."

Kingston turned his head sharply toward him. "Isn't that how all of this began in the first place?" He chuckled. "She crawled out of a window to get to you, and now you are scaling walls and crawling through windows to get to her. It really is comical. After you made it inside, how did it go?"

"Well, she didn't try to throw me out the window, but I think it was only because she physically couldn't, not because she didn't want to."

"Hmm, it went that well, did it?"

Cam heaved a heavy sigh. "I lost my head today, and I owe you an apology as well."

Cam saw a look of surprise cross his friend's face quickly replaced with what he was certain was guilt.

"Well, at least you have stopped denying your feelings for the girl."

Cam didn't want to discuss Abigail anymore tonight. "What is so interesting in this game that you have focused all of your attention on?"

Kingston crossed his arms over his chest as he watched the table. "Do you see the young lord wearing the bright green jacket and pink silk breeches?"

Cam looked at the young dandy. He couldn't be more than twenty years old and from the way he was dressed, he was trying his best to fit in with the other dandies in town. "Who is he?"

"That, my friend, is Lord Edward Pettigrew, Viscount Litchfield. He just came into his title a few months ago and has been rapidly losing his inheritance ever since. Last week he lost over a thousand pounds in one night. I tried to talk to him and reason with the idiot, but his arrogance is astounding. I believe he sees himself as an heir to the throne rather than viscount to a small estate in Hertfordshire."

Cam frowned as he watched the young fool lose again. "You are still going to try and intervene, aren't you?"

Kingston shrugged his shoulders. "I don't enjoy taking everything a man owns."

Cam nodded. "I'm going to sleep in your sitting room tonight."

Kingston looked over at him. "When are you going to reopen Stafford House? It is ridiculous to own a huge mansion in Grosvenor Square and never stay there."

Cam knew his friend was speaking the truth, but while his father had doted on him, regardless of his legitimacy, he still didn't feel like Stafford House belonged to him. "The house is not closed. There is a small staff that keeps everything ready in the event I choose to stay there, but I suppose you are right. It is nonsensical for me not to stay there."

Kingston grabbed his arm as he started to walk off. "One more thing, there was a man in here tonight. Sam heard him mention that he was waiting for an acquaintance to arrive from France."

"Is that all?"

Kingston frowned. "It's more than you have discovered. Sam will let me know if he returns. and if I feel it is necessary, I will have one of Harrison's men follow him."

"You will send word to me if you see him again?"

Kingston gave him a grin. "I will. Now, go get some rest, you have bigger problems than Toussaint. I'm afraid Abigail might kill you before the Frenchman gets a chance."

Cam ignored the comment and headed back down to Kingston's apartments. Tomorrow he would pay another visit to Avanley House, hopefully, this time through the front door.

Chapter Twelve

Davenport slept very little the night before and now as he stood on the steps of Avanley House like a damn 'wet behind the ears' suitor hoping Abigail would receive him this morning, he could feel his irritation rising. He reached up and pulled at his intricately tied cravat feeling as if the knot was growing tighter by the second. Finally, Avanley's butler opened the door.

The man had seen him a dozen times at least and still looked at him as if he was a stranger.

"Good morning, Jameson."

The older man bowed slightly in deference before resuming his rigid straight-back posture to examine him more closely.

"Is there something I can help you with, your grace?"

Davenport narrowed his eyes and refrained from clenching his teeth. "I am seeking an audience with Miss Bailey."

Unperturbed by his admission, Jameson still refused to stand aside and allow him admittance.

"Is the lady expecting a call from you, your grace?"

"Yes, Jameson she is expecting me. Now are you going to let me in, or should I stand out here all bloody morning?"

Jameson lifted his white-gloved hand and held it out to him, palm up. "Do you have a calling card, your grace?"

Davenport squeezed the life out of the stems of roses he was holding. "You know very well who I am, Jameson, and no I don't have a bloody calling card. Is Miss Bailey in or not?"

"I am not certain the lady is receiving visitors at this time."

Davenport watched in shocked outrage as the man tried to shut the door in his face. He stuck his foot in the opening and pushed it back open. "Avanley! Where the hell are you? Avanley!"

He heard his friend's deep laughter coming from inside the house. "That's enough, Jameson. I suppose we can admit him, although it might be wise to have some footmen ready to throw him out in case he can't behave properly with the young lady."

Jameson dutifully moved out of the way, and Davenport strode into the entranceway fuming with anger. His friend was standing off to the side and had heard the entire exchange between him and the ever vigilant Jameson.

"You think this is funny, Avanley? I should have known you were behind Jameson's behavior."

Charles stepped forward. "I most certainly do." He motioned his head at the bouquet he had gripped tightly in his hand. "Better than last night's attempt, but I always preferred gifting women jewelry or a bauble they had seen in a store window. That way they always had something to remember about our association. Of course, Miss Bailey may not wish to remember your association."

Davenport took a menacing step toward his friend. "How much did she tell you about last night?"

"She didn't tell me anything, it was Isobel she confided in, and of course, since my wife was concerned over the welfare of her new-found friend, she confided in me."

Davenport's frown became more pronounced. "Your security is shite, by the way."

"There is nothing wrong with my security. It is your skills that are under scrutiny. My men alerted me to your presence. I already knew you had snuck into the lovely lady's bedchamber, and I, being the friend that I am, chose not to interrupt you. My wife, however, will not be so lenient if she had discovered your presence. I suggest you not let her catch you. She will have you thrown out."

Davenport rolled his eyes. "Perhaps you can keep her distracted." He saw Avanley's rakish grin. "Where is Abigail? I didn't bring this ridiculously large bouquet of roses for you, nor do I wish to stand here and converse with you all day."

"Very well, I believe she is in the drawing room with Isobel. I will see if she is willing to see you."

Davenport narrowed his eyes. "Avanley, I am not in the mood. There are other things I need to see to today."

Cam followed his friend down the hall to the blue drawing room. Before they entered, Avanley leaned over and said in a softer voice, "Come to my study before you leave. I have some information you might find useful."

Cam nodded before following Avanley further into the room.

"My darling, we have a guest. Davenport is here to see Miss Bailey."

Both ladies turned and neither seemed pleased to see him.

Thankfully Avanley decided to help him out. "Isobel, darling may I speak with you about tonight's dinner arrangements?"

Isobel stood from where she had been seated beside Abigail and gracefully glided across the room toward them. "Are you certain we should leave them alone? A chaperone is most certainly required."

Charles reached over and took his wife's hand. "My love, chaperones ruin all the fun, besides, from the look on Miss Bailey's face, the only thing a chaperone would be good for is to keep her from doing Davenport harm."

Isobel smiled up at her husband, then turned to Cam. "At least the bouquet you brought with you this time is respectable." She turned back to look at Abigail. "We will not be far away, my dear."

Cam sighed heavily, feeling more annoyed by the second. He looked back over to Abigail who had risen from the settee and was standing before him wearing a 'not so happy to see him' look on her face. "I suppose I should be glad that you didn't make me scale a wall or climb down one of the chimneys."

"And you should be grateful that I haven't hit you over the head with something."

Davenport quickly crossed the room to take her into his arms before she had a chance to escape. She squirmed against him. "That's enough, Abigail. Since my rash and ill-advised behavior toward you in the park yesterday, I have found myself buying flowers, and begging butlers for admittance both here and at Aunt Louisa's townhouse. I have walked around London carrying bouquets of flowers like some foolish love-struck adolescent, I have climbed a wall, which was no easy feat I might add, only to receive a not-so-welcome reception when I finally made it through the window of your bedchamber. Do you not think I have done enough penance by now?"

Abigail bit her bottom lip to keep from smiling. He truly did look pathetic and maybe even a little bit repentant. "I don't know about that, but I suppose we should at least be civil. You can unhand me now."

Cam grinned. "I have no intention of ever unhanding you, love."

Abigail was surprised at his words. "Have you lost your mind? Yesterday you practically accused me of being a lady with little moral character, and today you are trying to accost me."

Cam chuckled, which only seemed to make her angrier. "Don't be so dramatic, Abigail. I am not accosting you; I am about to kiss you."

Abigail stared at him and thought perhaps the man was half crazy, but before she could voice another protest his lips had descended upon hers, and her body turned traitor against her as she felt herself giving in and melting against him.

Cam knew the moment she surrendered, he felt the rigidness in her body melt away and she softened against him. When she began returning his kiss with equal fervor, he knew he had been absolved. He broke the kiss and looked into her violet eyes before twisting a small curl of her hair between his fingers. "Am I forgiven?"

Abigail felt the corners of her mouth lift in a small grin. "I will think about it." She gently pushed against his chest, and he reluctantly released her. "Now weren't you here to tell me what you discovered from Mr. Harrison's office."

Cam shrugged his shoulders as he refused to give any ground, staying close to her. "I would much rather keep kissing you."

"You truly are a rake, aren't you? I had heard stories from Emma, and Bella has told me a few things since I arrived here, but you didn't seem that way on our journey here."

Cam sighed and stepped away. "On the journey here, I was worried for your safety."

Abigail raised her eyebrows. "You are no longer concerned for my safety?"

Cam took her hand and tugged her back into his chest. "I will always be concerned for your safety, but after meeting with Harrison, we now believe Toussaint isn't the danger to you I first believed him to be."

Abigail didn't try to pull away as Cam reached up to caress her cheek. "Yes, you told me that yesterday. Last night you said you would tell me more. What makes you believe that?"

Cam didn't want to talk about Toussaint, he didn't want to talk about his past, the war, or anything other than how much he wanted to get this woman into his bed.

"Harrison believes Toussaint might be in England in search of French sympathizers that still favor Napoleon, or at least his cause. Since he already has a vendetta against me, killing me was just a bonus."

"So, he is here trying to elicit support from others? That could be very dangerous."

Cam was surprised that she was so astute. "Yes, and if I can discover who he is meeting with, I can also discover what they have planned. That's why Harrison has asked me to help find and deal with Toussaint."

Abigail nodded her head. "I understand, it sounds intriguing. How can I help?"

This time Cam was the one to step back abruptly. "Help? Darling, it is much too dangerous for you to be involved. Keeping you out of Toussaint's sight and reach is the only reason I have permitted you to be around bloody Kingston. I would never endanger your life by asking for you to get involved in anything so risky."

Abigail shook her head slightly. "I'm not suggesting I take on Toussaint, but isn't there something I can do?" She instantly saw his eyes darken as he stalked toward her.

"Yes, you can stay here with Bella, and enjoy what London has to offer. Avanley has a box at the theater, there are plenty of shops on Bond Street, and there is always Vauxhall and Hyde Park. Once the ton returns for the season, you will have more than enough to keep you occupied."

Abigail huffed out an exasperated breath. "I'm not looking for entertainment. I simply want to help."

Cam shook his head and spoke clearly, and, in a tone, he hoped would convey to her that he would not capitulate. "No"

Abigail raised her eyebrows and tilted her head to the side. "Hmm, I don't know why you are so against a little bit of assistance."

Cam tapped down his irritation. "There are any number of reasons. You have no idea what you are doing. Because this can be dangerous, and damn it, Abigail, I care about you and will not risk you being hurt!" He cupped her face with his hands and pressed a kiss to her lips. "Harrison, Charles, and Cavendish will help me. I am not going into this alone." He watched as she lowered her eyes, her long lashes curling up as they touched her cheeks. "I have some things to do this morning, but I will come to see you tonight." He tilted her chin up. "Leave your window open, love."

He turned and left her, glad to have the incident in the park firmly behind him. Now he had to hope that she would abandon the idea of getting involved. He would have to ask Charles to make sure Bella kept her busy. He made his way through the house and down the hall to Charles' study. The door was open and he could see Charles sitting behind his huge mahogany desk that was positioned between two large almost floor to ceiling windows. It reminded him of being called into his father's study at Stafford Park when he was a young boy being disciplined for some sort of mischief he had gotten into. Charles was sitting behind his desk, drinking brandy, waiting for him.

"Shut the door, Davenport."

Cam walked inside, closing the door behind him. "You said you had some information for me?"

Charles nodded and then indicated that he should have a seat. "This theory that Toussaint is here in England to meet with people who are not quite as loyal as they should be to the crown, I felt was a bit outrageous." He leaned back in the chair with his elbows on the armrests and his fingers forming a pyramid under his chin. "But regardless, I felt I would see how it all played out; however, I have now been given reason to believe that the theory may have some credibility."

"And what has brought you to that conclusion?" Cam asked curiously as to where this conversation was going.

"I received an invitation to a dinner party tonight at Lord Darlington's estate just outside London. If you will remember, it had been suggested that he was a French sympathizer a few years ago before Napoleon's defeat at Waterloo, although nothing could be proven."

Cam narrowed his eyes as he regarded his friend. "And now you think he has connections to Toussaint?"

"I don't know if he even knows Toussaint, but I do know that there are some French businessmen expected to be at the dinner tonight."

Cam drew in a deep breath. "How did you garner an invitation?"

Charles grinned. "You don't believe that people just enjoy my company?"

"Not bloody likely."

"Kingston and I have made it known that we are looking for some lucrative investment opportunities. Darlington seems to think these men might have ideas that would interest us."

Cam stood from his seat. "You know these 'businessmen' might be after your money to fund their own interests, interests that might be detrimental to the country."

"I am not a fool, Davenport. I will be attending the dinner tonight and felt it would be an opportunity for you to snoop around and see if you can uncover anything that would be useful in finding Toussaint or any plotting that might be going on."

"Am I to attend as your guest?"

Charles frowned and he looked at him as if he had grown another head. "Miss Bailey must have you rattled. Of course, you will not attend with me. How can you move about the house looking for clues, if you are a dinner party guest? No, you must use this dinner as a distraction." He arched his eyebrows up higher. "Unless you think you have lost your touch."

"Go to hell, Avanley."

Charles laughed. "Let's hope you do a better job of sneaking into Darlington's home than you do of sneaking into mine."

Cam headed for the door ignoring the comment.

"Are you going to marry the girl?"

Charles' voice stopped him in his tracks.

"What are you talking about now, Avanley?"

Charles stood from behind his desk. "Don't pretend you are ignorant of what I mean. Do you plan on marrying her?"

Cam turned back around to face him. "What concern is it of yours?"

Charles moved around to stand in front of his desk. "I can't allow you to continue to sneak into her bedchamber if you don't intend to marry her."

Cam reached for the door handle. "Did Bella put you up to asking me this? Since when did you, the biggest rake London has seen since Brummel, become so interested in propriety?"

"Since I married Isobel. She made me see the error of my ways, so to speak. Just don't do anything that will cause my wife to become cross with me."

Later that evening, Darlington Estate

With Davenport's particular set of skills, he had no difficulty sneaking into Darlington's modest country manor house. There were few servants as most were occupied with the dinner party. He could hear the laughter and conversations from the guests drifting up the stairs as he made his way down the hallways undetected. He found Darlington's study easy enough. It was dark, no candles were burning, but there was enough moonlight shining through the windows that he could make out the desk and the papers strewn over the top of it. But he knew that what he was looking for would not be in plain sight. Experience had taught him that when people had something they didn't want anyone else to ever find, they would hide it in places that weren't obvious, places that were not easy to discover or get into. He searched around the desk, looking for any kind of hidden compartment.

When he was satisfied that there was nowhere else he could look on the desk, he heaved a heavy sigh and moved to the bookcases along the back wall. He scanned the shelves first looking for anything that seemed out of place. There was a small box on the third shelf, but he dismissed it as much too obvious and small to hold anything of significance. It was beginning to look as if Darlington's study would hold none of the answers he sought, and he was about to go explore other parts of the house when he heard the handle on the door turn. He looked around quickly for his easiest and quickest means of escape. There was another door on the other side of the room. He moved quickly, hoping it was another exit. Unfortunately, it turned out to be some sort of small storage closet. It was dark and he couldn't tell what it housed, but he did know there wasn't much room to move around. He heard light footsteps as they entered the study. He lowered his head and sighed heavily hoping whoever it was would move along quickly so he could get the hell out of there and continue his search of the house before the dinner party concluded.

Abigail felt better after she visited with Cam this morning. The flowers he gave her were very beautiful, in fact, they were the first flowers anyone had ever given her before. While she still didn't understand exactly why he acted so aggressively in the park, when he kissed her today, there was no trace of animosity between them, and she realized that she had missed him. After Cam had left Avanley House, she had gone upstairs to her bedchambers hoping to write Emma another letter when she remembered that she had wanted to get a few books from the library to keep in her room to have in case she wanted to read before bed. When she headed back down the stairs to the library, she moved past the duke's study. The door was partially opened and she heard Bella's voice as she and her husband discussed the dinner party they were to attend tonight.

She didn't think anything about it until she heard Charles mention the name Toussaint. She paused and pressed herself against the wall outside the door. Eavesdropping was not something to be proud of, but in this case, she couldn't help herself. When he mentioned to his wife that they would be attending the dinner party in order for him to evaluate Lord Darlington's French contacts, she knew this could be her chance to do some investigating on her own. She might even be able to find something that would be beneficial to Davenport.

Later that afternoon, when Emma asked her if she would like to attend with them, she gleefully agreed but made no mention that she was aware of the reasons they were attending. During the party, it had taken her longer than she would have liked to escape the attentions of their host, but eventually, she did manage to sneak away from the group undetected. She moved out of the salon where the others were enjoying drinks and conversation before dinner and into the hallway. All the servants were busy, so she made her way up the stairs. If she was discovered, she would just claim that she had gotten lost. Pretending to be an unsophisticated country girl would not be too difficult for anyone to believe given her circumstances.

She made it up the stairs unnoticed and peeked in a few rooms before she found the study. It was dark and she hesitated a moment before moving inside. She could barely see well enough to make her way over to the desk, and once she was there, she realized that she had no idea what she was supposed to be looking for. She leaned over the desk and rifled through the papers on top. This was ridiculous, she didn't know what she was doing. She was beginning to feel foolish, and if she were discovered snooping about, it would embarrass Charles and Emma, not to mention it could hurt Davenport's efforts to discover whatever it was he was looking for.

She turned and started for the door when she heard footsteps coming down the hall. She frantically looked around for a place to escape or hide when she saw a door on the opposite side of the room. She wasn't sure where it would lead, but right now she was desperate to escape. She tried the handle and was thankful it wasn't locked. When she opened the door, she was jerked inside. A large hand clamped down over her mouth, and strong arms hauled her against a firm, hard, wall of flesh. The door closed, and she felt a sickening feeling of panic course through her as the realization hit her that she was locked in a dark storage closet with a man that could very well kill her. At least she wouldn't have to see or hear Cam gloat about how he had warned her not to get involved. She supposed it served her right. Her inquisitive nature was bound to get the best of her one day.

Chapter Thirteen

Cam heard soft footsteps approaching and when the door opened, he did what came naturally, he grabbed the person physically subduing them to prevent them from giving away his location, but the instant he pulled her body against his own, he knew. He tightened his hold on her and pressed his hand against her mouth tighter. She squirmed against him but until he knew there wasn't anyone else that could discover them, he had to restrain her. Her muffled cries were getting louder despite his hand covering her mouth.

He leaned closer to her ear and whispered, "Shh, be quiet before someone hears you!"

He felt her instantly relax, but he kept his hand clamped over her mouth to keep her quiet until he knew it was safe, but once he was certain no one was in the study, he was about to wring the truth out of her pretty little neck.

He waited a few more minutes, then cracked the door open, and seeing the study still dark and empty, he opened the door further and pulled Abigail out behind him. He spun around keeping his hands on her shoulders wanting to shake her and demand answers.

"What the hell are you doing here?" he spoke harshly through clenched teeth.

Abigail didn't know if she should be relieved that Cam was the one who discovered her snooping about or if she should be afraid of his reaction at catching her. From the slant of his eyes and the firm set of his jaw, she decided she should be the latter.

"I should ask you the same thing, what are you doing here? And you scared me half to death, it certainly wouldn't have hurt to let me know sooner that you were the one that grabbed me."

Cam wanted to shake her until her teeth rattled. "Damn it, Abigail. This is not a game! Now tell me what you are doing snooping around Darlington's study. What were you hoping to find?"

Abigail tried to pull herself from his grip, but he refused to release her. "Very well, I don't know what I was looking for. It might not have been the best thought-out plan, but at least I was doing something. You know this is entirely your fault."

"My fault? How in the bloody hell is this my fault?"

Abigail huffed out a breath. "You knew I wanted to help and if you had told me what I could look for or given me another assignment, I wouldn't be here now.

He closed his eyes and took a deep breath to steady himself. "An assignment? Why are you talking like this? Listen to me carefully. You are not a spy, Abigail. You are a hardheaded woman that is going to get hurt. It scares the hell out of me thinking about what would happen if you were caught." He pulled her closer. "What do you know about Darlington? Why would it occur to you to be snooping about his study in the first place?"

Abigail was growing tired of being lectured. "I overheard a conversation between Charles and Bella. He told her that they would be attending the dinner party tonight because he suspected Lord Darlington might be involved with Toussaint." She bit her bottom lip when she saw her explanation was not making things any better. "I only thought that if I could sneak around in his study, I might find something that you would find helpful."

"Help, you were trying to help?"

Abigail stomped her tiny slippered foot in frustration. "Yes, but when I did manage to get away, I realized I had no idea what I should be looking for, then I heard footsteps, panicked, and found myself being accosted by you in that closet."

Cam ignored her comment. "How did you get away from the other guests?"

She shrugged her shoulders. "When the others were distracted, I left the room. I thought that if anyone caught me, I could say I was looking for the ladies retiring room and became lost. I needed to get out of there anyway, there is a man among the group who seems most enamored with me to the point that he is becoming a nuisance. While we were in the drawing room, he kept touching me. It was most bothersome."

Cam could feel the veins in his neck popping out. "Touching you?"

"Yes, but nowhere inappropriate just reaching for me constantly. I felt as if he was trying to maneuver me."

Cam released her, then put a hand up to his forehead and began kneading the area between his eyes as if trying to ward off a headache. "You have to hurry back downstairs and rejoin the group before people start looking for you."

Abigail nodded. "Are you here looking for something that would link Darlington to Toussaint? Did you find anything?"

Cam turned her toward the door. "Just go, Abigail. Find Charles and Bella and stay close to them. Stay away from the man who is bothering you and we will discuss this later. Right now, you must go."

Abigail took a step toward the door, then turned back to look at Cam as he stood back watching her. Even in the darkness of the study, she could tell he was furious, remarkably handsome, but furious. She hesitated, wondering if there was anything she could say that would make him any less angry.

"Go now, Abigail!"

The tone of his voice suggested there was not. She opened the door and slipped out into the hall. As she made her way back downstairs to where the others were gathered, she couldn't help but wonder what Cam was doing there and if he had found what she was unable to, and just how angry would he be when she saw him again.

She made it down the stairs undetected but just as she was about to reenter the drawing room a hand clamped down on her arm causing her to jump nearly out of her skin.

"Where have you been, Abigail?"

"Oh, Bella, I'm so glad it's you," Abigail replied as she put her hand over her heart.

"Of course, it's me, who else would it be?" She reached out and rubbed Abigail's arms. "What has happened? You're pale and you are shivering."

"I was just startled when you came up behind me. I promise I am alright." Abigail smiled, hoping that she was convincing.

Bella looked at her strangely. "Where did you go?"

"Lord Darlington's friend over there in the bright green coat, I believe his name is Mr. Franks, he has been overly attentive to me all night, and I find him rather bothersome. I just needed to step away for a few minutes."

Bella sighed in relief. "You should have come to me, Abigail. I would have found a way to extract you from Mr. Franks. I'm sorry he made you feel uncomfortable." She linked her arm through Abigail's. "You will stay by me the rest of the evening."

Abigail nodded and allowed Bella to lead her back inside the drawing room, she turned her head to look behind her, and although she didn't see him, she knew Cam was watching her.

Cam's anger had not dissipated at all by the time he reached Avanley House. It had started to rain and was well past the hour of receiving visitors and since he would more than likely be turned away at such a late hour, he knew he would have to climb the bloody wall again to sneak into her window. It was not an easy task, especially with the stones being wet, but he managed to reach her window on the second floor without falling and breaking his neck. The windows were shut, but to his relief when he went to open them, they were unlocked.

The room was dark, but he could see Abigail's form in the bed. After shrugging out of his wet greatcoat, he moved closer and reached out to shake her shoulder gently. She sat up abruptly with a squeal and he once again had to cover her mouth to keep her silent.

"Can you not keep quiet?" He removed his hand once he saw recognition in her eyes.

Abigail had not expected Cam to visit her tonight, even though he had told her to keep her window unlocked. With the rain and the late hour, she had assumed that he had changed his mind. She pushed the coverlet aside to stand up from the bed.

"Can you stop sneaking into my room? What are you doing here at this time of night?"

Cam's anger began to slowly fade as his gaze settled on Abigail standing before him wearing a diaphanous nightgown with delicate lace and ribbons. Her blonde hair hung loose down her back.

"We need to talk."

Abigail huffed out an exasperated breath. "At this hour! Could this not wait till tomorrow? I feel it is much too late for a lecture."

Cam narrowed his eyes, a bit of his irritation returning. "Do you still not realize how serious the consequences could have been if you had been caught tonight?"

Abigail crossed her arms over her chest, and Cam tried not to notice the way it pushed her breasts higher.

"You have already chastised me for that, and I admitted it wasn't the wisest choice I could have made, but don't you see how beneficial it would be if you would at least let me help in some small way?"

"No, I do not. Now I want your promise that you will stay out of this. No more snooping, no more eavesdropping, and no more putting yourself in danger!"

Abigail huffed out a slow breath. "Very well, no more snooping."

He took a step closer to her and gripped her arms. "I'm serious, Abigail."

She pushed away from him. "You are being ridiculous. I am the one who heard the plot to kill you in the first place. I am the one that traipsed all over England to escape Toussaint, and I should at least play a small role in seeing him brought to justice. There are so many ways I can be useful. I could distract a gentleman long enough for you to search their home, or I could casually keep watch at a party and alert you should someone head in your direction. All those ways are perfectly acceptable and not one bit dangerous. You are behaving like an overprotective father!"

Cam listened to her speech full of indignation holding on tightly to his temper but did not say anything.

Abigail stared at him hoping he would agree with what she had said. When he didn't respond she raised her chin a notch, stepped to the side, and pointed toward the window. "It's been a long night and I'm tired."

Cam's hands fisted at his side. The chit was dismissing him. He stalked toward her not giving her time to retreat but he did take pleasure in seeing the look on her face turn from outrage to fear. He wrapped an arm around her waist pulling her into his chest then with his free hand he took hold of her chin and forced her to look up at him.

"I am behaving like any man that wants to keep his woman safe."

Abigail bit her bottom lip stunned at the intensity she saw in his eyes but couldn't help responding. "I am not yours to protect."

Cam leaned down a little closer. There was no disguising his anger, the hard set of his jaw, the way his lips were set in a line, and the darkness of his eyes, all signs that she had pushed him as far as he would go.

He was only a breath away from her lips when he responded, "The hell you aren't!"

Then with a force that shocked her, he took her lips in an all-consuming kiss. He lifted her off her feet and carried her back to her bed, his lips never leaving hers even when he laid her back against the pillows. He knew he should stop; he knew she was an innocent, but all he wanted was her. His lips left her mouth and moved to the spot on her neck underneath her ear. He let his tongue flick over her earlobe and smiled at her sharp intake of breath.

"My God, Abigail, you are so beautiful!" He leaned up on his elbows to look down at her face. Even in the darkness, he could see her eyes shining as she looked back at him. He brushed her hair back away from her face. "If you want me to leave, tell me now. But know this, if I stay, I'm claiming you as mine, Abigail. There will be no going back and there will be no other man to possess you." He watched as her lips parted and he waited for what she would say, how she would react to his words.

Abigail felt as if her heart would beat out of her chest. Never before had she been kissed with such raw passion and never before had she ever felt the way she did just now. She was the daughter of a vicar, and she knew the consequences if she asked him to stay. She knew she had to pull herself together, she had to ask him to leave. Yes, she knew what she should do, but those were not the words that came from her lips.

"Please stay."

Her voice was but a whisper, but Cam had heard her. He let his fingers tug at the ribbon that was holding her gown together at her throat. It easily gave way. He parted the material exposing her collarbone and decolletage to his view. He bent down and feathered kisses to the base of her throat and along her collarbone. He felt her shiver as his hand reached inside her gown to cup her breast and tease her nipple into a tight nub. He looked at her one more time, hoping and praying she would not deny him.

"Are you very certain, Abigail?"

Abigail loved the feel of his hands on her skin and while she had no idea what occurred between a man and woman in bed, she could not imagine asking him to stop now.

"Are you going to continue to ask me?"

He grinned at the brusque comment. He pushed aside the material of her gown and exposed her breast to his view. He let his fingers caress her. "I won't ask anymore darling, but if you…"

Abigail reached up and pulled his head down to hers and pressed a quick hard kiss to his lips. "Will you please just stop talking?"

"As you request, my love." He bent his head and suckled her breast. A loud gasp escaped her lips, and her reaction spurred him forward. He moved to her other breast while he slipped the gown lower exposing her from the waist up. He paused long enough to whip the shirt he was wearing over his head and tossed it on the floor. He wanted to feel her skin against his own.

Abigail's eyes widened. His chest was covered with a spattering of dark hair and muscles rippled across his abdomen. He looked spectacular and her fingers itched to touch him. She didn't wait to ask, she reached up and placed her hand over his heart, then slowly slid lower. He was solid and his skin was warm to her touch.

Cam allowed her to explore with her hands, watching the way her eyes followed the path taken by her fingers and the expressions on her face. When she reached the waistband of his pants, he decided it was his turn. He gathered her gown in his hands and before she could protest had whipped it up to her waist, and then in one fluid movement, he had removed it completely leaving her naked, a feast laid out before him.

He pried his eyes away from the perfection of her body to see her face. Her eyes were wide and he could see the uncertainty behind them, but he was too far gone now. It would take an army to stop him from taking her now. He kissed her again, nudging her mouth open with his tongue. She tasted sweet, like honey. His hands moved up her legs, his fingers lightly paving the way up her thighs until he found what he was seeking. He urged her legs farther apart with his knee as his fingers found her slick folds. She bucked against him as he touched her, and he heard her cry out into his mouth as he slowly slipped a finger inside of her. Sweet heaven, she was so tight. He released her mouth and his lips moved down her neck to her breasts and then to her flat belly all while he moved his fingers inside her. Her breathing was heavy and she gripped his shoulders with her fingers, her nails digging into his flesh. When his mouth lowered further to lick her slit, she cried out. He gripped her hips with his hands as his mouth moved over her, his tongue tasting, licking her. He continued to press his finger deeper inside her, hoping it would stretch her so that when he did make love to her, it would not be as painful.

Abigail arched her back not knowing how much more she could take before she cried out again. She didn't know how to explain what she felt. There was a mixture of pleasure and pain, but also a feeling of euphoria as he continued stroking her. She had never imagined it would be like this, but when he stood from the bed and swiftly removed his trousers, she let out an audible gasp as his cock sprang free.

She immediately put a hand over her mouth and scooted further back as he moved toward her. He was naked, she was naked, what was she doing? She opened her mouth to protest but before she could do so, his hands were upon her again and she sank back against the pillows as his body covered hers. He kissed her as he settled between her thighs. His hands caressed her skin as if she were fragile and he was afraid she would break under his pressure.

"Abigail?" his voice was strained and low. "If we do this, I need to know that you understand, I need you to know that you will be mine. If you aren't certain, or if you don't wish for it to be, say so now. There will be no changing your mind once I have taken you."

Cam waited. She stared up at him, but her face was unreadable. It had been a long time since he had been with a woman, and he had never wanted a woman as bad as he wanted this one. His cocked throbbed in anticipation and if she said no, he was unsure how he would walk away.

"Abigail?" he reached up and cupped her cheek gently.

Abigail swallowed and chewed her bottom lip before answering in a soft trembly voice. "Please."

He breathed in a deep breath and summoned all his willpower and started to move away from her when she grabbed his hand.

"Please, don't stop, Cam."

A sense of relief that he had never felt before surged through him. He pressed another kiss to her lips as his body covered hers once again. He felt feverish with need, desire, and the knowledge that he needed to go slow was rapidly deserting him. He settled back down over her, pressing her legs farther apart. He kissed her possessively this time, she was his and there was no way he would allow another man to have what he claimed. He let his cock press slowly into her warm, wet, heat.

Abigail tensed at the intrusion into her body, but Cam continued to kiss her and touch her in ways that made her long for more. When he pushed further inside her, she began to feel pressure and while she was not afraid, she was a bit nervous.

Cam felt her body tense. He leaned up on his elbows and looked down into her face. "Hold onto me tight, Abigail." He leaned down pressing his nose into the side of her neck. Her fingers gripped his shoulders. He sucked her earlobe into his mouth and when she moaned softly, he thrust forward filling her completely.

Abigail couldn't help the sound that escaped her, half moaning, half screaming. She instinctively pulled her legs closer together and stiffened at the pain.

Cam kept still allowing her body to adjust to his invasion. He closed his eyes willing his body not to react to the way she felt. The urge to thrust into her hard and fast was almost more than he could resist, but he didn't want to hurt her.

He kissed her cheeks, kissing away a salty tear. "I'm sorry, Abigail. Does it still hurt?"

Abigail wasn't sure she could speak. Her breath was coming heavy and fast between her lips. "I...I don't know."

Cam kissed the tip of her nose and then pulled out of her and then pressed back in again slowly. "How does it feel?"

Abigail closed her eyes and shook her head.

Cam began moving slowly at first, but he wasn't sure how much longer he could hold himself back. She was so warm and tight around him. He heard Abigail sigh and moan beneath him, and his thrusts became harder and faster. Her hands had moved to his back and he was certain to have marks on his skin from her nails. Her cries became louder, and Cam was reminded that they were in Avanley's house.

"Shh, love. We don't want anyone to hear you."

Abigail tried to keep quiet, but with every movement he made, her body got closer to something she couldn't explain. "I'm trying."

She cried out again as her body began to convulse. It was a feeling of complete euphoria and at that moment she didn't care who heard her.

Cam pressed his mouth firmly to hers to swallow her cries as he drew nearer to his own climax, before pulling out and spilling himself into the sheets.

Both were breathing heavily. Cam rolled to the side and pulled her into his arms. She was still shivering, and he wrapped a leg over hers to hold her. He kissed her shoulders and neck as his breathing became more controlled.

"My darling, are you alright?"

Abigail nodded. "Is it always like this?"

Cam chuckled. "The next time will be even better, love. I promise."

Abigail turned so that she lay facing him. "What happens now?"

Cam snuggled her closer in his arms. "Lie beside me, listen to the rain and go to sleep. I'll take care of everything else."

Cam smiled when he heard her gently sigh. He held her while she slept as long as he dared to stay. He had to leave the house before dawn or take a chance at being seen. When he was certain she was asleep, he carefully moved away from her, dressed as quietly as he could, and moved to the door. He wasn't about to chance climbing from her window. The servants should all still be asleep, and he was fairly certain he could leave undetected.

He made his way down the hallway toward the stairs when a deep voice stopped him. "If you need help acquiring a special license, do let me know."

It was Avanley.

"What the devil are you doing lurking about this time of night?" Cam asked as he turned to face his friend.

Charles moved out of the shadows where he had been waiting. "I should be asking you the same thing, but from the noises coming from Miss Bailey's bedchamber, I have a fairly good idea what you have been up to. Did I not warn you about this?"

"No, you warned me not to let Bella catch me, and I do not see her anywhere about."

Charles grinned. "True, but you know I can't allow you to do this again. At least not without the knowledge that you will do the right thing."

Cam frowned. "Do you really think I would take that chance? I will seek a special license and be married as soon as it is granted."

Charles stepped forward and patted him on the back. "Excellent, if that is the case then I suppose you will be formally opening up Stafford House."

Cam sighed heavily. "Yes."

"If you would like, I can have my staff help with that."

Cam nodded. He didn't want to stand around and talk about this now. There were other things he had to do and while taking Abigail for his wife at this time might not be prudent, there was no other course of action he could take.

He looked to Charles. "I must go, but I will be back as soon as I have everything arranged. If you would be willing to do so, I would be grateful for your staff's assistance. There is a small staff at Stafford House already there, but I'm sure they would be grateful for the help and the addition of more staff."

Charles nodded but didn't reply and Cam turned to leave. There was so much to do but the first thing was to check with Mr. Cavendish to see if he had discovered anything more about Toussaint and then he had to make arrangements to take Abigail from Avanley House.

Chapter Fourteen

Abigail woke up the next morning alone and feeling as wretched as she could be. Cam had left her sometime during the night and other than the fact that she was naked lying in a rumpled bed, there were no other signs that he had even been there. Now she was by herself and trying to figure out how to deal with the storm of emotions she was experiencing.

She found her nightgown lying on the floor where Cam had tossed it. After slipping it back over her head, she called for her maid and asked for a tub of hot water to be filled for a bath, then dismissed her. While waiting on her bath to be prepared, she moved over to recline on the chaise beside the window. The streets below were quiet this time of the morning. She lay her head against the cool pane of glass and closed her eyes. What was she to do now? Cam had said that once he had taken her, she was his. But now in the light of morning, Abigail had to admit, she wasn't sure exactly what he meant. He could have very well meant that he would set her up as his mistress.

Last night, she had not thought beyond the yearning need for him to touch her.

Once the tub was filled, she whipped the nightgown over her head, grimacing a bit at the soreness she felt between her thighs. How would she ever explain this predicament to Emma? She slid down further into the water and cringed as she thought of how awkward things would be the next time she saw Cam. She dunked her head under the water. Perhaps it would be best to just drown herself now and avoid the embarrassment.

She had just emerged from the water when the door to her dressing room flung open and Bella came inside. "Oh my, Abigail. I'm sorry to disrupt you. I knocked but there was no answer."

Abigail wiped water from her face. "It's alright. Is something wrong?"

Bella shrugged her shoulders before clasping her hands in front of her. "I don't know. Davenport is here and he says he must speak with you right away. All he said was that it was urgent before he leaves town today."

Abigail's eyes widened. "Cam is leaving London? Where is he going?"

Bella walked over and handed Abigail some linens to dry with. "That's all he said. I know nothing else, but he is most insistent that he speak with you."

Abigail wrapped the linen around her as she stood from the tub. "Please let him know that I will be down as soon as possible."

Bella nodded and left the room.

Abigail knew there was no way around seeing Cam. If she refused, he would more than likely storm up to her room regardless of her wishes. She dressed as quickly as possible and pinned up her damp hair. She took a quick look in the mirror and cringed at her appearance.

She slowly walked down the stairs to the main entryway of the house. Bella was standing with her husband outside the drawing room. As she approached, Charles took his wife's hand and pulled her away.

"Miss Bailey, Davenport is inside the drawing room, we will leave the two of you alone for a short time."

Abigail glanced over at Bella who looked as if she wanted to say something, but her husband was practically dragging her away. She took a deep breath and hesitated before entering the drawing room hoping to prepare herself for whatever Cam was about to say. There was no need in stalling any longer, she clasped her hands in front of her and tried to paste a smile on her face, hoping he did not notice her discomfiture. When she entered, he was standing near the windows dressed elegantly with his back to her.

"You wished to see me, your grace?"

At her words, Cam turned to face her.

"Bella said that you needed to speak with me before you left. Where are you going?"

Cam remained where he stood. "Cavendish thinks he might have found someone that can give us information about Toussaint and his contacts here in England. I am leaving London with him today to question his source."

Abigail nodded but didn't dare try to speak.

"Come here, Abigail."

Abigail shook her head and looked away from him. "I hope you have a safe journey."

Cam watched her. She was fidgety, shifting her weight from one foot to another as if she were nervous. "Come here, Abigail."

She slowly stepped closer and when she was within arm's reach, he reached out and pulled her into his chest so he could wrap his arms around her. He kissed the top of her head then tilted her chin up to see her face.

"I have already seen about acquiring a special license and as soon as I return, we will be married."

Abigail's eyes widened and she thought there must be a mistake. She must have misunderstood what he just said. "Married?"

He leaned forward and pressed a kiss to her lips. "Yes, my love. Did you think I just came here to tell you I was leaving London?"

Abigail narrowed her eyes a bit and shook her head. "I'm not sure I…I."

Cam lightly ran a finger down her cheek. "Abigail, I told you last night that you were mine."

He reached into his coat pocket and pulled out a ring. He held it up for her to see. "This did not belong to my mother, but it is a part of the Stafford family collection and has been worn by the duchess' before you." He slipped it over her finger and pressed a kiss to her knuckles. "I want my duchess to wear it as well."

Abigail felt tears welling up in her eyes and try as she might, she could not hold them back. "When you said that I would belong to you if I allowed you to stay with me last night, I didn't know what you meant."

Cam frowned. "Did you think I would dishonor you with any proposal other than marriage?" He took her shoulders and held her a little away from him. "Abigail, I am a man of honor regardless of my parentage. I would never subject my child to what I endured not being the legitimate son of my father." He saw her face pale a bit, her eyes shimmering in tears.

"I just didn't know. After we…well, I fell asleep and then this morning you were gone."

He kissed her quickly. "I had some arrangements to make. A special license will be acquired in a day or two. The archbishop frequents *The Lair* and owes Kingston some money so he will not deny my request. Stafford House is just a few streets over from here, but it has only had a small staff since the death of my father. When in London I always stayed at The Lair, so I saw no need in opening a grand house just for me. Now I must see to it that everything is set right for your arrival."

Abigail felt as if her head was spinning. "I can't believe you wish to marry me. You are a duke and as such could have any of the unmarried ladies that came out this season. Why would you want me?"

He chuckled. "I did give it some thought, but I have decided I would be better suited to a lady that climbed from windows, would sneak about homes looking for spies, and would not bat an eye at having to travel across the continent with an army chasing after her." He saw her lips turn up slightly in a smile.

Abigail glanced at the ring he had placed on her finger and suddenly a terrible sense of nervousness overcame her. "I don't know how to be a duchess."

"I have a feeling you will be a quick learner, Abigail." He kissed her once more, then stepped back. "I should leave. Cavendish is waiting for me at *The Lair* and I am hoping the information will be valuable in my search for Toussaint."

He bent down to kiss her once again, but she pushed away. "You say you want to marry me, but if I am to be your wife, your duchess, I want something from you."

Cam tilted his head to the side as he regarded her with curiosity and amusement. "And what is it that you wish from me, Abigail?"

"If we are to be married, we must do things together. Your problems will become my problems."

Cam's smile turned into a frown. "I know what is running through that pretty little head of yours, Abigail. The answer is still no."

Abigail heaved a heavy sigh and stepped farther away from him. "If that is your decision., then I can't accept." She turned to walk away but had only taken a few steps before she was nearly whisked off her feet and pulled back into his arms. The smile was no longer on his face and for a minute she wondered if she had pushed him too far.

Cam didn't like how easily this woman could drive him mad. He gripped her chin and tilted it up none too gently as he leaned down so that his nose was nearly touching hers. Her eyes had widened, and she looked very much like a small animal caught in a trap. His voice was low and controlled as he tried to make her understand.

"I asked you last night when I took you to bed, when I took your innocence, if you understood that afterward you would belong to me. You are mine now, Abigail. I will protect what is mine. I will never agree to let you put your life in danger. Now, I'm leaving London, when I return to this house, I will have a bishop with me and you will marry me, Abigail. I don't care how much you protest. If I have to drag you out of your bath and marry you naked as you drip water on Avanley's Axminster rug, I will do it. Do not give me ultimatums, darling." He kissed her again, plundering her mouth with his tongue. When he felt her body relax, he stepped back and let her go.

Abigail couldn't have spoken even if she had known what to say. She placed a hand over her swollen lips and watched as he bowed to her before taking his leave. She wanted to scream at him, throw something at his retreating form, and rail against his arrogance and superiority, but before she could even form the words in her head, he was gone.

A hand went to her throat as she sank down on the settee, her fingers trembled as she held out her hand to see the large sapphire and diamond ring that rested on her finger. Her heart was beating wildly in her chest.

"Abigail? Are you alright?"

Abigail turned her head slowly at the sound of Bella's voice. "I think he means to marry me."

Cam knew he should not have left Abigail in the way that he had, but her insistence on becoming involved in anything related to Toussaint was beyond ridiculous and absolutely unthinkable. He would never allow her to put her life at risk regardless of her threats.

Cavendish was waiting for him outside the Lair. "Should I assume from your dark brooding look that the girl refused your suit?"

Cam's frown intensified. "No, she will marry me. She did, however, insist that if she was to be my duchess, she should also help me find Toussaint."

Davenport scoffed. "She is a brave woman, I will give her that, foolish but brave. I do hope you made it clear that would never happen."

"I did, but I will still have to keep an eye on her to keep her out of trouble."

Cavendish shook his head with a strong look of disapproval on his face. "Nevertheless, I think you should have stayed away from her, at least until this trouble with Toussaint was over. If you are distracted by her, Toussaint will use that to his advantage."

Cam had always confided in Cavendish and valued his opinion in most matters, and he knew that his friend had warned him to stay away from Miss Bailey on more than one occasion. "I couldn't stay away. I will just have to keep her occupied with other things."

At this, his friend rolled his eyes and grunted something under his breath. Cam chuckled as they rode on in search of a French woman, Molly Tremblay, who had made her living as a high-class prostitute in London, but after making her fortune had moved just outside the city to run her own brothel about five years ago.

According to Cavendish, Molly had seen Toussaint at her establishment and the men he had met there. Cam just hoped she could be trusted. He wanted to get this business over with as soon as possible, return to London, and claim Abigail. The thought of having her in his bed every night was beginning to make his ride uncomfortable, and while he knew she would be angry with him for the things he had said and his actions today, no matter what he demanded, she would still try to find a way to get involved with his investigation. He would just have to think of some creative ways to keep her mind elsewhere.

The brothel that Molly owned was nicer than he had expected, even if it was not the same caliber as Madame Laurent's. Molly's clientele were not the lords and aristocrats of London's elite, but rather the judges, wealthy landowners, and lower-level politicians that enjoyed the fact that her establishment was on the outskirts of London. It made it less likely that they would be seen.

As he entered, he was greeted by two ladies eager to ply their trade. He pushed their hands away as they moved to touch him. "I'm here to see Molly."

One of the girls pouted as she let one of her fingers trail down her neck to the valley between her breasts hoping to draw his attention. "Molly doesn't see gentlemen anymore. Why don't you let me take you upstairs where I can make you forget all about any other woman?"

Cam sighed and pushed her hands away again. "She will see me. Go tell her that Camden Davenport is here."

The woman shrugged her shoulders and walked away presumably to retrieve Molly. Her friend sidled up next to him and rubbed herself up against him. "You know I could keep you occupied until Molly returns. She might be awhile and there is no reason for you to stand here idle when you can enjoy yourself."

Cam smiled but pushed the lady away from him. "While I appreciate your exuberance, I am not interested, love. You will do better to find someone that is willing."

The woman frowned and stomped away.

"I wouldn't advise angering my girls, Davenport," an older lady said as she moved out of the shadows toward him.

"Hello, Molly, it's always a pleasure to see you." Cam moved over and took her hand. "You are looking as youthful as ever."

The older lady blushed as she put a hand to her pepper-gray hair. "And you are still a charmer I see." She gave him a crooked smile. "I had heard you were granted your father's title after his death, so what is a duke doing here? You were never one to partake in the pleasures my girls offered before you gained a title."

Cam grinned. "Cavendish says you may have information for me concerning a man named Toussaint." He took out a pouch of coins from his jacket pocket. "I will pay handsomely if the information proves to be useful."

Molly jerked her head to the side. "You know I don't conduct business in the open. Come with me to my private quarters."

Cam followed behind her up the stairs past several other rooms where the sounds of what was going on behind closed doors left no room for imagination. At the back of the hallway, she opened a door that led to an office of sorts and an attached apartment of her own. Cam watched as she moved to have a seat at a table beside the window. She held out her hand offering him the seat across from her, but while he moved further toward her, he declined the seat.

"I need to know if you have seen Toussaint and what you know about him being here in England."

The woman poured herself a glass of whiskey and chugged it down with no trouble. "Are you going to kill him?"

Cam narrowed his eyes. "Would it disturb you if I did?"

Molly chuckled. "I wish I could see him strung up by his intestines, filthy swine that he is. Yes, he was here. Paid handsomely to be with one of my girls. Got drunk and told her that he was here to meet with a Sir Hillebrand and to kill you. Not sure why he would share such information but afterward he did some things to her that

I do not allow in this house." She poured another glass and drank it the same way she had the first.

"He tied her and gagged her so we would not hear her cries. After she was raped brutally, he proceeded to beat her with a leather strap and then burned her. Sweet Alice will never be the same and like I said there may be pleasure houses around that cater to such perverse tastes, but I don't allow such things. I will tell you all I know, but if you get the chance to end his miserable life, make him suffer." She reached into a box on the edge of the table and pulled out a worn piece of paper.

We found this on the floor after he left Alice's room. Must have fallen out of a pocket. I kept it hoping he would come back for it, and I would kill him myself, but since you seem intent on completing that task, I will give it to you."

Cam took the paper and unfolded it. There was a list of names, some had been crossed off. This could be exactly what Harrison needed to discover the people sympathetic to the French cause.

He went over and took Molly's hand again, this time brushing a light kiss to her knuckles. "Thank you, Molly. This information will be most helpful, and I will kill him, not only for you but for the many people he has made suffer over the years."

Molly nodded before her lips turned up in a cheeky smile. "You know, I don't normally entertain clients anymore, but I have been known to make a few exceptions."

Cam gave her his best wicked grin before walking toward the door. "I'm afraid I will have to decline, Molly."

"She must be a special girl then."

Cam stopped and turned back to face her. "That she is."

Once he was outside the brothel, he moved to where Cavendish was holding his horse.

"Did Molly give you the information you needed?"

Cam mounted his horse. "It's a list of names. Names that might all be connected to Toussaint and the French movement."

"So do we head back to London?"

Cam frowned. That was what he wanted to do. He had told Abigail that he would return in a matter of days, but before he did so he needed to visit with the first name on the list, Sir Peter Hillebrand.

"I need to send this list to Harrison and a note to Abigail letting her know I will be longer than expected, then we are headed to Hertfordshire."

Cavendish nodded as he nudged his horse into a walk. "I knew you wouldn't be able to resist the urge to discover what was behind Toussaint's appearance."

Cam grinned. "I just want to end his miserable life so I can go about living mine. Harrison can deal with the rest of the people on this list. I'm merely after Toussaint."

Chapter Fifteen

Three months later

It had been three months since Abigail had received the note from Cam telling her he would be longer than expected due to the information he had received, but she never expected him to be this long.

After he had left, the day he had told her they would be married, she had gone through a whirlwind of emotions ranging from anger to elation. She had told Bella about her request to get involved with his investigation and his absolute refusal to allow her to. Bella had assured her that Cam was only looking out for her best interest. The talk with the duchess had eased her mind some and she began to get excited about becoming Cam's wife, even if the thought of becoming a duchess was a bit overwhelming, but that was three months ago. Now she feared something had gone terribly wrong.

She had expressed her concerns to Bella and even to Emma in her letters, and while at first, they had tried to reassure her that it would probably only be a few days longer, she could tell from the expressions on their faces anytime she entered the room, that they were beginning to become as worried as she. The days had turned to weeks and then to months. Now the season was about to begin in earnest, and she was expecting Emma and Ian to return from their home in Scotland any day now. Once they were back in London, she would have her things moved over to McDonough house which was just a few streets over.

She had attended a few dinner parties and even a garden party or two, but everywhere she went, she kept looking for him, hoping he would return. Had something gone wrong? Had Toussaint been successful in killing him? Did he walk into a trap? Or was it simply that he had changed his mind about her?

All those questions and more danced through her head as she tried to go about her life pretending not to continually search out the window or jump whenever the front door opened thinking it might be him. She looked down at the embroidery hoop lying in her lap and at the last few stitches she had made while her mind was distracted. She tossed the hoop aside, placing it on the settee beside her. She needed fresh air, a walk in the gardens, or perhaps through the park. She stood from her seat to make her way out to the gardens via the library terrace when the door was opened by Avanley's butler.

"Her grace, the Lady McDonough, Duchess of Sunbridge to see you, Miss Bailey."

Before the poor man could even step out of the way, Emma came rushing across the room nearly knocking Abigail over as she wrapped her in a tight hug.

"Oh Abigail, I am so sorry you have had such a bad time of it. I am furious with Davenport for taking you from McDonough Castle in the first place, especially now that we know it was unnecessary. From your letters I can't imagine how horrible the journey to get to London must have been. Thank heavens for Charles and Bella. I simply can't thank them enough for taking care of you until we could get back to London." Typical Emma, she had blown in like a storm and Abigail had yet to utter a word. "We will have the servants pack your things and you will come home with me this morning. We have much to discuss. Bella told me all about Davenport asking you to marry him and then running off deserting you here alone. I am so angry with him right now, and when I see him again, I will tell him exactly what I think about the abominable way he has treated you."

Abigail took a breath hoping her friend would finally let her speak, but that was not to be.

"You look thinner, Abby. Have you not been eating? I know you must be terribly upset and who wouldn't be in your situation. Thank goodness, you no longer have to worry about that assassin Toussaint."

"Emma!"

Abigail finally got her friend's attention.

"Please, slow down and have a seat. You are making me anxious with the way you are flittering about."

Emma sighed heavily and took a seat on the settee beside her friend. "Oh Abby, I have been so worried about you. I wanted to come to London sooner, but Ian had so many things he had to do. Being the chieftain of a Scottish clan carries with it so much responsibility. It was just impossible for us to come here any sooner. I'm sure you were in good hands with Charles and Bella though." She reached over and took Abigail's hand. "But I am here now and I am determined that you have the best season."

Abigail smiled at her friend. "I am happy to see you again, Emma."

Emma returned her smile. "My carriage is waiting outside to take us home."

Abigail stood. "I must speak with Bella before I go. She has been so kind to me and has made me feel very welcome. I also need to leave a letter for Cam should he come." She saw a concerning look in Emma's eyes before she lowered her head. "What is it, Emma? Do you know why he has not returned?"

Her friend sighed heavily. "He isn't coming back, Abigail, at least not any time soon."

Abigail felt the blood leave her face and her knees grew weak. "Do you know something that you aren't telling me, Emma?" She felt her hands begin to shake. "Has Toussaint….is he dead?"

Emma jumped from her seat. "Goodness, Abigail! I wasn't suggesting that. Sit down before you faint."

Abigail didn't return to her seat. She wanted to know exactly what her friend meant by that statement. "Why is Cam not coming back, Emma?"

She watched as her friend twisted her hands in front of her. "He has been gone for three months, Abigail and has not sent word to you. Ian says that Cam was one of the best spies that England had during the war with France. He says that there were times when Cam disappeared for months at a time. He becomes so involved in his work that he forgets everything else."

Abigail felt the tears gathering in her eyes. "And you think he has forgotten about me."

"I just think that he has gotten so caught up in searching for Toussaint that perhaps he may not be thinking clearly." She moved to wrap her arms around her friend. "Abigail, I am so sorry that all of this has happened. I would give anything if I had refused to allow you to leave McDonough Castle with him, then he never would have had a chance to…."

"Stop! It was a horrible journey from Scotland to London. You know what I suffered. I wrote to you about everything. But none of those things matter, I wouldn't trade any of it." She swiped at a lone tear that began to roll down her cheek. "Well, I could have done without the seasickness." She took a deep breath. "Cam will come back." She put her hands on her hips. "And you of all people should not make assumptions about someone leaving. You put your husband through hell on earth when you left London and it took him months to find you. What if he had given up, Emma? What if he had friends that told him that you would never be found?" Abigail saw the surprised look on her friend's face.

"I'm so sorry, Abigail. You are right, I never should have said that. You are so dear to me and the thought of you hurting, hurts me. I only want what's best for you. I know you have been watching by the windows searching for him, Bella told me. You just need to prepare yourself, Abigail. Prepare yourself for the possibility that he will not return." Emma shook her head slightly and moved to embrace her friend. "Let's speak no more about it today. I am just happy to see you and am anxious to show you about London. The season's first ball is Saturday, and we have much to do before that."

Abigail closed her eyes as Emma hugged her tightly. She would not believe that Cam had just forgotten about her, and she pushed any thoughts of him coming to harm completely out of her mind. She knew Emma was determined that she enjoy the season, and she would try her best, but until Cam returned, she would continue to watch out windows.

The first ball of the season, it was indeed a spectacle to behold, especially for a girl like her that had never attended anything more than a small country dance the local country gentry would hold no more than once or twice a year at the assembly rooms in Somerset.

Emma had wasted no time in making certain Abigail would have everything she needed for the season and after many fittings and trips to the modiste, she could say that she had more clothes than she would have ever thought one person could ever need. Emma was wearing a ballgown in a lovely shade of green, it actuated her eyes and Abigail thought she looked incredibly lovely. The gown Emma had picked out for her was peony pink. The skirt had a gauze overlay and tiny diamond like jewels sewn around the edge of the bodice. It was the loveliest dress she had ever owned.

The carriage ride to the Bennington's ball was taking longer than expected. The streets were much more crowded now that the ton had arrived back in London eager to partake in all the festivities the season had to offer. Abigail stared out the carriage window as she twisted the ring on her finger that Cam had given her before he left London three months earlier.

"Abigail, you look so melancholy. You really should try to enjoy yourself. Forget everything that has happened and just enjoy being here. I'm certain your dance card will fill up quickly and you might even have a bit of fun."

Abigail gave her friend a small smile. "I'm sorry if I appear ungrateful or as if I am not enjoying myself, Emma. It is just that I am worried."

Ian gave her a sympathetic smile. "I want you to know, lass that Davenport is not the kind of man that would desert you after asking you to be his bride. Things aren't always what they seem." He reached over and took his wife's hand. "I know Emma is anxious for you to enjoy yourself and I wish that for you too, but don't give up hope. Davenport is skilled at what he does, and I am certain he will return soon."

Abigail smiled, grateful for Ian's words. When the carriage finally came to a stop in front of the Bennington's house, she was feeling a bit better. Perhaps Emma was right, she should try to forget everything, at least for tonight, and enjoy herself. This was a moment that most young ladies dream of and one that she never imagined would be available to her.

The carriage door was opened, and the duke alighted first and after assisting Emma, held his hand out to her. Abigail was mesmerized the moment her feet touched the ground. Lanterns burned brightly lining the drive and leading up the large steps to the entrance. There were so many people, she wondered if all of London had turned out for the event.

She followed behind Ian and Emma, waiting patiently with them as the major domo announced their arrival. They moved through the throng of people and eventually came to find Persephone and Catherine standing beside their husbands.

Persephone was the first to move forward and greet her. "Miss Bailey, I am so pleased to see you again. Emma has relayed to me the stories of your journey to London, and we can only hope your time here is less strenuous."

Catherine also greeted her warmly. "Yes, and while you are here you must join us for some of the engagements. There is a particular garden party we attend every year, and I insist that you join us."

Abigail smiled brightly. "Thank you. I would be pleased to join you."

Emma leaned a bit closer. "I'm not sure if pleased is the correct word to use regarding the garden party to which Catherine is referring. Lady Weatherby's annual event is attended by many, but I'm not sure any of the people are pleased to be there."

Abigail narrowed her eyes wondering what her friend was trying to convey to her but before she could ask, a familiar voice caught her attention.

"Miss Bailey, you look remarkably lovely this evening. I hope I am not too late to request a dance. Surely your card has an empty space for me," Mr. Kingston said as he took her hand and raised it to his lips.

Abigail's eyes lit up. "Mr. Kingston, it has been a long time since I have seen you."

"Well, *The Lair* tends to occupy most of my time, but when I heard you would be attending, I couldn't miss the chance to see you. Would you do me the honor of allowing me to be the first to dance with you this evening?"

Abigail placed her hand in his and allowed him to lead her onto the dance floor. When the music started and they began their dance, she couldn't help but ask, "Mr. Kingston, have you heard from Cam? He was only to be gone for two or three days and it has been over three months now. I thought he might have written to you."

The sympathetic smile Mr. Kingston gave her was very similar to the ones she had been receiving from her friends for the past few weeks. "I'm sorry, love, but I do not know anything about his whereabouts. I know things have taken longer than anticipated, but I'm confident he will be back soon."

Abigail let her smile slip. "I'm sorry for asking. I just thought you might have heard from him."

Mr. Kingston spun her around the room. "Smile, Miss Bailey, or you will ruin my reputation."

Abigail did smile and even laugh a bit at his comment.

"That's more like it. Now that your dear friend the lovely Emma McDonough has returned to London, what exciting things do you have planned?"

Abigail shrugged her shoulders. "I am not certain. Emma has mentioned a garden party we must attend, but other than that I don't know. I am at her mercy, I'm afraid."

The music stopped and he led her back to the side of the room where Emma and the others were waiting, but before she could even speak, another gentleman was at her side asking for the next dance. Her gaze landed upon Emma, who was smiling and nodding encouragingly. She accepted the gentleman's hand and allowed him to lead her back onto the dance floor.

Cam watched from where he stood hidden in the shadows behind some ridiculously large plants Bennington had placed just outside the ballroom. He watched as Abigail danced with Kingston and then again with some other young lord who had no idea how close he was coming to an unfortunate end to his evening.

"Bloody hell, man! Why the devil are you lurking about ogling Miss Bailey from a distance? Should you not have made your arrival known to her by now? You have been in London for more than a week," Kingston said as he moved to stand in front of the plant to help Davenport avoid detection.

"I just wanted to see her."

"Then bloody well stop hiding behind this monstrous plant and claim her for the next dance."

Cam frowned as the young lord dancing with Abigail leaned closer to speak into her ear. "Damn it! Where is McDonough? He is supposed to be her guardian."

Kingston walked forward and took two glasses of champagne from a passing footman, then passed one through the foliage to Davenport. "McDonough is dancing with his lovely wife."

"I can't stay here. It is too big of a risk that she will see me."

Kingston drank the reminder of his champagne. "This is bloody ridiculous. Just tell me the reason you refuse to allow her to know you are back and let's do so elsewhere before everyone that sees me begins to think I have gone daft carrying on a conversation with this piece of damn foliage!"

Cam continued to watch Abigail as the dance came to an end and the young lord escorted her to the refreshment table closer to where he was hiding. Now he could see her clearer. She was a vision in pink, her cheeks nearly matching the shade of her gown. Her fair hair put up in an elegant coiffure that accentuated the graceful curve of her neck. Her bright violet eyes stood out as she laughed softly at something the young man had said. Her slender fingers gripped the stem of her champagne flute as she lifted the glass to her lips to take a sip. The tip of her tongue darting out to taste it on her lips. Cam nearly growled when another young man approached her.

At that moment, she turned and looked in his direction. She narrowed her eyes a fraction and tilted her pretty neck to the side and for a second, he thought she had seen him. The gentleman that was standing at her side reached for her hand and led her back onto the dance floor. Once he was sure it was safe to do so, he moved from his hiding place.

"Hurry, let's go somewhere we will not be disturbed."

Kingston nodded. "We can go out to the gardens. There should be a few places we can talk there without being noticed. It looks as if it might rain, so few will venture far from the house."

They moved undetected out one of the side doors and into Bennington's gardens. Once outside, Cam found an area toward the back that was well hidden by tall hedges.

"So now that we are well out of sight of the ball, a ball I was enjoying very much by the way, will you tell me what the hell is going on? Since I haven't seen you at *The Lair*, where have you been staying the past few days?" Kingston asked as he crossed his arms over his chest.

"I've been at Stafford House."

Kingston raised an eyebrow. "Hmm, so you finally decided to call it home. I'm surprised you have been able to keep your arrival in London secret, especially with the way servants talk." An insolent grin spread across his face. "You do have servants, don't you?"

Cam rolled his eyes. "Yes, Charles had his staff handle the arrangements and more staff was added while I was away. Since I proposed to Abigail, I thought it was time to officially open the house."

"I think you should tell me what has happened since you left London and why the hell have you not told Abigail that you were back in town?"

"Cavendish and I found out from Molly Tremblay that Toussaint had been in London and after abusing the girl he was with at her establishment, they found a piece of paper that he dropped on his way out. It was a list of names. I thought it prudent to visit some of those people on that list, the first of which was Sir Peter Hillebrand."

"So, what did Hillebrand have to say?"

Cam breathed deeply. "He was dead when we arrived. His steward said that they found him dead two days before we got to his estate. Apparently, he drowned in the garden fountain."

This information got Kingston's attention. "Toussaint?"

"I assume so. That night, I snuck back into the house and went through Hillebrand's study. All I found were some ledgers that indicated he had dealings with some French businesses. I sent them to Thomas Harrison at the War Department. Since I had the list of names, I thought I would move to the next name on the list, Sir Norman Whitburn."

Kingston cleared his throat. "Was he dead too?"

Cam grinned. "No, but he talked and said that the names on the list are all French sympathizers or those that had expressed an interest in the cause. He also said that Toussaint had returned to London. I intend to find him or at least find out if he is still here before I let Abigail know I am back. I wouldn't want to risk her knowing anything about Toussaint. I have been searching for the past three days, and I feel certain that I will discover him soon. Once I know she will be safe, we will be married."

"So, you intend on hiding from her until that time?"

"Do you have a better idea?"

Kingston shrugged his shoulders. "I suppose not, but what happens if she gives up waiting? It has been three months and from what Charles has said, she has been quite distraught."

"I know, he said as much to me when I met with him upon my return."

"Well, you should probably leave before anyone discovers you here, and you must realize that you can't sneak around following her throughout the entire season. Eventually, she will…" The sound of footsteps coming closer stopped his speech.

Cam quickly moved away finding a place where he would be out of sight, hoping that Kingston would get rid of the unwelcome intruder quickly.

Something was going on and Abigail was determined to get to the bottom of it. She had seen Kingston leave the ball and go out to the gardens and she was almost certain someone was with him. Since their dance, she could not escape the feeling that he was hiding something from her. So, when the dance ended and her partner escorted her back to the side of the ballroom, she decided it was the perfect time for a stroll through the garden herself, and if she just happened to meet Kingston while getting some fresh air, then she would satisfy her curiosity.

She cautiously moved through the crowd, trying not to draw any attention to herself and when she was sure no one was looking in her direction, she slipped out the terrace doors to the garden. She followed the path into the gardens away from the house where she heard voices speaking low. She couldn't tell exactly who was speaking but when she moved around one of the tall shrubs, she ran headlong into the arms of Mr. Kingston.

"Miss Bailey? What the devil are you doing out here alone?"

Abigail did not want to admit that she was stalking him, trying to find out if he had more information about her missing fiancé.

"The ballroom is so crowded and warm. I thought I would come get some air."

Kington glanced back over his shoulder and she followed his line of sight. "Did I disturb you? I certainly wouldn't want to intrude if you are with someone."

Kingston turned back to give her a bright smile. "Your company is never an intrusion, Miss Bailey, but you really should avoid venturing off by yourself. Not every gentleman is as gallant as I."

Abigail laughed softly. "Yes, of course you are right. Emma would certainly chastise me for being so bold." She started to move around him, but he gripped her arm.

"Allow me to escort you back inside, Miss Bailey. I'm certain you have many admirers eager for your return to the ball."

She narrowed her eyes just a bit. "Are you certain we are alone, Mr. Kingston? I could have sworn that I heard voices, as in more than one."

Kingston grinned. No wonder Davenport found her so irresistible, her cheeky tongue alone would keep a man on his toes. "Are you accusing me of having a tete-`a-tete?"

Abigail blushed. "I am not accusing you of anything, Mr. Kingston. I just simply stated that I was certain I heard another voice."

Kingston once again took her arm and began leading her back toward the ballroom. "Has your imagination always been this active, or is it merely enhanced since Davenport has been away?"

Abigail came to a stop and pulled her arm from his grasp. "It was not my imagination, but please do go on and keep trying to hide things from me. I promise you; I will discover what or who you are trying to conceal."

Kingston was more than a little impressed with Miss Bailey. "I apologize, Miss Bailey, if I have offended you. It was not my intention. Please let me make it up to you by allowing me to take you for a carriage ride tomorrow afternoon through the park. It will be crowded now that all the ton has descended upon London, and it will be the perfect time to showcase your beauty and to tell me exactly what you think I am keeping from you."

Abigail crossed her arms over her chest. "Very well. It has been over a week since I have been to the park. I will look forward to it, Mr. Kingston."

He reached for her hand, the hand where she wore Cam's ring. "As will I, my dear."

Abigail knew she would get no further tonight, and he was right about being in the gardens alone so she allowed him to lead her back to the ballroom, but tomorrow she would do her best to wear him down and find out what he knew about Cam's whereabouts.

Cam watched as Abigail walked away on the arm of his friend. The fact that she was suspicious was disturbing. The last thing he needed was for her to meddle and get involved with his investigation. The whole reason for staying away and not letting her know of his return was so she could occupy herself with the season and not risk her being hurt. Perhaps he should claim her now, at least as his bride, he could keep her under watch or even send her to his country estate and have her locked away under constant guard till he saw fit to release her.

His mind immediately filled with carnal pleasures of having Abigail locked away in his bedroom, naked and bound to his bed. A treasure for him to plunder at every opportunity. Those thoughts were going to have to wait. Right now, he had more important things to be concerned with, finding Toussaint. It was taking longer than he first imagined but he knew he was close to finding the madman. He just didn't realize how close.

Chapter Sixteen

A bigail woke early the next morning. Emma had told her that
during the season, they would be out late most evenings, and
while she should probably take advantage of some extra rest, she was
too anxious to stay in bed. After Mr. Kingston had escorted her back
inside, she had found Emma and spent the remainder of the ball either
in her company or dancing with gentlemen that she was introduced
to. At one point, Catherine and Persephone joined them and she was
given a brief, if not thorough, education of who was who in the ton.

Overall, it was an enjoyable evening, but by the end of the night,
her feet had ached mercilessly, and she was bone tired. So, when she
finally did make it to her bed at McDonough House, she had fallen
asleep almost instantly.

Now that she had finally awakened, she remembered that she
had accepted an invitation to go on a carriage ride with Mr. Kingston
later in the afternoon so if she hurried, she would have time to pay
a visit to see Bella before he arrived to collect her. Since the Duke
of Avanley had also been involved with the secret dealings of the

War Department, there was a chance that she might have knowledge of something that might help her unravel the mystery behind Cam's disappearance.

After dressing as quickly as she could, she hurried downstairs and was almost to the door when Emma's voice stopped her.

"Abigail, where are you going? You know you shouldn't go out alone. If you wait a few minutes, I will join you."

Abigail chewed her bottom lip nervously. She didn't want Emma to know about her conversation with Kingston or her suspicions. "I was just going for a walk this morning. I assure you that I have no intention of going very far."

Emma moved forward. "It isn't safe to go alone, I…"

Abigail crossed her arms over her chest. "Emma, do you hear yourself? Did you not go on walks alone when you first came to London with your aunt and uncle? How many times did you write to me saying how ridiculous it was that you were expected to always have a maid with you?"

Her friend sighed heavily. "Yes, I remember, but I also remember how I almost was accosted one night while out alone. If Ian had not been there, I could have been hurt. It was ridiculous of me not to realize the dangers of London."

Abigail rolled her eyes and tried a different tactic. "Emma, I know you are only wanting to protect me, but I just need some time alone. Ever since I left Somerset, my life has been turned upside down and the past three months have been hard for me. Please understand that I just want to talk a walk, clear my mind, and then I will return here in time for my carriage ride with Mr. Kingston. I promise not to venture far, I won't even leave Mayfair."

She saw the sympathy in her friend's eyes and knew she had won. "I know it has been hard for you, Abigail, and if I ever get my hands on Camden Davenport, I may wring his neck myself. I think you need a distraction. Why don't I talk to Ian and maybe we can go to the theater tonight or even plan a trip to Vauxhall this week."

Abigail grinned before walking out the door. "Thank you, Emma. I would like that."

Once she arrived at Avanley House, she was shown into the front drawing room by their butler where she waited patiently for Bella to arrive. She found herself nervously pacing about the room wondering what exactly she would ask Bella. She was so lost in her own thoughts that she didn't hear the duchess when she approached.

"Abigail? Is everything alright? I wasn't expecting to see you this morning."

Abigail clasped her hands together in front of her. "I came to talk to you, Bella. I have a problem, and I thought you might be able to help me."

"I certainly hope I can. What is it?"

"Your husband, Charles, he was…well… he has worked with Davenport in the past, and they have done some things for the War Department."

Bella smiled. "Yes, although he hasn't shared very much about what he did."

Abigail moved to sit beside her on the settee. "It's been three months, Bella. Cam said he was only going to be gone for two or three days. I talked to Mr. Kingston last night at the Bennington's ball and he seemed like he might be hiding something." She stood up again and then started pacing in front of the settee. "I suppose it could be my imagination, but I just can't shake the feeling that Cam is in danger and no one is willing to tell me." She glanced over and saw Bella's eyes drop and thought her friend instantly looked guilty. "Do you think I am overreacting, Bella?" She glanced over and saw her friend fidgeting, twisting her fingers around the material of the dress she was wearing. "Bella?"

"Abigail, I'm certain everything will work out. You really shouldn't worry about it."

Abigail narrowed her eyes a fraction. "Do you know something, Bella? If you do, please tell me."

Bella sighed heavily and patted the seat beside her. "Please sit down, Abigail."

Abigail sat beside her friend and waited for Bella to gather her thoughts.

"I really shouldn't say anything, but I do feel terrible that you are suffering with not knowing, and I think it is wrong for them to keep things from you."

Abigail felt her chest tighten. She was right. They were keeping something from her. "What is it, Bella?"

Bella sighed heavily and looked back toward the door. "Cam has been back in London for several days now."

Abigail gasped and covered her mouth with her hand. "How do you know?"

"He was here meeting with Charles. I wasn't supposed to be here, but I returned early from shopping, and I saw him in the study."

Abigail felt her heart drop into her stomach. "What were they talking about?"

"I didn't hear everything, just that he had been here for several days and didn't want you to know."

"Do you know where he is?"

Bella shook her head. "I don't, and I never questioned Charles about it, but if I had to guess, I would say he is either staying at *The Lair* or he has opened up Stafford House."

Abigail shot to her feet. "Kingston must know too. Last night he left the ball and went out to the garden. I followed him and as I got closer, I thought I heard two voices, but when I found him, he was alone, but I knew he was hiding something from me."

She hurried toward the door.

"Where are you going?"

"I'm going to find Camden Davenport and when I do, he is going to wish he had left me in Scotland!"

Abigail was angry and hurt. When she thought of the many sleepless nights she had endured worrying over that infuriating man she could scream. To think of all the hours, she had spent watching and waiting for him or worrying that he had met some terrible fate or had been hurt, but he was only hiding in London so he didn't have to be with her. If he didn't want to marry her, he should have had the guts to tell her himself, not hide like a coward.

It was not difficult to find Stafford House, Emma had pointed it out to her one day as they passed by. She marched up the steps so angry, she wasn't sure what she would say. She knocked loudly and the door was opened by an older man who she supposed was Cam's butler.

"May I help you, madam?"

Abigail raised her chin a notch higher. "I am here to see the Duke of Stafford."

The man's expression didn't change. "His grace is not receiving visitors."

"Is he in residence then?"

"Do you have a calling card I can present to his grace?"

Abigail put her hands on her hips. "No, I do not have…"

"Then you must return at another time, madam. Good day."

He tried to shut the door in her face, but Abigail pushed back. "I'm sorry, but I simply refuse to leave until I have been seen." She pushed forward and walked into the house leaving the older man sputtering orders to the footmen in attendance. Abigail moved down the hallway quickly looking from room to room with two footmen right behind her. Before she could reach the door of the library, the footmen grabbed her arms and began hauling her back toward the door.

"Take your hands off of me!"

The butler was holding the door open, and she suspected they were about to bodily throw her out. She tried to pull her arms free, but it was no use. Then a loud booming voice coming from the top of the stairs caused everyone to stop.

"Release her and leave us!"

The footmen released their hold on her, and along with the older butler, bowed deeply before rushing from the room. Abigail turned around to watch as a shirtless Cam moved slowly down the stairs toward her.

She narrowed her eyes trying to focus on her anger instead of her relief that he was alive.

"You!"

"Hello, darling."

"Do not call me that!"

He continued walking toward her until she was within reach. "Miss me?"

"You are despicable. How long have you been back In London?"

He tilted his head to the side. "Over a week. You are even beautiful when you are mad."

Abigail rolled her eyes. "Were you ever going to tell me?"

He shrugged his shoulders. "As soon as I knew it was safe to do so."

Abigail shook her head. "Don't tell me that! Keeping me safe was the reason I had to leave McDonough House, it was the reason you were going to leave me at *The Lair*, it is the reason you give me for everything, and I don't want to hear it anymore!"

She started to walk away, but she wasn't quite finished yet. "I waited for you, terrified that something had gone wrong and you had been hurt or even killed. Everyone told me not to worry, but no one bothered to say that you were the most wicked, horrible, rotten, abysmal man I would ever meet." She took a deep breath as she twisted the ring, he had given her off her finger. "You can take this back. I prefer to marry a man that doesn't sneak around hiding from me."

She held the ring out waiting for him to take it, but from the look on his face, he had no intention of doing anything she asked.

"Put it back on, Abigail." His voice was low and deep.

"No, it belongs to you, I do not!"

She held her hand out further arching her eyebrow in defiance.

He stepped closer, but Abigail refused to back down. She refused to acknowledge the fact that he smelled good like he had recently bathed with sandalwood soap. Even though he was close enough that she could feel the warmth from his body, she refused to let her body react to it, and she would not imagine how good it would feel for him to kiss her, no she would be strong.

"I'm not going to ask you again, Abigail. Put my ring back on your finger."

He obviously wasn't going to take the ring. She wrapped her fist around it, refusing to put it back on her finger. She would not give him the satisfaction. "Fine! I will leave it on the side table on my way out." She spun on her heel and headed to the door, but she had not gone more than two steps before Cam had pulled her back into his chest and wrapped his arms around her anchoring her to him.

She thrashed and kicked and tried her best to hit him, and if he had not wrapped his hand in her hair to pull her head back, she would have bitten him. "Are you done, Abigail? Are you ready to listen to me?"

"No, take your hands off me. I never want to see you again."

Cam hoisted her up in his arms and began carrying her up the stairs. "If you don't stop thrashing around you are going to cause both of us to fall down the stairs."

"You are a beast! You can't do this to me. Let me go!" She got one of her hands free and almost connected a decent punch.

He chuckled at her efforts which only made her fight him more. He reached his bedchambers and once he had the door shut and locked behind him, he finally set her on her feet.

Her hair had come loose in her struggles and cascaded down her back. Her cheeks were red and her face flushed. Her chest was heaving from her exertions, and he felt his cock stiffen. "If you will calm down, I will explain why I didn't tell you I was back."

She looked around the room frantically trying to find another exit. "You would never make it before I caught you, Abigail."

Abigail wanted to throw something at his head and wipe that incredibly appealing smirk from his face. "I don't want to hear anything you have to say."

He stalked toward her and while he could sense her urge to move away, he admired her courage. "You will hear what I have to say, and when I am done explaining, I am going to carry you to that bed and make love to you until you forget why you are mad at me."

Abigail couldn't help but gasp at his words. "You arrogant arse of a man. What makes you think the last time was memorable? Besides, I will never let you touch me again."

He reached out to touch her cheek, but she pulled away from him. "Yes, you will, Abigail." He glanced over to a chair that sat by the hearth. "Would you care to have a seat, or would you prefer to stand erect like you are about to throw yourself into some epic battle?"

Abigail straightened her shoulders and lifted her chin. "I will sit, but as soon as you have spouted your lies to me, I want the door unlocked."

He nodded. "Very well, you have my word that I will unlock the door."

Abigail walked stiffly to the chair and had a seat. "Go ahead, I'm listening." There was a table beside the chair, and he didn't miss her setting his ring on it before clasping her hands tightly in her lap.

He walked over to where he had a decanter of brandy sitting by his bed and poured a glass. "Did you have your maid wait for you outside, if so, I'll have my butler bring her in and she can wait for you downstairs?"

"I didn't bring a maid, I am alone."

His eyes narrowed slightly as he took a sip from his glass. "You came all the way here alone?"

"Don't you dare chastise me after what you have done."

"There are a few other things we will discuss later as well, but now that I have your attention I will…"

"Just tell me so I can leave." She crossed her arms over her chest ignoring the fact that he seemed to be getting as angry as she felt.

"When I left London, I thought it would only take a few days, I did not lie to you about that. In fact, I haven't lied to you at all."

She cast her eyes sideways, and he clenched his teeth growing tired of her petulance. Maybe he should have made love to her first, then explained himself.

"I received some information from a source that has had contact with Toussaint recently. He left behind a list of names. She gave the list to me, and I thought it best to visit some of the names on the list before returning to London."

"She?"

He grinned slightly at her obvious jealousy. "The first name on the list was dead by the time I got there. He had an unfortunate accident."

At this, she perked up. "An accident? Did Toussaint kill him?"

He arched his eyebrows. "Interested now? Yes, you are correct, love. Toussaint killed him before I could question him. There were other names on the list, however, and I did get to question them. It was a list of traitors, all those interested in supporting the French cause against our country."

Her mouth opened slightly. "What did you do to them?"

"I gave the list to Harrison. They will be dealt with according to the law."

"That doesn't explain why you didn't tell me you were back in London, nor why you did not send me any word. Do you have any idea what I have been through?"

He moved toward her intending to pull her into his arms, but she held up her hand to stop him.

"No. Don't."

He sighed heavily. "One of the men I questioned said that Toussaint had returned to London. I wanted to find him before I let you know I was back. I didn't want Toussaint to know anything about you. It was for your safety."

Abigail stood from her chair. "I'm so tired of hearing that. You could have let me know." She stood from her seat and took a step toward the door. "I listened, now unlock the door."

Cam wasn't about to let her leave. Other than his obsession with finding Toussaint, he had thought of little else but returning to London and taking Abigail as his wife. Her anger and stubbornness had not changed anything. She would still be his, and it was time he reminded her of that fact right now.

He moved with lightning speed and took her in his arms. "I meant what I said earlier, Abigail." He pressed a kiss to her lips before she could utter a protest. He was not surprised that she fought him, but he could already feel her body softening against his. His lips left hers to trail kisses down her neck. Her breathing increased and she stopped trying to push him away. He pulled the sleeve of her gown down to expose her shoulder and nipped at her soft skin. He felt his desire growing by the minute. She was wearing too much clothing. Any clothing was too much clothing.

"Christ, Abigail, I can't wait any longer." He swept her into his arms and carried her over to the bed.

Abigail had not meant for this to happen. She was still angry, and the moment his lips touched hers she knew she had lost the fight, but when her back hit his bed some of her reason returned. "I can't do this. I must go."

He moved over her, his hands moving over her body. "You aren't going anywhere, Abigail."

She closed her eyes as he ripped her bodice down to expose her breasts. "I can't do this, Cam. I told Emma I was just going to take a quick walk. I have been gone much longer than expected, and I wouldn't be surprised if she hasn't already sent servants out looking for me."

Cam continued pressing kisses across her breasts while his hands raised her skirts. "I don't give a damn how many servants are out looking for you or if Emma is going to be angry with me. I need you, Abigail." He pushed her skirts higher until his fingers found what he sought.

Abigail arched her back and gripped the coverlet tightly with her fingers. Oh God, this can't happen. "Cam, we can't do this. I have to leave." Somehow, he had managed to release the buttons at the back of her gown and now he was pulling it over her head leaving her in her chemise and stockings.

"You can leave, darling, after I have had my fill." He moved slowly pressing kisses from her ankles up to her thighs raising her chemise as he did so."

Abigail closed her eyes and cried out as his tongue flicked over her core. "Please, Cam." Her voice was partly a cry. "I can't stay."

Cam sighed heavily and raised up on his elbows to stare down into her eyes. "Is it because you are still mad at me or because Emma will be worried?"

She sucked in a deep breath before answering. "I am still angry with you, but Emma will be beside herself if I don't return soon, and Mr. Kingston is expecting me to join him on a carriage ride through the park this afternoon."

Cam moved off her and headed for the door. "I don't give a damn about Kingston, and I am not allowing you to leave, but if it will ease your mind, I'll have a message sent to McDonough House. Do not move from that bed, Abigail. I'm serious. I will haul you right back up here if you do." He turned and gave her a wicked grin, the one that made her toes curl. "And don't try the window either." He winked, then closed the door behind him.

Abigail was alone, alone, and partially naked. She sat up and pulled her knees into her chest. How could he so easily do this to her, reduce her anger to sheer lust, make her forget everything but how it feels to be in his arms? She had to pull herself together. She had to stiffen her spine and let Camden Davenport, Duke of Stafford know that she would not be so easily swayed. That he couldn't just disappear for weeks at a time and then swoop back in, taking her into his arms and making her forget her anger, her feelings, and everything she had been through with a kiss, or touch her in ways that made her feel as if she were on fire, making her long for more. No, he can't do this to her.

"You have to be stronger, Abigail," she said to herself as she kept her eyes on the door.

She was still sitting there with her arms wrapped around her knees when the door opened, and Cam walked back into the room. She immediately jumped from the bed angry at herself for not defying his orders.

She grabbed her dress and held it up before her like some sort of protective shield. "I can't stay."

"Yes, you can." He moved toward the table where she had set her ring and picked it up twisting it around his little finger as he stalked back toward her. "

"No, I'm angry with you. I can't let you distract me."

She started backing away from him, and he followed.

He stood before her and the look of burning intensity in his eyes made her knees buckle and her heart beat faster. He reached for her hand, and she didn't try to pull away from his grasp. He held the ring up in front of her face then slipped it back on her finger as he continued to hold her hand in his.

"I'm sorry you are angry with me, love. I'm sorry that I haven't been able to find Toussaint, I'm sorry that I couldn't think of a better way to protect you other than staying away, but I am not sorry for this."

Before she could even blink, he had her back on his bed flat on her back. The dress she had been holding in front of her had somehow managed to make it back to the floor. She didn't know if she had dropped it, or if he had ripped it away.

Abigail felt her body rebel against her, and she reached up to wrap her arms around his neck pulling his body down to hers. She let her fingers skim over his chest and down his abs to the waistband of his trousers.

Cam shivered at her touch knowing his restraint was not as strong as he needed it to be. He had not intended to see her today, but when he saw her standing downstairs ready to fight his butler and two footmen, he knew there was no way around it.

When their eyes had locked, and he saw the fury behind her violet orbs, his cock had instantly hardened. She was undeniably the most passionate, stubborn, headstrong, and beautiful woman he had ever met, and she belonged to him.

He slid her chemise slowly up her legs, letting his fingers graze the skin of her body as he moved it higher. He bent down to kiss her belly as it became exposed, then continued kissing up to her breasts, her collarbone, the place where he could feel her pulse beating in her neck. Once he had removed her chemise, he raised up on his knees just to look at her. She had nothing on but her stockings tied to her thighs with pink ribbon. He thought they made her look even more sensual and decided he would leave them on. Her fair hair had come loose and waves of it spread out around her like a halo. Her rose-colored nipples were tight, and her breasts rose and fell with each breath she took. She was a masterpiece. A painter's dream that should be put onto canvas. Of course, that would never happen. He would never let another man view the erotic vision laid out before him.

Abigail did not try to cover herself. She let Cam's eyes roam over her naked body strangely aroused by the look on his face as he skimmed over her most private places. She had come here to rage at him, to tell him that she never wanted to see him again, but she couldn't, because she…loved him.

She watched as he moved from the bed and removed the remainder of his clothing and when his body covered hers, she wrapped her legs around him to pull him into her. She sucked in a breath as the full length of him filled her. There was no pain this time, only pleasure.

Cam held himself rigid for a moment trying not to lose himself too quickly inside her. She felt so good, like a glove that fit him to perfection. Her body tightened around him as he pulled out and thrust back in again. He reached his hands under her hips to lift her so he could fully embed himself into her warm slick body. He moved faster, her rhythms matching his own. He suddenly flipped to his back taking her with him so she sat astride him. She looked at him in surprise, not knowing what to do. He lifted her hips and slid her back down along his length slowly gritting his teeth to maintain his control, but his little vixen didn't need much tutoring. She caught on quickly and started riding him while he squeezed her breasts. She raised her head to the ceiling and closed her eyes as he pumped inside her. He felt her shiver and the warm sensation of her sweet cuny as she climaxed. He couldn't have lasted longer if he had wanted to, one more thrust and he filled her then rolled her to her back lifting her hips as he finally found his release.

Abigail felt as if she couldn't catch her breath. Cam's body lay atop hers and he was breathing as hard as she was. While this had not been in her plan when she had stormed through his front doors, she could not say it wasn't what she had truly been seeking.

He raised off her and looked down into her eyes. He leaned down to kiss her lips but stopped when he heard loud voices and an ungodly commotion coming from downstairs. He moved from the bed quickly grabbing his clothes, and hastily throwing them on.

"What the devil is that?" Abigail asked as she struggled to get her chemise over her head.

Cam grabbed a pistol from the table by his bed. "I don't know, but I'm sure as hell going to find out." He looked back at her, the pistol held down by his side. "Stay here, Abigail."

"Wait for me, I'm going with you."

"No!"

The deep boom of his voice made her jump.

He took a step toward her and she instinctively retreated. Cam sighed heavily and reached for her hand. "I don't know who is downstairs, Abigail, nor do I know their intentions. Please, for the love of the Almighty, stay here so I know you are safe."

Abigail pulled her hand away and reached for her dress. "Fine, but if you get shot, it will be your own fault."

He grinned before raising her hand to his lips for a quick kiss. "Better for me to be shot than you, love. It would just be another hole added to my list of scars." He hurried from the room slamming the door behind him. Abigail put on her dress and slipped her shoes back on her feet. She had no intention of getting shot today but being left behind was not an option either.

Chapter Seventeen

C am moved cautiously down the hallway as the noises grew louder. He held his pistol up, pointing the barrel into the air, ready to fire if needed. He peered around the corner readying himself for a fight, but what he saw was much worse than anything he could imagine.

The Duchess of Sunbridge, Emma McDonough was standing in his entryway brandishing what he thought was a dirk she had obviously borrowed from her husband and had both footmen and his butler backed up against the wall with their hands held up as if she were some highwayman set out to rob them. He couldn't help but chuckle as Emma slashed the knife through the air in front of the men making them visibly nervous.

"Where is she? I know Stafford has her hidden here somewhere and I want her brought out right now!" the duchess said with as much authority as her five-foot, three-inch frame could muster.

Cam began walking down the stairs needing to take control of the situation before Emma felt the need to gut his servants on his freshly waxed tile floors.

"Emma, what a pleasant surprise. My day has been full of surprises. I wasn't expecting to see you so soon."

To the relief of his servants, she immediately turned her ire to him as she marched up the stairs to confront him.

"What have you done with her?"

Cam couldn't help the smile that spread across his face, and he was rewarded with a sharp slap across his cheek.

"You, lecherous whoreson. Tell me where Abigail is before I take this knife and make a few more holes in you."

For emphasis, she held the blade up a little higher and mimicked running him through.

Cam held up his hands in mock surrender. "If you will give me…"

"Emma!?"

Both he and the duchess turned to see Abigail running down the stairs toward them. He frowned wondering what he was going to have to do to get that woman to listen and obey his orders.

Emma took in the appearance of her friend and turned a deadly glare on Cam. "You were my friend and I trusted you. I allowed you to take my best friend away from McDonough Castle on the pretense that she would be safer in London with you than staying there with me. I trusted you to keep her safe, her person along with her virtue. You took advantage of her, Cam. She has no experience with men like you. I never should have allowed you near her." She turned to her friend. "Abigail, my carriage is outside. I will take you back home and make sure this villain never bothers you again."

Cam reached out and held onto Abigail's arm as she moved beside him as if he was afraid that she would do just as her friend suggested. "She isn't leaving, Emma. I will send for the bishop; I have the special license and we can be married this afternoon."

The duchess put her hands on her hips, the knife dangerously close. "She deserves better than that."

Cam wrapped his arm around Abigail's waist and pulled her to his side. "I won't argue that point, but I need her, I need her just as surely as I need to breathe, and I refuse to do without her."

Abigail looked over at him, her eyes widening at his declaration.

"Oh, so now you need her. You need her so much that you just left her behind, left her to wonder if you were even alive. Well, I was the one who had to watch her heart break more and more every day." She pointed the knife at him again. "I should cut you just for that alone."

Cam pushed Abigail behind him. If Emma did decide to slash away at him, he didn't want Abigail anywhere near the blade her friend held in her hand. "I didn't just abandon her. I had my reasons."

"Hmm, reasons that I'm sure will conveniently come up again the minute you want them to," Emma said as she rolled her eyes heavenward. "Come on, Abigail."

Cam narrowed his eyes. "She stays with me."

Abigail had listened as the two of them bickered back and forth discussing her future and what she was or wasn't going to do as if she were not there and she wasn't having it.

"That's enough from both of you!"

Both Emma and Cam turned in her direction, shocked at the look of anger on her face.

"Emma, I love you. You have been my best friend since we were little girls, but you are treating me as if I don't know my own mind and can't make my own decisions. I am twenty and one and I can decide my fate." She stepped forward and grabbed both of her friend's hands in her own avoiding the knife Emma still held. "I know you mean well, but I just need you to support my decision on this."

Emma frowned. "I just want to see you as happy as I am with Ian."

"I know that, and I will be happy. You just have to believe me."

She looked over to see Cam's smirk. "And you! If I am to be your wife, you have got to trust me. I want to know what is going on. I refuse to be kept in the dark anymore, and if you ever leave again making me wonder where you are, or what has happened to you, don't expect me to be here when you return. Understood?"

Cam hesitated. "I will not ever allow you to be in danger, Abigail. As your husband, it is my duty to keep you safe, but I will concede to share more information with you, and I will not leave you again."

Abigail nodded. "Very well. There is one more thing. While I may have never had designs on a large wedding ceremony at St. George's Cathedral, I do however wish to at least have the time to make myself presentable and invite a few of our friends."

Cam wasn't liking where this was going. He was hoping to have her in his bed again tonight, but he had a feeling Abigail had other ideas. "How much time do you need, Abigail?"

"A week will be enough time for me, and we can be married at McDonough House if it is alright and Emma is willing."

Emma sighed heavily. "You know it is, Abigail." She glanced over at Cam. "Do you still plan on being in London in a week?"

Cam frowned. "I'm not leaving again."

Abigail hated the tension between her best friend and her soon-to-be husband. "Please stop looking at each other that way."

Both Emma and Cam turned to face her and reluctantly they seemed to come to a truce.

"Excellent, now I have things I need to do today, and Mr. Kingston will be by to take me on a carriage ride this afternoon, so I have to hurry." Abigail started to walk down the stairs, but Cam reached out and grabbed her arm.

"I would like a few minutes alone with Abigail if you don't mind. If you will excuse us, Emma we will not be but a minute."

"From what I can see, you have had enough time alone with her."

Cam just turned a frown in her direction and walked with Abigail down the stairs only to thrust her behind him once more when the front door flung open, and Ian came tearing into the house.

"Oh, thank God. I was told that Emma was coming over here to kill you and since she took my dirk from the table by our bed, I thought I might not get here in time," Ian said as he glanced from Cam to his wife.

Emma moved down the stairs toward her husband. "Abigail talked me out of it."

Ian pulled his wife closer to his side and removed the dirk from her grasp before turning to give Cam a smirk. "Well, that's good because I do consider him a good friend."

Emma huffed out a sigh and rolled her eyes.

Cam raised his brow as he looked at Ian. "I would like a few minutes with Abigail, then she can return with you to McDonough House."

Ian nodded and took his wife by the arm. "We will wait for her in the carriage."

Emma started to protest, but at her husband's insistence, she willingly walked outside, giving Cam a few minutes alone with Abigail.

Cam looked down into her eyes and smiled as he tucked a stray curl behind her ear. He picked her hand up and kissed her knuckle above where his ring rested on her finger. "One week and you will be mine, Abigail."

She lowered her eyes. "I am already yours, Cam."

He tilted her chin up and placed a soft kiss on her lips. "I'm sorry for leaving you, Abigail. I promise to never allow you to hurt like that again. I will find Toussaint and end this, then I will take you to my country estate where I can have you all to myself. Even if I must have guards stationed around the estate to protect me from Emma."

He saw her lips turn up in a smile and her violet eyes flashed with amusement. "Emma has always been impulsive. You didn't truly believe she would have stabbed you?"

He rubbed his hands up and down her arms. "She was most convincing. I do believe that if I caused you any harm, she wouldn't hesitate to make me pay for my transgressions."

Abigail laughed softly. "I should go. I wouldn't want Mr. Kingston to be kept waiting."

Cam frowned. "Kingston can wait an eternity for all I care. I want to know how you knew I was here."

Abigail narrowed her eyes. "If I had not shown up here today, you would still be trying to keep your arrival back in London a secret, wouldn't you?"

Cam wasn't sure how to answer that question. After seeing her at the ball, he knew he couldn't be without her for much longer, but with the threat of Toussaint being in London, he also wasn't sure he would have revealed himself so soon.

Abigail's smile faltered just a bit when she realized he either wasn't going to answer her or the answer was not what she had hoped it would be.

"It was Isobel. She told me that she had seen you at Avanley House meeting with Charles. But don't be angry with her. I saw you at the ball last night and when in the garden with Kingston, I was certain it was you with whom he had been conversing before I ran into him. So, I suppose you could say that Isobel just confirmed my suspicions." She pulled out of his arms and walked toward the door. "If you are going to catch Toussaint, you might want to brush up on your skills. Because if I can find you with the little experience I have, someone with more knowledge in the art of subterfuge would not have any trouble either."

Cam watched the sway of her hips as she sashayed out the door to join Emma and Ian, but her words had given him pause. If Emma had figured out that he was in London, there was no doubt Toussaint knew as well. He called down the hallway to Gerald, the butler Charles had hired to run Stafford House.

The man hurried from around the corner where he had been waiting for the pandemonium to pass that Emma's arrival had ensued.

"You called, your grace?"

Cam ran a hand through his hair in frustration. "Send one of the footmen to the *Devil's Lair*. Find John Cavendish and ask him to come to see me here."

"Yes, your grace. Is there anything else?"

Cam inhaled deeply. "Yes, have the house and staff prepared to welcome their new duchess in a week."

"A duchess, your grace?" Gerald asked in surprise.

Cam started back up the stairs. "Yes, I'm getting married. Get a bottle of my father's finest wine and bring it up from the cellar. We will all share a toast in celebration."

He went back to his bedchamber where Abigail's scent still lingered. He smiled as he thought about having her in his bed every night and looked forward to showing her his other estates. Being born the bastard son of the Duke of Stafford, he had never dreamed of having a wife to call his duchess or even a spare thought of having a family. He had never expected to inherit his father's title. But now, knowing Abigail would be by his side, he knew he wanted it all. He wanted a home, a wife, and children to run through the halls. He wanted to take his place in the House of Lords and stand alongside his friends. He wanted to take his father's place and in order to do that, he had one more task to complete to keep his wife safe and be able to look to the future to make his dream a reality. He had to find and kill Toussaint.

One week later

The sun had barely risen casting the sky in shades of pink and yellow when he saddled his horse and started for Hyde Park. Last night he had received a letter from Leicester asking him to meet at Rotten Row at first light. While he would not say that the two of them were friends, they had, however, managed to be civil the past two years and he was curious as to why Leicester had chosen today, the day he was to wed Abigail, of all days to request a meeting. He was not involved with Harrison or his investigation into Toussaint so the reason for such an early morning summit had him curious. He saw a figure on a horse at the beginning of the row, but it was not Leicester waiting for him, it was Catherine.

He pulled his horse to a stop as he neared her and looked around wondering where her escorts were waiting. "Well, your grace, this is an unexpected surprise."

Catherine smiled brightly. "I wanted to offer my congratulations on your upcoming nuptials."

Cam narrowed his eyes while his lips turned up slightly at the corners. "Surely you did not request an early morning rendezvous just to grant me your best wishes." He looked around again. "Tell me you did not come out here alone, Catherine."

She leaned down and rubbed the neck of her horse when he began to move restlessly. "I have two grooms waiting for me. I assure you I am in their sight. Michael refuses to allow me to ride alone."

Cam nodded. "Well, Leicester and I agree on that at least. Does your husband know you are here meeting me?"

"Michael knows I enjoy my early morning rides and most of the time, he joins me but today he was sleeping soundly, I didn't dare wake him."

Cam's grin widened. "So, you snuck out without his knowledge. You know he will be furious if he finds out."

Catherine shrugged her shoulders. "I have no intention of hiding our meeting from him. How is the search coming for Toussaint?"

Cam nudged his horse into a walk. "I'm not discussing this with you, Catherine."

She moved her horse to walk alongside him. "I'm simply curious. Although I have already ascertained that you have had no luck."

"You are trying to get information from me, for what purpose I am unsure, but I have no intention of sharing anything with you. I know you, Catherine. You want to get involved, are you bored with being a wife and mother so soon?"

Catherine frowned. "I am not bored. I love my husband and my son very much. I was just trying to have a conversation with you."

"Why are we here, Catherine? Sending your best wishes for my marriage to Abigail or asking a simple question about Toussaint does not require the two of us to meet at dawn in a fairly empty park. What are you up to?"

Catherine huffed out a frustrated breath. "I came to offer my help and not in the way you are thinking. I would like to help your new duchess navigate the treacherous waters of the ton. I know you are not familiar with how vicious the people of the beau monde can be seeing that the last eight years you have been involved with other matters."

Cam laughed. "Are you referring to my time spent as a smuggler, assassin, spy, or the legitimacy of my birth?"

"I would be lying to you if I didn't tell you all of those things are a factor, but I was going to offer my help to Abigail."

Cam pulled his horse to a stop. "I'm sure Emma will be more than happy to aide Abigail in any way that is needed."

"Yes, I'm sure she will, but I must remind you that Emma is also new to the ton. She was not born into this life and has only been a duchess for less than a year. Not to mention, that she is now Scottish since her marriage to Ian. Persephone will still be helping Emma make her way." She glanced over and saw that he was listening. "I was born to this, Cam. I know all there is to know and will be influential in seeing her accepted."

He scoffed. "I am not concerned with being accepted. I know many still do not want to accept me due to my illegitimacy regardless of the fact that my father acknowledged me as his son, and the Prince Regent granted me the title upon my father's death."

"Yes, I can see that about you. You wouldn't care if people gossiped about you or shunned you. You are also a man. Things are not as easy for us women, and I would like to see Abigail accepted as your duchess."

Cam looked over at her as if to measure her sincerity. "Thank you, Catherine. I believe Abigail will be grateful for your assistance." He saw her smile grow, but he still was suspicious of her motives. "As you know, this conversation could have taken place at any time. Was there something else you wanted to discuss, Catherine?"

He saw her eyes dance with amusement. "You can read me too well." She looked down before casting her eyes back to him. "I was also curious about your search for Toussaint. You know I want to see him caught almost as much as you. The man he sent to Dover the night I went with you to retrieve information for Harrison, tried to kill both of us and would have if you had not reacted so swiftly."

Cam gave her a wink. "I would not let anything happen to you, Catherine, and that is the reason I refuse to give in to your inquisitive nature. The less you know, the better. Now, I think you should go home before your husband decides to end his truce with me. Although I never truly understood why he detested me so much when it was McDonough who paid addresses to you and offered for you, yet I am the one he wants to murder anytime I look in your direction."

Catherine laughed. "It's because you were the bigger threat. Ian was a sweet friend, you were mysterious, and he was afraid my thirst for adventure would lure me away."

Cam had always admired Catherine, Duchess of Leicester and at one time had been incredibly attracted to her, but at this moment he was glad Leicester had been the one to win her heart and fate had granted him Abigail. As the thought of her came to his mind he was reminded that he was just a few hours away from claiming her as his bride.

"Will we see you and Leicester later at McDonough's house?"

"Of course, I must return home. Michael will no doubt be upset with me, and I'm certain there are things you must do as well."

Cam watched as she turned her horse and galloped back to where she had instructed her two grooms to wait for her. Once he was certain she was safe in their protection, he turned his horse and headed back to Stafford House.

Cam handed off his horse to a groom that was waiting for his return and strode through the front door where his butler Gerald was standing at attention.

"Has everything been made ready for the new duchess?"

"It has indeed, your grace. Your valet has prepared your clothing and the duchess' chambers have fresh flowers and candles as you instructed. The staff will all be assembled waiting for your return to meet her grace."

"Excellent, I will require a hot bath before I dress and please see that cook has a meal prepared for us upon our return. Something light, as we will have already eaten at the wedding breakfast."

"Yes, your grace."

Cam moved past him and headed toward the stairs.

"Excuse me, your grace but you have a visitor. The Duke of Avanley is waiting for your arrival in your study."

Cam frowned wondering if Charles was here with information on Toussaint. While he was anxious to find the devil, he was hoping not to have anything disrupt his wedding day and more importantly, his wedding night.

"Thank you, Gerald."

Cam walked toward the study curious as to why Charles had chosen today to visit him. As he entered the room, he found Charles lounging, looking very relaxed, in a chair with his feet propped up on his desk, and he could see that he had also helped himself to his brandy. Considering the half-empty glass, he must have enjoyed it.

"Charles, are you here to bring me news from Harrison?"

Charles didn't bother standing as Cam entered the room. "No, my friend. Today I am on an even more important mission. I am to make certain that you do not leave London before you have said those all-important wedding vows."

Cam rolled his eyes as he made his way over to the decanter of brandy sitting on his desk. "Did Emma send you?"

Charles grinned. "No, it was my wife. She is feeling guilty for telling Abigail you were here in London."

Cam poured the amber-colored liquor into his glass and lifted it to his lips. "You may tell Isobel that she is forgiven. There is no need for her to be concerned that I am upset with her. In truth, I never should have kept hidden from Abigail in the first place."

At his words, Charles laughed. "Oh, you are not who she is concerned with. She is worried about Abigail. If she had not told Abigail, you were here, she wouldn't have come over and you wouldn't have seduced her."

Cam's grin spread.

"And since she feels somewhat responsible for this hasty marriage today, she asked me to make certain you actually attend."

"Trust me, there is no chance of me running out on my bride."

Charles raised his glass. "Then let's have another drink before you join the rest of us who have traded in our bachelor lifestyle for the women who have captured our hearts and our freedom."

272

Chapter Eighteen

The morning had been a flurry of activity. Emma had been running around the house giving instructions to the servants making sure everything was ready for the small ceremony that was to take place there this afternoon. Abigail had tried to deter her, reminding her that it was to be a small intimate ceremony and there was no need in making such a fuss. When she had insisted on waiting a week to marry Cam, it had only been so she could make herself presentable and have time to gather her wits about her. Not so that Emma would have time to throw the entire household into turmoil trying to decorate and put together a wedding breakfast at the last minute. Even Ian had tried to deter her, but Emma wouldn't hear of it.

Abigail had spent most of the morning downstairs arranging flowers while Emma directed the kitchen staff. She had never imagined her marriage to take place like this, under a special license because she couldn't control her lust for a man she had only known for a few months. She moved to place the vase of roses on the table by the window. It was a staggering truth that she was about to give herself to a man she truly didn't know. She knew very little about his past or what he was like before he worked for the War Department. She felt her knees get weak and she sank down onto the chair by the window. She knew nothing of his likes or dislikes, what he expected from her as his duchess. They had not even talked about where they would live once married. Would they stay in London, or would he like many of the men in the ton, deposit her at his country estate? Her head started to ache as her anxiety increased.

Emma hurried into the room. "Abigail, go upstairs. I have already had a bath prepared for you and it's time you start getting ready."

Abigail sighed heavily, her friend not even noticing her distress, and slowly walked up the stairs. There was no way to delay things now. If she tried, Cam would more than likely haul her off to Gretna Green. Perhaps a long soak in a warm tub was exactly what she needed right now. Her feet felt heavy as she moved and her mind was cluttered with thoughts and worries about her upcoming marriage.

When she got to her room, the steaming tub of water was waiting for her. She removed her clothes and slipped down into the tub letting the water cover her with its warmth and the scent of lavender. She closed her eyes as she leaned her head back against the rim and wondered how her life would be different right now if it had not been for the one night at the inn. If she had stayed in Somerset, would she have married one of the local men from the village, lived a simple life in a small cottage raising a half dozen children, never becoming immersed in the ton, never having her life threatened? Would being in bed with another man have been the same as with Cam? Would her body burn for his touch, would the sensations she felt between her thighs be all-consuming if another man's hands touched her there? She let her fingers move along her skin, over her breasts causing her nipples to peak. Tonight, she would be in his bed again and the thought of him taking her as his wife was thrilling. Her hands dipped lower into the water as she neared the junction between her thighs. A soft moan escaped her lips as her fingers dipped lower.

"Please for the love of God, tell me you are thinking of me right now, my love."

Abigail sat up quickly sloshing water out of the tub onto the floor as she turned to the sound of the voice. Cam stood back against the open window, his eyes dark and piercing as he stared back at her.

Abigail wrapped an arm around her breasts. "What the devil are you doing in here?"

He tilted his head to the side just a bit and narrowed his eyes. "Am I at the wrong address? I thought we were to be married today here at McDonough House." He pushed away from the window just as she lowered herself deeper into the tub to her neck.

Abigail blushed brightly. "Yes, but that doesn't explain why you are here now, in my room."

He knelt beside the tub letting his hands dip beneath the surface of the water to skim over the skin on her arm. "Something told me I should arrive early and thankfully my intuition was correct." He leaned forward and dropped a kiss to her lips before he whispered. "Tell me, Abigail, when your fingers were moving along your skin were you thinking of me?"

"I don't know."

"Oh, I think you do." He let his fingers dip down between her thighs and she sucked in her breath. "I think you were thinking of this." He slipped a finger inside her and she moaned softly.

"I wasn't thinking of you, and you shouldn't be here."

He removed his hand from her body and grinned at the pouty look on her face. "You are a terrible liar, my love. But I am glad I came early and even more glad that I shimmied up the tree to your room instead of going into the house first."

Abigail looked over at him and was once again struck by how incredibly handsome he was when he smiled. "You should leave by the same way you entered. It wouldn't do for them to see you leaving my room."

Cam stood. "Darling, with my reputation I don't think it would shock anyone to see me leaving your room, but since I do not want to enrage Emma anymore than I already have, I suppose I should do as you suggest."

He moved to walk away back toward the window when Abigail's wet hand came up and grabbed his wrist. "Cam, are you certain we should do this?" When she saw his eyes darken, she went on to better explain herself. "You don't really know me. What if I can never fit in with the ton? What if you decide later that we are not well-matched? What if…" Her next question was silenced when he placed a finger across her lips.

"Are you having doubts, Abigail? Because you do know that even now my child could be growing inside you."

She looked at him curiously. "Is that the reason you are marrying me?"

He moved back to the tub. "I'm marrying you because you are one of the bravest women I have ever met and because the thought of anyone else possessing what belongs to me drives me mad, because I want you in my bed and my life every day, Abigail. I want you to be my duchess and the mother of my children, and I don't give a damn about the ton and what the people surrounding the prince think about me, but there will not be anyone that disparages you, my love. I believe that in time, you will win the hearts of the beau monde just as you have won mine."

Abigail tried to turn her head away as a tear rolled down her cheek, but he gripped her chin to turn her face up to his. "Get dressed, Abigail." He leaned down and kissed her lips. "I am anxious to take you home."

He walked toward the door.

"Cam! You can't go out that way."

He turned and gave her a wink. "I'll take my chances, love. If you are not downstairs in an hour, I will come back to get you."

"But I thought the ceremony wasn't until this afternoon."

"I'm not a patient man, Abigail, and after seeing you as you are now, I am more anxious than ever."

Abigail decided that it would be a good experience for Cam if she made him wait. While he had threatened to drag her from her bedroom, she had never truly believed he would make her stand before the priest in nothing but her chemise. She sat before the mirror as Emma weaved a stand of pearls through her coiffure. She was wearing a lavender day dress that had a silver ribbon tied underneath her breasts. The color made her eyes look even brighter.

"You look beautiful, Abigail. I wish we had more time to give you a proper wedding ceremony," Emma said as she began threading a few small white flowers through her hair.

"You have done more for me than I ever expected, Emma."

Her friend sighed and sank into a chair beside her. "I just feel terrible about this, Abby. It's all my fault. I should have insisted that you stay with us at McDonough Castle. If I had, you wouldn't be about to marry a man you scarcely know." Emma glanced up quickly. "If you want, I could help you get away. I would even go with you."

Abigail laughed. "You would never leave Ian and you know it."

"I didn't mean I would leave him. I could let him know where we were going and he could join us as soon as he could."

Abigail rolled her eyes. "Do you even know how ridiculous that sounds? Emma, you have a husband that loves you very much. I can't stay with you forever. This is what fate has in store for me. I will be fine."

"Well, if you are absolutely certain this is what you want to do, I will not stand in your way." Her lips turned up into a wide grin. "I do so love that you made Cam wait. When he came downstairs earlier demanding for things to proceed right away, I almost smashed the punchbowl over his head."

Abigail covered her laughter with her hand. "Was he very demanding?"

"Yes, and he better be glad that Ian was here to take him into his study. I'm sure they are drinking brandy and telling stories. Avanley, Hawk, and Leicester joined them a while ago so I'm sure between all of them, they can keep him occupied until you are ready."

Abigail gave her friend a quick hug. "Thank you, Emma."

She saw her friend sniffle and blink her eyes quickly. "Everything is ready, but you take as much time as you need."

"I'm ready."

"I'll go tell Ian. He will escort you."

Abigail watched her friend leave. She picked up the small bouquet of white peonies and held them tightly in her hands as she walked toward the door. She made her way down the stairs to the landing where Ian was waiting for her.

"You look lovely, Abigail."

She placed her hand on his arm as he escorted her across the hallway to the drawing room where Cam was waiting for her. She looked around the room noting everyone that attended. Mr. Kingston gave her a wink as she passed, and Mr. Cavendish smiled and nodded to her. Cam was standing stoically in front of the bishop. When she reached his side, he took her hand in both of his and held it tightly as the bishop began the ceremony. She nervously bit her bottom lip as Cam repeated the words asked of him. When the time came for her to speak the words that would bind her to this man forever, she froze. Cam pulled her a bit closer and squeezed her hand gently. She swallowed and repeated the words asked of her. The ceremony concluded and Cam pulled her into his arms for a quick kiss.

As soon as he released her, she was swarmed by the good wishes of her friends and was pulled away as the men slapped Cam on the back and shook his hand while the ladies gave her hugs and bright smiles. She looked across the room as Cam kept his piercing eyes on her, holding her attention to him. She watched as he pushed through the others in the room and headed straight for her. The intensity she saw in his eyes made her shiver with excitement.

When he reached her, he took her hand and tugged her closer to his side. "We are leaving."

Abigail gasped as he tugged her through the crowd of people. "We can't leave now. There is the wedding breakfast, and our friends are here they will…"

"I'm not hungry and our friends, or at least mine, will know exactly why we are leaving."

He took a few steps toward the door when Emma came running up tugging on Abigail's arm. "Don't think for one minute you are dragging her out of here before the wedding breakfast."

Cam turned and gave her a smile as Ian removed his wife's hand from Abigail's arm. "We have plenty of guests to entertain, darling."

Emma turned to give her husband a deep frown. "This is what was planned when the two of you were locked in your study drinking all of the brandy, wasn't it?"

Ian tugged her closer to his side and gave Cam a nod. "I just know how he is feeling. Remember when I found you working in that dirty tavern."

Abigail watched as her friend blushed brightly.

"Thank you for everything, but I am anxious to have Abigail alone. I'm sure you understand."

Ian laughed as Emma shot Cam a look that said she would love nothing more than to wring his neck, but before any more words were said, Cam wrapped an arm around Abigail's waist and pulled her from the room and out the front doors where his carriage was waiting.

Once he had her bundled inside and the carriage began moving away from McDonough House, Abigail allowed herself to chuckle softly. Cam was seated across from her staring at her as if she were some sort of sweet treat.

"You do realize that it was terribly rude for us to leave before the wedding breakfast. Emma did put a great deal of time and effort into it." Abigail slowly removed her gloves, one finger at a time, as she continued to give him a seductive grin.

Cam watched her as she tugged the glove from one hand and then the other. His fingers were itching to pull her onto his lap, but it was not a long ride to Stafford House, and he knew once he got his hands on her, he would not be able to stop. So, he forced himself to stay on his side of the carriage and endure her teasing.

"I have never been one to worry about what others thought."

Abigail sighed as she leaned back against the cushions of the carriage, her eyes never leaving his. She was curious about his behavior. She had expected him to kiss her as soon as the carriage door closed, but instead, he sat stoically across from her. She slipped her foot out of her slippers and moved it slowly against his leg hoping to elicit a reaction from him.

"Perhaps I should have stayed, so our friends will not think both of us rude." Her foot moved to his knee but when she saw that his expression didn't change, she put her slipper back on. "Hmm, you aren't saying very much."

"What would you like me to say?" He clenched his hands into fists as she leaned forward a bit allowing him a view down the front of her dress. The dress he was going to rip off her as soon as he had her behind closed doors.

She smiled. "I'm not certain. This is my first marriage, but I would think that a bridegroom would do more than just sit across from his new bride with such a fierce look on his face."

His lips turned up on one corner. "You have objections to my face?"

She chuckled. "No, my objection is that you seem so serious."

"I apologize if my serious expressions have offended you, dear wife."

She gave him a flirtatious grin. "I'm not offended, just curious as to your behavior."

He sighed and tilted his head to the side as he regarded his new duchess. "Then allow me to enlighten you, my love. I am keeping my distance from you because I know that as soon as I touch you, I am going to rip that dress from your body, strip you naked, and feast on you with my mouth as well as my hands. There will be no part of you that I have not kissed, licked, bit, or touched. I plan on keeping you naked and in my bed for my pleasure for as long as possible, a week may not even be long enough." He shifted in his seat, his cock already growing hard in anticipation. "In light of the plans I have for you, and the fact that once we arrive at Stafford House, the servants will be assembled in the great hallway to greet their new duchess, I thought it best for you not to arrive naked."

He watched as her eyes widened and her cheeks flamed. It made him wonder if her blush would spread over her body. That was something he would discover shortly. "Was my answer sufficient, duchess?"

Abigail felt warm all over. "Yes, I suppose I should be grateful for that consideration."

He grinned at her as the carriage came to a stop.

Abigail placed a hand on her hair and patted her cheeks. "Do I look presentable? I mean, do I look as a duchess should look?"

Cam narrowed his eyes noting that for the first time that she was nervous. "You look gorgeous and exactly as I would wish my duchess to look."

A footman raced forward and opened the carriage door. Cam stepped out first, then held his hand out for Abigail. Once she had her feet on the ground, she turned and gave him a small smile. He led her up the gray stone steps to the front entrance of the house where Gerald stood at attention before dipping into a deep bow.

"Your grace, on behalf of everyone here at Stafford House, we welcome you. We are at your disposal and if you allow me, I will introduce you to the staff."

Abigail smiled, then gasped as she was swept into the arms of her husband as he headed directly to the stairs.

"The duchess will be indisposed until further notice. Have dinner delivered to my room and left outside the door."

Abigail shrieked as he jostled her when he came to the top of the stairs. "Cam!"

Cam reached his room and leaned down to fumble with the door handle. Once it was open, he strode inside kicking the door closed behind them.

Abigail chuckled as he set her back on her feet. "First, you leave before the wedding breakfast and now you disregard all your staff by refusing to allow them the customary introductions. Is there no end to your rudeness today?"

Cam gripped her face between his hands and leaned closer. "None." His lips descended upon hers in a kiss that was both brutal and possessive. Abigail Bailey, no, Abigail Davenport was now his. She belonged to him in both body and soul, and he was determined to mark her and claim her as his. His hand moved to grip the edge of her bodice and one a swift tug the material ripped free. He swallowed her gasps as he continued to tear the dress she was wearing from her body. The chemise she was wearing suffered a similar fate as he tossed the ragged strips of fabric to the floor. He took a moment to appreciate the picture she made standing there wearing only her slippers and stockings.

She was biting her bottom lip but made no move to cover herself. For that, he was thankful because her body was a masterpiece. Her porcelain skin was flawless, and her long blonde hair hung in curls down to her waist and her violet eyes were shining like jewels. Her breasts were high and firm, her tiny waist and flat belly made him want to kiss a trail from her neck to her navel. The curve of her hips, her perfectly rounded bottom, and long legs would be any artist's dream.

"Beautiful does not do you justice, love." He moved closer cradling her in his arms as he walked toward his bed. "You are exquisite." He laid her down against the thick pillows and placed a kiss on her lips before moving lower. He felt ravenous as if he couldn't get enough of her. He felt her small hands move over his arms. He stood and took off his coat throwing it to the floor then lowered himself back to the bed, his lips moving back to the skin above her breasts.

Abigail sighed as Cam's lips moved over her skin. When Cam had ripped her dress from her body, she had been shocked but found it to be incredibly sensual and her body shivered as his eyes had raked across her. But now it was her turn. She gripped his shirt and pulled as hard as she could sending buttons flying across the room. The surprised look on his face made her smile.

"I hope that wasn't one of your favorites." She let her hands move slowly over his chest before leaning up and pressing a kiss to his shoulder.

Cam jumped from the bed quickly discarding the remainder of his clothing. He came over her again, this time letting his cock settle between her thighs. He nipped at her hip before pressing kisses across her belly as his fingers moved lower to dip into the center of her heat, she was ready now, but he wanted to take this time to savor every inch of her. His kisses moved lower as he moved to the inside of her thighs, he dipped a finger into her core, and growled at the slick warmth he found there. He continued kissing down her legs, bringing her knees up and spreading them further apart before letting his tongue flick over her. He held her hips steady as he licked her, the moans escaping her lips driving him further.

Abigail had never felt anything like this before. Her hands delved into her husband's hair as his mouth consumed her. She cried out, but no complete, intelligible words would form as she tried to keep her body still while Cam's hands gripped her hips tightly.

Cam leaned up to see the expression of ecstasy on the face of his duchess. There were rosy patches on her cheeks and her chest was heaving as she tried to get her breathing under control. Her lips were slightly parted and when her tongue flicked out to moisten them, he knew he could wait no longer. He entered her in one swift thrust causing her to cry out as she clenched her body around his cock. He closed his eyes and willed himself to remain in control. Then he began sliding in and out of her, each thrust more powerful than the one before. Her cries grew louder until he felt her shiver beneath him as she found her release. He continued his thrusts finding his release soon after. He rolled to his side pulling her against him.

Abigail pressed her bottom against him as she snuggled closer and grinned at the growl her actions elicited from him. "I will never be able to look any of your servants in the face again. I'm certain they heard us."

Cam laughed as he placed a kiss on her bare shoulder. "If they don't like hearing you scream, dear wife, then they are welcome to find employment elsewhere because I plan on making you scream night after night." To emphasize his words, he sank his teeth into the side of her neck causing her to squeal.

"I'm serious, Cam. We must try to be more quiet in the future."

"Alright darling, Let's see how quiet you can be when I do this." He flipped her over onto her stomach and lifted her hips in the air and entered her again causing another cry to escape her lips. It did not take long for them both to reach their climax again.

Cam collapsed onto his back pulling her over his chest as he wrapped his arms around her. "Do you still think we should work on being quieter now, my duchess?"

Abigail didn't have the strength to lean up. She pressed a kiss to his chest. "I suppose they will grow used to it."

Cam leaned up to kiss the top of her head. His staff would indeed grow accustomed to it because his little wife was very vocal when he made love to her, and he loved that about her. There was no way he would try to stifle her cries of pleasure when he had her in his bed, and he intended to have her often.

Chapter Nineteen

Abigail blinked her eyes a few times seeing the first rays of sunshine peeking through the draperies that hung over the windows in the duke's bedchamber at Stafford House. Since she and Cam had been married three days ago, they had seldom left the bedroom and today would be the first day she had left Stafford House since her wedding. Cam's body was pressed close against hers and his deep breathing indicated that he was still sleeping. She knew she needed to get up so she could get ready to meet Catherine who had invited her to attend a garden party with her this afternoon.

Cam's arm was heavy as it lay across her waist. She wiggled out from under him, hoping she would be able to sneak out of the bed without waking him. She slipped one of her legs from under the covers and scooted closer to the edge of the bed. The tips of her toes had just touched the floor when a strong arm wrapped around her waist and yanked her back into the bed.

"Darling, did you really think that you could sneak away from me, that I wouldn't notice the minute your body was no longer touching mine?" His hand moved under the coverlet over the curve of her hip to her smooth flat belly.

Abigail grinned as she looked up into the face of her husband. "You can't keep me in this room forever. You know I promised Catherine that I would attend the garden party with her."

Cam moved the blanket away from her breasts as he dipped his head to pull her nipple into his mouth. "Hmm, I can have Gerald send a note with your regrets." He slipped a hand between her thighs.

Abigail sucked in her breath as Cam slipped a finger inside her. "I can't do that, Cam."

He positioned himself over her. "You don't think I can convince you to change your mind?"

Abigail laughed softly as she stared up into her husband's eyes. "You can be most convincing, but you know Catherine will not relent and Emma will be there. If people don't start seeing me about town soon, they will imagine all sorts of wicked things you have done to me."

Cam grabbed her wrists and pinned them above her head. "Wicked things, you say. I like the sound of that." He bent his head lower and nibbled at the sensitive skin below her ear. "I think that once you have returned home after your afternoon with Catherine that we should investigate these wicked things much further."

Abigail chuckled as he continued nibbling down her neck to her breasts. "You must let me out of bed so I can get ready. I can't attend Lady Weatherby's garden party looking as if you have just ravished me."

Cam leaned up and looked down into her face. "Is that where the two of you are going today? Lady Weatherby's garden party?"

Abigail nodded. "Yes, Catherine said that they attend every year, and it was simply one of the events in London I could not miss."

Cam moved away from her, laughter rumbling deep in his chest. "Well, it will certainly be something you will never forget." Then he said a bit under his breath. "No matter how hard you try."

Abigail sat up and studied her husband's expression. "I feel as if this is some kind of trap or trick. What aren't you telling me?"

Cam got up from the bed. "That is something you will have to discover for yourself, love."

Abigail watched as he moved from the bed. Her eyes following his naked form around the room. He really was the picture of masculine perfection. He was tall and lean, but his body was rippled with muscle. His body did carry a few scars from his time serving the War Department, but they did not detract from his appearance. She was beginning to rethink her outing with Catherine, maybe she should stay in bed with her husband one more day.

Cam looked back toward the bed as he wrapped his robe around his body, and Abigail sighed in disappointment. "While you are with Catherine enjoying the most talked about garden party of the season, I think I will venture to *The Devil's Lair* and see if Cavendish or Kingston have any new leads on the whereabouts of Toussaint."

Abigail moved to stand before him, her hand sliding just underneath the robe to move across his bare chest. "I have been so blissfully happy the past few days, I had forgotten about Toussaint."

He pressed a kiss to the top of her head. "I promise that soon we can all put him from our thoughts and minds forever. I'll have some breakfast sent up to you while your bath is being prepared."

He took a step away, but Abigail grabbed his arm. "Cam, you will be careful. You won't let Toussaint…"

Cam raised her hand to his lips. "I will be fine, Abigail. Do you know why Toussaint has been so difficult to find? Why he sent others to try and kill me?"

Abigail shook her head.

"It's because he is afraid of me. I am dangerous, a lethal killer, and now that I have something so precious to protect, I will be more deadly than ever. Don't worry about me, love."

Abigail watched as he walked out of the room, and she moved to take a seat by the window. She knew Cam was a capable man, a man to be feared, but she also knew how dangerous Toussaint could be. And while Cam may have meant for his arrogance to boost her confidence in his abilities and ease her worries, she couldn't help but be afraid. Because if she lost him, she would also lose her heart.

Lady Weatherby's Garden Party

"Oh, my goodness. This is worse than last year," Persephone said as she sat between Emma and Abigail.

Catherine chuckled behind her fan. "You have to give Lady Weatherby credit, she outdoes herself every year."

Emma and Abigail both covered their smiles as they looked at each other.

"At least the refreshments are good," Bella said as she tried to find something nice to say about the dreaded party they subjected themselves to every year.

"The program is twice as long as last year and she has added Emma's favorite poet, Phillip Cranston as a guest," Catherine said as she flipped her fan open and closed in boredom.

"Poor Phillip, I can't imagine him having anything of substance to write about. When I met him last season, he talked of nothing but his wardrobe and cake," Emma said causing Persephone to burst out laughing which in turn caused several heads to turn in their direction.

Bella wiped a tear from her eye as she tried to control her laughter. "You must tell me this story. I don't believe I have heard it."

Emma grinned. "I will tell you later."

"Shh. Lady Weatherby is about to begin another sonnet. Perhaps this one will be better than the last. You have to know that eventually she will get it right. One can't be this terrible forever, can they?"

All five ladies cringed when Lady Weatherby's high shrill voice belted out the line,

A flower is a friend to the nose,

And the friend knows its name shall be called Rose

"No, I suppose they can be," Persephone said as she moved to place her hands over her ears.

Abigail leaned over to whisper softly to Catherine. "If it is always so bad, why are there so many people here?"

Catherine shrugged her shoulders slightly. "Persephone says it is because the ton feels a sense of solidarity and bonding over the fact they can all agree on how terrible Lady Weatherby's poetry is. I personally think we all just feel the need to do some sort of penance for our sins and subjecting ourselves to this form of torture is our way of seeking redemption."

Bella groaned causing the ladies to turn in her direction. "I should have listened to Charles and pleaded some sort of ailment that kept me bedridden so Persephone wouldn't make me attend."

Persephone frowned at her friends. "We are all duchess' and as such it is our duty to support the arts."

"Art, are you seriously saying that you consider Lady Weatherby's caterwauling art?" Emma asked, causing Catherine to laugh loudly. Lady Weatherby paused long enough during the middle of her recitations to send them a fierce glare.

Catherine arched her brows as Lady Weatherby cleared her throat loudly gaining everyone's attention again.

"Lord Cranston is to recite next. I simply can't take much more. When will Lady Weatherby pause for refreshments?" Emma asked as she closed her eyes and squinted as if in agony.

"This is the last poem before the break," Persephone said just as Lady Weatherby took a bow to the applause and obvious sighs of relief from her guests.

"Finally! Come with me, Abigail. Let's take our time moving about the gardens and get some lemonade. We will let Persephone and the others perform their duchess duties. I have never been much for polite meaningless conversation." Catherine stood and waited for Abigail to join her and together they walked away from the crowd toward a quieter spot in the garden.

"Do your husbands ever join you for this particular garden party?" Abigail asked as she nodded to a group of ladies that were staring at her as if she were an unwelcome addition that had wandered into their midst.

"They have all attended at least once I suppose, but it is the one event they are adamant about us attending alone. They are more than likely all at The Devil's Lair or at Whites. I personally would not attend if Persephone did not drag me here every year." Catherine stopped beside an arbor where there was a bench and took a seat, Abigail joined her.

Catherine looked around before turning to Abigail. "Davenport is a good man, and I am happy for the two of you. I know the Frenchman Toussaint has been a thorn in his side for years and has come close to killing him in the past." She saw Abigail's face pale slightly. "Oh, I'm not telling you this so you will worry, my dear. Trust me, Cam is more than capable of killing Toussaint. In fact, he can be quite lethal when the occasion calls for it." She smiled remembering her adventure with Cam a few years ago. "Anyway, I know you have asked Cam to help in his search, to which he adamantly refused."

Abigail nodded her head. "Yes, it's not as if I want to hunt the man down myself, but I just wanted to be involved."

"You are a lady after my own heart, and I would like to offer my help. Of course, there is no way we can let either of our husbands know. Michael would be beyond furious with me as I am sure Cam would be with you."

Abigail liked Catherine but she was a bit confused about what she was suggesting and her reasons behind it. "Yes, Cam would be angry, that's for certain, but what do you think we can do and why do you want to be involved? Cam has told me how dangerous Toussaint can be."

Catherine grinned. "Yes, I am aware. I am only proposing that we do a bit of digging and questioning ourselves. If we find anything, we will immediately give the information to Cam. Toussaint is dangerous, and I am not suggesting putting ourselves in danger." She sighed heavily. "There are two reasons I am doing this, the first being I enjoy a good puzzle and an adventure, the second…I have a score to settle with Toussaint. He was the one that sent the man to kill Cam the night I traveled with him to Dover. He would have killed me too if Cam had not reacted quickly."

Abigail clasped her hands in her lap as she thought about the Duchess of Leicester's suggestion.

"Are you certain we can do this without anyone discovering our intentions? The last thing I want to do is have Cam angry with me. What if he left London again because of this?"

Catherine placed her hand over hers. "I understand your hesitation and if you do not want to become involved, I completely understand. I just know how worried you have been and the desire to protect and help your husband is strong. I was only offering you my help if you wish it."

Abigail nodded. She was worried about Toussaint and the sooner his hold over Cam was broken, they could begin living their lives without fear. "Alright, where do we begin?"

Catherine's smile widened. "We will start by asking questions around town. I will come by with the carriage tomorrow morning to pick you up for a shopping trip, but on our way to Bond Street we might make a few detours. Of course, I will have footmen with us. That way they can ask the questions and we will stay safely behind in the carriage."

Abigail gave her friend a small smile. "I will be ready. Shouldn't we rejoin the others before they think we have escaped?"

Catherine huffed out an exaggerated breath. "Yes, I suppose we should. Or we could make a hasty retreat. My carriage is right outside."

Abigail laughed as she followed Catherine down a path away from the worst garden party of the season.

Three Days Later

"Are we ever going to find out anything important?" Abigail asked Catherine as they sat outside another dockside tavern waiting for Catherine's footman to reemerge, hopefully with useful information this time.

Catherine sighed heavily. "I must admit, this all seemed much more exciting when I first suggested it."

Abigail leaned forward to peer out the carriage window. "Your footman is coming back to the carriage now."

Catherine leaned forward and opened the carriage door as the young man approached. "Anything on the Frenchman?"

"No, your grace. If anyone knows anything, they aren't talking."

Catherine nodded and closed the door. "Well, I guess we have exhausted our search for today. I will take you home and perhaps we can come up with some ideas of other places to search tomorrow."

The Leicester carriage came to a stop outside Stafford House. Footmen raced forward to assist her and after thanking Catherine, Abigail descended from the carriage. She moved past Gerald as he opened the front door for her. "Good afternoon, Gerald. Would it be possible for you to bring some tea into the drawing room and maybe a cheese sandwich? I am famished after spending the morning with the Duchess of Leicester."

The butler bowed deeply before taking her cloak. "Yes, your grace, but might I bring your refreshments into the duke's study. His grace is waiting and asked me to show you there upon your return."

Abigail gave the older man a sweet smile. "Certainly, but please bring his grace something to eat as well, Gerald, and you don't have to escort me, I know the way."

"Yes, your grace."

Abigail walked down the hallway toward her husband's study. Even after being married for over a week, she still struggled to grasp that this grand house was now her home. The door to the study was cracked open, and she knocked lightly before pushing the door open further.

"Cam, Gerald said that you wished to see me. I asked him to bring us some tea and sandwiches. I'm starving and if my guess is correct, you haven't eaten either."

Cam moved from where he stood looking out the window and turned toward his wife. "Yes, I suppose you and Catherine have worked up quite the appetite sneaking about London in search of Toussaint."

Abigail stopped where she stood noticing the fierce scowl on her husband's face. She had indeed spent the past few days with the Duchess of Leicester riding about London sending in Catherine's footman to various pubs and taverns to ask if anyone had seen or heard of the French assassin, and it seems like her husband has discovered her duplicity and looked quite furious.

Cam narrowed his eyes as he watched the realization that her and Catherine's scheme had been discovered cross her face. Her eyes widened and her face paled. "Shut the door, Abigail."

Abigail raised her chin a notch higher refusing to let his domineering stance intimidate her. She held herself up tall and straight as she gracefully crossed the room to have a seat in the chair he was looming over.

"You lied to me, Abigail."

At this her eyes shot up to him. "I most certainly did not!"

"You told me you were out shopping with Catherine, but instead you have been going to every tavern in London asking questions."

Abigail took a deep breath. "I have never lied. Catherine and I went shopping every day. You will see the truth of that statement when you receive the bill, and the packages begin to arrive."

Cam was beginning to lose his temper. "Damn it, Abigail! John Cavendish saw Catherine's carriage outside the Bow and Arrow, one of the filthiest establishments in London. He heard Catherine's footman asking about Toussaint and decided to ask a few questions of the man himself and was told that the two of you had been going about London looking for Toussaint for the past three days! Can you deny that, Abigail?"

Abigail clenched her jaw and gripped the edge of her seat. "No, I do not deny it, and stop raising your voice to me!"

Cam ran a hand over his face. "You have no idea the danger you have put yourself in, do you? Was this Catherine's idea? It must have been her idea. Leicester will deal with her when she arrives home."

"Catherine was only trying to help, that's all both of us wanted to do. We never got out of the carriage, and if we had discovered anything, we would have brought that information directly to you. It isn't like we were going to approach Toussaint ourselves; we are not simpleminded."

"It was simpleminded to do any of that. Toussaint is a professional killer. What if he had attacked you or followed the carriage?

This is for me to deal with, Abigail. You are to stay out of it, do I make myself clear?"

Abigail felt her own temper about to erupt. "Very! Now, if you are through with my interrogation, I will inform Gerald that I will take my tea in my room."

She stood up from her seat, but he reached out a hand to stop her. "You don't get to be angry with me over this, Abigail. When John told me what you had been up to, a hundred different scenarios popped into my mind and none of them were pleasant. You could be killed!"

Abigail pulled her arm from his grasp. "So could you! Can't you see that I did this for us, so we can both be free of this man?"

"You are my wife! It is my job and duty to protect you. I can't have you putting yourself at unnecessary risk. I am the one that is trained to deal with this, being a killer is second nature to me. When working for the War Department, I hunted down men and I will find and kill Toussaint. This was exactly why I didn't want to marry you until this problem was resolved, the very reason I stayed away from you when I returned to London."

Abigail's mouth dropped open at his words. "Well, I suppose it's too late to do anything about that now."

Cam bowed his head knowing he had hurt her feelings. "Abigail, I didn't..."

She held up her hand to stop him. "There is no need for you to expound your position on this matter further. I will do as you asked and no longer try to help with your search."

Cam stepped forward with a small grin as he went to place his arms around her, but she stepped out of his reach.

"If you are finished, I have other matters to attend. I will be joining Catherine and Emma at the Mallory's ball tonight. My ballgown will be delivered shortly, and I would like to have time to eat and bathe before Ian and Emma arrive to retrieve me."

Before he had a chance to utter another word, Abigail had swiveled around on her heels and made it out the door. He walked over and poured two glasses of brandy when he heard the door on the other side of his study open.

"I'm not certain you could have handled that any worse than you did, my friend," Kingston said as he moved across the room and took one of the glasses from Cam's hand.

Cam drained the brandy from his glass and poured another. "What the hell was I supposed to do? I should have known Catherine would get her into trouble."

Kingston took a seat on the edge of the desk. "I agree that it is dangerous for her to interfere, but you could have handled things with a bit more finesse. I personally would have taken her to bed and convinced her in a more pleasurable way to agree to my demands. Of course, my skill set differs from yours."

Cam took another drink from his glass. "Don't you have an appointment with a young lord who can't seem to control his urge for gambling?"

Kingston gave him a small grin. "Yes, I do have that to deal with now. Such a bore trying to save these young witless lords from themselves. Do you realize how rich I would be if I just allowed them to lose all their wealth?"

Cam rolled his eyes. "Are you looking for sainthood now?"

Kingston laughed at his comment. "Hardly. I do have one more question for you. Are you going to tell her that it is because of her and Catherine's misguided efforts that you now have the biggest lead so far on finding Toussaint?"

"If I tell her, it will just give her validation for what she and Catherine have done."

"But it might ease the tension between the two of you if you let her know all her efforts were not in vain."

Cam huffed out a heavy sigh. "It might also give her reason to continue on this ridiculous and dangerous quest."

Kingston moved toward the door. "Do what you will, my friend. I am just thankful that I do not have to face her wrath."

Cam took another sip from his glass after Kingston left and pondered his situation. Perhaps he should tell Abigail what her meddling had uncovered. It might soothe her anger.

He walked up the stairs to her room and frowned when he discovered the door was locked. He shook his head slightly thinking how amusing it was that his little wife would think a locked door would stop him, especially if she was on the other side. He quickly picked the lock, a skill he had perfected over the last few years and entered her bedchamber to find her pacing the floor at the foot of her bed. Hearing his approach, she turned to face him, her hands on her hips, and her petite frame positioned to do battle if need be. She looked adorable.

"The door was locked for a reason, your grace. Am I not to be granted some small measure of privacy?"

Cam moved toward watching as her small foot tapped impatiently against the carpet. "Darling, did you really think locking the door would deter me? I was a spy, Abigail. Picking locks is considered a necessary skill in that line of work." He chuckled as her eyes narrowed and lines appeared on her smooth forehead.

"I am not interested in hearing about your abilities or lack thereof, your grace." She swiveled away from him and started to move away when his next words stopped her.

"Well, I suppose you aren't interested in hearing the latest in my search. I probably shouldn't share such details with you anyway."

Abigail moved toward him standing on her tiptoes as she raised her face to him. "Now you want to share with me after chastising me for my involvement. Why?"

He wrapped his arm around her waist and pulled her into his chest. He leaned his head down to kiss her lips, but she turned her cheek to him instead, an action he found extremely irritating. His brow furrowed.

"I promised you that I would keep you informed, did I not?"

She nodded her head.

"As it happens, and as much as I hate to admit it, your snooping around with Catherine may have brought us our biggest lead on Toussaint since we arrived back in London."

Abigail tried to push herself out of his arms, but Cam refused to release her. "If that is the case, why were you so furious with me?"

Cam bent his head lower and nibbled lightly on her neck. "Because you are mine to protect, Abigail. You are my wife. I don't want you anywhere near danger and the thought that you took it upon yourself to hide your actions from me and it took me three days to discover what you and Catherine had been up to, still infuriates me." He moved to kiss her again, but again she turned her lips away. Cam wrapped his fingers in her hair and gripped tighter so she could not move away. "There will be none of that, Abigail." He pressed his lips to hers in a possessive if not punishing kiss. He felt her body tense at first, but it did not take her long for her to lean into his kiss.

Never leaving her lips, he bent down and lifted her into his arms and deposited her on the bed. His hands moved to her breasts and with a swift tug he had pulled her bodice so that they were free for his mouth to feast upon.

"Abigail, I need you."

Cam gathered her skirts letting his fingers skim along the skin of her thighs.

Abigail wanted to be angry, but his kisses and the way her body responded to his touch seemed to make the anger she was holding onto so desperately swiftly evaporate. "Cam, you are trying to distract me."

"I am trying to make love to you."

Abigail pushed against him again. "Cam, I want to know what you discovered."

Cam sighed heavily dropping his forehead to hers. "Can't I tell you after?"

Abigail giggled at the pained expression on his face. "No, I want to know now."

Cam looked down at her bare breasts and growled. "Last night a man came to the back door at the Lair. Sam refused him admittance, but he said he had information for the ladies that had been asking questions in St. Giles." He let his fingers circle her nipples watching them pucker tighter. "Kingston went to speak to the man and apparently he was coming to send you and Catherine a message."

Catherine tried to sit up, but Cam placed his hand in the center of her chest and pushed her back down onto the bed as he let his fingers continue to trace circles over her naked skin.

"What was the message?"

"The man said that Toussaint was staying at an inn near the Thames."

Abigail tried to sit up again. "What do you plan to do with that information?"

Cam moved atop her effectively trapping her legs beneath his own. "Cavendish is checking out the lead now. If the information proves to be true. I will go there tonight and find him."

Abigail reached up and placed her hands on either side of his head. "I am afraid, Cam."

Cam paused in his ministrations to stare down into the wide violet eyes. "Nothing is going to happen to you, my love."

Abigail took a deep breath. "I'm not worried about me. Cam. You must be careful. What if this is a trap?"

Cam pressed a kiss to each of her eyelids and then moved to her cheeks. "That is why Cavendish is going today to check out the situation. You have to trust me, Abigail."

"I do trust you, but I can't help but be afraid. I love you."

Cam stilled at her words and the sincerity he saw on her face. He didn't know what to say, but he did know that he would protect this woman with his life if need be, because she was the one thing he could not live without. She was his everything.

Chapter Twenty

Abigail tugged at the bodice of her ballgown hoping to cover herself just a bit more. Catherine had insisted that she wear one of Madame LaCroix's creations and now she was beginning to question her friend's judgement. The tops of her breasts were pushed up and she prayed that there would be no reason for her to bend over at any time tonight. Gerald had retrieved a diamond necklace and matching tiara for her to wear from the Stafford family collection. She had hesitated at wearing them, thinking them much too fine for her, but Cam had insisted. The jewels glittered against her skin and in her hair. Her gown was made of the finest deep purple silk with beading of the same color along the skirt and edge of her bodice. She reached for her white elbow length gloves and headed downstairs so Ian and Emma would not have to wait for her when they arrived.

She paused as she came to the bottom landing seeing Cam waiting for her dressed in his evening attire. He looked resplendent, his bright white cravat and shirt a drastic contrast to the black coat and pants he was wearing. He looked very much like a duke and she couldn't help but feel a bit inferior. He held his hand out to her and she placed her gloved hand in his.

"I didn't think you would be joining me tonight," Abigail said as she blushed at the intensity in his eyes.

"There is no way I would allow you to attend any function wearing one of Madame LaCroix's creations alone."

Abigail sighed and once again pulled at her bodice. "Is it truly indecent?"

Cam let his eyes linger on the swells of her breasts and the valley between. "Incredibly!"

Abigail's eyes widened. "Cam, be serious."

He took her wrap from Gerald and placed it around her shoulders. "I am extremely serious, darling and once we are in the carriage; I will show you exactly what I think of that dress."

Abigail tilted her head to the side. "Are we not riding with Ian and Emma?"

"No, once I decided to go with you, I sent a note to Ian telling him we would meet them there."

He escorted her outside to the waiting carriage and assisted her inside before climbing in to take the seat across from her. "I might have to leave the ball early and if that is the case, Ian and Emma will escort you home."

He instantly saw the light dim in her eyes, and he knew she was worried. "Everything will be alright, Abigail. I do not wish for you to worry."

"How can I not worry?"

Cam watched her as she twisted her hands on her lap and stared out the window. In all the years of working for the crown, he had never had anyone to worry for him. He had always taken care of whatever business he had been assigned and had no thoughts of anyone back home.

"You look incredibly lovely this evening, Abigail."

She turned to look back at him and gave him a small smile. "You look quite handsome yourself, your grace."

They remained quiet the remainder of the ride to the Mallory's residence. When the carriage came to a stop, he assisted her to the ground then linked her arm through his to escort her through the receiving line. He did not miss the eyes of the ton turning in their direction as they were announced. He kept Abigail close by his side as they moved through the crowd.

"I think I see Emma and Ian. Perhaps we should join them."

The strains of a waltz began to float upon the air as the orchestra began tuning their instruments. "Not now. First, I would like to waltz with my wife."

He wrapped his arms around her and pulled her incredibly close. Abigail placed her hand in his as he began twirling her about the room. "Cam, people are staring at us. You are holding me too close." She looked over his shoulder as a group of dowagers sent them disapproving looks. "Cam, you aren't listening to me."

"I am listening. You think I do not notice the way every gentleman in this room is staring at you. I am simply making certain they understand that you are mine and any attempt at trying to steal you away from me will be met with swift retribution."

Abigail couldn't help but laugh. "You are being ridiculous. I am married."

He leaned a bit closer and whispered in her ear. "Oh darling, your innocence both amuses me and excites me." He leaned back and grinned at the frown on her face.

"Don't make fun of me."

He wanted to kiss her pouty lips. "Darling, surely you know that being married in the ton does not mean you are off limits. There are many men here that would be more than eager to take a married woman to their bed. It is less complicated."

Abigail tilted her head to the side and narrowed her eyes slightly. "So, you are making a statement by dancing with me this way, marking your territory so to speak."

His grin was strictly predatory. "I thought it would be more subtle than announcing to everyone here that I will not hesitate to slit their throat if they so much as look at you the wrong way. You don't want to know what I would do if anyone had the nerve to touch you."

Abigail's grin spread wider on her face. "You are jesting with me."

"I am deadly serious, and my reputation precedes me. Nobody would dare approach you now."

Abigail almost faltered as he swung her around swiftly toward the edge of the ballroom. "So, now that you have successfully insured that my dance card will remain empty. Am I to just go stand with the dowagers now?"

Cam shrugged his shoulders. "You may do as you wish, my love."

"As long as it does not include dancing with anyone other than you."

"You may dance with Hawk, Ian, Charles, even Leicester is permissible, although I'm not certain of his dancing skills." He saw her frown. "Very well. I suppose I must learn to share you with others, at least on the dancefloor."

Abigail was about to say something else when she noticed Mr. Kingston standing by the terrace doors watching them. "What about Mr. Kingston?"

He turned her so that he could see where her focus had shifted. "Kingston is definitely off limits." He moved her off the floor before the dance ended. "Let me escort you to Emma and Ian. I'm sure Emma is anxious to talk to you. To make certain that I haven't been keeping you locked in a dungeon somewhere."

He escorted her through the crowd on the edge of the ballroom to where Ian and Emma were standing talking to Persephone and Hawk.

"Abigail!" Emma said excitedly as she spotted her friend. "I'm so glad to see you here tonight. I have been worried since you left Lady Weatherby's so early the other day."

"I would be worried if she didn't wish to leave Weatherby's early." Hawk said under his breath as he and Ian exchanged painful glances at each other.

Cam looked back to where Kingston still stood then turned back to speak to Ian. "Can I leave Abigail in your care until I return?"

Abigail looked over to him quickly and he leaned over to press a quick kiss to her cheek. "I must go talk to Kingston, and I am not certain if I will return before the end of the ball."

"We will be happy to take her home if you are longer than expected," Ian replied, and Emma moved forward and wrapped her arms through Abigail's.

"We will have fun, Abby. Persephone was telling me stories of some of the people here tonight. As we are both new to the ton, I'm sure her knowledge will be beneficial for you as well. You remember me writing to you last year about Lord Cranston and his absurd infatuation with cake, well as it so happens the ton is full of people and their insane addictions and fetishes. See the lady beside the refreshment table, that's Lady Roberts. She apparently collects bugs, dead ones that is, and her library is filled with their little bodies all pinned to the walls."

Abigail looked over at Cam, and he gave her a small smile and a nod as Emma started dragging her away.

"Be careful, Cam. I still wish you would let me come with you," Ian said in a soft voice so the ladies wouldn't hear.

"Just take care of her, Ian."

Ian nodded and Cam walked away to where Kingston was waiting for him.

Once he reached his side, Kingston's face took on a more serious look. "Does she know?"

"No, I didn't tell her everything. Ian will take care of her."

They walked out of the ball and down the street to where Kingston's carriage was waiting. "Are you certain he is there?"

"Cavendish laid eyes on him himself."

Cam nodded and as the carriage began moving his thoughts began to grow darker. He had never been concerned with death before. He had always known it was a possibility in the line of work that he did, but now it was different. Now he had Abigail.

He turned to Kingston and his voice turned pensive. "Promise me that if something happens to me that you will take care of Abigail."

Kingston frowned as he regarded his friend from across the carriage. "Don't start being melancholy now. I have known you for years and been involved in some of your exploits. I have never seen you look so somber."

"Just take care of my wife."

Kingston crossed his arms over his chest. "Alright, if something happens to you, I will gladly wed your beautiful young wife. Of course, we will wait for the customary mourning period to subside."

Cam nearly growled.

"If the thought disturbs you so much then make damn sure you don't get yourself killed tonight!" Kingston narrowed his eyes. "Bloody hell man, focus! Toussaint will not be daydreaming about a woman. He will be ready to kill you."

Cam nodded. "I'm focused. Tonight, I will send Toussaint to hell where he belongs."

Abigail moved in time to the music as she danced with Ian, but her eyes continued to watch for Cam's return.

"If I were not already married, my dear, your lack of attention would certainly be effecting my ego."

Abigail glanced up quickly, almost missing her step, to see Ian grinning at her. He was so tall she had to crane her neck to look into his eyes. "I'm sorry. I was just… do you think Cam has gone to find Toussaint?"

Ian sighed as they continued their dance. "I believe he has, Abigail."

"Why didn't he tell me?"

He escorted her away from the others to where Emma was standing by Catherine. "I know you are worried, but everything will be alright, lass."

He deposited her next to Catherine before reaching for Emma's hand. "My darling wife, may I have this dance?"

Emma grinned mischievously. "I'm sorry, but I believe this dance is taken and you wouldn't want me to disappoint my partner."

Ian swiftly pulled her into his arms. "If you think I will relinquish you into the arms of another man, you are the one that is going to be disappointed, my love."

Emma's laughter floated in the air as Ian swept her into his arms for a dance, making Abigail's belly tighten. Once she was alone with Catherine she turned to her friend. "Was Michael very angry with you?"

Catherine flipped open her fan. "Very much so. I had to listen to a lecture that stretched out well past what I felt was appropriate. He even threatened to pack us up and return to our country estate. Although, I knew he was bluffing. He means well, but he is so over-protective. Especially since I ran off on a mission with Cam a few years ago. What did Cam say to you?"

"He was angry, but he did tell me that our snooping, as he put it, actually did give him the lead he had been searching for and even now I believe he has gone to find Toussaint. That's why he brought me to the ball and left me with Ian and Emma. He thinks it will keep me out of trouble."

Catherine leaned a bit closer. "And will it?"

Abigail shrugged her shoulders. "I don't know what I can do now, and I certainly don't want to do anything that is going to make the situation worse."

Catherine nodded. "You are right, of course. I am glad you told me that our investigating was successful. I will make certain to tell Michael as soon as the opportunity presents itself."

Abigail smiled. "I think I will go onto the terrace. It is a bit warm in here, and I could use some fresh air."

"Would you like some company?"

"No, I will not stay out long, besides, it looks as if that opportunity you were speaking about will happen sooner than you think." She raised her chin a notch as Michael approached them.

She gave Catherine a wink and moved past her through the doors onto the terrace. She walked over to the railing and looked out at the garden below. She could smell the clean scent of rain on the wind. The clouds had obscured any stars that might be in the sky. It was dark without the light of the moon and the faint light coming from inside the house was not enough to illuminate the garden below. A breeze blew over her skin causing her to shiver but there was something else she detected in the wind, the faint scent of a cheroot. She tilted her head to the side then turned to see if someone had joined her on the terrace. Her hands clutched the railing behind her as a man materialized from the shadows. He was dressed in evening attire as the other men at the ball, but he had a thin mustache, and his eyes were assessing her as if she were going to be his next meal.

There was nowhere she could go. Her back was already against the stone railing. The hair on the back of her neck began to tingle and her instincts told her to run but her feet felt planted to the ground.

She raised her chin a notch higher waiting on the man to speak or make a move toward her.

"I have startled you, madame."

It was not a question and Abigail got the distinct impression that the man was pleased that she was afraid of him.

He moved closer, his eyes raking over her from her feet back up to her face. "Davenport has better taste than I would have given him credit for. You are beautiful, Mon Cherie."

Abigail felt her stomach flutter at his words. He was speaking French and his accent was true, not the exaggerated version used by some of the seamstresses about town.

"I assume you are Toussaint." Her voice faltered a bit, and she bit her bottom lip to keep it from trembling.

"Ah, my friend has mentioned me, I see."

Abigail didn't know what the man wanted with her. Perhaps he was there to kill her. She narrowed her eyes and squared her chin. "I wouldn't say he thought of you as a friend."

The man put a hand over his heart as if he were wounded by her words. "You are much too severe for one so young." He reached out as if he would touch her cheek and Abigail pulled away before his fingers could brush against her. The man took another puff of his cheroot before tossing it over the railing.

Abigail tried to move past him, but he swiftly stepped in her way. "What do you want from me?"

The way his lips curled up into a grin made her nauseous.

"What do I want? That is not a simple question, Mon Cherie, nor does it have a simple answer."

He moved swiftly for someone with a limp, pinning her back against the stone railing, but before she could cry out, his hand swiftly covered her mouth. Abigail felt tears forming in her eyes as the pain of the hard, cold, stone pressed painfully into her back. With his free hand he let his fingers trail along the edge of her bodice. "I do wish I had more time for play, but alas time is of the essence. You see it is imperative that I leave England right away. Thanks to your husband, it has become too risky for me to stay. But I couldn't leave without first getting a glimpse of you up close."

Abigail felt him lean in closer, his heated breath on her neck.

"You see, Davenport always thought he was one step ahead of me, always thought he was the clever one. But tonight, he will discover just how wrong he has been. Tonight, this will be over, and he will know before he dies, before I sever his head from his body, he will know that he was nothing. He will never defeat me. And when I have settled my score with your husband, I have some unfinished business with the lovely, Duchess of Leicester."

He moved his hand from her mouth but was still much too close to her. "Now, I know the first thing you will do when I release you, is to walk through those doors and head straight for your friends. You will plead for them to warn your husband, but it will too late, Mon Cherie. Everything will have already fallen into place."

Abigail thought she could hear her heart beating in her chest. Her hands were shaking and if what this man was saying was true, Cam and Mr. Kingston were walking into a trap. Toussaint knew they were coming for him. He knew everything. Her hands started to shake, and she clenched her fists together hoping he wouldn't notice her body trembling.

He leaned in closer, and Abigail turned her head away from him. "Enjoy the remainder of the ball. It would be a shame to kill someone as lovely as you."

He pressed his nose into her hair and Abigail squeezed her eyes closed tight. When she was brave enough to open them again, he was gone.

She looked around frantically expecting him to appear once again, but when she was sure he was gone, she hurried back inside. It was difficult for her to see over the heads of the people mingling around the ballroom. She looked to the left and thankfully saw Ian talking to a man she didn't recognize. She hurried over to him ignoring the comments of the people she shoved out of her way. When she reached his side, she grabbed hold of his arm to gain his attention.

"If you will excuse me, Lord Hennessy." Ian took her arm and escorted her away so they could speak privately. "What has happened, Abigail?"

"Toussaint is here! He found me on the terrace. Cam is walking into a trap. He knows everything. We must warn him!"

Ian's face transformed. "I will go. You stay with Emma."

"No! I am going with you, Ian. I must see him; I have to know." She saw him hesitate. "Don't think for one minute that you will be able to leave me behind."

"Cam will probably kill me for this, but I will take you with me." He started to walk off, but Abigail reached out and grabbed him again.

"There is more, Ian. He said he had some unfinished business with Catherine. We need to tell Michael so he can get her to safety."

"Bloody hell!" He looked around the room frantically. "I must find Hawk. Stay here, Abigail. I promise I will not leave you, but I have to make certain Hawk warns Michael and that he takes Emma home with him and Persephone."

Abigail nodded. "I will wait here." She watched as Ian pushed his way through the crowd. She had to reach Cam so she could warn him. It couldn't be too late. She waited for what seemed like an eternity, then when she saw Ian coming toward her, she raced forward taking his hand as they left the ballroom.

Chapter Twenty-One

It took much longer than Abigail would have liked for Ian's carriage to be brought around, and with each passing minute her anxiety grew. Once they were seated inside the carriage she turned to Ian. His jaw was set and his eyes narrowed causing deep lines to form on his forehead. He looked worried, which didn't make her feel any better.

"Do you know where they have gone?"

Ian looked at her for the first time since the carriage started moving. "Cam didn't tell me much. All I know is that he had information about where Toussaint was hiding here in London, and he was going there tonight to…well to take care of matters."

"If you don't know where they are, then where are we going?"

Ian gave her a sympathetic look. "The Devil's Lair. Kingston is with him and if Kingston has left the Lair, there is a good chance that Sam might know where they are. Kingston leaves Sam in charge when he is not there to watch the tables."

Abigail clasped her hands together in her lap. "And if Sam doesn't know?"

Ian turned away from her, his eyes looking out into the darkness as the carriage moved through the streets of London. "I don't know. Let's just hope that Sam knows something, otherwise, we will have to wait. I don't know what else to do."

Abigail would not accept that, but until they arrived at the Lair, she would just have to hope and pray they were successful in finding Cam before Toussaint could make good on his threats.

"Why do you think Toussaint found me tonight? What was his purpose? It was as if he wanted me to know what his next move would be."

Ian looked back at her, and she could tell from the expression on his face that he was confused about his motives as well. "Cam said Toussaint liked to play games. The man is a bastard, he probably wanted to see the pain and worry on your face when he told you those things. He is unstable."

Abigail couldn't shake the feeling that there was some other motive behind his actions, but for the life of her she had no idea what it could be.

Upon arrival at The Lair, they were immediately allowed entry and taken to Mr. Kingston's personal apartments to wait for Sam who was circulating through the gaming rooms.

Abigail found herself pacing back and forth knowing that every minute they waited was another minute closer to Toussaint finding

Cam before they did. When Sam walked into the room, she rushed over to him but before she could say anything, Ian had grabbed her arm and pulled her away.

"Good evening, Sam. We are looking for Davenport and Kingston and were hoping you would know where they might be," Ian asked as he continued to hold onto Abigail's arm.

Sam looked from Ian and back to Abigail.

"It's alright, you can speak in front of her. She knows about Toussaint."

Abigail was much too anxious about finding her husband to be offended by Sam's reluctance to speak in front of her.

"There is a set of warehouses down close to the docks. Davenport, along with Kingston and Cavendish went there to find Toussaint. Mr. Cavendish discovered that Toussaint was to meet someone there tonight, someone that was to help him escape back to France. It is Davenport's plan to intercept and stop him."

Abigail stepped froward. "It's a trap!"

Ian frowned down at her. "Will you keep an eye on her grace while I go warn the others?"

Abigail pulled away. "No! I'm going with you."

"Abigail, this is much too dangerous. When Cam left, he asked me to take care of you. I would not be keeping my promise if I brought you with me. You can stay here in Kingston's apartments and as soon as I have Cam and the others we will come straight here."

Abigail put her hands on her hips. "I'm not staying here and the more time we spend arguing about it, the less time we have to warn them." She moved past Ian and out the door.

Ian sighed heavily before looking at Sam. "That woman is almost as stubborn as my wife. If any of them return before we do, tell them what has happened."

Sam put a hand on Ian's shoulder. "Do you need me to come along? I can get someone else to watch the tables."

Ian shook his head. "No, Kingston would have my head if I took you away from the Lair. Besides, who needs additional support when you have an angry and strong-willed duchess to contend with. Wish us luck, my friend."

Ian hurried out to the carriage where Abigail was already waiting inside. "When we get there, Abigail, you are not to leave this carriage, do you understand?"

Abigail looked across the carriage at him. "Of course."

Ian narrowed his eyes. "I'm serious, lass. If you break your word, I will have my coachman tie you up and throw you back inside this carriage. I will already have Cam angry at me for bringing you, and if you get hurt, my wife will be furious. I will warn Cam. You stay in the carriage."

Abigail sighed heavily. "I promise that I will not follow you. Are you satisfied?"

Ian wasn't satisfied and was beginning to regret bringing her, but it was too late to turn back now.

Cam kept to the shadows as he moved through the empty warehouses by the docks. He did not like this. It was too open and too vast.

Toussaint could be anywhere. He had sent Kingston to search the warehouses on the far end and Cavendish to search the other buildings nearby. The information they had received had not been specific, just that Toussaint was meeting someone at these warehouses who would be able to get him back to France undetected. Cam was determined that Toussaint die on English soil. It would be justice for the lives the man had taken throughout the years. But Cam had not survived working for the war department all these years by being careless and right now he felt that something wasn't right.

He crept silently among the buildings, careful not to make any noise. Some of the buildings had been empty, but this one was lined with crates. It would be an easy place for someone to hide and ambush him. He stopped suddenly when he heard a sound, light footsteps, and whoever they belonged to was in a hurry. He moved backward pressing himself further against the wall of the warehouse, keeping himself partially hidden while he waited to see who the intruder could be. He readied the pistol in his hand, poised to strike as soon as the person was close enough. He leaned forward to get a better look and what he saw made his blood turn cold.

Abigail impatiently sat in the carriage outside the warehouses where Ian had left her. He had given the coachman strict instructions that she was not allowed to venture outside of the carriage. She peeked out the window at the dark shadows of buildings along the docks. There was a cluster of buildings to her right and the Thames to her left. The smell of the contaminated river was nauseating, and she covered her nose with a handkerchief to keep the smell from making her sick. The area was pretty much deserted or at least it was this time of night.

She hated just sitting there waiting, but she had promised Ian that she would not follow him into the warehouses. She opened the door of the carriage and looked both ways before stepping outside.

"Your grace, I was instructed that you were to stay inside the carriage."

Abigail turned to look at Ian's coachman. "I was just getting a breath of air."

When the coachman arched his eyebrows at her, she knew he did not believe that anyone would want to purposely breathe in the foul stench of the Thames. "I just wanted to stretch."

"I think it best if you get back inside the carriage, your grace."

Abigail rolled her eyes before climbing back inside and plopping down on the cushions. She would go crazy sitting here waiting, but how would she get away from her vigilant guardian? She had to distract him.

"Excuse me, but McDonough is waving to you from behind that building over there. She pointed in the opposite direction from where she intended to go.

The coachman stood and looked to where she had indicated. "I don't see anything."

Abigail frowned as she realized this was going to be harder than she thought. "Surely you saw him. He was right there waving for you to come to him. Do you think he is injured? Oh my! What if he needs help?"

The coachman climbed down. "I still don't see him. Are you sure it was him?"

"Yes, and now I am frantic with worry! What will I tell his duchess if he is injured and we do nothing?"

Abigail grew more desperate as the coachman did not appear to be falling for her ruse.

"You must go to his aide. I feel as if I will swoon if I don't discover that he is safe."

She saw the coachman's eyes widen. She knew men were fairly petrified of a woman swooning. It had always seemed ridiculous to her, but tonight she was thankful for it.

"I will go see if I can find him, your grace. I will not be long so stay here."

Abigail gave him her best worried, about-to-swoon look, and watched as he ran over to the building she had pointed to.

She quickly jumped down from the carriage and lifting her skirts, hurried across the street into the alley between the buildings. She technically had not broken her promise to Ian because she had promised not to follow him, and she was heading in the opposite direction he had gone. It was a technicality, and she would apologize later for it, but right now she had to find her husband and that wasn't going to happen sitting in Ian's carriage.

She moved a bit slower trying to keep as quiet as possible. There was a door on the side of the building. She slowly turned the knob and cringed when it squeaked as it opened. She stilled hoping her movements were not heard. She moved further into the room letting her eyes adjust to the darkness. The building was not as empty as she expected. There were barrels and crates stacked along the walls. She stopped long enough to see if voices could be heard over the silence, but all she heard was the soft squeak of a mouse. The sound made shivers creep up her spine.

There was obviously nobody in this building, but there were many more to search. She saw another door on the opposite side of the building and she hurried over to it, hoping it would lead to where Cam and the others were. She had almost reached the door when a hand reached out and wrapped around her mouth as another strong arm wrapped around her waist like a vise. The breath was nearly knocked from her lungs, and she slammed into a hard solid chest. She reached up to claw at the hand across her mouth but stilled at the harsh words whispered near her ear.

"What in the almighty hell are you doing here?!"

Abigail's body sagged in relief. Cam's hand fell away from her mouth as he whipped her around to face him. "You better have a good explanation for this, Abigail! I told Ian to keep an eye on you. I should have had you bound, gagged, and tied to a chair with fifty men to guard you." His hands were painfully gripping her upper arms.

Abigail swallowed the lump in her throat and pushed away the fear she had as she looked into the furious eyes of her husband. "It's a trap!"

"What the devil are you talking about?"

"Toussaint! He was at the ball, and he cornered me on the terrace."

Cam looked her over quickly. "Did the bastard hurt you?"

Abigail shook her head frantically. "No, but you must listen. He told me that he knew all about your plan for tonight. You and the others are walking into a trap, Cam. I had to warn you. He said that when he had killed you, he was going to settle a score with Catherine. Hawk and Leicester have been warned and are taking precautions to keep her safe."

"How did you know where to find me? Where the hell is McDonough?!"

"Ian came with me. He is searching for you. I was told to wait in the carriage, but I couldn't stand not knowing if you were safe. I couldn't wait another minute, I had to warn you. I suppose I will owe him an apology when we find him."

Cam grabbed her arm. "I have to get you out of here."

He took a step toward the door when the sound of boots clicking against the floor and the smell of a lit cheroot reached his nose. His body stiffened as he pushed Abigail behind him and faced the man he had been trying to kill for the past eight years.

Chapter Twenty-Two

"Ahh, I was beginning to think you would not join us this evening, Mon Cherie. We have been waiting for you," Toussaint said as he tilted his head slightly to the side and clucking his tongue before giving Abigail a wink while keeping his pistol aimed at Cam's heart.

Cam stiffened wondering what his best move would be now. Abigail being here put him at a disadvantage and her in danger. "My wife has nothing to do with this, Toussaint. She is going to walk out of here and we are going to settle this between us."

"Yes, your beautiful wife. I must commend you on finding such a gem. Who would have ever thought such a lovely lady would be traveling alone to Scotland of all places?" He looked over to where Abigail was peeping from behind Cam's back.

Cam narrowed his eyes and stepped so Toussaint could no longer see her. "Abigail, go through the doors and return to the carriage. Get out of here now!"

"Not so fast, Mon Cherie. I don't want you to miss anything especially after we had such an…. intimate conversation on the terrace tonight."

Cam never took his eyes from Toussaint. "If you touched her, I will see that you linger in death and make it as painful as possible."

Toussaint grinned as he moved closer. "It seems to me that I am the one holding all the cards here, Ange De La Mort." He looked at Abigail. "Were you aware of your husband's nickname? Ange De La Mort, the Angel of Death, but yet I am the one considered a criminal. Doesn't seem quite fair, does it, darling?"

"You came here for me, Toussaint, not for my wife. Let her go."

Toussaint took another pistol from inside his jacket pocket and pointed it at Abigail. "That might have been my original intent, but my plans have changed." He crooked his finger at Abigail. "Come to me, my sweet."

Abigail shook her head as Cam lunged forward. "I will rip your heart out of your chest while you still breathe if you dare to hurt her."

"Tsk, tsk, tsk, I told you that I have the upper hand in this. Perhaps you still believe that your friends are coming to help you. Unfortunately, they might be a bit distracted at the moment."

Cam felt Abigail grip his hand as fear began to seep into her.

"What the hell have you done?" Cam asked, hoping Toussaint had not ambushed his friends.

Toussaint grinned and Abigail couldn't help but think that the man was pure evil. Could he have killed the others? Were they alone with this madman?

"I truly was surprised that you underestimated me once again, Davenport. It was easy to take out Cavendish. I was surprised at his lack of skills. I suppose his age can count for that. Your other friend, Kingston, put up more of a fight."

Cam narrowed his eyes as he continued to watch Toussaint, waiting for his chance. He couldn't think of his friends now. He had to focus so he could get Abigail out of there safely.

"Unfortunately, the cause we supported has no possible way to gain the strength and support needed to bring France back to the glory our Emperor envisioned. The men here in England had hoped to gather enough funds to sponsor another rebellion, but the cause is lost. They were nothing more than a liability to me." He waved the pistol a bit through the air. "They are traitors to your country and not beneficial to mine so there was no need in furthering our acquaintance. I will say it was entertaining watching you try to find me. You had no idea how close you were at times. But it was your dear sweet wife that was within my grasp and never knew it. While you were traipsing across England following that list of names I left behind for you, sweet Abigail was left in London where I could have taken her at any moment." Toussaint glared at Abigail. "You should never make things a habit, love. Going to the park at the same time each morning or taking a walk outside Avanley's house each afternoon is much too dangerous. Being predictable will get you killed."

Cam heard Abigail suck in a deep breath.

Toussaint took a step forward and held out his hand. "Now come here, my sweet. I am not a patient man."

Abigail reached out and gripped Cam's hand as she looked from Cam to Toussaint trying to think of something she could do. "I will not leave my husband."

Toussaint let out a low growl clearly not liking that she did not jump to follow his commands. "Let me help make your decision easier. Do you not think that I know where to find your dear friend, the Duchess of Sunbridge? Sweet Emma. Do you really want me to pay her a visit? I assure you that I can be most brutal when I choose to be. If you don't believe me, ask your husband." He leveled the pistol at Cam's head.

Abigail felt her heart drop into her stomach. She could not allow Toussaint to hurt Emma. She felt her body begin to shake. How would Cam be able to save them both, especially since Toussaint said no one would be coming to their rescue? But there was some hope, Toussaint didn't know about Ian. Maybe she could distract him and give Cam an opportunity to strike or Ian enough time to find them. "If I come with you, will you promise not to hurt Emma and let my husband go?"

Cam gripped her hand. "You aren't going anywhere with this bastard, Abigail! And you know damn well he will not let either of us go free. Don't listen to anything he says."

Toussaint raised his pistol. "How trusting your young wife is, Camden. Tell me, have you told her everything? Does she know the number of people you have killed, including women, all in the name of your King? Does she know of your infatuation with the Duchess of Leicester?" Toussaint glanced over at Abigail and smiled at the lack of pallor on her face. "There is so much you don't know about your husband."

Cam wanted to see how Toussaint's words were affecting Abigail, but he didn't dare take his eyes off the man. "I never killed the way you have, Toussaint. You massacred entire families, people that didn't have anything to do with the war effort. You kill without conscious, but your reign of terror will come to an end tonight. I have no intention of letting you walk out of here alive." He narrowed his eyes and began stalking forward. "And if you think I needed the help of my friends to kill you, then you are a bigger fool than I first believed."

Abigail watched in horror as Cam moved toward Toussaint, completely unafraid of the pistol pointed at him. She stepped closer to Cam, but he must have sensed her movements.

"Stay put, Abigail!" His voice was deep and angry.

Abigail stepped backward and breathed a sigh of relief when Toussaint lowered the pistol. Her relief did not last for long when he pulled a knife from behind his back and slashed out at Cam leaving a red streak across his chest.

Abigail screamed as she watched blood ooze through the white of her husband's shirt. She swiftly covered her mouth with both hands and resisted the urge to move toward him, but to her disbelief, Cam merely laughed as he looked down at where Toussaint had slashed across his chest.

Cam heard Abigail's whimper but it seemed far away as he was now completely focused on his prey. He took his fingers and swiped at the blood on his chest. "That will be the last time you leave a scar across my body."

Toussaint laughed as he readied himself for Cam's move. "Know this, Davenport, after I carve you to ribbons, I am going to take your sweet wife."

Cam suppressed the feral growl that was rising from his chest, knowing Toussaint was taunting him hoping he would make a mistake, but he was too focused and the Frenchman's tricks would not distract him. He began to circle him keeping himself well out of range of another attack.

Abigail felt her chest tighten and when Toussaint lunged forward, the knife he held aimed right at Cam's heart, she grabbed up her skirts and started forward when a strong arm wrapped around her waist and pulled her back.

"No, Abigail!"

She whirled around at the sound of Ian's familiar Scottish brogue. "Ian! You must help him. Toussaint will kill him."

Ian looked from where Cam was fighting with Toussaint back to Abigail's worried face. "Do you have so little faith in your husband, lass?"

Abigail looked back to where the two men were locked together. She thought she would surely faint at the sight of all the blood. "Please, Ian."

She tried to pull away again, but Ian tightened his hold on her arms. "If you interfere, you will get him killed! Let him handle it."

Abigail watched in horror as her husband continued to dodge the blade Toussaint wielded in his hands. Somehow, he managed to keep clear but with each swipe Abigail felt her heart drop. Finally, Cam lunged forward gripping Toussaint's hand that held the knife. They struggled. While Cam was close enough, he landed a few punches to his opponent's gut causing Toussaint to gasp for breath. The Frenchman staggered back, his eyes dark and murderous as he charged Cam catching him in the midsection and shoving him against the crates along the wall. Cam beat his fists against Toussaint's back and punched his ribs to escape his grasp. The knife was still in Toussaint's hands and Abigail covered her mouth to stop her screams as she watched him once again slash at Cam. But he wasn't quick enough. Cam kicked up catching the Frenchman's chin with his knee. The knife Toussaint had been holding clattered as it hit the ground and Cam moved swiftly to grab it. Toussaint's anger overcame him as he saw Cam brandishing his own weapon against him. His hands and fingers curved into a claw like shape as he lunged for Cam's throat. But Cam anticipated his anger and stepped to the side before driving the knife deep into the Frenchman's chest.

Cam had been waiting for Toussaint to tire out so he could make his move and when he had the chance, he took it. He plunged the knife deep into his chest while looking into the man's eyes. He had never taken pleasure in killing a man, until now, but when he saw the realization that death was near come into Toussaint's eyes, he couldn't help but feel some measure of satisfaction that he had been the one to end his life.

He pulled the knife from his chest and watched as Toussaint crumbled to his knees. It was a mortal wound, but he was not dead yet. "Now it's over." He took a step back just as Toussaint fell face forward onto the floor.

Cam wiped the blood from his knife and put it away as he turned to face his wife. Her face was pale and her eyes wide as she looked over him. He glanced down and cringed at his appearance. The front of his shirt was covered in both his blood and Toussaint's. His hands were stained red as were his trousers. He watched as Abigail placed a hand over her mouth and he worried his appearance and what she had just witnessed had shocked her, but suddenly he watched as she pulled away from where McDonough still held her and ran into his arms.

He picked her up and whirled her around so her back was to Toussaint's body, and she could not see him lying on the warehouse floor.

Abigail let her hands rove over Cam's body searching for his injuries. She ripped his shirt open and grimaced at the large cut across his chest. "Are you hurt anywhere else?"

Cam kissed her cheek and took both her hands in his. "No, he never touched me again."

He turned to look over his shoulder as they were joined by Cavendish and Kingston. "Did we miss all the fun?"

"I thought Toussaint had killed the both of you."

Cavendish placed a hand over the place where blood dripped from his skull. "Bastard gave me a hell of a headache, but I see he won't be hurting anyone else ever again."

Kingston looked much worse. His arm was at an odd angle and his face was bloody and swollen. "I think my shoulder is dislocated but nothing that won't heal with time. Although, the ladies may not find me as handsome for a few weeks."

Cam chuckled and tuned back to his wife. "I told you I would take care of him, love. You worried for nothing. It's over."

He watched as her worried little face transformed and a smile began to spread across her lips.

Then.... it was as if the floor fell out from under him. He smelled the unmistakable acrid smoke from the shot and the loud report of the pistol echoed around the warehouse.

He saw Abigail's eyes widen as she looked down at the red stain spreading across her chest. Cam heard the others running toward them and he caught Abigail as she fell forward. He glanced over to where a smoking pistol lay on the ground beside Toussaint. The bastard raised up just enough to give him a weak smile before lowering his head in death.

Cam held Abigail gently in his arms as he lowered her to the ground. She was alive, her eyes open and full of fear. He ripped open her dress at the shoulder to see her wound. The bullet had entered through her back. It had not gone through her heart, but it was close. He looked up to see Ian standing over him.

"My carriage is right outside. We can load her up in it and take her to the Lair. It's closer than any of our homes. Kingston can you ride out to find Dr. Hawkins?"

"I'm on my way."

Ian nodded. "Before we move her, we must stop the bleeding and Cam you have to be careful, if the bullet moves…"

Cam had seen men die around him. He had even come face to face with his own mortality a time or two but the thought of something happening to Abigail scared the hell out of him. "Abigail, look at me." She blinked and her tongue darted out to wet her lips. "I should have cut his throat, I'm sorry, love." He kissed her cheek. "You are going to be alright, Abigail. Do you hear me?"

McDonough had already removed his coat and ripped the sleeve off his shirt. He handed the material to Cavendish who had bent down to examine her wound. He pressed the material hard against the jagged opening in her shoulder. "Carefully lift her so I can see where it entered through her back."

Cam lifted her carefully grimacing when she let out a soft groan of pain. If Toussaint was not already dead, he would kill him all over again and if anything happened to Abigail, he would follow him into the depths of hell to heap more torment on his doomed soul.

"I'm not a physician but it looks as if it might have missed anything vital. Dr. Hawkins will certainly know more than I. Come on, let's get her inside the carriage."

Cam lifted her as carefully as he could. "I know it hurts, love, but we will have you patched up and back at home soon where I can better take care of you."

Abigail closed her eyes and gritted her teeth as the movement sent hot streaks of fire shooting through her shoulder and chest. Was she going to die? It was dark and she couldn't see Cam's face clearly, but she could tell from the sound of his voice that he was worried.

When they reached the carriage, Cam continued to hold her close, trying to keep the ride back to The Devil's Lair from jostling her overly much. Cavendish was riding with them as was McDonough. He hoped Kingston had been successful in finding Dr. Hawkins. Abigail was being very quiet, and her breathing was getting slower.

"She is strong, Cam. I'm sure she will be fine," McDonough said as he sat across from them in the carriage.

Cam didn't say anything. He couldn't say anything. He held Abigail close, his chest tightening with every breath she took. She had closed her eyes and her hand had fallen down by her side.

When the carriage came to a stop outside of the Devil's Lair, Kingston was standing in the alley waiting for them. Cam carried her down the alley to the back of the gaming establishment where Sam held the door open for them. "Hawkins is waiting in my private apartments. I'm afraid he is wearing his dressing gown and robe. I didn't give him time to dress."

Cam nodded and carried her through the rooms to Kingston's bedchamber. The doctor was waiting for them. He gently laid her down on the bed as the doctor began barking orders to everyone around him. Cam stepped back as her dress was stripped from her body, her bloody chemise still clinging to her skin.

"Your grace, please leave the room. I have work to do, and I can do it better if you aren't glaring over my shoulder."

Cam moved to stand beside the bed and reached for her hand. "If you let her die, I will kill you myself."

The doctor was getting his instruments ready and paused at Cam's words. "Your threats do not frighten me, your grace. It is not the first time I have been threatened with death by an anxious husband. But I do insist that you leave, so the sooner you get out of this room, the sooner I can get to work."

Cam nodded solemnly before leaning down and pressing a kiss to his wife's cheek. "If she wakes, you will come get me. I will be just outside the door in Kingston's apartments."

Dr. Hawkins sighed heavily. "I will inform you the minute I am finished and give you my best prognosis."

"Cam, come with us. Kingston has already poured some drinks. I will wait with you. McDonough has gone to get Emma." Cavendish was standing just outside the door along with Charles. Cam had been so concerned with Abigail that he had not noticed Avanley's arrival.

Avanley stepped forward. "I came as soon as I heard that you had gone in search of Toussaint. How is she?"

Cam looked back toward the room just as Dr. Hawkins closed the door. "I don't know. Toussaint shot her. It was my fault. I didn't make certain the bastard was dead and now Abigail is paying for my mistake."

"You can't blame yourself, Cam," Avanley offered trying to help console his friend.

"Who the hell do I blame then?! My wife could die tonight because I made a mistake, a mistake that very well might take her life. I should have left her at McDonough Castle. I never should have brought her to London, and I damn well should never have married her. She is lying in there, a bullet in her back, because of me."

Kingston was standing off to the side listening to the conversation. "You need a drink. We all need a drink. There is no use talking about what you should or should not have done. She is your wife now and you bloody well know you would marry her all over again if given the chance. I saw the way you looked at her when you first came to The Lair. Abigail will recover and then you can spend the rest of your life being the obnoxious, overprotective husband all of us happy bachelors grow to detest."

Cam pressed his fingers to the bridge of his nose. He didn't want to leave Abigail alone with the doctor. He wanted to be as close to her as the doctor would allow, but he also knew Kingston was right. No matter what he might think, Abigail was always meant to belong to him and if she survived this. He would spend the rest of his life loving her and taking care of her.

He moved past Avanley and Cavendish to where Kingston stood holding a glass of brandy out to him. He would wait for the doctor to do his work, but he wasn't certain how long he could remain outside the bedroom door.

It had been three hours….three of what seemed like endless hours. Emma had arrived and upon entering the Lair, had gone straight into the bedroom not sparing a word for anyone else. If the doctor had requested her to leave, she obviously didn't listen. Cam and the others had finished a bottle of brandy and were working on the second. The rug in front of Kingston's desk was beginning to look threadbare as he paced.

"Bloody hell! Hawkins should have been finished by now. What could be taking so long?" Cam threw the glass of brandy he was holding against the wall causing the glass to shatter and brandy to drip down to the floor.

"Hawkins is the best in London. I'm certain he is doing everything he can to make sure she heals properly," Avanley said as he stood from where he had been sitting to pace alongside his friend.

They both turned as the door opened and a grim-faced Emma walked inside. Cam rushed toward her. "The doctor is finishing up now and requests that you send him home in a carriage since Kingston drug him out of his bed only allowing him to put on a robe."

Cam raked his hand through his hair. "Hell, I will give him my carriage. I don't really give a damn how he gets home. How is Abigail?"

Emma frowned. "She is very lucky. The bullet was retrieved and did not severe any arteries or hit anything major along the way. She lost a lot of blood and is weak, but she is most upset about having a nasty scar on her shoulder. The only danger she faces now is from sepsis, but I assured the doctor that we would keep her wound clean and change the bandages daily."

Cam gripped her shoulders. "She is going to be alright then?"

Emma rolled her eyes. "As I said, she is weak and upset about the scar she will carry. As long as the wound is kept cleaned and does not turn septic, she will be fine after a few weeks of rest."

Cam ran from the room narrowly missing the doctor as he was coming out of Kingston's bedchamber. He hurried into the room quietly closing the door behind him.

Cam stared at where Abigail lay very still in the bed propped up on the pillows. Her eyes were closed, and her face very pale. She was still very beautiful. There was a bandage across her shoulder hiding the injury Toussaint had inflicted upon her flawless body. He took a small tentative step forward not wanting to startle her.

Abigail opened her eyes and turned her head toward where her husband was standing looking as if he were afraid to touch her. Perhaps he thought she was dead. She tried to sit up a little bit and grimaced at the pain it caused her shoulder. He was at her side in less than a second.

"Don't move, Abigail."

She rolled her eyes. "I just want to sit up a bit more. You can't expect me to lie on my back and look at that for the next few days." She raised her good arm a bit higher and pointed toward the indecent scene painted on the ceiling above the bed. "I simply refuse to die underneath a mural of a Roman orgy."

She smiled weakly and Cam gripped her hand and brought it to his lips. "My God, Abigail. You scared the hell out of me. I was so afraid."

Abigail's smile faltered a bit at the anguished look on her husband's face. "I am alright, but I'm afraid Madame Lacroix's dresses will no longer look good on me. The doctor said I will have a scar from the wound."

Cam frowned as he stared down at her. "Darling, do you really think a scar will make you any less beautiful or any less desirable?"

She closed her eyes and took a deep breath. "That's because you haven't seen it."

Cam climbed into Kingston's bed to lay beside her. "I will see it everyday for the rest of our lives. I will kiss it every time I make love to you and when our children ask about it, I will tell them how brave their mother was against a villain that it took eight years to finally kill." He moved her hair back away from her eyes. She was brave, not a tear, no hysterics, just sheer determination, and strength.

Abigail turned her head into his palm. "The doctor says I will be alright. Emma wants to take me to McDonough House when I am able to leave the Lair. She says it will be easier to care for me there."

Cam stiffened. He didn't like the way Emma continued to try and take Abigail away from him, but in this instance, it might be for the best. "What do you want to do, Abigail?"

She reached over and squeezed his hand. "I want to go home, but if it is easier for you to have Emma care for me until I am able to do so myself, I will go to McDonough House. I'm sure now that Toussaint has been killed and the men he was meeting with captured, there must be things you need to take care of, things that need your attention."

Cam leaned over and kissed her cheek. "There is nothing more important than taking care of you, Abigail. Avanley and Cavendish can see to everything. If they need anything from me, it can wait until you are completely healed."

Abigail snuggled against him as they both stared up at Kingston's erotic and extremely inappropriate ceiling. "It truly is a work of art, even if it is a bit shocking."

Cam chuckled. "I have always admired it." That earned him a fierce scowl, but it made him happy to see a spark once again in her violet eyes. "I was thinking that we should find the artist that painted it and commission him to paint the ceiling in our bedroom at Stafford Hall in Yorkshire.

Abigail laughed softly then groaned a bit as a pain radiated down her arm. "Well, we certainly don't need him painting the nursery."

Cam laughed a bit louder at that. "If he painted a mural like that in the bedroom, it certainly would help to fill the nursery."

"Do you really think we need a mural for that?"

Cam let his fingers move along her bare arm. "No, but we do need that shoulder to heal." His voice deepened and his face turned serious suddenly. "I'm sorry, Abigail. I should have done a better job at keeping you safe. When I heard that shot…" He squeezed his eyes shut. "I thought I had lost you and I never want to feel that again." He lightly kissed her lips. "I love you, Abigail. I have never said those words to another living soul before. I love you and I will spend the rest of my life proving to you how much."

Abigail felt tears gathering in her eyes, but she pushed them back. "It's going to be different now, Cam. Things have changed for us."

Cam felt his chest tighten. What was she about to say?

"I'm not sure we will know how to handle our future."

Cam took her hand in his. "Abigail…"

She stopped him from saying any more by putting a finger to his lips. "You do realize that from the moment we met at the inn, we have been running for our lives, been in constant danger, and always looking behind us. What are we going to do with ourselves now that the danger has passed and Toussaint is dead?"

Cam let out a sigh of relief when he realized she was teasing him. "Darling, you get better and I will show you exactly how we are going to spend the majority of our time."

Abigail smiled and gave him a wink. "You don't think you will be bored; I mean now that your time as a spy is over. It is over, isn't it?"

"Yes, darling it is over. No more intrigue or espionage for me. We will be the typical and boring Duke and Duchess of Stafford."

"I like being your duchess, but I'm not sure about the boring part. I think I may have gotten used to the dangerous lifestyle of a spy."

Cam laughed again. "Don't worry darling. I plan on keeping you occupied."

Epilogue

Eight Weeks Later

Abigail reached up to touch the pink puckered skin on her shoulder. The back of her gown covered most of it, and even though Cam reassured her every day and told her that the scar made her even more beautiful, she was still a little self-conscious.

"With the way you look tonight, I think we should send Hawk and Persephone a note and let them know we must decline their invitation to dinner." Cam moved forward and wrapped his arms around his wife's waist as he leaned down and began nibbling at her exposed neck.

Abigail turned in her husband's arms. "We can't do that. Tonight, is the last night we will have before everyone goes to their country estates. Ian and Emma are leaving first thing in the morning to return to Scotland, and we will not see them again until next season. Charles and Isobel are leaving by the end of the week, as are Michael and Catherine."

"And we are leaving for Stafford Hall in two days' time, but you can't expect me to control myself when my wife looks so tempting." He let his fingers move to the shoulder of her gown. He pulled it further down and placed a kiss to the wound on her back where the bullet had entered.

Abigail closed her eyes. "We really should be leaving." Her words came out as a breathy whisper as Cam continued kissing her. Her skin prickling under his touch.

Cam lifted her into his arms and carried her over to the bed. "We will be late."

He sat her on the edge of the bed and gathered her skirts to bunch around her waist. His fingers easily finding what he sought. He yanked down her bodice exposing her breasts just as his fingers entered her. When she sighed in pleasure at his touch, he quickly unbuttoned the flap on his breeches and drove into her.

It didn't take either of them long to reach their climax. After Abigail's injury, Cam had been afraid to touch her. Even after the doctor had assured them that all danger had passed and there was no reason to think that she would develop sepsis from her wound, Cam had still been afraid to make love to her. It was only after she had come to his room completely naked that he finally realized he did not possess the willpower to resist his wife any longer. After that night, he had been ravenous for her. If it was up to him, they would have left London last week and moved back to Stafford Hall. Once he had her all to himself at his country estate, he would do whatever it took to satisfy his craving for his wife, if that was even possible.

"Cam, we are going to be very late now. I will have to redo my coiffure and my dress is wrinkled."

Cam leaned down to bury his face between her breasts. "You look ravishingly beautiful."

Abigail pushed him off her. "You mean I look ravished."

Cam shrugged his shoulders. "Just a play on words. And don't think that the reputations of Hawksford, Avanley, and Leicester are overexaggerated. I'm sure we will not be the only ones late for dinner."

Hawksford House

"I truly do hate that when the season is over, we don't see each other as often as we do when we are all in London," Persephone, Duchess of Hawksford said as she looked across the room at her sister-in-law.

Catherine, Duchess of Leicester rolled her eyes and grinned. "If you want to host a house party this summer just say so Persephone."

"Charles and I would love for all of you to join us at Avanley this summer," Isobel, Duchess of Avanley replied as she looked up at her husband.

"Is that right, Charles? Are you anxious to host a house party?" Michael, Duke of Leicester stated flatly as he took a sip of his port.

Charles raised his eyebrows at the comment. "If Isobel wishes to host riff raff at our estate, who am I to deny her?"

"It will be fun. I do hate that you will not be there, Emma. Do you and Ian really have to leave for Scotland so soon?"

Emma smiled as Ian moved to envelope her in his arms. "While we will miss all of you terribly, we really should return to McDonough Castle. But we will return to London for the season."

Cam watched everyone in the room thinking how odd it was that now he was one of them, a member of the most elite society in the world, a world that he was never meant to be a part of, but here he was. Abigail sat beside her friend Emma and even though she was never meant to be a part of the ton, she certainly looked the part. How was he fortunate enough to have her for his bride?

"You will join us at Avanley, will you not Cam?" Isobel asked, causing everyone in the room to look in his direction.

Cam took a sip of his drink as he looked across the room at his wife. "I'm not certain we will be able to make it."

Abigail watched as his eyes focused on her and her body warmed just as if he were touching her, and she had a strong desire to come up with an excuse to leave early. "I'm sure we can find a way to visit for a few days."

Cam narrowed his eyes just a bit indicating that he was not very pleased with her response, but before anyone could respond, they were interrupted as Hawk's butler Billings came into the room.

"Your grace, Mr. Benedict Kingston to see you."

Hawk stood and walked forward. "Send him in please, Billings."

Kingston walked into the room dressed more fashionably than any of them had seen him. Dressed in a dark suit obviously made by Worth or Weston, his white cravat styled in one of the styles made popular by Brummel years earlier.

"Good evening, my friends. Excuse me as I try to hide my disappointment at not being invited to your gathering."

Persephone came forward and offered her hand to which he raised to his lips. "You are always welcome, Mr. Kingston. We were simply having one last dinner together before we all return to our country estates."

"Yes, Charles and I are hosting a house party this summer. We would be delighted if you choose to join us," Isobel said as she gave him her brightest smile.

Kingston bowed regally at her invitation. "Well, I am afraid that I am about to ruin your plans. I have just left Carlton House after an evening with our Prince Regent and future King, and he is summoning all of you to Brighton this summer for two weeks to be spent at the Pavilion."

"Two weeks? What on earth are we to do with Prinny for two weeks?" Michael said as he lunged to his feet.

Kingston moved forward, taking a moment to greet the other ladies in the room. "He seems to think that we would all be amusing. I told him that I didn't think that you would be any fun anymore since you all have been domesticated, but he could not be persuaded." He paused as he moved by Cam. "He is most interested in making certain that the newest Duke of Stafford is present along with his lovely new bride. You all know a summons from Prinny can't be ignored."

Cam stood from his seat and moved closer to Abigail. "When the hell did you get so chummy with the prince?"

Kingston shrugged his shoulders, a slight grin on his face. "The prince likes to gamble. At the Devil's Lair he can play and lose as much as he pleases. I forgive his debts, and he considers me a close confidant. It's an arrangement I find most beneficial."

"Was it your idea for us to go to Brighton?" Charles asked.

"Me? No, I have no desire to spend two weeks away from The Lair. I might have to shutdown the establishment all together. I'm not sure if Sam can handle things for that length of time. Of course, I could always plan a grand reopening once the season is upon us again. It might actually be good for business."

"So, you will be joining us in Brighton?"

"Yes, I will be joining you, much to my dismay."

"I think it will be another grand adventure," Catherine said excitedly. "I found Brighton to be rather exhilerating and a great place for a distraction from the restrictions of the season. It will be fun."

Cam wasn't relishing losing two weeks in the country alone with Abigail, but as Kingston said, there was no way to refuse a royal summons. "Since we will all be seeing each other again sooner than any of us expected, I think Abigail and I will retire early."

Emma jumped to her feet and went to hug Abigail. "I am so glad you are feeling better, Abby. I will miss you, but I can't wait to see you next season. Perhaps you and Cam can travel to McDonough Castle. You are always welcome and this time you get to stay and see Scotland."

Abigail hugged her friend back. "Maybe next summer, Emma. This year I am looking forward to a peaceful, quiet summer in the country." She kissed her friend on the cheek and said hasty goodbyes to everyone else as Cam hurried her out the entrance to the carriage.

Once they were alone and the carriage started moving, Cam pulled her into his arms.

"Is this the reason you so hastily rushed away from Persephone's party?"

Cam kissed her. "We made an appearance, that was all that was required."

Abigail laughed as his hands began to slide up her skirts. "You aren't upset about the prince requesting our presence at Brighton?"

"I'm not happy about having to share you, that is why we left early. We must make up for the time we are going to miss."

Abigail laughed softly. "You are incorrigible, your grace."

"And you are overdressed, dear wife."

Later that same evening, The Devil's Lair

Kingston untied his cravat as he walked into his apartments at the Lair. He had a long night at Carlton House entertaining the prince. It was always exhausting keeping Prinny's spirits up while he dealt with the declining health of his father, his unpopularity with Parliament and the populace, not to mention his estranged wife Princess Caroline who was constantly trying to stir trouble for him. Prinny's moods were difficult to manage as well, and now he was expected to travel with him to Brighton for two weeks at the end of the season. He would have to close the Lair for that time and lose revenue because of it unless Sam was willing to take on the task of managing the gaming establishment. He could afford the loss of revenue; he just didn't like the idea of leaving London. At least his friends would be going as well.

He walked over to the decanter of brandy sitting on the table and poured himself a drink just as Sam entered the room.

"Evening Sam, how were the tables tonight? Did we have a good take?"

Sam nodded. "Better than average, but you have a visitor."

Kingston let his head drop to his chest. "Not tonight, Prinny has exhausted me. Although if it is a woman, I might could be persuaded."

"It's young Viscount Litchfield, Lord Pettigrew. He refused to leave."

Kingston growled in disgust. "You should have had him thrown out. Where is he?"

"I made him wait outside your office."

"Very well, bring him here. It will be a brief meeting and then you can throw him out the back door."

Sam nodded and left the room to retrieve the young lord.

Kingston took off his jacket and tossed it aside as he took a seat facing the door. Pettigrew had become a nuisance and he would be happy to see the last of the pompous fool. When Sam opened the door and Lord Pettigrew came inside, his first thought was that in the predicament the young man caused solely from his own ignorance, he would at least try to appear humble, but that was not the case. Pettigrew walked inside and casually tossed his hat on the table in front of Kingston before taking a stance that just oozed arrogance. The young lord stood there with one leg forward and his arms crossed over his chest. Kingston just grinned at the stern expression on the young man's face.

"Pettigrew, I thought we had matters settled between us. If I remember correctly, you were instructed not to set foot inside the Lair again."

"I am here to negotiate, Mr. Kingston."

At this even Sam harrumphed behind him.

Kingston leaned back in his seat regarding the young man standing across from him. "Negotiate indicates that you have something I wish to possess. I assure you that is not the case."

"You have taken everything from me! Everything I own and any money my family might have had. The only thing left me are my clothes and the small Abbey that belonged to my mother. I want it back. There must be some kind of agreement we can come to between gentlemen."

"You were warned multiple times, Pettigrew. I saw what was coming and I tried to get you to stop. I was told to mind my bloody business. Even after the insult, I tried to discourage your gaming. I saw what you were losing, but you could not be helped. Now I own everything, and I am not inclined to be generous at this time."

Pettigrew grew frustrated and his face became red and blotchy. "I have a sister!"

"I pity her for having a fool for a brother, but I have no sympathy for you."

Pettigrew clenched his fists. "If you ran an honest establishment, this would never have happened."

Kingston stood from his seat so fast that it flew backward, crashing against the floor. "You are young and stupid so I will overlook that comment once, but if you ever imply that the Liar is anything but an honest gaming establishment, I will call you out. Now get the hell out of here before I have Sam throw you out!"

He watched as Pettigrew hesitated and he wondered if the man was foolish enough to say anything else. Luckily, the young lord thought better of it and walked out on his own. When Sam returned from escorting Pettigrew out, Kingston poured him a drink and handed it to his right-hand man.

"Did Pettigrew give you any trouble after you left?"

Sam took a sip of the brandy. "No, he was as docile as a lamb."

"Good, don't allow him entrance again."

Sam nodded. "Is he telling the truth about his sister?"

Kingston looked up quickly. "Don't start being sentimental, Sam. He isn't the first person to lose their fortune here that had families to support. We are not in the business of running a charity." He took a drink and walked toward the door that led to his bedchamber. "His sister is none of my concern."

Sam shrugged his shoulders. "Whatever you say boss. By the way, you received a letter from your uncle."

Kingston stopped in his tracks. "Where is it?"

Sam reached into his coat and pulled the letter out. "I kept it close. I knew you wouldn't want anyone else to know about it."

He took the letter from him, and Sam walked out leaving him alone. Kingston walked into his bedchamber and looked down at the letter in his hand that bore the seal of the Duke of Kenworth. It was the fifth such letter he had received from his mother's dear brother. He held it out once more looking at the ducal seal on it before promptly tossing it in the fire, just as he had the previous letters before.

Thank you for reading Cam and Abigail's story. Please look for Benedict Kingston's story in the final installment of the **A Duke Always Series**, *A Duke is Always Wicked*, coming soon!